ADDRESS:

HOUSE OF

CORRECTIONS

a novel inspired

MONICE MITCHELL SIMMS

flower girl publishing

los angeles

APR - 2011

for grandma

THANK-YOUS AND
ACKNOWLEDGEMENTS

I've long since recognized that whenever I write, I'm not doing it alone. I am a vessel and God writes through me. Yes, there's that.

But I also wouldn't be able to be the writer that I am nor be able to pen the stories that I tell without the assistance, gifts and experiences I glean from others.

To all of them, family, friends and strangers, I say – Thank You. Specifically ---

Granny, I may have many hyphenates to my name, but I am proudest to be your great-grand.

Grandma, your touch continues to warm and inform me every day.

Grandma Mitchell, I often hear your whisper in the wind --- I know you're still with me.

Auntie, you taught me not just how to win, but how to *lose*. A crucial life lesson. Thank you.

Momma, my first friend, my first love, you're my shero.

Ryeal, I cherish loving and growing with you every second as your wife. Thank you for taking care of me.

Gina, my life began the day I became your sister. Thank you for always being there for me.

Moyya, I fell in love with you when daddy first placed you in my arms. Though years and distance separate us, know that we are one, sistah.

Daddy, it's not lost on me that my love for words began with all of the wild stories you spun just to amuse me. Thanks for loving me and making magic real.

And finally, other important folks who have made differences – big and small – in my life: (For anyone I've forgotten, please charge it to my head and not my heart.)

Beverly Armbrister, Margaret Bernstein, Kyle Bowser, Tamiko Brooks, Dr. Hattie Cason, Daphne Coleman, Denise Davis Cotton, Mary Cox, Cherise Davis, Delores Davis, Sheila Ducksworth, Denver Dowridge and Shanie Evans, Sheryl Flowers, Jacqueline Hackett, Karama Horne, Lyah Beth LeFlore, Mel Jackson, Quincy Lenear, Kamau Marable, Mary McNabb, Ron Milner, Charlene Mitchell, Judith Paige Mitchell, Joy DeMichelle Moore, Darren Nichols, Sevil Omer, Vonda Paige, Denise Pines, Tracy Ponder, Carolyn Printup, Collette Ramsey, Davida Rice, Neeyah Lynn Rose, Paul Rybicki, Ruth Seymour, Tricia Skinner, Bruce and Shani Simms, Tavis Smiley, Glenn and Juanita Towery, Delores Thompson, Tracy Truitt, Sonya Vann, Dr. Cornel West, September Williams and Julie Chenault Woods.

ADDRESS:
HOUSE OF
CORRECTIONS

KENTUCKY,
1965

She had never seen a sky so blue.

Well, aqua really. Like in those old National Geographic magazines in the nuns' library where the African savages bathed in the unmolested island lagoon.

And the sun, a glaucoma orangish hue, was hiding behind a cloud shaped like a wounded elephant with only a splash of pink trailing behind it, just to let her know it was there.

Merry swallowed hard and inhaled, the Kentucky dirt filling her wide nostrils. It burned. The smell of freedom.

"Where the bus?"

Merry eyed the blistered face guard eyeballing her ass from the other side of the barbed wired fence.

"One left 'bout 10 minutes ago. 'Notha one should be makin' it's way 'round here 'bout noon."

Merry bit her lip. That motherfucker. Still screwing her and trying to keep her on her back. She wondered the exact time, but wasn't about to give him the satisfaction of asking.

Besides, the look of her old sharecropping friend, the sun, where it halfway hung in the sky and the growl of her empty stomach told her the time for breakfast had been come and gone. Even with her bad legs, she could make it into town to hustle up something to eat before the next bus came.

"Where you goin', gal? Town's duh other way."

Angry, Merry picked up her pace, fire slowly creeping into the bones of her legs and the hole in her left shoe, exposing her flat foot to the hot country road with each step. If only his fat, cracker ass would just leave the gate, then she could turn around and go the right way. But Merry knew better. She knew that stinking piece of white trash would just stand there out of spite.

And watch her go nowhere fast.

LOCUST GROVE,
1944

"Where we goin'?"

"We ain't goin' nowhere."

Merry looked straight ahead and picked up her pace. Her baby brother Johnson, buzzing in her ear like a honeybee, beat her stride for stride, though. She was nine, a petite chocolate brown Colored gal with ballerina sized flat feet, but Johnson was eight, the color of sweet molasses with pearly white teeth and a whole foot taller.

Both had oily black good hair. And it glistened with sweat under the sweltering Locust Grove sun. Their momma told them they got their hair from their daddy, who got killed, liquored up on the town's railroad tracks before Merry was two. Rumor had it, he was part Blackfoot. Merry took pride in that. She and Johnson were Indian and Colored. Special. Not just some regular old sharecropping niggers like everybody else.

"Oooh, you goin' tuh town. Momma said we ain't 'sposed tuh go tuh town."

"You gotta do everythin' Momma say?"

"Naw, but she said..."

"Well, gone home den, Momma's boy. Gone hide back under her skirt and let me 'lone!"

Johnson stopped, hurt, his eyes already starting to tear.

"You really don't want me to go wit' you, Merry?"

Merry sighed and turned around to look at her baby brother. Johnson just wasn't cut like the other boys she knew. Every since he was born, Johnson never strayed too far from their momma's tit. And he was always clinging to Merry, following her around like a frightened piglet.

Merry tried more than once to get Johnson to play with the other sharecropping boys, but Johnson didn't like playing the stupid games they played and he always ended up running home, crying, because some boy had hit him and called him a sissy. Merry got tired of beating up every boy and girl who knew what she knew. To keep the peace, she just let Johnson follow her around. But today, Merry needed him to go back home.

"John John, stop cryin'. I want you tuh come, but you sho' to git us both in a heap of trouble if you come wit' me dis time. Momma already gone be lookin' fo' me, 'cuz I only picked half a bag dis morning, but if you gone, too, she gone send duh hounds out afta' us."

"I'll go back and finish pickin' fo' me and you...if you tell me where you goin'."

Merry thought about it. Johnson's slight hands and long fingers made cotton picking easy for him. Every day, he picked three bags to Merry's one. It was a game to her brother. He would squat low to the wet ground and be so quick snatching the soggy bulbs, that the thorns didn't have time to stick him. But Merry, short, stubby fingers and all, knew cotton picking wasn't a game. It was work. And every morning, she nearly bled to death just so she could fill up one bag.

"Merry, you hear whut I say?"

"I ain't deaf, boy. I heard you."

"Den why you ain't talkin'?"

Johnson stood in her face, demanding an answer. Merry heard the familiar sound of Mr. Sammy's old horse and wagon trotting up the road and quickly decided he didn't need one. She shoved Johnson, sending him flailing into a neighbor's tobacco field, then knelt down to tie her frayed shoelaces.

"Merry! Why you..."

"Stay down, boy. Don't move."

Merry tied, then retied her shoes, thinking fast about what she was going to say to Mr. Sammy.

Mr. Sammy, a gray eyed cracker with dirty blonde hair and a mean streak, was the head deacon of the white folks church in town and the owner of most of the farms in Locust Grove, including theirs. Merry was too young to figure it out, but somehow she knew that something wasn't right about Mr. Sammy.

It wasn't just the fact that he kept the Colored sharecroppers in debt to him, robbing them blind every week and barely giving them a slave's share of the profits from the bags of cotton and other crops they broke their backs picking. That, and Mr. Sammy being a Southern white man in 1944 would have been enough for Merry not to like or trust him.

But it was more than that. Something deeper.

"Merry? Merry Paine, is that you, gal?"

Automatically, Merry lowered her eyes to the ground, then slightly peeked up at Mr. Sammy sitting high in the wagon seat to flash him her best smile. He was wearing his true and tried straw hat and chomping on tobacco. Nothing out of the ordinary. Except that Merry couldn't tell if he was smiling back or not, because of how the sun was hitting him. It was hanging at an angle in the sky behind him, and the way Mr. Sammy stopped on the road made him look like a hillbilly Jesus with a halo over his head, his face in shadow.

"Yes, suh."

"What you doin' this far away from home? Dora know you gone from the farm?"

"Yes, suh, she sent me into town tuh fetch some medicine. She ain't been feelin' good."

"That ain't gone 'fect how much you pick, now is it? Dora owes me the same number of sacks 'gardless and I ain't gone have no mercy when you fall short tomorrow just 'cuz Teenie and everybody's gone and you say Dora's sick again."

"Don't worry, suh. We gone have our sacks and den some. Me and Johnson takin' up the slack. Johnson mostly."

Mr. Sammy nodded, lifting the brim of his hat. One look at his money-grubbing face told Merry all she needed to know. She had succeeding in assuring him that he would get his money by using the magic word - Johnson.

"You and Dora takin' care of my boy, Johnson? Feedin' him good?"

"Yes, suh. He growin' like a weed."

"Good. Good. Alright now, hurry on to town, so you can get back to pickin'."

"Yes, suh. I'ma hurry."

Mr. Sammy and his old horse scuttled off, the horse leaving behind a stinking present on the road. Merry wrinkled up her nose from the stench and watched them kick up dirt down the dusty trail.

"Come on out now. He gone."

"Whut you go and tell him that fo'? Momma ain't sick."

"So."

"So? Mistah Sammy gone find out!"

"Not if you go back home and finish pickin'."

"Aw, Merry!"

"You heard what Mistah Sammy said. He ain't gone have no mercy on us if we short again. You want us tuh lose duh farm?"

"No. But why you goin'...."

"Boy! Jus' go home! Dag! Gone!"

Merry glared at Johnson and balled up her little fist like she was going to hit him. And Johnson, convinced he was about to get a licking, bolted away from her, back down the road for home.

Merry looked up at the sun. She could tell it was half past the hour just by the way the sun hung in the sky. At nine, Merry may not have known many things, but the one thing she was smarter at calculating than most grown folks was time. Before she even knew how to count or spell, her momma had taught her how to tell time by the sun and moon. That's the way the slaves had to keep track of precious hours and minutes when they were out in the fields picking cotton or other crops. If they didn't pick enough at a certain time every day, Massa's foreman would bring the whip down on their backs or worse.

To this day, even though the scars were healed, Merry's momma's back looked like someone had played an old game of tic- tac-toe on it. Dora told Merry that she had been forced to learn the lesson about the white man's time the hard way, but she made sure that Merry and Johnson would never have to. Yes, her babies were Colored and the way of the world made sure that they would always have to depend on the white man for his money and his land. But his time? Never.

Merry walked faster. She had to hurry.

Fooling with Johnson had made her lose too much time.

COULD BE HER TIME

Merry's legs throbbed something awful. To make it into town in time, she darn near ran the rest of the way, and it felt like the bones of her legs were roasting over a slow fire, smoldering underneath her skin. She wanted to find a safe place to sit down and rest, give the pain time to pass. But she knew she couldn't. The good white folks of Locust Grove wouldn't take kindly to a young, healthy Colored gal lounging around on her high tail when she could be in the fields making money for one of them. Merry was just going to have to choke back the tears and keep moving.

Merry tried not to look as afraid as she was. In all of her nine years, she had never ventured far away from the safeness of home and she had only been into town once or twice that she could remember.

On their farm, they had a cow, some pigs and chickens and pretty much grew all of the fruits, spices, herbs and vegetables they needed. And her momma only ever went into town to buy medicine or something for special occasions. The last time was last year, when she brought Merry with her and bought material from the general store to make a new Easter dress for Merry and long pants for Johnson.

Johnson's long pants now hovered halfway between his ankles and his knees and Merry's dress still hung off her a bit. Dora always made Merry's and Johnson's clothes larger, so that they could grow into them over the seasons. But it looked like to Merry that every morning, her baby brother woke up hungrier, taller, his feet a bit wider and his arms a little longer. Merry, though, was hardly growing at all.

Merry wondered if she would ever grow up into a beautiful Colored woman like the one now walking out of the general store. The young woman, carrying a small bag of licorice candies, wore a pretty navy blue dress and matching gloves. She was also petite, and curvy, not straight and flat chested like Merry. The color of coffee and cream, she wore her hair pulled back into a bun underneath a blue and white hat that matched her blue and white pumps.

The woman smiled hello to Merry over her shoulder as they passed each other, a brief moment of recognition. Captivated, Merry watched her drive off with a handsome Colored Army man at the wheel of a beautiful jet black 1940 Ford two-door deluxe sedan - a car she had only seen in picture books from up North.

"Gal, you standin' in my doorway attractin' flies. You comin' in or not?"

Merry turned and entered the store, immediately casting her eyes to the floor before she answered.

"Oh, yes, suh. Sorry, suh. I came to fetch my Momma's mail."

"Don't your mammy rent a box at your farm?"

"Well, yes, suh. But she ain't got mail in so long, over a month or more. She was 'spectin' somethin' important from up North and I thought maybe the mailman left somethin' here..."

"You accusin' me of stealin' your nigga mammy's mail?"

Nigga. Nobody called her momma nigga. The fire in Merry's legs sept into her blood, boiling it. She looked up at the storekeeper, stared him in the eye.

"No, suh. I just thought maybe somethin' got left behind. By mistake."

The storekeeper stammered, the venom in little Merry's eyes momentarily choking the breath out of him.

"Well, she ain't got no mail here. And you best to learn not to eyeball white folks, gal. You might find you and your mammy hangin' from a tree. You understand me?"

Merry looked down and nodded. The storekeeper's eyes, suddenly cold and dead, were scarier to her than his lethal threat. She backed out of the store's door, tripping down the stairs.

"Yes, suh. Sorry, suh."

Too frightened to be embarrassed and the fire in her legs forgotten, Merry ran home as fast as her short legs would carry her.

*

Merry knew exactly which switch from the tree in her yard she was going to pick. She had been gone so long, Johnson with his chicken self had probably told her momma already where she had been, so it didn't make no sense to lie about it. No, this time, she was going to be a big girl, march into the house with her switch, get her licking and get it over with.

That was her plan, at least, as Merry walked up to her house, fully expecting to see her angry momma standing on the porch waiting to beat her. Instead, Merry saw something she never dreamed she'd ever see parked in her front yard - the car from up North that she saw earlier in town. And its handsome military driver, muscular, tall and the color of sweet buttermilk, stood outside on the porch smoking a cigarette.

Merry smiled, excited. The handsome man smiled back.

"Oh, my. I'd recognized that pretty smile anywhere. You must be Merry."

"Yes, suh."

"No, no, baby, my daddy's suh. I'm Cornelius. Folks call me Corn."

"Hi, Mr. Corn. Do I know you?"

Corn chuckled, exposing a gap in his front teeth large enough for Merry to stick her fist through.

"Straight out just like yo' momma. No, you don't know me, but I know yo' momma. Baby Girl, you look just like she spit you out."

Merry's heart skipped a beat, then she glanced toward the doorway, remembering her licking.

Army soldier or not, this fine stranger wasn't going to be able to save her from her momma's wrath

"Is my Momma inside?"

"Yes, Baby Girl. She's been lookin' for you."

The air inside the house felt hotter than usual. Stickier. The windows in the front room were open, but there was no breeze. Not that it would have mattered anyway. By all white folks accounts, Merry's small shack of a home wasn't really a house. It was more like an old hot box, a wooden makeshift three room shelter, in danger of tumbling over from the next high wind, with a leaky tin roof and rotting floor. Not fit enough for a white man's beloved family hound to live in.

But to Merry, it was home. All she knew. All she had. But here lately for reasons she wasn't consciously aware of, didn't understand, nor could explain, she had been yearning for more.

Dora and the pretty woman sat in two chairs by the radio, sipping on lemonade. Johnson panted at the woman's feet, gazing up at her like a lovesick puppy dog. Merry quietly entered, hoping no one would notice her. The screen door creaked. All eyes turned on her.

"Merry! Gurl, you alright?"

Dora rose and walked over to Merry, who stood frozen. Dora was what Colored folks called red bone. Two years shy of 60, but not looking a day over 40, Dora was the color of Georgia clay, her weary face randomly spotted with freckles.

She was willowy, tall, and always wore her wavy black hair plaited into two long ponytails.

Dora felt Merry's forehead and pushed her hand into her daughter's soaked shirt, touching her flat chest and back. Her touch was rough. Like her love.

Merry knew her momma loved her. No doubt about it. But Momma Blankface - that's what folks called Dora, because her face so called showed no emotion and was hard to read - didn't love like other folks with flowery words and hugs and kisses. Instead she showed what was in her heart to Merry, Johnson and those around her through her hands.

Merry wiggled from her momma's touch. It tickled.

"Well, you hot, but you ain't got a fever. I swear, if you had been gone five mo' minutes, I was gone come afta you mysef."

Merry peeked around Dora to read Johnson's face to see how she should answer, but he was still starring up at the pretty stranger. The woman, nervous and just as surprised to see Merry, looked at her with knowing eyes and smiled hello. Again.

"Momma, I'm sorry."

"Sorry 'bout whut?"

The love spell with the woman suddenly broken, Johnson shot Merry a petrified look she couldn't decipher.

"Merry, whut you sorry 'bout?"

"'Cuz I was gone..."

"Merry mus' still be sick, Momma! She was worried you would be mad, 'cuz I had tuh pick fo' her, 'cuz she was gone so long in duh outhouse."

Johnson stood up, eye balling his sister, telling her not to say another word. Merry glanced at the pretty woman. She nodded. Merry bit her tongue.

"Why would I be mad at you 'bout dat, girl? If you was sick, you shoulda come and tol' me."

"Well, maybe she was scared to. Could be her time. I started 'bout her age."

The pretty woman's voice sounded strange to Merry, yet familiar. She looked at her, hoping she would speak again.

"Lawd, dat's all I need. Jesus, gurl, you bleedin'?"

"Ma'am?

Dora spun Merry around to examine her backside.

"I said, did yo' monthly come? You bleedin'?"

Merry peered at her fingers. The fresh cuts from this morning's cotton picking were already healing.

"No, momma. Not no more."

Dora paused, then laughed. Relieved. Merry loved to hear her Momma's laugh. These days, she didn't get to hear it often enough.

Dora shook her finger, fussing at the woman.

"Don't you be comin' down here startin' no mess. Merry gettin' her monthly. Lawd, have mercy! You almost gave me a heart 'tack."

Dora, still chuckling, sat down with a thud and took a sip of her lemonade. Merry didn't move. Johnson and the pretty woman also stayed where they were.

No one said it, but they were all waiting for Dora to tell them what they could do next.

"Whut wrong wit' yaw? It ain't been dat long, for yaw tuh be actin' like yaw don't know each other. Merry, Johnson, stop actin' silly and come ovah here and give yo' momma a propuh greetin'."

Merry and Johnson looked at each other, confused.

"I said, come say hello to yo' momma. You hear me? Or do you want tuh go outside and git a switch. Merry..."

"Momma, don't. It has been a long time. Too long."

The woman walked over to Merry. Merry starred up at her, nearly overwhelmed by the painful questions and powerful emotions racing through her nine-year-old mind.

This was her mother? The woman she hadn't seen since she was not even three years old? The woman who had left her and Johnson when they were both still in diapers down in Locust Grove with their grandmother to go up North with her new Army husband to get a good job and build a better life? The woman who had promised to send for her and Johnson just as soon as she got on her feet and settled?

Merry didn't know how to feel. She had convinced herself that she would never meet this woman that now stood before her. This woman called Excellent. Her momma's first born. The oldest of nine brothers and sisters. The first to exodus North to the land of milk and honey. And the only one to leave her children behind.

Merry held out her hand to introduce herself, her fingers slightly trembling.

"Nice to meet you."

Excellent gasped. Tears rolled down her face as she gingerly shook her daughter's small hand.

"Nice to meet you, too, Merry."

Excellent's hand was warm and soft. Her fingers were trembling, too. She knelt down in front of Merry and tenderly moved the hair out of her face. Merry inhaled her mother's sweet scent. She smelled good. Like violets.

"You got so big. So pretty."

Merry wanted to say thank you, but couldn't. Johnson, in a quiet but sure voice, spoke for her.

"You real pretty, too."

"Oh, thank you, Baby. Such a big, handsome boy. Come here."

Excellent reached for Johnson and he ran to her, wrapping his arms around her neck so tight, she could hardly breathe. Slowly, Merry joined the embrace. Excellent rocked her children in her arms. Her heart so full, she sobbed.

"I got good news. I came here to get you today. You comin' home to Detroit with me."

"We are?!"

"Yes, Babies."

"We gone live wit' you and Auntie Teenie?"

"Well...Teenie don't live with me anymore..."

"Whut happened wit' you and Teenie?"

"Nothin', Momma."

"Had tuh be somethin', you kicked her out..."

"I didn't kick her out, Momma. Teenie left. Now, I didn't come here today to talk 'bout her. I'm takin' Merry and Johnson. Got it all arranged."

"You a lie. We ain't got nothin' 'ranged."

"But in yo' letter, you said..."

"We ain't got nuthin' tuh talk 'bout, you hear me? You run off with duh first high yella nigga you see and leave these chirren under my roof tuh raise up all by mysef. Den without askin' nobody, you come down here wit' yo' hand-me-down white folks clothes and fancy car and gone tell me dat you takin' my babies? Excellent, dese babies is mine. You might of birthed 'em, but I know whut's best fo' 'em."

"They my kids, Momma. I don't need yo' permission to take 'em."

"I don't give a damn, Excellent! I said dey ain't goin', dey ain't goin'!"

Dora starred at Excellent and Excellent met her eyes with such intensity that Merry felt the hot, sticky air get heavier in the room. Dora sliced through it.

"Merry, you and Johnson gone outside and finish pickin'. Dis grown folks business."

"Momma, please!"

"Yaw betta get duh hell..."

Dora took one threatening step toward Merry and Johnson, and before she could raise her hand good, they shot out of the house, the creaky screen door slamming behind them.

Corn barely had time to step out of the way before they ran into him.

"Whoa! Whoa! Where you goin' so fast? Yo' momma still inside?"

Merry and Johnson didn't stop to answer. Johnson ran straight ahead for the cotton field, just like Dora told him, but Merry, stubborn as ever, headed around the side of the house. Johnson found her eavesdropping through the open kitchen window.

"Girl, whut you doin'? Momma tol' us..."

"Ssh, I can't hear what dey sayin'."

Merry could see Dora and Excellent good, because the view gave her a straight shot through to the sitting room where they were arguing, but she couldn't really hear them. They were talking in harsh whispers as if what they were saying was too painful to speak out loud.

Excellent snatched a letter out of her purse and handed it to Dora. Dora tore the letter in two and threw it to the floor. Johnson tried to push Merry out of the way to get a better look inside.

"Whut they sayin'?"

"Stop it, boy! I can't see!"

Merry shoved Johnson and looked back through the window just as Excellent was walking out. She was leaving.

Merry and Johnson ran to the front of the house. Excellent stood with her back to them, talking to Corn. Sensing her children behind her, she turned to them. The look in her mother's eyes made Merry want to cry. It was a look of regret.

A look of goodbye. A look that Merry recognized, because Dora was looking at Excellent the same way through the screen door.

Johnson took a step toward Excellent to hug her goodbye. Merry stopped him with her arm. When their mother left them the first time, she couldn't protect him. Today, she would.

Excellent reached into her purse, handed the bag of licorice to Corn and sorrowfully walked to the car. Johnson, standing still behind his big sister's small arm, followed Excellent with his eyes. Merry looked back to the screen door for Dora. She was gone.

"Li'l Man and Baby Girl, yo' Momma wanted you to have this. She's real sorry it didn't work out."

Corn handed Merry the candy and stood before them a moment, looking uneasy. He was a big, bad soldier that had killed his share of Jap soldiers and been to war and back, but today, Excellent's children made him nervous. Merry and Johnson starred at Excellent in the car.

Excellent couldn't look at them.

"Well, now, yaw take care."

Take care. Corn's last two words hung in the air like a thick cloud of smoke from one of his city cigarettes as Merry and Johnson watched him and Excellent drive off.

Merry tenderly took Johnson's quivering hand and squeezed it. No one had to tell her to take care of her baby brother. She always had.

And she always would.

LOCUST GROVE,
1947

Merry closed her eyes, took a deep breath. She hated the smell of their outhouse. Johnson did a good enough job emptying the bucket when it needed it, but no amount of lemon juice, ammonia or lye could get rid of the staleness that lived in the outhouse's planks of wood that were supposed to be walls.

At least, the outhouse was dry, though. A welcome shelter from the rain pouring outside. Thank God it was Sunday and they didn't have to work in the fields. Dora never made them work on the Lord's day, because she said, even God, Himself, rested on the seventh day. That's why Merry always looked forward to Sunday. Because it was a break away from the field - the place she hated the most.

Truth be told, even though Merry was now twelve and should have improved at picking cotton just because she was forced to do it everyday, Merry - still small for her age - was a pitiful field hand.

But Johnson? He was a master cotton picker now and he looked every bit of fifteen or sixteen, because of his height, but behaved like every other silly eleven-year-old boy that Merry knew. The other sharecropping kids, grown folk and even Dora had also quietly accepted her brother's slight ways and Merry was glad for that. She didn't have to fight or take up for him as much anymore.

Not that Merry had time to protect Johnson these days anyway. Between schooling, sharecropping from can see to can't see and helping her momma keep house, Merry barely had enough time to get everything done before the sun set.

Merry was also a woman now. She would never be able to prove it, but somehow she knew that Excellent was responsible. The day she met her mother three years ago, something changed in her. Merry had always known the truth about who she was, but on that fateful day, she actually laid hands on who she came from, only to have her mother leave her again.

Merry's monthly started the next day.

Merry heard the footsteps slopping through the mud to the outhouse. If it was Johnson, he was going to have to wait.

"Merry, Momma said come on."

Merry hated to do it, but she had to stop holding her breath to answer. She spoke to her brother through the door.

"Tell her all I gotta do is pull on my dress and I'll be ready to go."

"She said come right now. Yaw gotta leave early, so yaw won't be late, 'cuz of the rain. Hurry up in deer. I gotta go!"

Merry yanked open the door. She found Johnson soaked and hopping back and forth on each foot doing the 'gotta pee' dance. But he wasn't wearing his Sunday best. He was wearing his work overalls.

"Why you not dressed?"

"'Cuz I ain't goin'. I'm workin' wit' Mistuh Sammy again today. You done made me late!"

Johnson pushed past Merry into the outhouse and slammed the door shut behind him. Not too long ago, her baby brother would have been too afraid to shove her out the way like he just did, but these days, ever since he had been doing extra work by himself for Mr. Sammy, Merry noticed that Johnson didn't seem as afraid as he used to be. Maybe it was because Johnson was acting like the man of the house. Him working extra with Mr. Sammy was helping to pay off Dora's debt so they wouldn't lose the farm. Merry didn't know how much her momma owed, but figured it must be a lot, because Dora let Johnson miss school and work on Sundays whenever Mr. Sammy needed him.

Here lately, Mr. Sammy needed Johnson more and more. And Merry still didn't like the man, but couldn't help but be grateful to him. Her momma laughed around the house now and Johnson wasn't up under her all the time anymore. Yes, thanks to Mr. Sammy, life was better for her family.

But in a weird, selfish way, Merry wanted things back the way they were. Her mother's laughter warmed her heart, but she missed her brother pestering and clinging to her. It's like when Johnson was born, her momma anchored him to Merry's leg and she had been dragging him around with her since before she could walk. But now the weight of her brother was lifting, forcing Merry to learn how to walk all over again. Alone. And she was having a hard time of it.

Merry even felt odd sitting alone with Dora on the church pew. Her momma always sat on the end seat of the third pew, on the outside, like she was either on guard or preparing to be the first soul from the aisle to escape. And Johnson, ever since Merry could remember, sat between them.

Without Johnson there, Merry had to fill the gap and sit next to her momma. Even if she wanted to, Merry couldn't dare sit on Dora's lap like her brother had been doing all of his life. She was a woman now. And women folk, her momma told her, have to hold their own, take care of themselves. They can never depend on a man to be there.

"Not even Jesus?"

Dora was surprised by Merry's blunt question. They were snapping Kentucky Wonders in the kitchen for last week's Sunday dinner and Merry hadn't said a word the whole while Dora was talking.

"Not even Jesus whut?"

"You can't even depend on Jesus, Momma?"

Dora stopped snapping and looked at Merry like she was seeing right through her to a painful memory.

"Not always, Baby. No."

"But Momma you told me dat Jesus loves me and I can always hold onto his unchangin' hand."

"I know and I was wrong tuh nurse you so long like dat. But you a woman now and it's time I tell you duh truth."

Dora pulled out a chair from the table. Merry pulled out the other chair to sit across from her.

"No, sit here."

Obedient, Merry walked over and turned her back to sit in the chair just when Dora pulled it out from under her. Merry's bottom hit the floor with a thud.

"Momma!"

"Whut?"

"Why you take duh chair away!"

"Oh. You was dependin' on dat chair tuh be dere?"

"Yes, ma'am."

"Uh huh."

Dora stepped over Merry to the kitchen table and started snapping beans again. Merry, rubbing her tailbone, looked up at her momma's back, confused.

"You break somethin'?"

"No, ma'am."

"Den git up here and hep me finish dese beans."

Merry silently rose and took her place at her mother's side. Dora cut her eyes at Merry, hiding a smile forming at corners of her mouth. Merry reached into the bowl.

Dora stopped picking and gently held her daughter's hand.

"Church folks are lazy, Merry. Jesus died fo' us and loves us, jus' like I tol' you. But sanctified fools take Jesus fo' granted, 'spectin' him tuh always be dere fo' 'em and take care of 'em like he owes 'em. Dey don't want tuh or don't dink dey need tuh stand on they own feets and do duh work. You know, meet Jesus halfway. But sometimes, 'cuz Jesus loves you, he'll snatch duh chair out from unda you when you need it. He'll let you fall and break you down so low, dat all you can do is either stay down in duh dirt, grovel and cry, or pray and pick yoursef up. No matter whut you do or where you go, you can always depend on Him to break you down, understand?"

Merry nodded, but the perplexed look in her eyes prompted Dora to make it plain.

"Don't take nuthin' for granted, Baby. Nobody's gonna give you nothin'. Nobody owes you nuthin'. Not even Jesus."

Merry squirmed in the church pew. The bench seemed sturdy enough this morning. Besides, as good as she had been and as hard as she had worked this past week, Merry figured God's baby boy would have to be the twin brother of the devil himself to yank her seat out from under her.

Merry looked above Rev. Tender's greasy head to the old hand-me-down portrait of Jesus hanging over the pulpit. He looked as benevolent as she remembered: Lilly white. Flowing blonde hair. Piercing blue eyes. Merry learned in bible school that Jesus was the Good Shepherd and she, along with the other Colored folks in her church, were His obedient sheep, His treasured flock. He protected them from slobbering wolves and the slaughterhouse.

But after what her momma told her, Merry wasn't so sure anymore. Dora continued to make her and Johnson say grace before every meal, but at night, Merry had secretly stopped saying her prayers before she went to bed. She fell to her knees, closed her eyes and clasped her hands like she was supposed to, but when it came to saying the words she had been reciting since she learned to talk, she couldn't do it. It's like Merry didn't know how to speak to Jesus anymore. In a way, she was scared to.

And so, it shouldn't have been a surprise to Merry that her legs didn't move when Reverend Tender called the church up to the altar for prayer.

Dora looked at Merry with a look of hell fire that would have made Jesus hop off the cross, but still Merry couldn't unroot her feet.

"You done lost yo' mind?"

"No, Momma, I can't..."

"Can't whut?"

"Move."

Obviously, Dora didn't believe the seriousness of the situation, because she yanked Merry up by her ear to the altar. Merry rubbed her ear, half expecting there to be a river of blood or a gaping hole where her ear used to be, and bowed her head.

Her momma grabbed one hand and another church member - a man, it felt like - took her other one and squeezed. Merry wanted to pull away, but knew better than to cause another scene, so she just peeked at the man sideways to get a better view of who was molesting her hand.

It wasn't a man at all. It was a boy that looked about her age with the prettiest hazel eyes she had ever seen. He was tall and dark chocolate like Johnson, but thicker around the chest and arms. And he smelled good. Like sweet cocoa butter.

The boy she didn't know softly squeezed Merry's hand again to say hello. Too shy to look up at him, Merry dropped her eyes to her feet and squeezed back.

She prayed for the altar prayer not to end. But Jesus, probably mad that she hadn't been speaking to him, ignored her and Reverend Tender said 'Amen' anyway. Merry let go of the boy's hand as slow as she could and they both filed back to their seats. She watched him walk to the back of the church and sit down next to a thick, big bosom woman that looked like she could be his mother and a stair step of children, probably his brothers and sisters.

Just as Merry turned her head back around, she felt her momma's eyes on her. Dora looked to see what Merry was looking at and grunted to herself. Merry knew that grunt, but felt too alive right now to be afraid. If Merry had to pick a switch when she got home just because she was holding that boy's hand, she would. She'd pick a switch every Sunday if she had to.

"Reveren', you out did yoursef dis Sunday."

"Sistah Combs, I'm just a humble servant. All glory goes tuh duh Lawd."

"Well, den as head of duh church's Homecoming Committee and on behaf of all duh saints, dank you fo' sharin'."

Reverend Tender and Dora shared a familiar laugh outside the church after service as Merry waited off to the side. They were standing in front of the door and all the other church members filed out, parting around them like the Red Sea. Some folks stopped or touched the Reverend's shoulder as they passed hoping to steal his attention, but Rev. Tender with his married self paid them no mind. He just nodded, sing-songed goodbye in a key that sounded like hello and kept his eyes on the sparrow - Dora.

And her momma was enjoying the attention. Reverend Tender wasn't a fine man, Merry had overheard Dora tell someone at church one Sunday, but there was just something about him. He was short and stout and dark as night with big bright eyes and teeth too small for a grown man's mouth. Nothing that any woman with any sense would find appealing. But when Reverend Tender preached, it was like God opened up the sky and poured sunshine on him. And Dora wanted to take a bath in his rays.

It usually made Merry uncomfortable when her momma flirted with men in front of her. Over the years, when folks didn't think she was in earshot, she had heard whisperings about her momma. How Dora never had a man of her own and was always stealing somebody else's. They said that's why Henry, Dora's first husband and Merry's grandfather, died of consumption. He was already married nine years when her momma seduced him away, and because Dora had done so much dirt, God took him away from her as punishment.

Merry never believed the stories. She figured that the women folk were just jealous of her momma, because she looked like she could be one of their daughters and she had a young man, her second husband, Jesse. Dora and Merry's step-grandfather fought like cats and dogs and stayed apart more than they did together, but they loved each other. And even though Jesse had stayed gone a good little while this time, everybody knew that any day now, he'd be coming back to take his place with Dora.

Today, though, those same women, some of them Dora's so-called friends, were eyeballing Dora and Reverend Tender. And Merry was glad, because it freed her up to wander off and look for the boy she didn't know.

Merry whirled around, trying not to look so obvious. Folks had gathered into pockets of groups to chat and catch up on the local news and rumors before they headed off for home. The Willing Women Workers with dresses down to their ankles and pulled back gray and black hair hidden under big colorful straw hats were cackling over who was going to cook what for the annual church picnic at the end of the month. The deacons, young and old men who really didn't do anything from what Merry could tell, but count the church's pennies, talk loud and stick their chests out like they were important were holding a quick Come to Jesus meeting in the shade under the tree. And the children - the few young folks were long gone to Sweetheart Lake to go "fishin'" - were running around, playing and giggling.

The boy was nowhere to be seen.

Merry was disappointed and frustrated. A 12-year-old in Locust Grove was a rock caught in a hard place. Too old to play with the children, but not old enough to go "fishin'" with the young folks, Merry really didn't have any friends her age that lived in town anymore, and she almost always spent the little bit of free time that she had by herself. And now with Johnson working with Mr. Sammy so much, she felt even more lonely.

She turned around to walk back over to her momma and there the boy was, right in front of her. He was breathing hard, like he had been running. Merry waited for him to catch his breath before she spoke.

"Hi."

Merry wanted him to say more, but all he did was smile. Just as excited, she smiled back, her face getting warm.

"You s--s--sho do h--h--have a puh--puh--pretty smile. Al---Al--most as puh--puh--pretty as mine."

Merry laughed. The sweetness falling off his full lips was so tasty to her thirsty ears that she didn't mind his stop and go talk. She liked him. In fact, she was liking the boy so much that she didn't notice that he was studying her at that moment, trying to figure out if her laughter meant that she liked him.

"Merry, what you dink you doin'?"

Merry, busted, spun around right into her momma's chest.

"Momma, I..."

"Momma, I nuthin'. Whut you doin' up in dis boy's face fo'?"

Merry and the boy looked at each other, as if what they were doing wasn't natural, but wrong.

"My boy got a name, Miz Dora."

The boy's momma stepped up behind him like a lioness protecting her cub.

She and Dora sized up one another like they knew each other and Merry could tell by looking at them that what they knew about each other, they didn't like.

"His name is James. If anybody should know dat, it's you."

Merry saw her momma's eyes flash. She and James glanced at each other, nervous. Dora spoke, friendliness in her voice.

"Leila, I wouldn't of known duh boy. He done grown so big. Yaw back fo' a visit?"

"No, we back to stay. Just me and my babies."

Dora and Leila smiled at each other, looking pleasant, cordial even. But if Merry peered real close, she could see the switchblades behind their eyes. Leila placed her hand on her wide hip.

"I see you still keepin' yo' grandbabies. How old is she now?"

"I'm twelve...Ma'am."

Merry looked up at Leila, defiant. She never did like the notion of being seen and not heard. Child or not.

Leila settled her sights on Merry and chuckled slightly to herself.

"James twelve, too."

"You are?"

Merry looked to James, excited. But Dora yanked her away before he could get the words out.

"Good seein' you, Leila. Tell yo' momma I said hello."

"Sho' will, Miz Dora. Sho' will."

Merry had to walk twice as fast to keep up with her momma's long, angry strides.

"Momma, who was dat lady?"

"Never mind who she is. You stay 'way from dat boy."

Merry's silence made Dora stop and turn around. She bent down so close in Merry's face, Merry could smell a whiff of peppermint every time Dora spoke a word.

"If I evah see you wit' dat boy again, I'm gone beat yo' ass to duh white meat. You hear me?"

Merry nodded. She wanted to speak her answer, but she was so scared of her momma right now, that her lips wouldn't move.

"Alright den, let's git home tuh finish suppa 'fore yo' brotha git home."

Dora turned and started off again. Merry quickly followed. She could feel James watching her, and she wanted to peek over her shoulder at least to look at him, but fear kept her neck from turning. If only she had eyes in the back of her head like her momma, then she could see him again.

Merry kept walking, looking straight ahead, but she decided right then and there to ask God for an extra pair of eyes. Now that she knew James, she was going to need them.

MISSUS SAMMY'S
DO NOTHIN' SHOES

"**Johnson**, that you?"

"Gone back tuh sleep."

"Where you goin'?"

Merry groggily rose up halfway, knocking over a brown paper bag lying by her head on her flat pillow. Johnson dove to catch it before it hit the floor.

"Dag, Girl! Can't give you nuthin' nice."

"Whut is it?"

Merry snatched the bag out of Johnson's hand and ripped it open. Inside was a vinyl record with small printing on it. She roughly picked up the record and squinted at it, trying to adjust her eyes to darkness of the room. Johnson quickly took it back from her, gingerly holding the record by its' smooth edges.

"Dat ain't how you hold a Lucy Sass record, Girl. You gots tuh be careful wit' it, so you don't git no scratches on it."

Merry looked at how Johnson was sticking his scrawny chest out all proud like, and bust out laughing.

"Fool! How we 'sposed tuh lissen tuh it? We ain't got no player!"

Johnson's chest deflated and he carefully put the record back into the torn paper bag.

"Not yet, we don't. Wit' duh extra money I'm earnin' from Mistah Sammy, I'll be able tuh buy one real soon."

"Ain't nuthin' extra 'bout dat money, boy."

Dora's voice rung out from their bedroom doorway, scaring Johnson and Merry half to death. They jumped as she entered the room and tossed a shoebox at Johnson's feet.

"You workin' wit Mistah Sammy tuh hep give us whut we need. Dis roof ovah our head. Dis land unda our feet. I ain't lettin' you miss school and church jus' so you can waste dis family's hard-earned money on mess!"

"But, Momma, I ain't waste nuthin'. I just wanted you tuh have some pretty shoes. Is dat wrong?"

The sun hadn't rose yet, so Merry couldn't make out her momma's face to read her reaction. But she did feel the temperature shift in the room. Dora leaned against their rickety nightstand, looking at her sweet son. She didn't have the heart to fuss at him.

And Merry didn't have the heart to be jealous. Johnson seemed different to her this morning. Maybe he was becoming a man. Or maybe it was because he was twelve now. The same age as she was.

Once a year, a strange thing happened to Merry and her brother. She was born on December 9, 1935 - a year before Johnson - but every September when his birthday came, they became the same age. Johnson loved that time of the year. It made him feel like he was as grown as she was. Merry, though, usually never paid Johnson any mind, because she knew in three months, she'd be oldest again.

Today, though, Merry didn't mind sharing her age with her brother. She was almost proud of him.

Johnson took their momma's hand and pulled her to sit down on the bed. He opened up the shoebox like a department store shoe salesman and slipped a pair of pretty pink house slippers on Dora's tired, callused feet.

"Missus Sammy calls 'em house shoes. But I calls 'em do-nuthin' shoes, 'cuz dat's all she does all day. I'm gone keep workin' hard, Momma, so one day, you can be like Missus Sammy and do nuthin'. You like 'em?"

"Dey nice, John John. Real nice."

"Good. Merry, play your record, so me and momma can dance."

"Boy, what I'm gone play it on?! My finger?"

"Sang the song. Pretend."

"Johnson, we ain't got time fo' dis mess..."

"Naw, Momma, Merry sing the song all duh time when it don't matter none. She can sing it dis once fo' us. Right, Merry?"

Johnson and Dora looked to Merry, hopeful. Lord knows she felt silly just thinking about it, but the looks on both of their faces made Merry start tapping her bare foot to the blues melody playing in her head. With the light from the rising sun shining through the window as her spotlight, Merry opened her mouth and began to sing.

Johnson bowed in front of Dora and held out his hand like the finest English gentleman.

"Momma, can I have dis dance?"

Dora playfully grabbed his hand and stood.

"Boy, you a mess!"

Almost shy like, Dora and Johnson swayed to Merry's off-key tune. Merry, offended by their timidness, stomped her feet and sang louder with more gusto. Johnson, taking Merry's cue, spun Dora and caught her in his arms before she had a chance to protest.

Johnson winked at her, his upper body swaying and his feet sliding back and forth underneath him, challenging her. Dora smiled, let go of his hand and copied his moves, every step, every sway. Merry and Johnson fell out, laughing.

"Yaw chirren ain't got nuthin' on me! Nuthin'!"

CRAZY AND SWEET,
HONEY BEE

"Mer--Mer--Merry, wait up!"

The Lord hadn't blessed Merry yet with those eyes in the back of her head, but she knew who was calling after her.

She pretended to walk faster. James caught up with her, winded. The boy was always winded.

"Where you goin'?"

"Home."

"But I--I--I walk you home. You--you--you mad at me?"

Merry hesitated. James had been walking her home from school every day since they met that Sunday. They always took the back road and were careful to only hold hands when no one was around. Merry also only let James walk her halfway home, so that Dora wouldn't see them.

But Merry was starting to feel uneasy about the whole thing. Her momma knew everything. Wouldn't be long before Dora knew about her and James, too.

James took her hand.

"I--I--I got some--some--thin' for you."

"Whut is it?"

"I--I--I ain't got it wit' me. You got--got--ta come wit' me to the lake to--to--tonight to get it."

"Sweetheart Lake?"

"Yeah, sn--sn--sneak out to--to--night wit' me."

Lord knows wasn't nobody else in the whole world Merry wanted to go fishing with but James, but her excitement right now was all tangled up in fear and forming a throbbing knot in her stomach.

"I don't know."

"Why n--n--not? You can sn--sn--sneak out afta yo' mo--mo--momma go tuh bed."

"Whut we gone do at duh lake?"

"It's a sur--sur--surprise. Dag, Girl, don't y--y--you like sur--sur--surprises?"

Merry loved surprises and what surprised her most was what she said next.

"O.K."

"Yeah?"

Merry, suddenly shy, nodded her head. James broke out into a huge grin.

"Girl, y--y--you just l--l--like a bee and hon--hon--honey."

"Shut up talkin' silly, boy, 'fo I change my mind."

"Naw, y--y--you won't, Hon--hon--honey Bee. Y--y--you can't say n--n--no to me. I--I--I'm too sw--sw--sweet."

Merry playfully shoved James and he dramatically fell flat to the ground, like the biggest giant had just slapped him. He laid there in the red Georgia dirt, his arms and legs spread every which-a-way and faked like he was dying. Merry stood over him, laughing so hard, she was crying.

They strolled the rest of the way, hand in hand, laughing. James told Merry more tales about living up North. Six years ago, his momma packed him and his three little brothers up and followed his daddy to Chicago. James' father had left them two years earlier to get everything in order so he could send for them, but when they got there, his father was boozing and gambling again and shacked up with some other woman. James' momma kicked her out, his daddy promised to make things right and life was good for the family. For awhile.

Then his father left them again. He claimed he was going up to Jacksonville, Florida to find work planting and picking crops. He promised to wire money every week and send for them once he got things in order. But this time, James and his momma knew he was lying. James wanted to come home then, but his momma took up with a sweet talking hustler, whose only job was to con Colored women out of their hard-earned money. And two years later, when his momma's money was gone, the only thing the hustler left behind was his momma's broken heart and James' two baby sisters.

Reaching the fork in the road, they stopped and looked at each other. This was as far as James could go.

Up ahead a piece, Merry saw Johnson plowing Mr. Sammy's backfield. If James didn't leave right now, Johnson could look up and spot him with her. James began to pull his hand away to go. Merry held on.

"Let's say hi tuh Johnson."

"Y--y--you sh--sh--sho'?"

"Yeah. Come on."

Merry walked hand in hand with a nervous James up to Mr. Sammy's backfield, then leaned on the gate in front of Johnson.

"Boy, you stay out in dis sun too much longer, you gone be blacker dan duh bottom of duh devil's feet."

Johnson stopped the mule and looked up, happy to see his sister. Then, he noticed James.

"Who dis?"

Merry smiled, proud to make the overdue introduction.

"Dis is James. James, dis is my brotha Johnson."

Johnson, protective and jealous, eyeballed James. Merry looked at them standing in front of each other and noticed how much they really did look alike. They were both dark chocolate boys, stood at the same height and both were slightly bow-legged.

Johnson gripped the handle of the plow and was the first to speak.

"Hi."

"H--H--H---"

Johnson looked at Merry as James fought a losing battle with his tongue, started to laugh.

Not a hee hee laugh, but a belly- aching laugh that starts tingling at your toes, then runs all the way up your body and shoots out your mouth like a bullet from a gun. James looked down to the ground, embarrassed. Merry grabbed Johnson and pulled him off to the side. Her brother was laughing so hard, he was choking.

"Duh boy is s--s--slow?!"

"No, you jus' rattled him. It's worst when he's rattled."

"Dis duh boy Momma tol' you tuh stay 'way from, ain't it?"

"Momma ain't got tuh know about dis."

"Why not?"

"'Cuz deer's some thangs I know 'bout you dat Momma don't. Or maybe you was gone tell Momma yo'sef dat you ain't always workin' here when you say and you been smokin' and playin' cards wit' our money 'cross duh tracks?"

Johnson swallowed his laugh, looked back to James. Merry saw Mr. Sammy come out of the barn. She waved to him.

"Hi there, Mistah Sammy!"

Mr. Sammy looked from Johnson to James, said nothing. Johnson rambled to fill up the silence.

"Mistah Sammy, suh, Merry jus' stopped by tuh say hello on her way home from school."

"I need you in the barn."

"Yassuh. Right away, suh."

Johnson glared at Merry. James touched her on the shoulder.

"See y--y--you later?"

Merry nodded. James smiled, then disappeared through a field. Johnson growled.

"Whut Slow Boy mean by dat, Merry, huh?"

Merry walked away, her smile so big, she didn't want to answer.

COOKIN' WIT
GREASE!

Merry opened the mailbox with her eyes closed. It was a game she played with herself, so that she could be surprised by what she found inside. Usually, it was a leaflet picturing a blonde, blue eyed white woman with straight teeth and perfect hair advertising some new appliance or clothes that her momma couldn't afford. Sometimes, it was a religious pamphlet selling the last tears of Jesus in an eyedropper or sanctified holy cooking oil.

Maybe today, Merry prayed, she'd be lucky and find a letter from Excellent, who had finally come to her senses and wanted her and Johnson to come up to Detroit and live with her. It had been three years after all since her mother's visit, and Excellent hadn't even sent as much as a postcard to them.

Merry reached inside the mailbox and felt around. From the feel of things, it was the same old junk - leaflets, a pamphlet. Then a ragged edge of cardboard scratched against her finger. It was a postcard.

Excited, Merry opened her eyes and yanked out the postcard, letting the other mail fall to the ground. There was a picture of a beautiful Colored woman on the front holding up a shot glass for a toast and dressed to the nines in a tight red dress, gloves, high heels, and a wide-brim black hat with a white gardenia pinned to it. Across the photo, in letters written in red lipstick was: *Let the Good Times Roll!*

Merry smiled. Only person fool enough to send this was her Auntie Teenie. She was the gypsy of the family – the only one allowed to pick up and go anywhere when her feet started itching. None of the other brothers and sisters were given a choice. Like a mailman delivering parcels, Dora took turns sending her youngest daughters off to Atlanta for school and the boys to Savannah and Macon to work for higher wages. But Teenie, who was tall like Dora and fair-skinned enough to pass for white, was free to go to school in town and find her own work, always managing to get friendly with a white family just long enough for her to get what she wanted.

Teenie had traveled all over the world that way and always stayed in touch with a postcard, never a letter. Sometimes the note on the back would be one sentence or if Merry was lucky, a whole paragraph. Once, Teenie was in such a rush, she even sent a blank postcard!

Merry turned to run into the house, then remembered to pick up the rest of the mail on the ground, when the front door of her house opened. Merry looked upside down between her legs and saw her momma and Reverend Tender step out on the porch together. Dora, standing close and smiling, was helping the Reverend straighten his tie and shirt collar.

Merry stood up and turned around, to make sure she was seeing what she was seeing. That's when Rev. Tender noticed her. Like a slick snake in oil, he laughed and slid back from Dora.

"Merry! God bless yo' heart! How long you been standin' deer?"

"I jus' got home."

"School let out early today, Baby?"

Merry shifted her weight onto her left foot. Uneasy. Her momma was in a good mood and she called her baby. Dora and the good Reverend were definitely up to no good.

"Yes, Momma, 'cuz e'erybody's gotta help get things ready for duh homecomin' on Sunday."

"See, Reveren', tol' you e'erybody lookin' forward tuh duh church homecomin' dis year. Don't know what it is."

"Aw, dat's simple, Miz. Dora. They're all 'cited, 'cause of the three F's - Fellowship, food and fun. I was tol' folks are comin' from as far as three counties over. God is good."

"Yes, he is and he got duh whole worl' in his hands. But God ain't in charge of dis homecomin'. I am. You best git gone, so I can git back tuh it."

Dora winked and Reverend Tender, the obedient gentleman, flashed his tiny teeth smile and headed down the road. Merry watched him walk away. The man waddled like a pigeon-toed penguin. Why did her momma bother with him?

Dora turned her attention back to Merry.

"What's dat dere you carryin'?"

Merry looked at her hands. Reverend Tender and her momma had thrown her off so much that she had forgot all about Teenie's postcard.

"Got another card from Teenie."

"Lawd, whut dat girl done got hersef into now? Whut she say?"

"Don't know yet."

"Well, den come read it to me. Den you can make my letters back tuh her when you done. She leave a address dis time?"

Merry looked at the back of the postcard. Teenie was back in Detroit. That was a surprise, especially since she and Excellent had fallen out. Plus, Teenie never could stay anywhere for long and she never visited any place twice. Detroit had to be some place special or home to somebody special to stop Teenie's feet from itching.

Dora rocked in her chair and listened like a child hearing her favorite bedtime story while Merry read Teenie's postcard to her:

Family! How yaw doing? As you can see, I'm cooking with grease! I'm working for this nice Jewish family in a clothing store downtown.

They trust me to run everything by myself, so naturally, I share the wealth with my peoples when they not looking! Momma, I got some fine things for you. And I know Johnson with his handsome self is asking why Auntie Teenie back in Detroit? Well, not too long ago, I was in Belgium (Merry I got some chocolates for you!) and while I was there, I met the finest soldier from Detroit of all places! He asked me to marry him. I told him no, but said I would come back to get to know him for awhile. What the hell, right?! Well, so far so good. Can't wait to see yaw soon. Love yaw like a fat child love cake! Teenie.

Dora laughed and took the postcard from Merry to get a closer look at the picture of the Colored woman on the front.

"Uhm, uhm, hum. Teenie sho' got her daddy's ways. It's like he took all duh life he had left in him and gave it tuh her 'of' he died. My Chile! My Chile!"

Merry laughed, too, but her thoughts drifted to her mother. Why didn't Teenie mention Excellent in her card?

"Momma?"

"Uhm?"

"Did Excellent die and you jus' didn't tell me?"

"Chile, whut duh hell kinda question is dat?!"

"I was jus' wonderin' dat's all."

"Why you wonderin'?"

Merry lowered her head. Dora pressed her.

"You dink I would let yo' momma die and not tell you?"

"No, Momma, I just don't know why she never wrote us again. Why she never came back."

"Came back for whut? Yaw don't want tuh stay here wit' me no mo', Merry? Dat why you wishin' so hard on yo' momma?"

Merry looked at Dora. Her tone and words still sounded angry, defensive even, but her eyes gave her away. Her momma was scared to be alone.

Merry took Teenie's postcard, deciding not to answer the question she and her momma already knew the answer to.

"Let's jus' write Teenie back, Momma, O.K.?"

Not waiting for Dora's answer, Merry got up to get a piece of paper and a pencil off the table, afraid that if she looked at her momma any longer, Dora would look into her eyes and figure out what she was really feeling.

TURN. ME. LOOSE.

Nighttime wasn't coming fast enough.

Merry, anxious, was still dressed and lying under the covers starring up at the tin roof. Where was James? Did he get caught? Or worst yet - Did he change his mind?

Johnson turned over in his bed. Merry held her breath, hoping her brother wouldn't wake up. He had come home early today from work, took a bath and went straight to bed without speaking to them. He hadn't even eaten dinner.

Merry felt kind of bad. He must have gotten into trouble with Mr. Sammy after she and James left. Mr. Sammy always worked Johnson like a slave, but today, he ran her poor brother down so bad that he had to let him come home early to heal up.

Merry yawned. If James didn't come soon, he'd be going to Sweetheart Lake by himself. She closed her eyes and drifted off to sleep as a hot breeze blew past her face. She opened her eyes. Johnson was sitting next to her on the floor by her bed.

"Johnson, whut you doin' on duh floor?"

"I ain't sleepy no mo'."

"You mad at me?"

"What fo'?"

"Fo' whut happened today wit' Mistah Sammy. Did he git mad at you?"

"Naw, he ain't mad. Ain't mad at all."

"Den why you actin' like dis?"

"'Cuz I gotta go back tomorrow."

"Tell Momma you too sick to work."

"I ain't sick, Merry."

Merry rose up, frustrated. If Johnson wasn't sleepy and he wasn't sick, then what the heck was wrong with him? She didn't have time for her brother's silliness. Not tonight.

Outside, she heard a low whistle. James' whistle. Merry climbed out of the bed and hopped over Johnson to James who was waiting for her at the window. Angry and hurt, Johnson grabbed her arm.

"Where you goin' wit' him?"

"Gone back tuh sleep, Johnson."

"I said I ain't sleepy no mo'."

James, seeing the fire in Johnson's eyes, wilted.

"M--M--Mer--ry, m-m-maybe..."

Johnson stepped forward, threatening.

"Shut up, Stupid. Ain't nobody talkin' tuh you."

Merry blocked Johnson, snapped.

"He. Ain't. Stupid."

Merry stood face to face with Johnson, the look in her eyes and tone of her voice telling her brother that it wasn't up to him to let her go. She was already gone.

Merry shook her arm free from Johnson's grip and without saying another word, climbed right out the window into the night with James.

****

Merry's hand was sweating so bad, it was any wonder that James was able to still hold on to it. Just when she thought her heart couldn't take it no more, they broke through to the clearing and Merry, who wasn't a stranger to Sweetheart Lake in the daytime, saw a wonder that she couldn't believe. The lake looked as smooth as a sheet of clear ice and the night sky's bright moon and twinkling stars were reflecting in it like the finest mirror. She let go of James' hand and ran to the lake's edge to look at herself in the water. Even Sweetheart Lake made her look pretty.

"Y--y--you l--l--like cake?"

Merry had gotten so caught up in the moment, she had almost forgot that James was there. Behind her, underneath a Weeping Willow Tree was a blanket with a small covered basket setting on top of it. Merry looked at him, suspicious.

"Where you git cake from?"

"B--b--borrowed two p--p--pieces from my m--m--momma, b--b--but I canned th--th--the b--b--berries my--s--s--sef."

Merry dug into the basket and found two pieces of fresh pound cake wrapped in wax paper, a newly open can of strawberry preserves and a pickle jar filled with strawberry lemonade. James took the cake, plopped some strawberries on top of it and gave it to her. Merry took a bite and frowned.

"Y--y--you don't l--l--like it?"

"Yeah, but you wrong fo' sayin' you did dese strawberries when you know yo' momma did."

"D--D--Dose m--m--my b--b--berries and I'm gone win a rib--rib--ribbon f-f-fo' 'em, too! You--you--you'll s--s--see when you go wit' m--m--me to duh--duh--duh chu--chu--church homecom--com--comin'."

Merry gulped down a big bite of pound cake. James couldn't have just said what she thought he did.

James continued, made it plain.

"Will y--y--you go wit' m--m--me to the homecom---com--comin', Hon--hon--honey B--b--bee?"

"But your momma and my momma..."

"S--s--so? As l--l--long as we know we d--d--dere tuh--get--get--gether, d--d--dat's all d--d--dat count. Right?"

Merry hated when James made sense. She already couldn't resist him, but when he dropped his cute country logic in her lap like a handful of pretty, wild flowers, it made her feel dumb for even thinking about saying no to him.

James eyed her, wanting an answer.

"S--s--so, whut y--y--you s--s--say?"

"I say you crazy and gone get us both killed."

"Whut I--I--I look l--l--like git--git--gitting m--m--my girl kil--kil--killed?"

"Who said I'm yo' girl?"

"Y--y--you did, 'mem--mem--member?"

"Nope. Must of slipped my mind."

"Well, l--l--let m--m--me glue it b--b--back d--d--den."

James dug in the basket and pulled out a single clip-on ruby earring. Merry couldn't take her eyes off of it. She had only seen white women wearing beautiful jewelry like that in the leaflets she found in her momma's mailbox. James nervously dropped the earring in her hand.

"M--m--my daddy gave m--m--my mom--mom--momma d--d--dis when d--d--dye got mar--mar--married. To--to--told her when he got s--s--some mo' mon--mon--money, he'd b--b--buy her d--d--duh oth--th--tha one."

"Did he?"

"Nope."

Exited, Merry clipped the earring onto her right ear and modeled it for him.

"Well, I don't need duh otha one. It's mo' special dis way, anyhow."

"Yeah?"

"Yeah."

Merry and James looked at each other, both knowing what they wanted to do, what they came there to do. But each suddenly too shy too to do it.

***

Merry's bedroom window didn't seem that far off the ground when she snuck out with James, but for some reason she was having the darnest time climbing back through it. It's like she was tipsy from all the fun they just had, and she was trying to hold in her giggles so bad that it was throwing her off balance. And James? He wasn't no help, because he was crouching down a few steps away in the grass, buckled over from muffling his laughing.

Merry steadied herself like a drunk trying to walk straight in front of the sheriff and finally pulled herself up into the window. But before she could swing her leg over the ledge and step on the floor, someone - felt like the hot hand of the devil, himself - yanked her inside. She landed hard on her back and looked up, ready to swing on Johnson, but instead found her momma towering over her. Dora plopped her heavy foot down on Merry's chest, knocking the wind out of her.

"Ain't I tell you stay away from dat boy?"

Merry wanted to answer. Lord's knows she did. But it felt like her lungs were deflated like a balloon and all the air had been sucked out of her body.

"Answer me, gurl!"

Merry tried to gasp for air and wildly grabbed at her momma's foot, but Dora wouldn't budge.

"Momma, you killin' her!"

Merry heard her brother's voice ring out faintly from the darkness, but she couldn't see him through her tears.

"Gone outside, git a good switch fo' your sistah like I said."

"Momma, please..."

"Do like I tol' you, boy, 'fo' I beat your ass!"

Merry barely heard Johnson run out the room, the weight of her momma's foot now causing a ringing in her ears and a dull, burning sensation in her chest. She tried to move Dora's foot again, but she didn't have the strength. All

Merry could do was give in to the stillness that was tugging on her. Panicked, Dora lifted her foot and shook Merry.

"Lawd, Jesus! Merry!"

"Momma..."

"You shoulda jus' done whut I tol' you. Why didn't you, Merry? Why you hurt me like dis?"

"I'm sorry, Momma. I'm sorry."

Merry laid her head in Dora's lap. Dora looked down at her, wanting to stroke her face, but she didn't.

"I'd ratha kill you dead, Merry, 'for I see you broke down and pregnant wit' a whole heap of babies and no man to call yo' own. You heah what I say?"

Merry sniffled, quickly nodded her head and wrapped her arms around her momma's waist. If she could just get her momma to hug her back, then maybe Dora would forget that she sent Johnson outside to find a switch for her. Merry laced her fingers together behind Dora's back, pulled herself closer and whimpered.

"Momma, please. I won't do it no more. I promise I won't."

Merry felt Dora's arms jerk a bit. Her momma was weakening. Merry sobbed and buried her head into Dora's chest like a two-year-old crying herself out of deserved whipping.

"I'll do whatevah you want, Momma. Please jus' don't beat me. Please."

Merry felt Dora's arms jerk again. She squeezed a few more teardrops out of her eyes and looked up to her momma with the most pitiful face she could muster. But Dora was already peering down at her with angry, disappointed eyes.

"Boy, git yo' ass from behind dat do' and brin' dat switch to me right now!"

Johnson hurried into the bedroom with a switch so sharp that it cut the air in half. Merry tried to hold onto Dora even tighter, but Dora pulled Merry's hands apart and pushed her back onto the floor. She could barely stand up for Merry grabbing at her feet.

"Take yo' clothes off and git in duh bed."

"Please, Momma. Momma, please!"

"Merry, turn me loose!"

Merry heard her momma's deadly order, but all she could think to do was grab hold of her momma so that Dora couldn't get a hold of that switch Johnson was holding.

Dora snatched the switch from Johnson and lit into Merry, her words landing with each lash.

"I. Said. Turn. Me. Loose!"

Merry cried out and tried to dart away. But every which way she moved, Dora tagged her with the switch, each lash stinging and drawing trickles of blood as it sliced Merry's clothes and ripped through her tender skin. All Merry could do was curl her body into a tight ball like a water bug to protect herself. But that still left her back, arms and legs exposed, and Dora, who was getting angrier and more tired with each swing of her arm, was too far gone now to show Merry mercy.

Dora struck Merry again, the lash stinging so deep that it stole the scream right out of Merry's mouth and replaced it with the bitter taste of blood and salty tears.

Merry moaned, in so much pain that silence had swallowed everything in the room. Dora had told her that she would kill her dead. And her momma was guilty of doing a lot of things, but one thing she never did was break a promise.

**

Merry opened her eyes that evening, surprised to still be in the Land of the Living. She tried to lift up in her bed and sharp pains shot through her weak body. Dora gingerly eased her head back down onto her sweaty pillow.

"Be still. You gone make it worse, you keep movin'."

Dora poured alcohol onto a cloth and dabbed Merry's fresh shoulder wounds. Merry nearly jumped out of the bed.

"Gurl, stop! So damn hardhead. I gotta change dese dressins now, so you don't git 'fected."

Merry winced and tried to will the tears to dry up in her eyes.

"You hungry?"

Merry shook her head no.

"Well, you need to be. You ain't ate all day. You gotta eat tuh keep your strength up. You gonna help Missus Sammy tomorrow wit' a dinner she's givin'."

"But, Momma..."

"Don't you momma me, gurl. I beat yo' ass half tuh death tuh keep you from dat boy. You dink I'm gone let you go tuh duh homecomin' where he gone be?! Mistah Sammy need Johnson tuh work tomorrow, so you gone work, too."

"Momma..."

"Don't say nuthin' else, Merry. Not anotha word."

Merry fell silent, her will broken and the salty tears falling from her eyes. She was in pain again. Not the pain from her wounds that her momma just covered with fresh dressing. A new pain of never seeing James again.

*

Merry's eyes sprung open. Her bladder was full. Too full. She needed to get to the outhouse. Quick.

She took a deep breath and braced herself. She raised up and just like before, sharp pains shot through her arms, back and legs. She yelped out loud. Johnson turned over in his bed.

"Merry?"

Merry ignored him and struggled to stand up. It felt like her skin was tearing open all over again, but she had to hurry. If she didn't, she was going to pee on herself and Dora would surely beat her again.

"Where you goin'?"

Merry still ignored her brother.

"Whut you tryin' tuh do? You gotta pee?"

Merry paid Johnson no mind and headed for the window. She didn't have enough time to go out the back door to the outhouse like a person with sense.

Johnson stood up to help her.

"Fool, whut you doin'? Let me carry you."

"Leave me 'lone, Johnson."

"C'mon, Merry..."

"Boy, I said, leave me 'lone!"

Merry felt a trickle run down her leg. She wasn't going to make it. And it was all Johnson's fault.

"Gone pee on yoursef den. Dat's whut you get. Shoulda stayed home wit' me."

Johnson snorted and laid back down in the bed. Merry looked at him, her bladder on the verge of busting wide open like a dam, but suddenly, she didn't have to pee so bad anymore.

"Whut you say?"

Johnson turned his back to her and didn't answer. Merry stepped over and stood next to his bed, her blistered hand balled into a fist.

"Whut. You. Say?"

Johnson still didn't answer. Merry knew he heard her question and she knew that he could feel her standing over him. But none of that mattered. Her brother wasn't scared of her. In fact, he was acting like he didn't even care about her at all.

Merry felt her face get wet, not with sweat, but with tears. She couldn't even remember how many beatings she had taken for Johnson. How many times she had protected him and went without just so that he could have.

Merry unballed her fist. She couldn't smash his face in like he deserved. Because the truth was, Johnson had already beaten her. He had wounded her someplace deep inside.

And the boy hadn't even laid a finger on her.

ON YO' BACK
LONG 'NUF

Merry winced as she reached for the fancy flowered teacups in Mrs. Sammy's china cabinet. Her skin was still tender from Dora's beating and the heavy starch in the maid's uniform that was nearly falling off of her was irritating her cuts something awful. She wanted to call out for help, but knew that M'Dear Beulah, Mrs. Sammy's head and oldest maid, would run and tell everybody in town that she was lazy and no good, just so she could embarrass her momma.

Merry peeked around the corner to make sure M'Dear Beaulah wasn't looking, then quickly slipped off her fraying shoes and pulled one of the dining room chairs over to the cabinet. She wobbled as she stepped on to it, the cushion so soft that she sunk a little.

She gingerly grabbed the teacups, cradled them in her arms and was just about to step down when she saw a small crumpled black and white photo sticking out of a corner on the cabinet shelf. It was a photo of two girls. One white. One Colored. The Colored girl looked just like her.

"Merry, either I caught you stealing my teacups or Ms. Dora raised a heathen. Which is it, child?"

Merry turned and saw Mrs. Sammy standing in the dining room doorway with her hands on her wide hips. Mrs. Sammy wasn't exactly what folks would call pretty. With thick brown hair and a fat, flat face, Mrs. Sammy didn't look like the beautiful white women in the magazines that Merry liked. But still there was something nice about her. Maybe it was her sky blue eyes or the way she talked. Her family had sent her away to school to become a teacher and escape Locust Grove. Mrs. Sammy ended up coming back, though, to marry her childhood sweetheart, Mr. Sammy, and she never did teach one minute of school. But to this day, she still carried her parents' good intentions in every proper word that she spoke.

"Missus Sammy, I was jus'..."

"You were just stepping on my very expensive chair. That's what you were doing. Let me help you with those cups before you hurt yourself."

Mrs. Sammy took the cups out of Merry's arms and Merry stepped down, nearly tripping over her uniform's apron, because it was so long.

"That dress is too big for you, isn't it, child? Beaulah couldn't find something that fits?"

"Dis usta be Viola's. Duh smallest one she had."

"Well, she could have pinned it at least. My Lord, it's falling off of you."

"Dat's o.k. I'm usta my clothes not fittin'. Won't keep me from workin' none."

"You mean, it won't keep you from working at all."

"Yes, Ma'am."

"Well, it isn't proper. What was Beaulah thinking? Beaulah!"

"No, Missus Sammy, it's o.k."

"It is not O.K. Your clothing must fit."

M'Dear Beaulah, a senior gray-haired, round hipped, bow-legged woman, just a few years shy of doing the right hand of fellowship with Jesus, scuffled into the dining room. She shot Merry a mean look, then settled her eyes to the floor.

"Yes, Missus?"

"Why didn't you pin this child's dress?"

"Missus, I didn't have time. Viola was 'sposed tuh..."

"Viola is lazier than a garden snake with a full stomach. You know that! If your daughter was worth her salt, I wouldn't have needed this child's extra help today."

"I'm sorry, Missus..."

"You should be. You know how important this supper is today, Beaulah. Reverend Warso, the First Lady and the Church founders will be here. Why do I have to do everything?! Jesus Christ."

Mrs. Sammy opened one of the china cabinet drawers, took out a pincushion covered in straight pins and pulled Merry over to her. M'Dear Beaulah stood there giving Merry the evil eye and waiting for Mrs. Sammy to dismiss her. Mrs. Sammy started pinning Merry's uniform and didn't say another word.

In a way, Mrs. Sammy's silent dismissal of M'Dear Beaulah was harsher and louder than any words she could ever say. Merry looked at M'Dear Beaulah, grinning mischievously with her eyes. Humiliated, M'Dear Beulah hurried out of the room.

Mrs. Sammy swiveled Merry around to pin the other side of her dress. It stung Merry a little every time she moved the material over her scabbing cuts, but she didn't let on, because Mrs. Sammy fussing over her made her feel special. Like she was a princess being fitted for the finest fairy tale gown, not an itchy hand-me-down maid uniform.

"Now you look presentable. We'll just fold up these sleeves..."

Merry lowered her eyes to the floor. She knew it was wrong to pull back from any white woman, especially Mrs. Sammy. So, she didn't.

"What happened, Child?"

"I...fell."

"It must have been a really bad fall."

"Yes, Ma'am."

"Well. We'll leave these sleeves down then. You finish putting those teacups on the table and I'll go remind my husband to freshen up. Our guests will be arriving soon."

"Missus Sammy?"

"Yes?"

Merry paused, suddenly nervous. She wanted to ask her about the two girls in the picture. But if her momma told her once, she told her a hundred times - colored folks don't ask white folks questions. In fact, Merry wasn't even supposed to be looking Mrs. Sammy in the face at all right now. But Mrs. Sammy's sky blue eyes just seemed so kind, so calm, that Merry, right or wrong, felt it was safe this one time to cross the thick invisible line that separated them.

"Who are duh girls in duh picture?"

"What picture, Child?"

"Duh one on duh shelf in duh cabinet. I saw it when I got duh cups."

Mrs. Sammy stepped over to the cabinet and peeked inside. She chuckled as she picked up and smoothed out the wrinkled photo.

"My Lord, I haven't seen this in years. This, my child, is a photograph of myself and my best friend. Your mother. Excellent. We were closer than two peas in a pod!"

"You were?"

"Oh, yes. You know, Ms. Dora worked for my family for years. Well, more often, than not, she brought Excellent along to help out and keep me company. You see, I was an only child and Ms. Dora quite frankly had more of a hand in raising me than my own parents, really. They were both so busy. Father with his businesses and mother with her many society and church functions. Anyhow, every year my parents paid for a photographer to come to our home and take my annual spring portrait. On this particular day, Excellent was here with Ms. Dora and I begged and begged my parents to let her sit with me for my portrait. They, of course, said no. But I can be quite persistent when I want to be and that year, I'm proud to say, my parents paid for two spring portraits. One of myself alone and one with my Excellent."

"She looks like me."

"She does, doesn't she."

Merry and Mrs. Sammy stood, admiring the old black and white photograph in silence. The girls looked to be a little older than Merry and appeared to be happy. Smiling for the camera, young Mrs. Sammy was seated in a white wicker chair and wearing a beautiful ruffled blouse and petticoat with matching gloves, and Excellent, dressed in a drab work dress and barefoot, stood next to Mrs. Sammy, holding an umbrella shielding her from the sun.

The longer Merry gazed at the photo, the more questions she had. Were Mrs. Sammy and Excellent still friends? If not, then why? Why was this photograph that Mrs. Sammy cherished so much crammed in the back corner of her china cabinet and not framed like all of the other ones in her home?

Merry turned to ask Mrs. Sammy all of the questions running through her head. If anybody could and would tell her the truth about the mother she wanted to know, but didn't, it would be her. But the pained, far-a-way look painted on Mrs. Sammy's face silenced Merry's tongue. It wasn't safe to ask her now. The intimate moment she and Mrs. Sammy were sharing was gone and just like that, the imaginary line was again drawn between them.

Merry stepped back as Mrs. Sammy folded the photo and stuck it into her dress front pocket. The grandfather clock chimed three times.

"My Lord, I've tarried too long with you. I'm not nearly ready. Mr. Sammy hasn't even bathed..."

"I can go fetch Mistah Sammy, Ma'am, so you can finish preparin' yourself."

"Thank you, Merry. That would be a great help. Be quick now. We don't have much time."

Merry hurried outside, her mind still racing with thoughts about Excellent. Her momma had never told her that Mrs. Sammy and Excellent were friends. Why was this and everything about Excellent a secret?

Ever since Merry could remember, Dora had kept the reality of her mother from her by telling her just enough about Excellent so that she would remain a question and not become rooted in her fertile mind. But meeting Excellent that fateful day changed everything. Seeing herself in her mother's eyes planted an impatient seed in Merry's mind and now thoughts and questions about Excellent grew and survived on their own inside of her like wild desert flowers.

Merry wiped sweat from her face. It was hot for October. Indian Summer is what folks called it. She called out for Mr. Sammy. Where could his mean tail be? Mr. Sammy wasn't in the front or backfields. And Johnson wasn't around either. They couldn't have gone into town, because Mr. Sammy's old horse and wagon was parked outside the barn as usual.

Merry stepped through the cracked opened barn door without moving it. It was cool and quiet inside. And other than some scattered tools, a rusty plow and tall stacks of horse feed, the barn was empty.

Merry turned to leave and then heard a sound. It was a man's voice, real low like, moaning. The grown folks sound was coming from behind the horse feed.

Merry smiled. She couldn't have prayed for better luck. She was going to find Mr. Sammy with another woman. He'd probably buy her anything she wanted to keep her quiet. He might even give them back the farm if she made him.

Merry stepped behind the horse feed. Mr. Sammy was standing, his pants down around his ankles, his eyes closed. And Johnson was kneeling in front of him.

Johnson looked to Merry and stopped. Mr. Sammy growled.

"Boy, why you stop?"

Mr. Sammy opened his eyes and saw Merry. Johnson scooted away, ashamed. Mr. Sammy pulled up his pants and started to laugh. Merry reached out her hand to her brother.

"Johnson, come on go wit' me."

"Oh, no, Merry, me and Johnson got some business to finish here."

"He finished wit' you, Mistah Sammy."

"Who said?"

"I said..."

Before Merry could finish her word good, Mr. Sammy closed fist slapped her hard in the mouth, knocking her over the horse feed. Johnson ran to her side.

"Merry!"

"Gone get my whip, boy. I'm gonna teach your sister a lesson for sassin' me."

"Leave her 'lone!"

"Leave her 'lone?!"

Mr. Sammy stomped up to Johnson, about to smack him, too. Instead, he tenderly caressed Johnson's face.

"Boy, you lucky, your mouth's too important to me or I'd smack the taste outta your's, too."

Merry tasted her blood as it dripped down her busted lip and down her chin. She was winded and so angry, she was sick to her stomach.

"Let him go."

"What that you say, Merry?"

"Let. Him. Go."

"You don't tell me what to do, gal. I own you. The both of you. Your momma. Your farm. I can take it away just like that. You hear me?"

Merry wanted to cry. Mr. Sammy was right. He was in control. That, Merry couldn't change. But she could change who he was controlling.

"You right, Mistah Sammy. We awful grateful."

Johnson's eyes bucked out, shocked.

"Merry? Whut you sayin'?"

"Johnson, I'm sayin', it's my turn tuh thank Mr. Sammy."

Johnson grabbed her arm, pleading.

"No, Merry! I won't let you."

"It's O.K., Johnson. Mistah Sammy gone let you go and I'm gonna thank him. It's our new 'rangement. Right, Mistah Sammy? Unless...you don't like girls no mo'."

Mr. Sammy's gray eyes flashed. Everybody's got a button that you don't want to push. For some folks, it's calling them a liar. For a short man, it's making fun of his height. For Mr. Sammy, it was calling him a fairy. A sissy. Queer. Even though, Merry had caught him with his pants down and they all knew the truth, it was still important to him live a lie and be in control. Merry knew that.

Mr. Sammy grinned.

"Well...it has been a while since I had some nigga gal tail. Let me see if the apple don't fall far from the tree."

"Merry, don't..."

"Gone, Boy. You gone watch next time. Me and your sister got some business."

Merry nodded to Johnson and rose up to her knees. Mr. Sammy kicked her back down.

"Stay right where you are, gal. I'm lookin' forward to this. You ain't spoiled yet. I can still smell the freshness on you."

Mr. Sammy unzipped his pants. Merry, seeing no light in his dead, pillaging eyes, panicked. She had made a horrible mistake. Mr. Sammy wasn't interested in her mouth. The man wanted her womb.

Trapped, Merry tried to scamper away. Mr. Sammy fell hard on top of her and grabbed her roughly around the neck.

"You scream, I'll kill you."

Merry, tears springing from her eyes, darted a horrified look up to Johnson, begging her brother to help her. Johnson, guilty with a trail of fear dripping down his pants leg, slowly backed out of the barn.

Merry heard the barn door close. Mr. Sammy, wet with sweat and stinking of manure and tobacco, flung up her dress, ripped off her underwear and forced himself inside her.

She screamed. The man was shredding her insides with thorns, splitting her in two.

Mr. Sammy clamped his dirty, bulky hand over her bloody mouth and continued to plow himself through her. Merry gasped for air. Her chest tightening. Her ribs breaking. Mr. Sammy had her pinned to the ground and his nasty skinny fingers were all over her mouth and covering her nose.

She was going to die with this white man taking her.

Merry's body went limp. Her back bleeding from re-opened sores. Her heart about the explode. She prayed for the Lord to strike Mr. Sammy dead. Right then and there.

Merry peered up at Mr. Sammy, the room suddenly soundless. Her whole body numb, and her soul on watch from the outside, Merry looked down at herself. She couldn't die. Not this way. Her momma and Johnson needed her. And if God was like His baby boy Jesus and didn't owe her nothing like Dora had told her, then He wasn't about to come down from Heaven to help a sinner like her. Merry was going to have to do what she'd always done. Save herself.

Merry bit hard into Mr. Sammy's fingers.

"Argh! 'Lil nigga bitch!"

Mr. Sammy raised up to slap her, but Merry kicked him in his groin first. He toppled over in pain and Merry scrambled away. He yanked her back by her hair.

"You done messed up, gal. I'm gone flog you. And I'm gone ride your sweet brother some more. Then, I'm gone burn down your shack of a home and put your old momma back out into my fields and work her 'til she fall out and die. And they got you to thank for all of it."

Mr. Sammy, ice cold, threw Merry down to the ground. Merry rolled over and curled up into a ball, in too much pain to cry. He stood up, pulled up his pants and headed for the barn door.

"Clean yourself up 'fore you come back in the house to help Mrs. Sammy. Don't take long neither."

Merry gagged. The stench of Mr. Sammy covered her and the taste of blood from his hand was fresh in her mouth. She grabbed her throbbing stomach and threw up, her body doubling over from cramps. Out the corner of her eye, she saw her torn underwear. She reached for it and her hand was bloody. Frantic, she searched herself for the wound. The blood was deep red, too red to be coming from her busted lip. Did Mr. Sammy cut her somewhere?

Merry ran her hands up and down her legs to find the cut. Then, she felt it. A wetness dripping down her legs that wasn't sweat.

Merry panicked. It wasn't her time. She wasn't supposed to be bleeding for a week or more. What was happening to her?

Outside, Merry heard Mr. and Mrs. Sammy quietly arguing next to the barn. She painfully rose to her feet. Mr. Sammy had hurt her, but Mrs. Sammy was Excellent's friend. Mrs. Sammy would help her.

"'Lizabeth, relax yourself. You unnervin' Johnson."

"You're more concerned about that boy, Robert? What am I saying? Of course you are. You just couldn't help yourself, could you? You live to embarrass me at every turn. Rev. Warso and our guests are here and you smell like horse shit."

"That's not horse shit, darlin'. That's nigga. And it'll wash right off. Let's go inside."

Merry struggled to stay on her feet and push open the barn door. She saw Johnson first and Mr. and Mrs. Sammy were walking away from them, toward the house. Merry looked to her brother to speak out for her. He didn't.

"Missus Sammy?"

Mrs. Sammy turned back to answer Johnson. He looked down to the ground. Her eyes floated over to Merry standing weakly in the barn doorway.

"Merry?"

"Yes, Ma'am."

Merry released the barn door handle and stood bravely on her own. In the light of the afternoon sun, she looked like a survivor of a battle. A busted lip, swelling eye and her uniform wet with blood.

Mrs. Sammy took a step over to Merry. Mr. Sammy grabbed her arm.

"Your guests are waitin', 'Lizabeth."

Mrs. Sammy shook her arm loose and walked over to Merry. Kneeling in front of Merry, Mrs. Sammy looked at Merry sorrowfully, afraid to touch her. Mr. Sammy stomped up behind her.

"'Lizabeth, Reveren' Warso and his Mrs. need your 'tention on the porch. You need to tend to your guests now."

"What happened, Robert? What did you do to this child?"

"I ain't done nuthin' to her she ain't deserve."

"Lord have mercy on your soul, Robert. You think she deserves to be beaten this way?"

Merry's eyes darted to Mr. Sammy, who was nervously looking to their nosey guests starting to gather around them. Merry sighed. These folks were Mrs. Sammy's church family. They would protect her from Mr. Sammy. Just like Mrs. Sammy.

Rev. Warso, a lanky, benevolent looking red-faced man with a crown of long white hair, stepped up and touched Mr. Sammy on the shoulder.

"Is everything alright, Robert?"

"Everything's fine, Reveren'. Me and 'Lizabeth'll be inside directly."

Rev. Warso's eyes settled on Merry. Then, he turned to Mrs. Sammy.

"Elizabeth, is there anything I can do?"

Mrs. Sammy looked to Merry, saddened and embarrassed. She rose with a forced a grin on her face.

"No, Reverend. Robert's right. Please go inside. All of you. We'll be right in."

Rev. Warso hesitated for a sanctified second, then started for the house with their other guests. Merry darted Johnson a worried look. Why did Mrs. Sammy send the white church folks away? Who was going to protect her now?

"Hold on now, Reveren'. 'Lizabeth, you wrong, darlin'. There is somethin' the Good Reveren' can do. He can pray. Pray for this nigga whore's soul."

Mrs. Sammy's body stiffened as she slowly turned back to Merry. Mr. Sammy took her hand, dramatically putting on a show for Rev. Warso and their guests.

"Darlin', forgive me. My flesh was weak to her black magic. Must of been the same black magic from when I was a boy, 'cuz I was weak she took me. Took me jus' like that Devil of a snake took Eve. That's why I beat her. The Good Lord heard my prayer even while I was sinnin' and gave me the strength to beat her. Beat her off of me."

Mrs. Sammy starred hard at Merry, her compassionate eyes now cold, distant, furious.

"This is the nigga I smell on you?"

Mr. Sammy nodded, pretending that he was too choked up to answer. Merry shook her head.

"No, Missus Sammy, no..."

Mrs. Sammy, seething, pounced all over her like a mad dog on an unprotected, newborn child.

"Are. You. Calling. My. Husband. A. Liar?"

Merry stammered. Mrs. Sammy was in her face, close enough for her to touch. But Merry knew by looking into her soul-less sky blue eyes, that she couldn't be any further away from Excellent's childhood friend right now. The thick, invisible line was again a wall between them. And now, the wall was on fire.

Merry glanced at Johnson for help. Her brother sorrowfully looked away, too scared to speak, too scared to move.

"Gurl, whut is wrong wit' you? Didn't you heah Missus Sammy?"

Reverend Warso and the guests parted like the Red Sea as Dora stepped up. Reverend Tender and other Colored folks from the picnic trailed behind her. She walked up to Merry and Mrs. Sammy.

"Momma, I didn't do nothin'..."

Dora slapped Merry so hard, she fell to the ground.

"You jus' a lie. Jus' a goddamn lie."

Merry covered her face and started to cry. Dora turned to Mrs. Sammy.

"Missus, I'm sorry."

Mrs. Sammy, her face beat red and eyes bloodshot with anger, peered through Dora, unmoved. Mr. Sammy chimed in.

"Ms. Dora, if it's all the same to you, you apologizin' for your grandbaby whore don't change the fact of what need to be done. Now, you best be goin', so we can give Merry the punishment she deserve."

Mr. Sammy stepped toward Merry. Dora jumped in between him and Merry and reached out for Mrs. Sammy.

"Mrs., she just a chile. Let Merry go and I'll teach her her lesson good."

Mrs. Sammy looked at Dora like she was a nigga. Not the woman who raised and loved her. Desperate, Dora dropped to her knees.

"Missus, she wrong! I know she wrong. Jus' please, please have mercy and let her live. I know dis hurts you in a wounded place deep down inside. But I know yo' heart. And duh Lawd know yo' heart. You don't want tuh hurt dis chile. I know you don't."

Dora starred up at Mrs. Sammy, trying to grab hold of her soul somehow with her pleading eyes. Merry looked at Dora through her tears. Her mother was the strongest woman she had ever known and now Dora was on her knees begging Mrs. Sammy for her life with everyone watching.

The moment felt frozen in time. The white folks didn't want to help and the black folks were afraid to. Merry wanted to cry out. Her momma believed she was a whore and it hurt her when Dora called her a lie and slapped her in front of everyone. But seeing her momma begging a white woman on her knees now was a worst pain. A pain that cut deeper than any wound.

"Git on up from there, Dora. You done wasted enough time wit' your carryin' on."

Dora kept her stare locked on Mrs. Sammy. Mr. Sammy, impatient, addressed his captivated audience.

"This nigga gal ain't no more a chile than I am. She snared me like a whore does a man. She broke the law, Reverend. Law of man. Law of God. And today, she gone pay for her sins."

Mr. Sammy rushed toward Merry. Dora lunged to stop him. Mrs. Sammy raised her hand.

"Robert, leave her be."

Mr. Sammy stopped, aggravated.

"Woman..."

Merry looked to Mrs. Sammy, grateful. Mrs. Sammy paused, choosing her words carefully.

"This child is Ms. Dora's responsibility, Robert. It's not our place."

"Not our place?! After what this nigga did to me?!"

Mrs. Sammy held out her hand to help Dora up. Dora appreciatively took it and rose.

"Thank you, Missus."

Mrs. Sammy nodded, but there was no warmth in her eyes. Flashing a smile, she turned her Southern charm on for the attentive crowd.

"Everyone, we apologize for this disturbance. Reverend and First Lady Warso, everyone, please join us inside. Supper's ready."

Mr. Sammy still stood towering over Merry, blocking the path for Dora. He glared menacingly at them, then stepped aside and followed Mrs. Sammy and their guests into the house.

Dora hurried to Merry's side. Rev. Tender and the others crowded around them.

"Where you cut?"

"On duh inside."

Dora took a staggered breath like she was reliving Merry's pain herself.

"Momma, I..."

"Hush wit' dat. Can you walk?"

"Yes, Momma."

"Den stand on yo' own. You been on yo' back long 'nuf."

GONE

Merry stood naked in the kitchen while Dora poured the last pot of hot water into their rusty tin tub.

She was cold, shivering. Not so much from the chill creeping through the drafty room, but from the frost covering her momma. Dora hadn't looked Merry in the face once since they got home from Mr. Sammy's.

"Git in 'fo' it git cold."

Merry saw the steam fuming up from the tub. That hot water was going to boil her and her sores alive. She didn't move.

"Can you add some cold water tuh it?"

"Gurl, you need it hot tuh clean you right! Stop sassin' me and git in."

Merry took a breath and dipped her big toe into the water. The water was so hot, it felt like it seared the skin on her toe clean off. She yanked back her foot.

"It's too hot!"

"Merry, I swear tuh God, you don't git in dis tub, I'm gone hang you mysef."

"But, Momma, it hurts!"

"Ain't gone hurt no mo' dan Mr. Sammy bustin' you open. Git in dis damn tub!"

Tired of the mess, Dora grabbed Merry and angrily plopped her in the tin tub. Merry screamed and flopped around like a live crab cooking in boiling water. She starred up at her momma standing over her. Dora looked away, turned to leave the room.

"Hurry up and clean yo'sef. 'Fo' dey come."

"'Fo' who come?"

Merry's unanswered question hit her momma's exiting back and slid down to the kitchen's wooden floor with a thud. Merry looked at her question lying there dead like a possum on a country road. Then, grabbed the bar of soap, her see-through bath rag and quickly washed herself.

When Merry got into her bedroom, her momma and Johnson were packing.

"What yaw doin'?"

"What it look like? Johnson, you got everythang in dat bag?"

"Yes, Momma."

Merry stood in the doorway, watching Johnson and Dora bustling about the room. She couldn't help but stare at her brother.

Johnson was such a coward today. He knew what Mr. Sammy was going to do. The boy knew she didn't know what Mr. Sammy was going to do. And still he didn't do anything. All his sorry self could do was piss his pants.

Dora fussed.

"Merry, stop standin' there eyeballin' us and finish dis up."

"Momma, where we goin'?"

"We ain't goin' nowhere. Jus' you and Johnson. Somewhere safe."

"Why, Momma? Mrs. Sammy, she..."

"Dat white woman want you dead, Merry. She jus' didn't want to strin' you up in duh light of day is all. I'm sendin' yaw up tuh Detroit wit' yo' momma. Tonight."

Merry, so excited about the last thing Dora just said, forgot to be scared about Mr. Sammy coming to kill her. She and Johnson were going to Detroit? That meant that Excellent wasn't dead and now Merry could live the life with her mother that she had been dreaming of.

Merry found herself smiling before she realized it.

"Uh huh, happy now, ain't you? Writin' dat letta tuh yo' momma ain't work, so you had tuh go and spread yo' legs fo' dat damn white man."

Merry's heart stopped beating. Her momma knew she wrote the letter to Excellent three years ago. Dora peered through Merry with a look as cold as ice.

"All 'cuz you wanted to leave me, I gotta lose everythang I got in dis worl'. You oughta be happy, gurl. You done got yo' wish."

Dora glared at Merry with such bitterness that Merry couldn't think of any words to defend herself. She wanted to tell her momma what really happened. Maybe if Dora knew why she did what she did with Mr. Sammy, then she'd understand and would even be proud of her for protecting Johnson.

But looking into her momma's weary eyes, Merry knew her truth wasn't going to set her free. Dora would think she was lying no matter what she said.

Merry starred at Johnson.

"Whut you lookin' at Johnson fo'?"

Merry peered defiantly at her brother, burning a hole in the back of his head and finally making him turn around and look at her.

She might as well been looking at a stranger. Her brother stood there, eyeing her blankly. He wasn't sorry. And he damn sure wasn't going to admit what they both knew. The only reason Merry had been on her back was because he had been on his knees.

"Momma, Johnson and Mistah Sammy..."

Johnson reached out for Dora, frantic.

"Mr. Sammy wasn't nothin' but kind tuh me, Momma. I was workin' hard tuh get you duh farm. I was workin' hard."

"I know you wuz, Baby. I know you wuz."

Dora proudly draped her arms around Johnson's shoulders, soothing him. Merry wanted to scream. Her momma was hugging and rocking Johnson, making him feel better? And the only touch she felt from her momma today? A slap Merry still felt stinging on her cheek.

A knock at the front door quieted the scream bubbling in Merry's stomach. Merry and Johnson looked to Dora, afraid. Dora put her finger to her lips and carefully peeked outside the bedroom window.

"Momma, is it Mistah Sammy?"

Dora rested against the wall, thinking. Another knock at the front door. Merry and Johnson ran to her. Johnson held Dora tight, clinging on for dear life.

"Momma! Momma!"

Dora rocked Johnson and calmly gave instructions to Merry.

"Reveren' Tender's comin' tuh fetch you in his wagon. He'll be waitin' on duh otha side of duh field. He gone whistle real low like, so you gotta lissen."

Merry nodded. Dora peeled herself away from Johnson.

"John John, momma need you tuh be strong now. I gotta answer duh do'."

"No, Momma. Mistah Sammy gone kill you."

"Dat fool ain't gone waste no rope on my old bones. Let me go now. Yaw listen fo' duh Reveren's whistle and don't pay no mind tuh whut's happenin' in duh sittin' room. Stay here, no matter whut you hear. Alright?"

Merry and Johnson sniffled. Another knock. Dora left, softly pulling the bedroom door closed behind her.

Merry couldn't stand still. She put her ear to the door and could hear her momma talking with someone. Sounded like a woman's voice. Did Mrs. Sammy come with Mr. Sammy to hang her? Merry reached for the doorknob.

"Merry, whut you doin'? Momma said..."

"You was gone let dem kill me. You gone let dem kill Momma, too?"

Johnson, ashamed, didn't answer. Merry quietly opened the door and walked right into Dora.

"Didn't I tell you not tuh come out here?"

"But Momma…"

Dora pushed Merry back into the room.

"James and his momma is here. She said you got somethin' dat belon' tuh her. Where is it?"

Merry knew exactly where James' mother's beautiful ruby earring was. But it was hers now. James gift-wrapped it with his love that wonderful night and Merry didn't want to let it go.

"You stealin' now?"

"No, Momma. James gave it to me."

"Wasn't his tuh give. Brin' it out and give it back."

Dora walked out, not closing the door behind her. Merry pulled a shoebox out from under the bed. Inside, were all of her most precious valuables - her postcards from Teenie, a few rusty coins and her ruby earring. She picked up the earring and paused, admiring it one last time.

As soon as she turned the corner into the sitting room, she saw James. Merry walked towards them, trying to stop her lips from turning up into a smile. She was happy to see him. Even under these circumstances. But James didn't look happy to see her. The light that he held in his eyes just for Merry was gone.

Merry stopped and stood next to a seated Dora.

"You have somethin' for Leila?"

Merry nodded and handed Leila the ruby earring. She held up the piece of rose-colored glass and examined it in the moonlight streaking through the open window.

"James got no business meddlin' wit' my valuables. Dis here is a fine piece of jewelry. My husband bought it. It's fo' a lady, not a..."

Dora eyeballed Leila, making the word get stuck behind her teeth. Leila cleared her throat.

"...A child. James know betta. Don't you, James?"

"Yes, Mom--Mom--Momma. It's f--f--fo'...a lady."

Lady. The last word rolled off of James' tongue without him stuttering. Merry now knew that he thought of her just like everyone else did. She was a whore.

Dora eyed Leila's ruby earring.

"That is fine. 'Bout how much dat cos', Leila?"

Merry shot her momma a look of complete shock. Leila boastfully cut her eyes at Dora and sucked her tooth.

"Cos' duh nigga everythan' he had."

"Hmmph. Can I see it?"

Leila cockily handed Dora the ruby earring. Dora held it up and admired it, all the while glancing at Merry sideways.

Then before anyone knew it, Dora was up out of her chair and throwing the junk jewelry out the open flinging front door. Leila jumped to her feet.

"Dora, what the hell..."

"Git duh hell outta my house, Leila. 'Fo' I thro' you and yo' slow boy out."

Leila arrogantly smoothed out her dress and picked up her tattered coin purse.

"C'mon, James. Tol' you duh girl wasn't even worth wipin' yo' dirty feet on. She take afta' her momma."

Dora slammed the door behind them. Leila yelped loudly as the doorknob hit her where the Good Lord split her. And Dora and Merry looked at each other, both trying to hold in the contagious chuckles gurgling in their bellies. But just like a body fights a losing battle when it tries to hold in gas, the giggles escaped and they busted out laughing.

Their final giggles dripping from their lips, Dora and Merry smiled at each other. Merry wanted to fill the silence. She wanted to thank her momma for protecting her today. And tell her she's sorry that she ever made her lose faith in her or made her cry. But most of all, Merry wanted to tell Dora that she loved her more than she could ever know.

Johnson ran into the sitting room with their bags.

"Momma! Duh whistle!"

"You got everythang?"

"Yes, Momma."

Johnson handed Merry her bag. She grabbed it, but wasn't sure how she was holding on to it. She was suddenly so sad, her arms felt like dead weights.

Dora started for the bedroom, then remembered.

"Wait. Yo' food."

Dora packed two shoeboxes of food into his bag. Johnson pulled the bag's drawstring closed and headed for the side door. Dora stopped him.

"No, out duh bedroom window. Dey won't be able tuh see you from duh road."

Merry followed them, a few steps behind.

"You be a good boy and lissen tuh whut yo' momma tell ya, hear?"

Dora hugged Johnson goodbye. Johnson held on, crying.

"Come wit' us, momma."

"I gots tuh be here when dey come, so dey won't catch up wit' you."

"But dey gone...Dey gone..."

"Dey ain't gone nuthin'. Hmmph. You dink I can't hol' my own wit' some white folks, boy? Gone tuh duh wagon, now."

Johnson climbed out the bedroom window and ran through the field to the wagon. Dora turned to Merry, reached into her bosom and pulled out a safety pinned handkerchief.

"Teenie gone meet you when you git dere and carry you tuh yo' momma's. Hear whut I say?"

"Uh huh."

Dora partially unfolded the safety pinned handkerchief and showed it to Merry. Inside, was a wad of money.

"Now, dis here yo' money. Fo' you and Johnson. Give mos' of it tuh yo' momma when you get dere and put tuh rest 'way in a place only you know."

She fastened the money inside Merry's underwear.

"Whut's gone happen tuh you, Momma? Who gone help you?"

"Don't wurry 'bout me. I got nine chirren. I'm gone be alright."

"I'm scared."

Dora paused, trying to stop her own fear from falling out of her mouth.

"Ain't nuthin' tuh be scared about. Jus' look afta yo' brotha. He ain't stron' like you."

Merry hugged her momma tightly. Dora held her fragily. Rev. Tender whistled. Dora patted Merry's back.

"Gone."

Dora helped Merry climb out the window and Merry landed on the ground, slowly backing with her eyes glued on her momma. Dora nodded goodbye.

Then, Merry turned and disappeared into the field.

KENTUCKY,
1947

Merry gasped for air. Her chest tightening. Her ribs breaking. She was pinned to the ground. Being choked. And raped. By him.

Merry screamed. Mr. Sammy clamped his dirty, bulky hand over her bloody mouth, smothering her. Merry desperately grabbed at his hand. It wasn't dirty or bulky at all. Mr. Sammy's hand was brown, slight, with long fingers. She peered up. Her brother. Johnson. Was on top of her.

Merry jumped up, awake.

It took a moment for her to realize where she was. She was safe, headed to Detroit on a half-empty, broken down bus.

Crammed in the last three rows with the other seven or so Colored passengers, Merry and Johnson were the only children. And the white section, which took up the front and the rest of the bus, was completely empty.

Merry tried to shift herself. Johnson was sleeping and drooling on her shoulder. Angry, she pushed him off of her.

"Oww, Merry! Whut you do dat fo'?!"

The other Colored passengers stirred from their slumber to witness the ruckus. The bus driver starred at Merry and Johnson through the rearview mirror.

"Everthin' alright back there, gal?"

"Yessuh. My brotha jus' fell out his seat."

Johnson climbed back up, mumbling.

"Whut wrong wit' you?"

"Stay on yo' side."

"Stop hoggin' duh seat, den."

Johnson knocked Merry's feet off the seat. Merry plopped them back up.

"Girl, move yo' feet."

"No! It's my turn tuh stretch out."

A young husky man sitting behind them cleared his throat. Merry and Johnson looked up to the front of the bus. The driver was eyeing them through the rearview mirror again.

Merry and Johnson flashed wide smiles to the driver like they were the best of friends. And Johnson scooted away from her to the other side of the seat.

Battle won, Merry leaned her head against the cool window and watched the shadowy country landscape roll by. It was still dark outside, but a little splash of pink was peeking over the road up ahead. The sun was rising.

Merry's thoughts turned to her momma. Reverend Tender had promised them he wouldn't let anything happen to Dora. But Merry's guilt wouldn't let her rest. Her momma was right. Ever since she could remember, Merry's wish was to leave Locust Grove and move to Detroit with Excellent. But she never wanted to do it this way. She'd always imagined there'd be a party. Not that she'd have to run away in the night and abandon her momma to fight a losing battle. Alone.

Merry closed her eyes to pray for her momma. But instead of feeling the presence of a God she no longer trusted, Merry felt Mr. Sammy. All over her.

Merry flung open her eyes and tried to focus on something, anything, outside her window. First thing she saw was a sign. It read: Kentucky State Women's Correctional Institution. A cluster of one story, red concrete buildings, the facility oddly enough looked more like little homes than a prison. At least, that's how Merry saw it. To her, the barbed wired fence that surrounded the prison was protection to keep bad folks like Mr. Sammy from getting in, not punishment to keep bad folks from getting out.

Merry touched the window, wishing at that moment that her momma had a barbed wire fence to protect her. The bus rolled past the prison.

"Ten minutes."

The driver yanked on a lever, which opened the back door of the bus and lit an unfiltered cigarette.

A greasy spoon diner waited in front of them.

Merry glanced at the young husky man sitting behind her, the cruel joke not lost on them. The diner was 'Whites Only.' What the driver even stop for? The young husky man shrugged and headed off the bus.

"No use gettin' your drawers in a knot. You betta use it. He ain't stoppin' again 'til Toledo."

Merry and Johnson followed.

Spotting a baby tree fighting to grow among the weeds, Merry found a safe place to squat. She lifted her dress and slowly pulled down her underwear, wincing as the cotton fabric tugged at her healing skin. Merry took a breath, released and the same fire that set her legs ablaze, trickled between her legs.

Tears sprang to Merry's eyes as she tightly held onto her knees, trying to keep the pain from toppling her over.

Something rustled in the bushes next to her. Merry froze. Maybe she had wandered near one of the Colored ladies and they were finishing their business, or there was a wild, killer animal waiting to eat her. Whatever it was, Merry wasn't going to make a move until she knew she was safe. She silently pulled up her panties, kneeled by the baby tree and listened.

The rustling sound moved closer to her. Merry backed up against the baby tree and grabbed a rock by her foot. Took aim. A chicken poked its head through the grass.

Merry jumped, then chuckled to herself. The dumb chicken stood in front of her and blinked.

"You. Dumb. Ass."

Merry peeked over the tall blades and saw two young white women carrying on in the back of the diner. They were twins and one was waving an ax.

"I can't believe you done left the gate open again, Alice."

"I ain't mean to, Aileen."

"Well, you gone tell her, Alice. You gone tell Betty we lost our last chicken."

"Oh, shut up, Aileen! I saw the dang thang. Over there."

The young women headed in Merry's and the chicken's direction. Merry looked at the chicken blinking at her. She could do one of two things right now. Turn the chicken in or help it escape. Merry picked up the chicken and crawled in the opposite direction of the twin sisters. Those crackers in the diner wouldn't let her come in and eat with them, then she was going to make sure they didn't have no chicken.

One of the hick twins cackled.

"I hear it rustlin'!"

Merry plopped the chicken down and tried to shoo it away. The stupid bird cawed.

"Alice, over here!"

Merry bolted, her chicken buddy on her heels.

"Aileen, he runnin' that way! Cut him off!"

Merry, her escape locked in her sights, saw the opening in the grass. Then out of nowhere, one of the twin sisters jumped in front of her. And like Jackie Robinson stealing second base, Merry slid right in between her bowed legs.

"What the hell?!"

Merry winked over her shoulder as the twin sister turned around, confused. The chicken shot past her.

"The chicken, Aileen! Git the chicken!"

Merry rounded the corner with the cawing crazy chicken chasing and the cackling twin white women stumbling behind her. She must of been a sight to see, because the Colored passengers on the bus couldn't stop laughing. The driver started the bus and flipped the lever to close the back door. Johnson stood in the door and waved Merry on.

"Merry, c'mon!"

Merry took a running leap and dove onto the back of the bus. Johnson quickly got out of the way of the door, letting it slam shut. The chicken ran into it.

Johnson and Merry fell all over each other, cracking up. The bus driver eyed them through the rearview mirror. They scurried to sit down and the rest of the bus also swallowed their chuckles. Johnson, pretending to tie his shoe, whispered as the bus pulled off.

"You a fool, Merry. A fool."

Merry smiled and looked out the window back at Alice and Aileen, who were still chasing after the chicken. She nudged her brother.

"Git the rest of Momma's chicken out. I'm starvin'."

KENTUCKY,
1965

"Shit."

Merry saw the bus driving off in front of her, too far ahead for her to run and catch.

She looked at the greasy spoon diner in front of her and tugged at her dress. Her favorite royal blue dress didn't fit her like it did four years ago before she landed back in the joint. She was a 26-year-old stinking sack of skin and bones then and a stone cold regular at Detroit's Wayne County Jail who stole and forged checks to get money for her next fix. But after being locked away in a Kentucky rat hole and surviving off of dirty potatoes, grits and biscuits, Merry had packed her weight back on.

Merry checked the diner window for a sign. This was 1965 Kentucky. And there was no Whites Only sign? Merry wiped her brow, the sun baking straight through her uncovered oily head down to her toes. She was hungry and thirsty. And the real nitty gritty? Merry had been to hell and back, kicked the monkey off her back in a windowless, prison hot box surrounded by shit, rats and roaches and all these crackers could do was tell her to leave? Please.

Merry strolled into the diner. All eyes turned. She sat at the counter, folded her hands and waited.

A chunky white woman with splotchy pink skin peeked around the corner at Merry, wiped her doughy hands on her apron and suspiciously shuffled up to her. Merry smiled.

"How you doin'?"

The woman grinned slightly, amused enough to play Merry's little game.

"Good. You."

Merry glanced at the woman's name on her uniform, knowing full well all the gun-toting hillbillies were watching her.

"I'm good, Alice. Real good. I don't even need a menu. I already know what I want."

"That right?"

Alice and the white customers chuckled. Merry joined in, not one bit nervous.

"Yes, Alice. Give me the special."

Merry looked Alice dead in the eye and winked. Alice's smile dissolved like sugar cubes in boiling water. She leaned in on the counter.

"Nigga, the only special I'm gone give your black ass is the sheriff dragging you back to that goddamn prison you just crawled out from under."

Merry smiled, disguising her first instinct. To smack the fat, cracker bitch in the face. Calmly, she got up to leave. Alice sucked her tooth and headed back into the kitchen.

Merry took one step and stopped. She had never seen or smelled anything so wonderful. It was a whole barbecue chicken right out of the pit, behind the counter in the kitchen. Merry licked her lips. All of the good sense her momma had drilled into her hard head was screaming for her to leave, but her gut, which was flipping upside down and inside out from hunger wasn't listening.

Merry sat back down. Alice turned around, damn near foaming at the mouth.

"Did. You. Hear. What. I. Said. Nigga?"

"Yes. And, Alice, it's real nice of you to arrange a ride with the sheriff and all, but I changed my mind. Never mind the special. Give me the chicken."

Alice's eyes turned red and she shot back over to the Merry.

"Look, I don't know how long you been locked up or what yo' damn problem is, Gal, but this ain't no game."

"Oh, you right, Alice. Absolutely. So how 'bout we make a deal? Since it looks like this gone be my last meal, why don't you bring me that barbecue chicken and then whatever I do to that chicken, you, the sheriff, everybody in here can do to me."

Merry folded her hands and waited. Alice glanced around the diner to everyone, suspicious. They silently nodded their approval. Alice smiled, her eyes sparkling mischievously.

"You the dumbest nigga I done seen in a long time. Aileen, bring me the barbecue chicken!"

All of the white customers left their seats and gathered around Merry. Alice handed her a napkin, knife and fork. Merry folded the napkin across her lap, like a lady.

"Alice, I been on that damn pit all day. What the hell you want the whole chicken for?"

Merry looked just as the bow legged woman entered with her dinner. If she had already been eating, she would of choked. Aileen looked just like Alice. They were identical.

Merry dropped her fork, the memory rushing back to her. How could she have forgotten that day when she was twelve-years-old on her way up to the Big City and she was chased by that stupid chicken with Alice and Aileen waving an ax on her heels? Easy. Merry handled memories like garbage. She threw out good and bad memories the same, like they were eggs or fish parts, so they wouldn't start stinking and rotting in her mind. And any stubborn memories she couldn't trash or ghosts she couldn't shake, Merry personally incinerated with booze, horse and pills. Anything she could get her hands on to stop the pain.

That's why Merry didn't remember Alice and Aileen until just now. They were the tail end part of her most painful memory. A memory that was still real to her every time she closed her eyes.

Merry reached down and picked up her fork.

"Alice, think I can have another fork?"

"Sho. Least I can do. This being yo' last meal and all."

Alice set the chicken down in front of Merry and handed her another fork.

Merry looked at the barbecue chicken, her stomach growling loud enough for all the white folks to hear. She put her knife in place to cut into the chicken. Then, she set her knife and fork down, turned the plate around, picked up the backwards chicken and kissed it. Square on the ass!

Merry set the chicken back down on the plate. Poker-faced. The diner silent. Then, just when those crackers couldn't take it no more, they busted up laughing. Alice looked around, embarrassed. Even her own sister, Aileen, was laughing! Alice lunged for Merry. Aileen stepped in, still chuckling.

"Stop all that foolin'! We can't sell the damn bird. Might as well let her have it."

"But, Aileen, she..."

"...Beat you fair and square. Stop foolin', fo' we make you keep yo' end of the deal."

Alice huffed, completely red-faced, and stormed out the back of the diner. Aileen settled everyone down.

"Alright, everybody, food's gone cost the same, even when it's cold. Sit down and finish eating."

Merry pulled two dollars out of a handkerchief in her bosom to pay just as the bus pulled up outside.

"How much I owe you?"

Aileen smiled.

"Five dollars."

Merry looked at Aileen, shocked but trying to hide it. Five dollars was half of everything she had in the whole world. The most this sorry chicken was worth was $1.50.

Merry felt the temperature in the room start to rise again. Aileen had laid out two choices for her. She could either walk out of there with her head held high and a chicken under her arm or she could be dragged out of that diner with her neck in a noose.

Merry flashed a smile, peeled off the five dollar bill like she had plenty where that came from and placed it on the counter.

"Thank you, Aileen."

Aileen nodded, not touching the money. Merry stood and picked up her $5 barbecue chicken with her small bare hands. She had just gotten off cheap with the deal for her life, she wasn't about to blow it all by asking the cracker waitress for a napkin or brown paper bag to carry her meal in.

No, her hands worked just fine enough.

DETROIT,
1947

Thunder. Thunder. Lightning. Thunder. Thunder. Lightning.

The rain was pouring down so hard that the bus was rocking. Back and forth. Like a mother rocking a cradle.

But Merry wasn't a baby. And Merry wasn't sleeping. She was wide-awake.

Merry rubbed the mist off the inside of her window to take a look outside. It was still dark, but it felt like at any minute, God was going to pull back the drapes of the night and turn the sun on.

Merry peered out at Detroit's dark city streets. The only things stirring were the shadows of the buildings and cars outlined by the streetlights as the bus passed by. She sat up, excited as the bus turned the corner. A Colored boy sold newspapers as a steady stream of Colored men carrying lunchboxes and wearing blue work pants and shirts darted in and out of the rain into a gray building, changing shifts at an auto factory. And Colored women, all with their straightened hair pulled back into buns and wearing crisp white maid uniforms, chatted as they hurried to catch city buses to raise white folks' children and clean white folks' homes on the Westside.

Merry nudged Johnson. He was snoring.

"Git up."

"Wake me when we get there."

"We here, Fool! Git up!"

Merry jumped to her feet. The bus driver eyed her through the rearview mirror. Johnson pulled her back down.

"Girl, what's wrong wit' you? You tryin' to git thrown off the bus 'fo' you even get deer?"

"We home, Johnson. We home."

Merry hopped back up, too happy to sit still. Johnson shook his head and closed his eyes for a few more winks.

The bus soon pulled into the terminal. Merry grabbed her bag and was the first one out the back door.

The moment her feet hit the wet pavement, Merry knew she was safe. It didn't matter that she was standing in the pouring rain getting as wet as a dog.

Johnson ran for cover under the bus terminal's doorway. "Merry, come on!"

Johnson might as well had been speaking to Merry in another language. She wasn't coming out of that rain. Merry was baptizing herself. Trying to wash herself clean of Locust Grove. Clean of Mr. Sammy. Clean of Johnson, even.

"You taking a bath, Girl?"

Merry opened her eyes and found Teenie smiling and standing in front of her. All five-foot-nine inches of her. Dressed in a white polka-dot raincoat, a nice fitting pink dress, stockings, pumps and carrying a black handbag and an umbrella, Teenie sure was a pretty sight for sore eyes.

Merry and Johnson tackled her. Teenie, smothering them with kisses, ushered Merry and Johnson underneath the bus terminal's doorway to get out of the rain and get a better look at them.

"My God, John John, you big and handsome enough now for me to date. I'm goin' to have to beat the ladies off of you!"

Johnson smiled bashfully. Merry rolled her eyes.

"And Merry, you jus' a pretty as you want to be. But what the hell were you doin' out there in the rain?"

Merry looked into Teenie's beaming face. She wanted to tell her everything. Before she left, Teenie had helped raise Merry and Johnson. More than Merry's other eight aunts and uncles, Teenie took care of them, played games with them and shielded them from anybody and anything that tried to harm them.

Teenie would do any and everything for her. Merry knew that.

But Merry also knew she was only thinking of herself right now. Telling Teenie the truth would only make Merry feel good. And Teenie would hate herself that she wasn't there to protect her.

Merry shrugged her shoulders.

"I jus' like duh rain, I guess."

"Yeah, well, see how much you like it when you laid up in the bed sick with the flu."

Teenie playfully popped Merry on her nose.
"You hungry?"
Merry and Johnson nodded.
"Good. I know jus' the place."

PASS THE SYRUP

"**What's** your song, King Kong?"

Merry couldn't take her eyes off the little chocolate man with the long scar on the right side of his face. He was a black eye-pea of a man wearing pinstriped gray pants, a red silk rolled up shirt, gray suspenders and a scuffed pair of red alligator shoes. Taking a long puff of a sweet smelling cigarette, he ran his burgundy beady eyes all the way up Teenie's long legs to her knockout face. Then, he blew out a ring of smoke and drowsily grinned. Teenie sensually rubbed his small, scarred face and sashayed by him with Merry and Johnson heading for the building's hidden back alley door.

The little man slid in her way.

"Where you think you stridin' with Junior and Jail Bait, Slim?"

"Come on now, Handsome. Don't snap your cap. These my babies, Merry and John John. We gonna knock us a scarf."

"Scottie don't have no crumbs for your snatchers, baby."

"Don't be getting brand new, Daddy. I draped your ole lady and ofay main squeeze for two's and few's just last week and now you got your glasses on?"

"Naw, naw, Queen, don't get salty. I ain't tryin' to beef with you. It's jus' that The Man been doggin' us all night. Thangs ain't been copacetic."

"But now everything's cool. And these lovelies? Are with me. Dig?"

The little man took another long drag of his sweet smelling cigarette and nodded, the smoke leaking out the sides of his mouth.

"You aces with me, Teenie."

Merry didn't know what the little man meant by that, but the music passing for conversation between him and

Teenie sounded a million times better than her slow, country drawl, so it had to be a good thing.

Merry and Johnson laughed as they walked up to the joint's back door with Teenie. She reached for the doorknob, looked at Merry and Johnson and chuckled.

"Ooh, Babies! You know you look country! Almost as bad as I did when I first got here. Teenie's gonna take care of that. But right now, when you walk in here, you walk with your back straight and head held high. You are Detroit Royalty! And nobody better mess with you. If they do, you send them straight to me. O.K.?"

"O.K., Teenie!"

Johnson jumped up and down, excited. And Merry smiled, too full to answer. She didn't have to worry or be afraid of anything or anyone again. Teenie was going to protect her from now on.

Inside, it took a second for Merry's eyes to adjust. They were leaving the morning sunshine in the alley, but in Scottie's, it was still nighttime.

But not just any nighttime. Christmas Eve. There wasn't a tree, or lights or presents, but it was definitely a party. Merry smiled. A child being allowed to come to this secret after-hours party must mean that she was Detroit Royalty. Just like Teenie said.

Up ahead, the band jammed on stage. A drummer, horn player, piano man and some cat plucking a giant stand-up banjo looked like they were playing the fast, swinging music in their sleep. Eyes closed. Fingers flying. Sweat popping off their mellow, greasy faces.

Merry looked around at the beautiful Colored people dressed in their Sunday's best, smoking, drinking, laughing and dancing to the new music. Whatever this strange music that made grown folks party instead of working was, it didn't sound like Lucy Sass crying or Mahalia laying it all on the altar. No, this music felt closer to God. Holier than gospel, more real than the blues.

And although this was Merry's first time hearing it, she knew in that moment that this music had to be God's favorite. This was the music He stole away and listened to in secret. The music that made Him tap his foot, snap His fingers and close His eyes just like the musicians in a trance on the stage. Merry knew this, because she felt it in her young bones.

"Teenie!"

Everyone in the joint hollered as Teenie, Merry and Johnson made their way over to the bar.

"Was wonderin' when you was gone show up. Ain't seen much of yo' yella ass since you hooked dat square Uncle Sam pet wit' the long bread."

"Please. We jus' took a trip for a few days. You act like I'm back from the dead. Wit' your jealous ass!"

Teenie and the woman exploded with laughter and affectionately grabbed each other's hands. They were friends. Merry had never seen anyone Teenie considered a 'friend' before. Teenie had always moved around so much that she never took root with anybody. And even when she was back home, Teenie had the knack of keeping to herself, but everyone was just so attracted to her that they didn't notice that Teenie didn't like them as much as they liked her.

But this woman she liked. This woman had the voice of a man and was thick in the hips and large in the chest. Not tall, but not short either, she was the color of walnuts that you get in Salvation Army Christmas baskets and she wore her shitty brown hair hot combed and in waves that didn't move.

They held hands across the bar, laughing. The woman was missing her right pinky finger.

"Where'd good ole' Lou take you?"

"Chicago. We drove over in his Lincoln."

"Oh! That's why your nose so high in the clouds, it's bleedin'!"

Teenie playfully yanked her hands away and pulled a large yellow dress with the sales tags still on out of her bag.

"Heffer, I went all the way to Chicago to get your color and size. You know how much material this is?!"

"Lou don't mind. He told me he likes a thick fly chick."

The woman struck a sexy pose and sucked her tooth. Merry and Johnson laughed. Teenie threw the dress at her.

"Put that damn tent away before everybody think you goin' campin'."

"If my threads is the tent, your skinny ass is the pole. How much bread I owe you?"

"Nothin'. Jus' feed my babies. Scottie, this is Merry and Johnson."

"Hmph, alright. But I don't see no babies, Baby. I see a pretty young lady and handsome young man."

Scottie smiled at a blushing Johnson. And Merry, who didn't think she could, stood up taller, straighter. She had walked into the joint a girl, but now she was a young lady.

Scottie extended her hand over the bar to Johnson. He shook it, nervous.

"Baby, this is my place and you and your sister are welcome here any time. Wit' or wit'out your triflin' auntie. You know what you want to eat?"

"'Sho do! Pancakes!"

Scottie chuckled and leaned on the bar, her large breasts about to pop out of her blouse. Johnson couldn't take his eyes off of them.

"Ooh, ain't you the cutest, country thing!"

"Yes, ma'am!"

Scottie and Teenie laughed. Merry frowned. Her fool, fairy brother. It's bad enough Johnson was acting like he liked titties, but did he have to sound like a country bumpkin, too? Merry decided right then and there, she was never going to give these slick, city folks a chance to laugh at her. No matter how long it took, she wasn't going to open her mouth until she learned how to talk just like them.

Scottie softly touched Johnson's face and disappeared through the swinging doors into the kitchen. Johnson watched her go. Merry climbed up on the stool next to Teenie, who was eying Johnson.

"Uh, uh, John John. Scottie's too much for you, now. Pick your tongue up off the floor before somebody trip over it."

"She's nice, Teenie."

"Nice. Right. Sit down, boy."

Johnson tripped to his stool, nearly knocking Merry off of hers. She grabbed hold of the bar to steady to herself and caught sight of a tall caramel-colored man in the mirror above the bar. Merry quickly swiveled around to get a better look. She had eyeballed everyone and everything in the joint when she got there, but this man must of just appeared out of thin air, because there was no way she would of missed him. He was handsome. The kind of handsome the devil had to have been to turn the angels against God.

The man ran his fingers through his uncombed short hair and lit a cigarette. Merry starred at him, wondering if he was smoking a sweet cigarette like the little man out in the alley. What did it taste like? She had snuck snuff once, but it burned her mouth something awful and made her so sick behind it, that she never wanted to try cigarettes. Until now.

The man, as if hearing what Merry was thinking, rolled down his sleeves and looked at her. Nervous, Merry darted her eyes to the floor, then quickly peeked back up. He was strolling over. Right for her.

Merry fidgeted in her stool, straightened her wrinkled dress and crossed and uncrossed her hands on her lap. Johnson noticed.

"Whut's wrong wit' you?"

"Shut up."

Merry snapped at Johnson through her smile. He swiveled around to see what Merry was looking at.

"Whut you dink dat man gone do wit' yo' flat chested butt?"

"Why you care? You like him?"

Merry looked to Johnson and winked. She might as well slapped him in the face. Johnson swiveled back around to the bar. Wounded.

Merry chuckled, proud of herself. The sight of the handsome Colored man in front of her, though, quickly made her stop patting herself on the back. She smiled wider, ready to shake the man's hand real lady-like when he introduced himself.

But the handsome Colored man didn't stop to talk to Merry. He walked right past her and stopped boldly in front of Teenie.

"If I didn't know better, I'd think you was iggin' me, Baby. My bread ain't no good no mo'?"

"If it's green, it's mean, Jack."

"Oh, it's leprechaun gold, Baby. Thanks to those lame gators in the back, I'm swimmin' in it."

The handsome Colored man pulled out a wad of money the size of Merry's head, peeled off a few bills and held out the cash to Teenie. She looked at him, blankly. He chuckled and peeled off a few more dollars. Teenie took the money and coolly slipped it into her purse. Then, she turned her back to him, took a sip of her drink.

"What's your count?"

"What's my count? Baby, don't you remember?"

"I always remember."

"I know you used to. But word on the line is, ever since you robbed the cradle and bagged that married Army slave, you been slippin'."

If the handsome Colored man and Teenie were at Merry's old school back in Locust Grove, they'd be fighting in the schoolyard right now. Teenie held her drink up to her mouth, frozen in the air, her eyes sparkling with anger. Then, she smiled. Merry shook her head. Poor handsome Colored man. Her auntie angry was one thing, but Teenie smiling *and* angry, Scottie better call the undertaker.

Teenie softly placed her drink down on the bar and faced the handsome Colored man.

"257 box and straight, Detroit and Cleveland. That it?"

The handsome Colored man starred at Teenie. Didn't answer. And Teenie gazed right back at him. Not dropping her smile. Merry wanted to jump out of her skin. Was Teenie right? Or did she get the man's count wrong? Whatever a count was, it had to be serious judging by that giant roll of money the handsome Colored man was carrying around in his pocket. So serious, that Merry didn't notice when Scottie brought their pancake breakfast out to the bar.

"Young Lady, you better eat before these cakes get cold. I didn't cook 'em for my health."

"Yes, ma'am."

Merry obediently swiveled around to eat her breakfast, hoping to watch the rest of Teenie's and the handsome Colored man's showdown in the mirror above the bar. But in that split second, he was gone. Merry looked to the front of the joint and saw him sauntering out the door into the morning.

"Merry, Baby, pass me the syrup."

Teenie's pancakes were buttered and perfectly cut into bite size squares. Now all she needed was the syrup.

Merry wanted to ask Teenie who the handsome Colored man was and if she was right about his count.

But Merry bit her tongue, her growling stomach telling her everything she needed to know. Now wasn't the time to be bothering Teenie with questions about grown men.

It was time for breakfast.

RUINED

Excellent was rich. That's all there was to it.

Merry couldn't come up with no other explanation as she stood in front of her mother's two-story brick home with Teenie and Johnson. Excellent's house with a neatly manicured lawn framed by pink and purple double petunias was larger and nicer than any building in all of Locust Grove. The house even had two front doors! Merry smiled, excited. With a home this big, they could send for her momma and she, Johnson, Dora and Excellent could all live the rich, white folk life together.

Merry and Johnson anxiously waited on the walkway as Teenie stepped up on the front porch and knocked on the first door. No answer. She tapped on the window and peeked inside.

Merry heard a creak above her. Someone was standing on the top porch of the house next door, watching them. Merry looked up. Right into the wrinkled face of a toothless old Colored lady with wild snow-white hair and clouded over gray eyes.

Merry took a step back, afraid.

"Call yourself out. Whoever you are. I can hear you breathin'."

Merry shoved Johnson to answer the scary old lady. He pushed Merry right back and tagged her to speak. The old lady leaned over the porch banister.

"You hear me down there?"

Teenie stepped off the porch with her finger to her lips, telling Merry and Johnson to be quiet.

"I hear you, Ms. Ruthie."

"Teenie! That you? Thought you was gone?"

"I was, but I'm back now and I'm lookin' for Excellent. Have you seen her?"

"She's cleanin' house at her second job, I think. Shame that man left her high and dry like he did. Your sister's too good a woman to have to work so hard."

"Yeah. Well, when Excellent gets home, will you tell her I stopped by?"

"Sure will. And, Teenie, don't you stay gone so long next time."

"I won't, Ms. Ruthie."

"Alright."

Teenie put her hand on both Merry's and Johnson's shoulders, signaling them to wait quietly for Ms. Ruthie to leave.

All three of them looked up at the old woman silently as she slowly shuffled inside her house and slammed the porch door behind her.

Teenie tiptoed back up to the front porch. Merry and Johnson followed her, curious. Teenie pulled open the unlocked screen door and took a bobby pin out of her hair.

"I hate to do this to you, Babies. But I have to get to work and Mrs. Lowenstein will pitch a fit if I bring you with me to the store."

Teenie stuck the bobby pin into the front door lock, jimmying it around while she kept her eyes on Merry and Johnson. Merry moved closer to get a better look.

"Teenie, whut you doin'?"

"Somethin' you better not ever do."

Teenie was so quick, though, she didn't have to worry about Merry copying her. The lock clicked. And like magic, Teenie turned the doorknob. She held the door open for Merry and Johnson to walk in first.

It was quiet and cool inside. From the front doorway, Merry could see down a long hall that seemed to stretch on for days. Johnson took off running.

"Merry, come here! Look!"

Merry and Teenie followed Johnson's excited voice to the sitting room. Merry's feet sunk into the soft brown carpet as she soaked it all in. The room, looking just like a picture from one of her magazines, was decorated with a couch that all white folks would love to have, fancy wooden coffee tables and a record player.

Johnson cut a step and waved the record in the air.

"She got records. Lots of 'em. Teenie, think she'll let me play 'em?"

"Well, that depends. Are you gonna be dancin' like that?"

Johnson stuck out his tongue and wiggled over to Teenie. She playfully shooed him off. Merry drifted back out into the hallway to explore, but she didn't find what she was looking for.

"Teenie, how you get upstairs? Is there a secret door?"

"A secret door? Merry, what are you talkin' about?"

"I want tuh go upstairs tuh see my room. I ain't got tuh share wit' Johnson, do I?"

"Yeah, Teenie, I ain't sharin' with Merry neither. She fart in her sleep. I'd ratha sleep outside."

"Hush, Boy. You don't have to sleep outside, but you won't be sleepin' upstairs either. See, this is what they call a two-family flat. You live wit' your momma down here and another family lives upstairs."

Merry looked to her brother, disappointed. Their mother wasn't as rich as she thought after all. Teenie bopped Merry on her head.

"Girl, why do you have your lip poked out? This house is still bigger than anything you ever seen. You and Johnson go pick your rooms."

Merry shot down the hall, beating Johnson to the first bedroom. A black leather purse hung heavily on the doorknob and gospel music played softly from a radio on a nightstand inside the room. This was Excellent's room.

Merry stepped inside, feeling as though she shouldn't be there. Back home, she never went into her momma's room without getting permission first. Even when Dora was sick and Merry helped Teenie take care of her, Merry always knocked before she came in. Her momma's bedroom was private. A sanctuary.

Merry wondered if Excellent thought of her bedroom the same way. The bed, made with a bright colored patchwork quilt laid neatly across the bottom of it, looked comfortable. Merry sat down and placed her feet into a pair of worn slippers on the floor. Merry's small feet got lost in the wide, flat house shoes. They were men's shoes. Corn's house shoes.

Merry tripped out of the shoes and skipped over to the dresser. On top was an open jewelry box, overflowing with costume gems, a string of pearls, a gold bracelet and a ruby earring. Just like the one James had given her. Merry spotted a diamond ring, slipped it on and struck her best Teenie pose in the mirror. With fine jewelry like this and the new clothes Teenie was going to buy her, no one would ever know that she was a country girl from Locust Grove. Now, all she had to do was get her mouth right.

"What's yo' song, King Kong. Now don't you be gettin' brand new. These lovelies are wit' me. Dig?"

Merry heard a chuckle from the hallway. Teenie peeked her head around the corner.

"What do you think you're doin'?"

"The door was open and..."

"And you decided to help yourself to your momma's jewelry. Girl, put her wedding ring back and come walk me to the door."

Merry slipped off the ring, dropped it back into the box and followed Teenie into the hallway.

"O.K. I'm not sure when Excellent will be back, but there's some chicken in the ice box when you get hungry. And, Merry, you and John John, be quiet over here. Ms. Ruthie is as nosey as she is blind. It wasn't my place to tell her that you were here. But if Excellent wants to, she will. Understand?"

Merry nodded that she understood, even though she didn't. Teenie headed for the front door. Merry grabbed her hand.

"Merry, Baby, I'll be back."

Merry threw her arms around Teenie, afraid to let her out of her sight again. Teenie had left home when Merry was four years old and drifted back through every now and again when she was in between stops. But the last time Teenie had promised Merry that she'd be back, Merry was eight years old.

Teenie patted Merry, gentle.

"I'll come by after work, O.K.?"

Merry held on tighter. And Teenie, her favorite auntie, held and rocked her. She was already late for work. Five more minutes wouldn't hurt.

***

"Whut time is it?"

"Time tuh get up."

Merry floured the last piece of chicken and dropped it into the hot pool of shortening sizzling in the large black iron skillet on the gas stove.

Johnson yawned and shuffled in, plopping down at the kitchen table that Merry had set. Besides a golden mound of fried chicken, Merry had also snapped some Kentucky Wonders, made some crackling corn bread and squeezed some fresh lemonade.

Johnson eyeballed everything, greedy.

"Where you find all dis food?"

"Duh chicken and lemons were in duh box and she got a garden out back. If you hadn't been sleepin' all day, you woulda known that."

"I was tired. 'Sides, I only woke up, 'cuz I thought you was burnin' down duh house."

"Boy, does it look like I'm burnin' down duh house?"

"Naw, but whut 'bout dat chicken in duh skillet?"

Merry whirled around to check the chicken. It was fine. She shot back around just in time to catch Johnson biting into a big, juicy drumstick.

"Boy! Stop! We not eatin' 'til she git home!"

"I'm hungry now!"

"Put it back!"

Johnson dropped the bitten drumstick back onto the chicken pile on the platter and looked at Merry, pouting.

"Now go wash up and change yo' shirt or somethin'."

"Why?"

"Dis is our first meal wit' her. I want it to be special."

Johnson stuck out his chest and leaned back in the chair like he was the man of the house.

"Girl, tuhnight's already special. 'Cuz I'm here."

Merry threw some lemon peels at him. Johnson dodged them and fell backwards in the chair. They heard the front door open in the hallway. Johnson sprung up.

"She's here!"

Johnson ran out of the room to the front door. Merry hurriedly took the last piece of chicken out of the skillet and took one last scan of the kitchen table. Everything was perfect.

She heard Johnson talking and coming up the hallway with Excellent. Merry fidgeted nervously.

"Oh, Son, what's that smellin' so good?"

"It's a surprise we put together just for you, Ma. No peekin'!"

Merry rested her hand on the kitchen counter, then glanced down and saw that she was still wearing the apron.

She snatched it off and flung it up on the hook just as Johnson stepped into the kitchen with Excellent. He proudly held their mother's right hand and she had her eyes covered with her left one.

Merry drank in the long awaited sight of her mother. Excellent looked silly standing there with her hand over her eyes, her mouth turned up into a half grin. She was wearing broken in white nurse's shoes and a black and white maid's uniform, not unlike the one Mrs. Sammy had given Merry to wear that horrible day. Her fine black hair pulled back and fastened with bobby pins, Excellent was still the color of coffee and cream, but she looked watered down to Merry, somehow. Sad and watered down.

Johnson swung Excellent's arm back and forth, playfully.

"You can look at the count of three, Ma. You ready?"

"Ready to see my Merry. Yes, I am."

Merry beamed. Johnson held up three fingers and nodded. Happily, he and Merry counted together.

"One! Two! Three! Surprise!"

Excellent lifted her hand away from her eyes and couldn't say a word. She was so full. Merry and Johnson looked at each other, not sure what to do. Merry stepped up to the kitchen table.

"Momma taught me how to cook real good, so you don't have tuh worry 'bout eatin'. Unless you don't like string beans. If you don't, you can jus' eat duh chicken and cornbread."

Merry paused and waited for Excellent to say something, anything. But her mother just wiped at the tears welling in the corners of her eyes. Johnson eyed Merry to keep talking.

"Or maybe you thirsty? I made some lemonade."

Excellent sniffed, her voice soft and pregnant with shame.

"Lemonade?"

"Uh, huh. It's in duh ice box."

Johnson scampered over to the icebox and Merry pulled the chair out from the head of the table.

"We better eat 'fo' it git cold."

Obedient, Excellent walked over to the chair to take her seat. She stopped in front of Merry, uncomfortable. And

Merry gazed up at her mother. Excellent was no longer a dream, but living and breathing. Flesh and blood.

They hugged.

**

Merry gasped for air. Her chest tightening. Her ribs breaking. She was anchored, pinned down by a familiar force she couldn't see. She was being choked. And raped. By Mr. Sammy. Again.

Merry lunged up, soaking wet with sweat and shaking. Merry pulled her knees up to her chest, wrapped her skinny arms around them and rocked herself back and forth. Desperate, she looked around the strange, shadowy room, trying to convince herself she was the only one there.

Slowly, Merry stood up on her bed and hugged the wall over to the light switch. She flicked it on and the low-watt bulb on the ceiling washed the small room with light. Aside from a twin bed, wooden dresser and a chair setting in the corner, she was alone.

No more shadows. No Mr. Sammy.

Merry leaned against the wall, relieved. For the moment. Because the truth was, deep down in a place that would take her years to talk about, Merry knew she wasn't safe. And the real shadows? The real shadows weren't the ones that ran like cowards from the light, but the shadows that had taken root and were growing in her mind.

Merry wiped her face, thirsty. She headed for the kitchen. Once in the hallway, she heard Excellent's and Teenie's hushed voices. They were arguing.

"Why didn't Momma tell me?"

"There was no time. Excellent, I told you. They got ran out in the middle of the night."

"And Momma had enough time to get word to you, but not to me?! That don't make no damn sense, Teenie."

"Well, whether it make sense or not, they're here now. And you have to raise them."

Excellent paused, her eyes narrow and furious. Merry peeked around the corner to get a look at the thick tension between her mother and auntie that was hemorrhaging into the hallway.

"You sayin' I didn't want to raise my children?"

"I can't call your wants, Excellent."

"Why not? I can call yours. Corn's gone. You want Merry and Johnson, too?"

Teenie leaned in, damn near spitting through her gritted teeth.

"You left those babies cryin' for your milk before they were out of diapers. If it wasn't for me and Momma..."

"Thank you, Teenie. Thanks to you and Momma, Merry ended up spreadin' her legs for Sammy. And now you send her hot tail to me? What am I gone do with her bad ass? She's ruined."

Teenie opened her mouth to fire back at Excellent, but then saw Merry standing, shocked, in the kitchen doorway. Excellent followed Teenie's gaze and found Merry starring right through her.

"Merry, Baby, what you doin' up?"

Merry heard Teenie's question, but she couldn't answer. She was still starring at her mother, wishing Excellent would peer through to her soul and see that she wasn't ruined.

Excellent reached for the leftover cornbread on the table and wrapped it in wax paper. Dejected, Merry faced Teenie.

"I was thirsty."

"Oh, O.K. How about some water?"

Merry nodded. Teenie got a glass out of the cabinet and filled it with water from the faucet. Merry stepped past Excellent, took the glass of water from Teenie and drank.

The silence in the room was unnerving. Aside from the sound of Merry gulping, the only other sound was Excellent's nervous rustling of the wax paper. She rose and put the wrapped up cornbread in the icebox.

Merry handed Teenie her empty glass.

"Is Momma, O.K.?"

Excellent glanced at Teenie over her shoulder. Merry noticed. Teenie tenderly popped Merry on the nose, a smile in her voice.

"Momma's always gonna be alright. She's stayin' in Atlanta with your aunt Rosemary."

Merry eyed Excellent's turned back. Her auntie was keeping something from her. She could feel it.

"Is Momma sick?"

"No, she's good. Just worryin' Rosemary to death, because she misses you and John John so much."

Her momma misses her. That, whether it was true or not, made Merry smile just like Teenie knew it would.

"When is Momma gonna come see us?"

Excellent, brimming over from jealousy, closed the icebox door harder than she needed to.

"As soon as she can, Merry. You need to get back in the bed now. It's late."

Merry jumped from Excellent's bark and shot a look at her, more confused, than afraid. And Excellent, not knowing the looks of her child, reacted like any adult would from that look from any child. With anger.

"You hear me, Merry?"

Teenie reached for Merry, a mother bear protecting her cub.

"Excellent, she's standing right in front of you, she can't help but hear you. Merry, Baby, your momma's right. You start school in the morning. You need your rest."

Merry turned away from Excellent and tightly hugged her auntie.

"Goodnight, Teenie."

"Goodnight, Baby."

Teenie kissed Merry on the forehead and whispered in her ear.

"Say goodnight to your momma."

Merry froze. She knew the same truth that Teeenie and Excellent did. Her momma was hundreds of miles away in Atlanta. Not this angry woman in the kitchen.

Merry faced Excellent, determined, like a child who just discovered there was no Santa Claus and didn't want to cry about it.

"Goodnight. Excellent."

Then, she turned and left. Not giving her mother a chance to correct her.

MORE THAN A DOG
SCRATCHES FLEAS

Merry wanted to sit down. She was uncomfortable, standing there in front of Mrs. Arnold's seventh grade class, 23 pairs of strange, brown eyes focused on her and Johnson. It felt like she was a slave on an auction block and at any moment, Mrs. Arnold was going to stick her white fingers into Merry's mouth and show everyone her teeth.

Not that that would of been an all bad thing. Merry felt her teeth looked a heap of lot better than the clothes she was wearing. All of the other children were dressed like city folks. Boys wearing creased slacks and shirts and girls wearing nice pleated skirts and dresses.

Merry crossed her arms and looked straight ahead. She wasn't happy and she wasn't going to pretend.

"Boys and Girls, I'd like to introduce to you Merry and Johnson Paine. They just moved here from Atlanta..."

Merry spoke, before she realized, breaking the promise she made to herself.

"No, Ma'am. Locust Grove."

Mrs. Arnold, paused, confused.

"I'm sorry, where?"

The class rippled with laughter, each chuckle pelting Merry like pebbles. Did she sound that country that her teacher didn't even know that she was speaking English? Merry didn't answer.

"No, really, Merry. I just want to get it right and I've never heard..."

Johnson chimed in.

"Missus Arnold, Locust Grove's a couple hours outside of Atlanta, Ma'am. All our peoples come from deer."

The class broke out in laughter again. This time, the joke was on Johnson. But instead of being embarrassed like Merry, he was laughing with them.

"O.K., Class, I have been corrected. Merry and Johnson Paine just moved here from Locust Grove, Georgia. And now they're going to be joining our class. Why don't you two find a seat?"

There were only two empty seats in the classroom. One in the front and one in the back. Both Johnson and Merry headed for the back of the room. But not before the light skinned, thin girl with a long face in the front row shot up her hand.

"Mrs. Arnold, Johnson can sit next to me if he wants."

Johnson paused, trapped. The thin girl smiled up at him and fluttered her long eyelashes. Merry kept stepping for the back of the classroom.

"Why thank you, Dolores. But Johnson is so tall. If he sits in the front, it'd be unfair to the students behind him. I think Merry should sit next to you. Merry?"

Merry stopped, one step away from the Promised Land. She turned and faced Mrs. Arnold.

"Merry, you're going to take the seat up here next to Dolores. And why don't you take the seat in the back, Johnson."

Merry shuffled past Johnson as he gladly hightailed it to the rear of the classroom. Merry plopped down next to Dolores, unhappy. Dolores was just as disappointed.

Dolores' disappointment didn't last, though. She was too curious.

"You don't talk much, do you?"

Merry looked at her, her mouth full of sandwich.

"I think it was wrong that everybody laughed at you. I like the way you and Johnson talk. It reminds me of my grandmother. She's down in Youngstown. Do you know where that is?"

Merry swallowed her bite of sandwich and shook her head no. No use ignoring Dolores. This girl was going to talk to her whether she liked it or not.

"Youngstown is in Ohio. My grandmother moved everybody there after she left South Carolina. My momma didn't like it, though, so she and my daddy came to Detroit. I was born here. In Herman Keefer Hospital. Me and my sister both. Do you have any sisters?"

Merry shook her head no again and took another bite of her sandwich.

"I have four of them. Three older. One younger. That makes five of us. No brothers, though. My momma says, my daddy can't make boys. My daddy always wanted a boy.

That's why they kept trying, but all he got was the five of us."

Merry chewed, as Dolores babbled on, wondering if all of Dolores' sisters talked as much as she did. She looked across the schoolyard and saw Johnson playing basketball with some of the other boys.

"Does Johnson have a girlfriend?"

Merry coughed, nearly choking on her sandwich. Dolores patted her on the back.

"Are you O.K.?"

Merry started laughing. Dolores frowned.

"What's so funny? You don't think Johnson would like me?"

"It's because I talk too much, isn't it? My momma tells me all the time, 'Dolores, you run your mouth more than a dog scratches fleas.' Maybe my momma's right. She's right, isn't she?"

Dolores' mother was right, but Merry just didn't have the heart to tell her. Dolores stomped her feet.

"I knew it! I'm a blabbermouth! A stupid, ugly blabbermouth! Johnson would never like me."

Again, Dolores was right. But this time, Merry decided to unsilence her country tongue and have some fun.

"My brother likes you."

"He does?!"

Dolores shrieked from delight and hugged Merry. Merry looked at her cross-eyed.

"Oooh, Merry. Do you know what this means? Johnson likes me, so that means he's going to ask me to go with him. Then we go together from now all through high school and then he asks me to marry him. And then we get married and have lots and lots of babies! Does Johnson make boys?"

Merry had no idea what her fairy brother could make. But whatever it was, she knew he wouldn't be making it with Dolores.

Dolores clapped her hands, excited.

"Thank you! Thank you, Merry! What can I do for you? There has to be something. Hey! You and me are about the same size. I can give you some of my clothes. I have a closet full of them!"

Merry bristled. She wasn't no charity case. Even if she was dressed like one.

"I have my own clothes."

"I know. It's just..."

Merry peered at her, daring her to say out loud what they both were thinking. Dolores continued, cautious.

"You just moved here and I thought maybe...I didn't mean nothing by it, Merry."

Merry bit hard into her sandwich. Yes, she did. Dolores did mean something by it. And Merry knew exactly who to go to fix it.

THE FIRST LADY
OF WHUT?

"Ma'am, is dis where you catch duh bus downtown?"

The young Colored woman, dressed professionally in a tweed skirt and white blouse, diagonally folded her newspaper back and looked at Merry, curious.

"Well, this bus will get you halfway there. Then, you'll have to transfer. Why are you going downtown alone?"

Merry sat down and crossed her legs, matter-of-factly.

"I'm goin' shopping."

The woman chuckled, amused by Merry's attempt to act grown.

"Oh. Well, then you're going to need five cents for bus fare and another five cents for a Downtown transfer. Just be sure to ask the driver for one when you get on."

"Thank you."

"You're welcome."

The professional Colored Woman went back to reading her paper and Merry looked down the street for the bus. She hoped it was coming soon. Merry took off from school as soon as it was over at 3 o'clock and didn't tell Johnson where she was going. She needed to get downtown to Teenie's job before 5 o'clock. Before Lowenstein's closed. At least that's what Merry thought the name of store was where Teenie worked. She knew that was the name of Teenie's boss and just figured that the white name sounded so important, that it had to be the name of the store, too.

Merry rolled some coins back and forth in her pocket, excited. Ten cents wasn't even going to put a dent in all of the money that her momma gave her. The handkerchief treasure chest was still safety-pinned to Merry's underwear, safe and sound like her momma wanted. Truth was, after what she overheard Excellent say last night, Merry hadn't even thought of giving the money to her mother like Dora told her. She wasn't sure she ever would.

The bus turned the corner up ahead. Merry shot up out of her seat. She wanted to be first to get on. The Colored seats in the back of the bus always filled fast.

The bus pulled up and the white man driver opened the doors. Merry was smiling. Surprisingly, he smiled back.

"Good afternoon, young lady."

Merry stammered, shocked that this white man was actually being nice to her. Then, she remembered her manners.

"Good afternoon, sir."

Merry stepped on and dropped her ten cents into the fare box.

"I'd like a Downtown transfer, please."

The bus driver ripped a thin piece of white paper with numbered boxes on it off a pad on the fare box and handed it to her.

"Here you go."

"Thank you!"

Merry took the transfer and whipped around to hop off the bus. She bounced right off of the professional Colored woman.

"Where are you going? Did you change your mind?"

"No, ma'am. I'm sorry. I'm goin' to the back."

The woman looked at Merry, her voice lowered to a whisper.

"You don't have to."

Merry finally looked into the bus. Coloreds and whites were sitting in the front and throughout the bus. Together. Some white folks were even seated in the back of the bus!

Fifty-three minutes and two buses later, Merry arrived Downtown, smack dab in the middle of majestic Woodward Avenue. Gazing up at all of the glorious buildings, Merry took note of all of the department stores that had impressive names chiseled on them - J.L. Hudson, Sacks Fifth Avenue, Hughs and Hatcher, Winkleman's, Lerners, Federals, Crowley's and Jacobson's. Every store's display window was also beautiful. So beautiful, she stopped to admire all of them.

In fact, Merry was having so much fun mimicking the poses of the mannequins, that she almost forgot why she was Downtown in the first place.

Then, she saw it - a small, three-story red brick building, sandwiched in between two giant department stores.

Lowenstein's Women's Apparel.   Its display window was closed off with red draping.

Merry hurried inside, the silver bell above the door announcing her arrival. A pale white woman with reddish brown hair and a slightly humped back fluttered around the display window platform to the right of Merry. She had colorful silk scarves wrapped around her short neck and was just a little taller than Merry, but Merry could look in her face and tell she was old. And annoyed.

"May I help you?"

The woman flung the question at Merry as she walked over to the counter. Merry followed.

"Yes, Ma'am. I'm lookin' fo' my Auntie Teenie. Is she here?"

"A lot of girls work for me, but I can't say I ever heard that name. Are you sure you're in the right place?"

Before Merry could answer, the woman tossed the scarves to the floor and hit a bell on the counter.

"Henrietta, what's taking so long? I need that fabric!"

Merry looked at the impatient white woman, sure she was in the right place. But maybe she didn't have the right person.

"Are you Missus Lowenstein?"

The woman turned to her, curious.

"I am. Who are you?"

"I'm Merry and..."

"...And she's in big trouble."

Teenie entered the showroom with fabric and material draped over her arms.

"Henrietta, you know this child?"

"Yes, Mrs. Lowenstein. Merry's my niece. She and her brother just moved here from Georgia."

"Oh. But she called you..."

"It's a silly name my family calls me..."

"I like it. Imagine someone as big and tall as you...Teenie!"

Mrs. Lowenstein laughed. A high pitch, light chortle that filtered out of her nose like steam out of teapot. Teenie shot Merry the evil eye.

Merry didn't know what Teenie was so mad about. Everybody on both sides of the Mississippi called her Teenie. Merry even suspected God himself would call her auntie Teenie when she arrived at the Pearly Gates. How was she supposed to know that Teenie had gotten uppity in Detroit and was going by her given name with the white folks?

Years ago, before Merry was a tear in Excellent's and her dead daddy's eyes, Dora named Teenie after Merry's granddaddy, Henry. Not because she liked the name -- Dora was always fond of her mother's name, Delilah -- but because Teenie was a miracle. Granddaddy Henry was dying from consumption when Dora found out she was pregnant with Teenie. And Teenie, born so sickly and teeny, never should have survived. So as Granddaddy Henry's dying wish, Dora named her sixth child Henrietta. And until the day he died three months later, he was the only one that ever called Teenie that.

Mrs. Lowenstein reined in her laughter and leaned on the counter, spent.

"Oh my! I haven't laughed like this in months."

Teenie crossed her arms, irritated.

"Oh, Teenie! Don't get your feathers ruffled. I think it's a cute name. It's fun."

Mrs. Lowenstein smiled to Merry. Merry grinned back. Unamused, Teenie laid out the fabrics on the counter.

"Mrs. Lowenstein, here's the material you wanted. I picked out a few samples, so you could have a choice. Lenora and I finished the books, too."

Mrs. Lowenstein shuffled through the fabrics and Teenie eyed Merry, still angry. Frustrated, Mrs. Lowenstein pushed the material onto the floor.

"These fabrics are all wrong! That's it, Henrietta. I'm washing my hands of this window. You're just going to have to finish it."

Mrs. Lowenstein pulled her coat and purse off the rack behind the counter and headed for the front door.

"But Mrs. Lowenstein, I can't stay late tonight, remember? Louis and I have plans."

"Are your plans with Louis more important than your job, Henrietta?"

"No, Mrs. Lowenstein."

"Good. I need that window up and running first thing tomorrow morning when we open. And make it fabulous as always."

She turned to Merry, a slight smile returning to her lips.

"Nice meeting you, Merry."

Merry glanced at Teenie before answering. For some reason, she felt guilty for being polite to this white woman. Like she was choosing sides.

"Nice tuh meet you, too, Missus Lowenstein."

Mrs. Lowenstein looked at Teenie and shook her head, tickled.

"Teenie. Funny...Funny."

Mrs. Lowenstein left and Teenie snatched up the fabric off the floor. Merry helped her. She wanted to apologize to her auntie for intruding, but Teenie kept her head down and wouldn't look at her. Teenie stood and carried the fabric over to the display window. Merry followed her.

"Teenie, you mad at me?"

"Yes."

"But I got a good reason why I came."

"Oh, I can look at you and tell why you came, but it's not a good reason. Let me guess, I wasn't moving fast enough for you, so you asked Excellent if you could ride the bus down here by yourself to pick out your own clothes and she said you could."

Merry lowered her eyes.

"Damn it, Merry!"

Merry looked at Teenie, surprised. Even when she deserved it, Teenie never got angry with her. Teenie sat down on the display window platform and picked up the scissors.

"Get away from while me while I fix this mess. I'll deal with you when I'm done."

"Teenie..."

Teenie shot Merry a look that made her suck her words back into her mouth. The telephone rang. Teenie looked up at the clock on the wall - 6:03 p.m. She went back to work. The telephone rang again. Teenie slammed down the scissors and stomped behind the counter to answer it.

"Lowenstein's Women's...Louis?"

Merry craned her neck and perked up her ears. She couldn't see Teenie from where she was standing. A rack of clothes blocked her view. But Merry could hear Teenie's side of the heated telephone conversation.

"I know, but you're headin' out Sunday. Why can't you...The kids...Why is she jus' now...When are you gonna tell her... Right. Your family...I know that, Louis...That's three months from now...Wait...I'm tired of...Look, Louis, you go have a good time with your family and be safe in Italy. No, really, be safe."

Teenie slammed down the phone, upset. It rang again before she even made it around the counter. She stood in front of the display window in deep thought. The phone continued to ring. And Teenie continued to ignore it.

"Have you kissed a boy yet, Merry?"

Merry looked at her, confused. She thought about telling Teenie about James. If anybody would understand why she still thought and cared about him, Teenie would. Teenie would, because the same feeling of pain and love were etched all over her face, too. Like birthmarks. And Merry wanted an explanation. Instead, she just answered her auntie's question.

"No."

Teenie sighed.

"Good."

Teenie sat down on the display window platform. Merry looked at her, her mind racing. How in the world was it good that she was almost 13-years-old and had never kissed a boy? She didn't know the city girls in her class, but she could tell by just looking at their fast tails, that they had all kissed boys. Even Dolores with her big mouth had probably closed her lips just long enough to do it.

Teenie patted a spot next to her on the platform.

Merry sat down. Teenie leaned against her.

"I'm sorry I yelled at you."

"That's O.K."

"No, it's wrong and I'm gonna make it up to you. Want to paint the town with Auntie Teenie tonight?"

"Really?"

"Uh huh. You can be my date. Detroit Royalty style! I'll let you pick out a new, snazzy dress up stairs. Do your hair. Maybe put on a little makeup..."

"But whut 'bout Excellent? Whut are we gonna tell her?"

Teenie winked, mischievously and handed Merry the scissors.

"Don't you worry about your momma. I'll handle her. All you have to do is help me decorate this window, then I'll take you to see Ella."

Merry hopped up and down from excitement, then stopped.

"Who's Ella?"

"Who's Ella! Oh my God. Did you just say, 'Who's Ella?!'"

Teenie dramatically put her hands on her hips, shocked. Merry nodded, embarrassed. Teenie placed her hands on Merry's small shoulders, starred her straight in the eye.

"Baby, this is probably the most important thing that I've ever told you in life. The lady I'm taking you to see tonight is none other than Ms. Ella Fitzgerald. The First Lady."

Merry starred back at Teenie, letting the importance of what her auntie just said sink into her head. Too bad she had to ruin the moment with another stupid question.

"First Lady of whut?"

Teenie shook her head and laughed.

"Of Jazz, Baby."

Jazz. So, that was the music she heard the musicians playing at Scottie's? Merry repeated the word again out loud. She liked the way it rolled off her tongue. It was both heavy and light at the same time. Like a whisper. To say it right, you had to open your whole mouth and let the word float up and trail off your tongue like a butterfly in flight.

Merry sat down, too excited to cut the fabric straight. She wanted to leave Lowenstein's right now and go hear The First Lady sing jazz.

She was ready to fly.

A TISKET. A TASKET.

Merry felt grown. Here she was strutting down Paradise Valley's vibrant Hasting's street, hand in hand with her auntie Teenie. Wearing a little makeup and donning a pretty lavender dress, stockings, matching pumps, Teenie's pearl earrings and her hair in an upsweep, Merry knew she looked too good for words. Gone was that country bumpkin girl from Locust Grove. She was now a young lady. Detroit Royalty.

And tonight, Paradise Valley was her kingdom. If New Orleans had Bourbon Street, than Detroit's Hastings Street was definitely its first cousin.

Like a carnival, the street was lined with cars and packed with handsome men and women out for a night on the town. Jazz music, laughter and the fragrant scent of fried chicken, powder, cigarettes and cologne bled into the crisp night air as the beautiful Colored people strolled in and out of Hasting Street's plentiful restaurants, theatres and clubs.

"Ma'am, these are front row tickets. For the eight o'clock show."

A young man, tall, the color of almonds and no more than seventeen years old, stood in the ticket booth of the Paradise Valley Theater with Teenie's tickets in his hand. He wore a blood red suit jacket, bow tie and hat and looked like he wanted to be anywhere, but there. Teenie smiled, turning on the charm.

"I know. I wasn't able to make the eight o'clock show, but my niece has never seen Ella..."

The young man looked at Teenie, unmoved.

"The eleven o'clock show is sold out."

"I know. But...I used to work here. I sold tickets just like you. Spending hours on my feet, smiling in that musty booth for no money. But the shows..."

Teenie leaned in closer to the booth, like she was sharing a secret with the young man.

"Ella started singing twenty minutes ago and you're about to close down the ticket booth and go stand in the back and listen with the ushers, right?"

The young man's eyes flickered, guilty. Teenie pulled back, draped her arm around Merry's shoulders.

"I just want to share Ella with my niece. You and I both know there are always some seats left. Can't I just exchange my tickets?"

The young man darted a curious glance to Merry, then handed Teenie two tickets and flipped the ticket booth sign over from open to closed in one sweep.

"Balcony. Last row."

Teenie flashed a grateful smile and tapped the tickets twice against the booth's window.

"Thank you."

The young man nodded. And Teenie walked into the theatre. Merry floated in behind her. This was Merry's first time ever in a theater. Whether they were sitting in the balcony or front row didn't matter to her. Teenie, though, wanted no parts of that nonsense. Spotting an old man usher, with slicked back gray hair and a big belly that looked like it was going to topple him over, Teenie steered her away from the balcony stairs. The old man did a double take, then threw up his hands in mock shock.

"My Lord! I must of died and gone to heaven. Is that my Lilly of Paradise Valley?"

Teenie planted a big, fat wet kiss on old man usher's cheek.

"Yancy, I swear if you get any more handsome, I'm gonna have to give Marjorie a run for her money."

"No, Baby, Marjorie play dirty. She don't want to lose her good thing."

Teenie and Yancy held hands and laughed. Yancy rested his friendly, brown eyes on Merry.

"Teenie, who is this lovely, young lady?"

"This is my niece Merry. I'm treatin' her to her first Ella concert. Can you show us to our seats?"

Yancy smiled. His teeth so straight and white, they couldn't be real.

"Ladies, I would be honored to. Right this way."

Yancy turned and strutted in the opposite direction. Teenie and Merry followed. Merry noticed Teenie didn't show Yancy their tickets. She grabbed Teenie's hand.

"Teenie, how does Mr. Yancy know where we're sittin'? You didn't give him duh tickets."

Teenie grinned like a child with a secret. Yancy stopped and pulled back the curtain to the middle row of the theater's main floor. Merry froze. Onstage, singing directly in front of her was Ella Fitzgerald. The First Lady.

Teenie whispered in Merry's ear.

"Baby, when you have friends, you don't need tickets."

A tisket. A tasket. A green and yellow basket. I bought a basket for my mommie. On the way, I dropped it...

Teenie tugged Merry's hand and they followed Yancy down the lush, red carpet to their seats. With each step, they got closer and closer to the stage.

I dropped it. I dropped it. Yes, on the way I dropped it. A little girlie picked it up and took it to the market...

Five rows in danger of running out of red carpet, Yancy stopped and extended his arm toward two empty seats.

Schooby doobie doo bop bop tweetie tweet tweet dee dee boop boop doobie do schoop doobie do schoop...

Merry got to her seat, but she couldn't sit down. What was the First Lady doing? Her smooth, warm voice, at perfect pitch, sounded like one of the band's instruments. But Ella wasn't singing words. She was ratta-tat-tatting sounds like a machine gun, each sound connected by the rhythm, tied together by the beat.

"Teenie, whut is she doin'?"

"She's scattin', Baby."

"Can you teach me to do it? Please, Teenie? Please?"

Teenie laughed and bumped Merry with her hip. Merry bumped her back.

Dee dee boop boop doobie do schoop doobie do schoop tweet tweet tweet tweet tweet tweeday

Merry still flying high heard Ella Fitzgerald scatting in her head as she and Teenie took their seats at Scottie's two hours later.

"Scottie, Duh First Lady wuz so beautiful and duh band wuz so handsome. She sang *A Tisket, A Tasket*. A whole bunch of good songs. But my favorites was *Flying Home* and *Lady, Be Good*. Ella scatted on dose duh best..."

"My, my, Merry, you must of really loved Ella tonight. Talking so fast and excited, you sound just like Johnson."

Merry stopped talking. She didn't want to be compared to her brother. She was a beautiful princess. Not a country bumpkin.

Teenie eyed her.

"Go ahead, Merry. Finish tellin' Scottie about Ella."

Silence. Scottie's smile dropped. She hadn't meant to hurt the girl's feelings.

"Merry, Baby, I didn't mean nothing by it. You know I love you and Johnson..."

Teenie patted Merry's hand.

"Merry, when I first came to Detroit, I sounded worst than a donkey in heat every time I opened my mouth."

Merry smirked. Scottie chimed in, agreeing.

"Naw, Baby, it was baaad."

Teenie cut her eyes at Scottie.

"But after awhile, I got better. And Baby, you're going to get better even faster. You know why? Because you have me. I'm gonna teach you how to talk, how to walk, how to dress, how to scat and..."

Teenie's eyes floated to the crowded dance floor. Merry followed her gaze.

"How tuh dance?"

Teenie stood up, smoothed the wrinkles out of her form fitting burgundy dress.

"But, Teenie..."

"Uh uh. After what I saw you doin' tonight at the show, you need lessons. Let's go."

Merry nervously followed Teenie to a spot she carved out on the dance floor. Surrounded on all sides by sweaty bodies swaying, bopping and grinding to the hopping jazz music, she instantly felt self-conscious.

Teenie pointed to her feet and took both of Merry's pasty hands. Merry mirrored her auntie's smooth steps, keeping up with Teenie as she moved faster. Merry smiled. She was starting to get into it now.

Teenie nudged up Merry's chin and dropped her hands. No more looking down at her feet. Merry stiffly kept in time with her steps as she watched Teenie's bent arms swing rhythmically in front of her curvy chest and her womanly hips rock from side to side. Merry swung her arms easy enough, but her straight hips weren't cooperating. Teenie playfully grabbed Merry at her small waist and shook her hips to the beat.

"Come on, Baby! Shake what your momma gave you!"

Teenie twirled around. Merry copied her and came out of the turn rocking her little hips like a natural grown woman. Teenie clapped her hands, pleased. Merry curtsied, totally proud of herself.

Danced out, Merry headed to the bathroom. Turning into the hallway, she stopped. In the dark corner by the back door was a man and a woman. But not just any man. It was the handsome Colored man that Merry saw the first night she came to Scottie's. He was roughly kissing the pound cake colored woman. She had a rubber hose tied around her right arm and was pinned up against the wall, her legs wrapped around his waist, his hands grabbing her thick behind.

Merry knew she should be a good girl and go into the bathroom, but she was frozen by the sight of the handsome Colored man. Doing what grown folks do.

The woman, as if sensing the primal urges Merry was feeling, rolled opened her eyes as the handsome Colored man gripped and kissed her neck. A second or two passed before the slurred words spilled out of her slanted, slow moving mouth.

"Silas...a...girl..."

Silas continued pushing himself inside the slow talking woman.

With more effort than it should have taken, the woman pulled her face away and pushed Silas in his chest, getting his attention.

"Stop..."

Silas, still holding the woman up against the wall, slyly looked over his shoulder. Merry starred back, her feet stubbornly cemented to the floor. He smiled and lowered the woman down to the ground. Embarrassed, the woman straightened her red dress as Silas adjusted and zipped up his pants. The woman stumbled out the back door and Silas turned around, his intense eyes locked on Merry. He took a funny cigarette out of his pocket, lit it and took a slow drag.

Uncomfortable, Merry scampered into the bathroom. She rested against the door, suddenly no longer needing to release herself. She was too hot and bothered about what she just saw to pee.

Titillated, she creaked open the bathroom door, peeked out and into the face of Silas.

"What's your name?"

Still standing in the same spot where she had left him, Silas was shorter and younger than she remembered. About 25, he was deliciously caramel in color like her favorite penny store chew candy and he smelled sweet and spicy, like cayenne peppers.

Silas, wickedly enjoying watching her watch him, took one last drag of his funny cigarette, then stomped it out on the wall. Merry heard her voice before she opened her mouth.

"My name's Merry."

Silas coolly put the butt in his pocket and slightly tilted his head to the side.

"Merry, Merry, quite contrary. How old are you, Merry?"

Merry stumbled. She wondered how old he thought she was. And did he think she was as pretty as the slow talking woman she had watched him having sex with in the hallway?

"I'm fifteen."

Silas smiled. And Merry stood up straighter. He believed her.

"Shit...Girl, you so flat chested. If you wasn't wearin' that dress, I would of thought you was a boy."

Merry starred at him, humiliated. Silas busted out laughing. Merry scurried out of the hallway. Right into Teenie.

"Baby, you were takin' so long, I was scared you fell in."

Teenie chuckled. Merry didn't. Teenie looked at Merry, concerned.

"You O.K.?"

Merry, not wanting her auntie to find Silas laughing at her around the corner, quickly rubbed her stomach and moaned.

"I don't feel good, Teenie. Can we go home?"

"Yeah, O.K., Baby. Whatever you want."

Merry heard the back door in the hallway open. She started to walk away. But not before Teenie peeked her head around the corner, just as the backdoor swung close.

"Merry...Who were you talkin' to?"

Merry kept stepping, throwing the lie over her shoulder that she wouldn't dare say to her auntie's face.

"Nobody."

IN ROLLED
THE CLOUDS

"Teenie, she's twelve years old!"

Teenie picked up the new clothes that Excellent had thrown on the sitting room floor and calmly began folding them. Merry held back at the archway, cautious. Excellent continued to fuss.

"The dresses for Merry too short, blouses too tight..."

Teenie folded the clothes more briskly.

"There's nothin' wrong with these clothes, Excellent."

"You would say that, bringin' these stolen, grown ass clothes in my house..."

Teenie stopped, one of Merry's new blouses wrinkled in her hands.

"I bought these clothes. With my own money."

Excellent snorted a sarcastic chuckle.

"Since when your ass stop boostin'? Running numbers too much for you?"

Merry looked at Teenie, searching for any sign that Excellent had hurt her. She didn't know what boosting or running numbers was, but from the way Excellent flung the words at Teenie like poisonous darts, Merry figured neither one could be a good thing.

Teenie, too angry to give Excellent the satisfaction, deliberately finished folding Merry's blouse.

"Merry and Johnson needed new clothes, so I bought some."

Teenie placed Merry's folded blouse on top of the pile of clothes, then reached in her purse and took out a receipt.

"If you don't want Merry's clothes, you have thirty days to return them."

Teenie dropped the receipt on the pile and got up to leave. Merry walked her to the front door.

"Teenie, do you have tuh go?"

"Uh huh, I forgot I have some runs to make."

Merry knew that was a lie. When they were shopping earlier at Lowenstein's, Teenie had promised to stay for dinner and play cards with her and Johnson. But, right or wrong, Excellent had made Teenie feel so bad for doing a good thing that her auntie wanted to get as far away from there as fast as she could.

"Can I go, too?"

Teenie paused with her hand on the doorknob. Her eyes floated to Excellent as she appeared in the sitting room archway.

"See you later, Baby. Tell Johnson to call me, tell me how his clothes fit. O.K.?"

Merry nodded, closed the door behind Teenie, then turned around with her eyes focused on the floor. Maybe if she didn't look directly at Excellent, she could become invisible and walk right by her.

"This ain't no vacation, Merry."

Merry stopped. Excellent had spotted her.

"I'm not gone have yo' fast ass runnin' the streets, chasin' behind Teenie. All you gone do is go to school and church. And you gone work. Just like me."

Merry sighed. She didn't want to be like Excellent. Cleaning white folks houses for a living. All she wanted to do was have fun and go to school like the other city kids.

"As soon as you get settled at school, I'll see if Mrs. Benson can use you on the weekends."

"Why?!"

"'Cause I said so! Now gone outside and hang up those clothes I just washed on the line, and do the dishes when you're through."

Merry stomped past Excellent and out the kitchen's back door. The weathered wooden steps wobbled a little as she walked down them into the small yard. Pink and purple double petunias lined the neatly manicured lawn, forming a colorful border between it and the dirt alley on the other side of the silver wire fence. A clothesline dotted with wooden clothespins hung between two metal crosses and swung back and forth in the crisp October breeze. Merry marched over to the clothes line and bent down to pick a damp towel out of the clothes basket. Hanging the towel up on the line, her eyes, for a second, attracted upward to the sky. It was cloudless and blue.

She had never seen a sky so blue.

Merry picked a blue dress out of the basket and pinned it on the line. It didn't look anything like the maid's uniform and housedresses Merry had seen Excellent wearing. Made of soft, but sturdy cotton-like material, with a round neckline and a frilly hemline, the classic dress actually looked like something Merry might see a mannequin wearing in a department store display window downtown. It might even be from Lowensteins!

Merry checked the label. There wasn't one. Didn't matter. She had seen all she needed to see. It was O.K. for Excellent to dress nice and wear pretty city things, but Merry wasn't good enough to.

Merry kicked over the clothesbasket. Excellent could hang up her own damn clothes.

Since before she could remember, Merry had dreamt of living happily ever after with her mother. They'd eat the best foods, wear the best clothes, laugh, joke and love each other. But only two days in and Merry knew her fantasy was never going to come true. Excellent was mean.

And yes, Merry was the first to admit, her momma had a way about her, too. But no matter what, even when Dora was fussing and beating her, Merry always felt her momma's love.

She didn't feel anything from Excellent, though. Not love. Not hate. Merry just knew her mother didn't want her there. Excellent thought she was ruined, just like the wet clothes sinking into the grass at her feet.

The back door of the house swung open. Excellent stepped out on the porch, carrying measuring tape and dangling a blue dress across her scarred left arm.

"Merry, come here."

Merry slouched up to the porch. Excellent handed her the dress. It was one of the dresses that Teenie had bought her.

"Hold this up 'gainst you. Let me see where it falls."

Merry held the dress up against her body, confused. Excellent didn't want her to have the clothes Teenie gave her. So, why was she doing this?

Excellent looked at Merry, not pleased. She knelt in front of her, measured the length of the dress from the waist to the hem and made note of the measurement. Then, Excellent flipped up the bottom of the dress and examined the faulty hem.

"Damn shame. As much as this dress cost."

Excellent stood up, disgusted, and snatched the dress away from Merry's body. Merry, rocking forward from the force of her mother's pull, grabbed Excellent's hand and caught her balance. In that second, Merry and Excellent locked eyes. But both, uncomfortable with the love neither recognized in each other's gaze, looked away. Excellent's eyes landed on the kicked over basket and wet clothes in the grass. Merry hurried down the steps, her lie spilling out her mouth faster than she could run.

"The wind knocked it over..."

Merry grabbed up the clothes and dropped them into the basket. Excellent headed back inside.

"Bring those clothes inside and hang them up in the basement. It's 'bout to rain."

Merry looked up. Her clear, blue sky was gone. In rolled the clouds.

GLAD TO BE
IN HIS SERVICE

I'm glad to be in his service. Glad to be in his service. Glad to be in his service. One more tiiiiiime. Didn't have to let me live. Didn't have to let me live. I'm glad to be in his service. One more time....

As the choir sang and the congregation clapped along, Merry looked around. Corinthian Baptist Church wasn't so bad. A two-story red brick sanctuary, it was three times bigger than her church back home with an elevated pulpit, deep enough to seat the minister and a choir.

A strip of green carpet stretched down the three main aisles, leading to the pews that were wooden, but comfortable. And an old faithful portrait of Jesus hung on the wall next to the First Lady wailing on the organ.

Merry brushed a piece of lint off of her dress. It was the pretty blue dress that Teenie had bought her, but Excellent had made the hem, now bordered with silky, pink material, longer. She also added pink material to the collar and sleeves and switched out the gold buttons for pink, Mother of Pearl ones.

Merry tugged at her irritated earlobes. Excellent had let her wear a pair of her clip-on, costume pearl earrings and her earlobes were itching. Teenie's pearl earrings didn't irritate her, not once. Why were her earlobes on fire now? Maybe she was allergic to these earrings like she was allergic to her mother.

Merry pulled off the right earring and Johnson nudged her. He was bored and wanted to play with it. Merry ignored him and dropped it in her purse. Merry wasn't about to let him play with Excellent's itchy earring. He might lose it or worst yet, break it, and then she'd have to do more chores and suffer under their mother's sternness, while Johnson, Excellent's baby boy prince, did nothing.

Merry pinched her brother's arm and he yelped like a little girl. Excellent eyeballed them. Merry stopped. And

Johnson slouched down, pouting. Excellent slapped the church fan against the pew. Johnson sat up straight.

Merry grinned to herself. Excellent had her brother trained like a dog. Now only if she would make the boy do some chores, maybe he'd stop believing his mess didn't stink.

"Oh, Lord, you been so good to me...Hallelujah...So good, Jesus...So good...So good..."

Merry heard the mumblings before she realized where the voice was coming from. A large Colored woman with massive arms and legs was sitting on the pew alone in front of her. She was moaning and rocking, moving the wooden pew with each heavy sway. Wouldn't be long now before she...

"Thank ya, Jesus! Thank ya! Thank ya! Thank ya! Thank ya!"

The large woman leapt to her swelled feet, her fat head rolling back and forth, round and round as if her thick neck was made out of spaghetti. And Merry watched her. Not just because she couldn't look away, but because she was jealous. Merry wasn't talking to God's Baby Boy, because she was mad at Him for not helping her. But deep down, she missed Jesus.

The large woman, suddenly spent, threw back her head and fell back as if the sanctified air, itself, was going to catch her. Merry scurried to run out the aisle, but couldn't. Excellent was standing in her way, holding up one of the large woman's gigantic arms and cradling her head. Gently, she eased the limp woman back into her seat, pulled her glasses off of her face and dropped them into her pocket. Then, she dabbed the woman's damp forehead with Kleenex and started to hum.

Merry strained to hear. Excellent's hum was so soft, that if she wasn't paying attention, she would have missed it.

Excellent pulled a church fan out of the shelf on the back of the pew and fanned the large woman, comforting her. The woman moaned and muttered something that Merry didn't understand. Excellent rubbed the woman's neck and spoke into her ear.

"It's alright. Ain't nothin' wrong in callin' is name."

The large woman, as if releasing a long carried burden, sighed and let go. Excellent hummed louder as the tears streamed down the woman's now peaceful face.

Merry looked to Excellent and saw the same peaceful expression on her mother's glowing face. Dressed head to toe in a white nurses uniform, Excellent looked like one of God's chosen Christian Soldiers. And in that moment, Merry saw the sadness roll away from her mother's tired face like the stone from Jesus' tomb.

"Sister Mavis, was it just my imagination or did I see two of your lemon cakes downstairs in the kitchen?"

Last in line at the head of the church, Merry, Johnson and Excellent were waiting to shake hands with Reverend McKeever. Handsome and broad shouldered, he was already reaching out for Excellent's hand before they could step up to him good.

"You saw two, Reverend, but I made three. One just for you and Susie."

"Bless your heart. Did these fine children of yours help you bake them?"

Reverend McKeever shifted his tired, but large friendly eyes to Merry and Johnson. Merry stepped up, on cue. Ready to play her part in the story. Of course, not the true story.

No one could ever know how Excellent left her and Johnson behind to follow Corn, who then ran out on her. Corinthian's Christian Soldiers could never find out that Merry was a whore and Johnson was a queer. No, Merry and Johnson had to be perfect. Sinless. Fake.

Excellent touched Merry on the shoulder. Merry bristled.

"Merry'll help me with next week's cakes. She's a good little cook. Johnson just eats."

Reverend McKeever laughed and shook Johnson's hand.

"That's alright, Johnson. You're a growing boy. That's what you're supposed to do. Besides, if I was blessed with your mother's food, eating's all I'd be doing, too."

Johnson smiled and Excellent beamed. Merry took half a step back. She wasn't going to be able to take too much more of this charade.

"Johnson's 12 and eats like his daddy, but Merry takes after me. She'll be thirteen in December. December 9th."

"December 9th? That's three days before Katherine's."

Reverend McKeever looked around and spotted a shapely Colored girl, a little taller than Merry, picking up church programs left behind on the pews. He called out to her.

"Kat, come here, Baby. I want you to meet someone."

Katherine quickly walked over. She was brown skin, plain faced and wore her wavy black hair pulled back with a pearl headband. She stepped up , a pleasant smile on her face.

"Hi, Sister Mavis."

"Hi, Katherine."

Reverend McKeever affectionately wrapped his arm around his daughter's shoulders.

"Kat, these are Sister Mavis' children, Johnson and Merry. Merry's birthday is three days before yours."

"It is! Are you going to be thirteen, too?"

Merry nodded. Finally, somebody was as excited about her turning thirteen as she was. Katherine playfully poked her father.

"That makes twelve, Daddy."

The Reverend cleared his throat. Katherine stomped her foot like the spoiled Daddy's girl that she was.

"Daddy, you promised!"

Reverend McKeever sighed and shook his head. His baby girl had him wrapped around her little finger and they all could see it.

"Sister Mavis, Kat has it in her mind to start a choir for the young folks. Ages thirteen to eighteen. I told her that she'd have to gather at least the same amount of disciples as Jesus did before I'd bothered her mother to rehearse with them every Saturday. Susie already has so much on her plate."

"I asked mother. She said she would. Come on, Daddy. Johnson and Merry make twelve."

Reverend McKeever grinned, mischievously.

"Well, actually, Johnson's not thirteen yet. So technically, Kat, you only have eleven."

Katherine looked at Johnson in disbelief. Johnson shrugged. Merry thought fast. She really didn't care about singing in the young people choir. But truth was, if Merry was busy rehearsing with the choir, Excellent couldn't make her clean Mrs. Benson's house on Saturdays.

Merry spoke up.

"Reveren', doesn't duh Bible say dat where two or mo' are gathered tuhgether in Jesus' name, he's right dere wit' dem?"

Reverend McKeever smiled at Merry, impressed.

"Yes, it does, Merry. In the book of Matthew. Chapter twenty, verse eighteen."

"Well, Katherine's choir has eleven. Dat should be enough for Jesus, right?"

Merry wasn't sure if the Reverend heard her, because he just looked at her, his smile frozen on his face. And Excellent? She must of stopped breathing. Merry had to glance at her, just to make sure she was still standing there. Katherine grinned at her father and crossed her arms, justified. Excellent grabbed Merry's arm.

"Merry, you apologize to the Reverend right now..."

Reverend McKeever chuckled.

"No, no, Sister Mavis, Merry's right. Out of the mouths of babes. My Lord."

Katherine jumped up and down.

"Daddy, you mean it? I can have my choir?!"

"Yes, Baby. And you need to thank Merry for it. Child came up in my church and put me in my place, she better know how to sing!"

Johnson grumbled. Merry nudged him. True, she couldn't carry a note in a bucket. But that didn't matter. Katherine's young people choir wasn't about singing. It was about freedom to hold onto her childhood for just a little while longer.

And that, alone, was worth singing about.

MERRY, MERRY

Life in the big city was turning around for Merry. She had been living with Excellent a month now and had pretty much fallen into a boring, predictable rhythm.

Monday through Friday, Merry went to Deggin Junior High School and attended Mrs. Arnold's 7th grade class. The work was easy. Often times, Merry finished before everybody else and when Mrs. Arnold didn't give her extra work to do, she'd spend the rest of the class time practicing how to talk right in her head. She still wasn't talking much these days. Not so much that Merry didn't trust her improving tongue, but because it hadn't taken her long to realize that she found out more about folks and what they were really thinking, if she just kept her mouth shut. So most of the time, she did.

Except at Church. Merry didn't really believe the words any more, but she still liked singing the church hymns. They reminded her of her momma. Dora couldn't carry a tune either, but Merry remembered how her momma used to sing with everything she had. So every Sunday, Merry used every bit of what she saved throughout the week and lifted her voice up in song. For Excellent's sake. It made Excellent happy to see Merry surrender and throw herself on the altar. And Merry was more than happy to make the sacrifice, because a happy Excellent at church meant a happy Excellent at home.

The only thing missing from her new, good life was Teenie. Her auntie hadn't come around since the day she and Excellent argued about the new clothes. She called to check in every Wednesday and Sunday, though, and at the end of each call, she promised to visit them as soon as her work as Mrs. Lowenstein's new head bookkeeper slowed down. But Teenie hadn't been by yet. And Merry was starting to worry if she ever would.

Merry nodded hard, snapping back her neck right before her head bounced on her desk. Embarrassed, she quickly looked around class to see if anybody noticed. Dolores smirked at Merry, teasing. Merry shrugged and gazed out the classroom window again.

She was still having nightmares about Mr. Sammy. The only time Merry really got a few safe winks was when she snuck naps in class, at church or after school before Excellent got home from work. She just couldn't sleep in the darkness of her room. At night, she tried keeping her bedroom light on and reading, but Excellent always made her cut it off. Merry wondered why her mother never once asked her what she was afraid of.

Maybe if she had, Merry would have told her.

"Merry, Principal Bennett needs to see you in his office."

Merry hesitated. Mrs. Arnold eyed her, stern.

"Now, Merry. And take your things with you."

Merry gathered her supplies. Dolores leaned over, digging for dirt.

"What'd you do?"

"Nothin'."

"Are you sure?"

Was she sure? Merry left without answering Dolores' retarded question. For a month now, she had been as close to perfect as possible. She had no idea why Principal Bennett wanted to see her. But maybe her mother did. Why else was Excellent waiting in the principal's office for her?

Merry hung back at the door, not sure whether to run or go in. Principal Bennett, a balding white man who wore small, square spectacles, made the decision for her.

"Come in, Merry. Take a seat."

Merry obeyed and sat in the chair next to Excellent.

"Your mother and I have been having a lovely conversation about you. You're a very bright girl."

"I am?"

Merry glanced at Excellent, nervous. Her mother wasn't mad that she had to take off work and come to the school. She actually looked pleased sitting there.

"Yes. I understand Mrs. Arnold has been giving you extra work to do. Has the work been easy for you, dear?"

Easy wasn't even the word. Mrs. Arnold's assignments were simpler than counting to ten. But Merry was bright enough not to say that.

"No, I jus' finish faster, I guess."

Merry looked at Principal Bennet, sheepishly, hoping he would buy it. He didn't.

"Well, I shared your test scores with your mother and you did extraordinarily well. Especially in math and English. We both agree that you need something to challenge you more. So, starting today, I'm double promoting you to the ninth grade."

Merry gulped. Promotion? The only thing she knew about promotion was that Teenie had just gotten one and she was slaving day and night because of it. A double promotion had to be twice as much work.

"Why?! Why can't I stay where I am?"

Merry slapped her hands on the chairs arm rests, upset. Excellent grabbed Merry's wrist, speaking through her gritted tooth smile.

"This. Is. A. Good. Thing. Merry."

"But I like my class! I like Missus Arnold!"

Excellent clamped down harder on Merry's wiggling wrist, darn near cutting off the child's circulation.

"This isn't about what you like. This is about what you're going to do. Understand?"

Merry winced and nodded. She was bright just like Principal Bennett said, but it would take her years to understand that Excellent was doing this for her own good.

In that moment, with her fingers tingling, Merry only understood one thing. If she ever wanted to feel or use her left hand again, she'd better do what her mother told her to do.

Period.

***

The boy's goofy face was the first thing Merry saw when she stepped into Mr. Lewis' 9th grade classroom. He was tall and wirey, so skinny that when he stood sideways, he disappeared. Red bone like Merry's Momma, the 15-year-old boy wore thick, black eyeglasses and had ears so big that they stuck out from his thin face like catcher's mitts. When Mr. Lewis introduced her, all of the other older kids gave her the cold shoulder, but the skinny boy? He looked right at Merry, his shy, brown eyes whistling hello from behind his glasses.

"Sorry. 'Scuse me. Sorry."

Merry tried to pick up her dropped books and dodge getting trampled by the grumbling students in her row as they stepped over her and hurried out the classroom. These new ninth grade books were thicker and heavier than her old seventh grade books. Too big for her book bag. She was going to have to ask Excellent to buy her a new one.

A pair of long hands reached down to help her. She looked up. It was the skinny boy.

"Thanks."

"You're welcome."

Merry looked at the skinny boy, expecting him to hand her the books, but he just stood there with that goofy look on his face.

Merry snapped at him, impatient.

"Can I have my books?"

He jerked back to life, nervous.

"Oh. Yes. Absolutely."

The skinny boy clumsily handed Merry her books. Her chest caved in a little from the weight of them, but Merry knew the boy was watching her and she wasn't about to embarrass herself and drop the books again. No matter how heavy they were.

The skinny boy ran to hold open the door for her, breathless, like he needed to blurt out something important.

"My name is Felton."

Merry starred at him, blankly.

"May I carry your books for you?"

**

Merry didn't have a lot of experience with boys, but she knew she didn't like Felton. He didn't give her butterflies and didn't make her laugh like James did. But she did like to listen to him talk. Hearing him softly patter on as he carried her books and walk her home from school was like listening to a talking dictionary. He spoke so properly and pronounced words so well, that Merry knew she could learn to talk right from him. If only she could survive the boy's silent treatments.

Yes, her sweetheart James stuttered something awful, but conversations with him were still always lively and fun like a game of hot potato. But talking to Felton was like skipping rocks by yourself on a pond. If you were lucky and found a smooth, flat rock, you could fling it and get a few, good hops out of it. But most of the time, the rocks were ragged, too heavy and just sunk to the bottom. That's how

Felton sounded to Merry. When he did talk, his few words were like smooth, flat rocks. But when he fell quiet, his silence was ragged and heavy. Heavier than the books he was carrying for her, even.

They walked in silence and Merry counted in her head how many more blocks they had to go to get to her house. They were coming up on the soda shop where a lot of the kids went after school. The halfway point. Merry decided that she would ask for her books back before they passed it. She would rather suffer and carry her books home by herself, than suffer one more second of in Felton's quietude.

Merry turned to tell Felton to give her back her books, then stopped. Silas, wearing a rumpled Chrysler auto plant uniform and black worker's shoes, was getting out of a new, maroon Chevrolet Fleetmaster coupe and crossing the street. Merry looked away, hoping he didn't see her. He did.

Silas stopped in front of Merry and Felton, coolly, his hands in his pockets.

"Well, well, well. Merry, Merry, quite contrary."

Merry eyed Silas, still angry with him for making fun of her that night at Scottie's. Silas eyes shifted to Felton.

"Who's your friend?"

Merry cringed.

"He's not my friend."

Silas didn't even blink. Merry kicked herself. He knew she was going to say that. Silas thinks she's a kid and he knew she was going to say that. She grabbed Felton's hand, sending the books he was carrying tumbling.

"He's my boy friend."

Felton's mouth dropped and Silas' full lips turned up into a slight grin. Merry swung Felton's skinny arm back and forth.

"His name is Felton. Felton, dis is Silas."

Felton, so overwhelmed, could barely croak out   a greeting.

"Hi."

Silas chuckled, amused that Merry wanted to play their little game. Again.

"Jack, you must be one bad square to bag this frantic bait minor chick. How old are you?"

Merry gripped Felton's hand. She knew that Silas had just insulted her, but even she didn't really understand what he just said. There was no way Felton could have.

The last question, though, she and Felton both understood. The only difference? Merry knew that Silas' question wasn't about Felton's age. Silas was poking fun at her again, making a mean point about how young she was. How young she would always be.

Merry dragged Felton past Silas.

"We have to go. Felton's takin' me to the soda shop."

"Really. I'm goin' there, too."

Silas stepped ahead and held open the soda shop's front door for them. Merry and Felton walked in, hand in hand. Merry, uncomfortable. Felton, proud to be with the prettiest girl in school. Dolores waved them over to a booth she was sharing with some classmates.

"Hey, Merry! Over here!"

Silas headed over to the counter and Merry and Felton joined Dolores in the booth. Merry shook Felton's hand loose. He looked at her, confused. Dolores leaned over the table and whispered loudly to Merry.

"Isn't he in the ninth grade?!"

Merry nodded.

"I knew it! He's so cute!"

Merry wrinkled up her face and peeked around the booth to see if Silas was still at the counter. She nearly got her head knocked off by a mid-sized teenage soda jerk carrying a half dozen bottles of orange Faygos. Not looking a day over 18 and the color of roasted almonds, the young man with dimples set the first pop down in front of Merry.

"What's dis?"

"Orange pop. For you and all your friends. Thanks to my man at the counter."

Dolores and the other girls squealed, all of them climbing over each other to get a peek at Merry's gift-bearing mystery man. Merry didn't bother. She wasn't about to give Silas the satisfaction. She twisted off the top and took a swig of the orange flavored pop. It was good.

Dolores plopped back down into the booth, excited.

"Merry, who was that?!"

Merry took another swig of her pop. This lie was getting easier to tell.

"Nobody."

*

As soon as Merry stepped into the house, she knew something was different. Excellent wasn't home from work yet and Johnson was still at basketball practice, so the stillness greeting her was normal. A pair of man's brown work shoes strewn about the hallway, though? Not normal at all.

Merry stepped over the shoes and headed to her room. Excellent's bedroom door was closed. Her mother didn't go back to work after she left the school. She came home.

Merry heard scuffling and giggling voices from behind the bedroom door.

"Woman, you better keep your hands to yourself or we ain't gone ever make it out of here. Get off me!"

The bedroom door flung open and a shirtless Corn stumbled out with Excellent's arms seductively wrapped around his waist. His brown pants were half zipped and Excellent was barely dressed in a white polyester full slip.

Merry looked at them, just as shocked to see them as they were to see her. Corn was so embarrassed, the man turned red.

"Hey! Merry! Look, Baby. It's Merry."

Excellent dropped her arms and chuckled. Corn darted back into the bedroom to zip up his pants and put on his shirt. Merry started to walk away.

"How was school today?"

How was school? Merry couldn't believe her mother. Was Excellent really asking her this with the long lost husband who left her high and dry over three years ago suddenly back in her bedroom?

"It was O.K."

"O.K.?!"

Corn stepped back out into the hallway, fully dressed now.

"Getting pushed up from the seventh to the ninth grade is more than O.K., Baby Girl. It's great. Excellent told me all 'bout it. If I hadn't made special plans for yo' momma tonight, I'd take you out to celebrate.

Excellent slipped her arm through Corn's, playful.

"Come on, Honey. Where you taking me?"

"Woman, it's a surprise! Don't you know what a surprise is?"

Merry took one look at her laughing mother and knew that Excellent knew what a surprise was. Just like Merry did. Earlier today, she was surprised to find her mother in Principal Bennett's office. She didn't understand then why

Excellent wasn't upset about losing pay and coming down to the school for her. But it all made sense to Merry now.

Her mother hadn't taken off work for her.

She had taken it off for Corn.

MIND STAYED
ON JESUS

"Shut up, Kat. Shut up..."

Merry doubled over, trying so hard not to laugh loud, she couldn't sit up. Kat gasped for breath. Her contagious giggles were falling out of her mouth so fast, she could hardly talk.

"I swear...Donnie's breath smell like neck bones...and he kiss... like a fish."

Kat poked out her lips and bugged her eyes like a cross-eyed goldfish, tears of laughter rolling down her face. Then she grabbed the silver crucifix of Jesus hanging from her chain and dramatically swatted her neck.

"Then...he was slobbering...all down my neck....spitting all over Jesus..."

Merry hollered and knocked the playing cards every which-a-way. It was Saturday night and she and Kat were in their pajamas in Kat's bedroom cracking up and playing Tunk. Again.

Ever since Corn floated back into her mother's life, Merry was free to have a life of her own. Every weekend, Corn returned from his job as a baker for the Railway Passenger Train Company to visit. On Friday, he and Excellent would throw Tunk parties for the neighbors and Pullman porters and cooks from Corn's job. Then, Saturday, Excellent would let her and Johnson spend the night at friends' houses and meet her at church on Sunday.

Merry loved it when her mother wanted Corn all to herself, because it meant she could spend Saturday night with Kat after choir rehearsal. Kat was the sister Merry never had. Born only three days after her, Kat thought just like her, liked the same things Merry did and made her holler. And Merry didn't have to worry that Kat was just being nice to her to get next to Johnson like other girls at church and school were. No, just as Merry knew her name, she knew that Kat was her friend.

"Katherine! Go. To. Sleep."

Kat's stepmother Susie's voice shrieked through the bedroom walls. Merry and Kat covered their mouths, trying to stop laughing. That made it worst.

"Now. Katherine!"

Merry and Kat looked at each other and took their hands off of their mouths. Merry's lip was still twitching. Kat pointed at her to stop. Merry gulped down her last chortle and she and Kat sat still to listen. The other side of the wall was silent.

Kat gathered the cards and whispered.

"Whose turn is it?"

"Mine."

Kat handed the deck to Merry. She shuffled and dealt them both five cards.

"What about Carl and Ronald?"

Kat rolled her eyes and arranged her hand.

"I'm tired of those fools at church. There's this boy Nathan at my school..."

Merry peeked over her cards at Kat, suspicious.

"A white boy?"

Kat smiled, wickedly, threw down a Queen of Hearts and picked a card from the deck.

"He kisses better than all of them. He does this thing with his tongue..."

Kat stuck out her tongue and rolled it around. Merry scrunched up her face, disgusted. Kat smiled.

"How does Felton kiss?"

"I don't know and I don't want to know."

Merry threw down a Three of Clubs and picked up Kat's Queen of Hearts. Kat looked at her, surprised.

"Wait, Felton's been walking you home from school..."

"...He follows me. I'm walkin'."

Kat starred at Merry, her eyes getting big.

"You never kissed a boy."

Merry wanted to, but couldn't lie. Merry shook her head. Kat plopped down her cards.

"Do you know how?"

Merry shrugged. Kat hopped over her bed to her toy trunk and returned with a teddy bear. Well loved, his left paw was flat and he was missing one eye.

"Merry, this is Mr. Snuggles."

Merry snickered. Kat eyed her, offended.

"What's so funny? My mom gave this to me."

Merry stopped laughing. Kat's real mother died three years ago in her sleep and Kat didn't talk about her much. Merry listened to her friend's important introduction, attentive.

"Me and Mr. Snuggles have been through a lot together. Now you can use him."

"Use him for what?"

"For practice."

Kat handed Merry the bear. Merry didn't reach for it.

"Are you crazy?"

"Merry, you need to know how, so you don't make a fool of yourself when it happens."

"I'm not kissin' that bear."

"Why? You want to be like Donnie? Slobbering all over the place like a fish?"

Kat held up Mr. Snuggles to Merry's face and puckered. Merry crossed her arms, unmoved. Kat dropped Mr. Snuggles.

"O.K. Use the back of your hand, then. Can you at least use your dang hand?"

Merry thought about, then raised the back of her hand to her face, awkward. Kat egged her on.

"Kiss it."

Merry gave her hand a quick peck. Kat sighed.

"No, Merry, do it right. Kiss your hand like it's James."

Merry grinned, despite herself. Just the sound of the boy's name still gave her butterflies. Merry puckered, softly pressed her lips against her hand and landed a long, tender smooch. Kat smiled, glad Merry was finally catching on.

"O.K. Now stick out your tongue."

Merry stopped mid-kiss.

"What?"

"Like this."

Kat rolled her tongue around on the back of her hand. Merry watched, confused.

"Boys like that?"

"Uh huh. You do it."

Merry brought her hand back up to her face and poked her tongue out at it. Slowly, she started to roll her tongue around like Kat. She closed her eyes. It was easier to imagine that James was her hand if she wasn't looking into Kat's face. Merry kissed her hand faster. She was beginning to get into it now.

That is, until she heard Reverend McKeever clear his throat in Kat's bedroom. Merry's and Kat's eyes sprung open and they dropped their hands like they had just stolen something. Kat stumbled out an explanation.

"Daddy, we...we were just..."

Reverend McKeever, half-full tumbler glass in hand and pencil behind his ear, eyed the mound of playing cards between them and took a sip of his drink, letting Merry and Kat dangle on a little longer. Kat rambled on.

"We were playing a game."

"Really? What's it called?"

Merry looked at Kat, expectant. She had witnessed her friend melt Reverend McKeever like taffy candy before. But what was Kat possibly going to say now to explain the silliness he just walked in on? Kat scratched her head, stalling.

"What's it called?"

"That's right. The game's name."

Kat's face lit up like the light bulb suddenly going off in her head.

"Simon Says, Daddy. We were playing Simon Says."

Kat smiled. Merry searched the Reverend's tired face, trying to see if he bought it. Reverend McKeever set his glass down on dresser.

"I know that game. Let's see. Simon says, it's way past you girls' bedtime and get in bed."

"Aw, Daddy."

"Aw, Daddy, nothing. Simon said it. Let's go."

Merry and Kat hopped into the bed and climbed under the covers. Reverend McKeever tucked both of them in. His words tumbled out of his mouth less crisp than usual.

"O.K., now, you girls go to sleep. You need rest for your choir's big day tomorrow. Mother told me you have something real special planned."

Merry beamed.

"We've been practicin' real hard, Reveren' McKeever."

"I heard. That's all Mrs. McKeever can talk about. She also said you like to tickle the ivories, Merry. A natural, if she ever saw one."

"I wish I could play like her."

"Well, you must be half way there, because Susie can't stop talking about you."

Kat chimed in, jealous.

"What about me, Daddy? Did mother say anything about me?"

Reverend McKeever looked at Kat lovingly.

"Your mother said you're so anointed, so divine, that the Good Lord, Himself is going to come down from Heaven and sit on the front pew to hear you. Why do you think I dry cleaned my good robe?"

Kat smiled and gazed back at Reverend McKeever. Merry felt a tinge of jealousy. If only she had a daddy she could look at like that. Her own daddy she never knew was long dead, and her momma and her second husband, Jesse, fell out so much, that he was never around long enough to establish any ties with Merry and Johnson.

Sad truth was, Corn was the closest thing resembling a father that Merry had. Corn kept his distance and never took up any time with her or Johnson, though. He was her mother's husband. There on the weekends for Excellent and Excellent, alone.

Reverend McKeever tenderly kissed Kat on the forehead.

"Goodnight, Baby."

"Goodnight, Daddy."

The Reverend headed out, picked up his glass and paused at the light switch.

"Oh and Kat, if I ever catch you kissing a boy like you were kissing your hand, I'm going to lock you in the basement until you're forty. Understand?"

"Daddy, that's forever!"

"I know."

Reverend McKeever turned off the light and pulled the door closed. Kat and Merry turned on their sides, back to back. Merry nudged Kat.

"Kat, you awake?"

"Uh uh."

"You sleep that fast?"

Kat didn't answer and Merry looked to Mr. Snuggles on the floor. She didn't want to kiss the bear. She didn't want to talk to him, either. She turned onto her back.

"Kat."

"What."

"Do you still miss your mom?"

Merry's question stung like cold water on her friend's face. Kat opened her eyes, didn't turn over.

"Yeah."

"You still mad at her?"

"For what?"

"For leaving you."

Kat slowly turned over. She looked at Merry and nodded, ashamed. Kat had never admitted that she was angry with her mother for dying to anyone, but somehow Merry knew. Merry knew, because she had been abandoned, too.

Kat laid her head on Merry's shoulder and Merry's eyes floated up to the ceiling. Silent.

**

"What are you doing?"

Merry looked up from Kat's fairy tale adventure book and found her groggy friend standing in front of her. She was sitting cross-legged on the floor in the closet. How long she had been in there, she didn't know.

"I'm readin'."

"Why?"

"I'm not sleepy."

That was a lie. Merry was sleepy as hell. She had just trained her body not to shut down at night to keep that monster, Mr. Sammy, out of her head. To keep herself awake, Merry read books. At home, she devoured her schoolbooks, the Bible and Excellent's secret stash of romance novels. Kat's books were the best, though. Every story was a fantasy or an exciting adventure that sparked Merry's imagination, made her forget her own problems and took her places beyond her wildest dreams.

Kat wiped her eyes.

"I can't sleep either. Did you have a bad dream, too?"

Merry nodded. Once again, Kat sensed Merry's truth and she didn't have to tell her.

"My daddy used to have bad dreams. After my mom died."

"What did your daddy do?"

Kat answered Merry's question by taking her down to the kitchen and pouring some clear liquid into two mugs shaped like strawberries. Merry starred at it, blankly.

"What is it?"

"My daddy calls it a nightcap."

Merry sniffed it.

"It doesn't smell like anythin'. Is it water?"

"No. My daddy drinks it every night and he sleeps like a baby. You want to sleep, don't you?"

Lord knows Merry wanted to sleep. She just wasn't sure about the strange liquid in front of her. Kat did get the strange liquid from a pint-sized, green glass bottle under the kitchen sink. How'd the girl know it wasn't some new kind of citified bleach?

Kat raised her mug.

"Ready?"

Merry picked up her mug, unsure.

"Remember, Merry. Drink the whole swallow fast."

Merry nodded and she and Kat counted together.

"One...two...three."

Merry threw back her head and downed the clear liquid in one gulp. It tasted like nothing and felt cool like ice water on her tongue. At first. Then, came the burn in her throat straight from the fires of hell. Like identical twins, Merry and Kat gagged, grabbed at their inflamed throats and stumbled over each other to the kitchen sink.

Merry, face soaked and throat smoldering, looked at Kat, suddenly dizzy. It was a warm, happy feeling, her head spinning like she had just hopped off a playground merry-go-round. Kat grabbed Merry's face and slurred.

"Merry... stop...moving...your...head.   You're making...me...dizzy."

Kat and Merry starred at each other, their contagious giggles bubbling up with the hot, hard liquor in their bellies. They fell out, laughing. Upstairs, they heard a creak. Kat brought her finger up to her mouth, sloppily grabbing onto the sink to keep her balance.

"Ssh, Merry...we have...to be...quiet."

Merry held onto the sink, too. The room was still spinning.

"O.K. Let's...go to...bed."

"Right...bed."

Merry and Kat held onto each other and tumbled out of the kitchen, arm in arm. At the staircase, they climbed each step slowly and deliberately. Setting their unsteady feet down on the top landing, Merry jetted for the bathroom, barely making it to the sink. And Kat? Poor child completely missed the toilet.

*

"Feeling better now, Merry?"

Mrs. McKeever's question echoed like high-pitched sledgehammers in Merry's rattling head. It was Sunday morning and just like Kat promised, she hadn't had a nightmare about Mr. Sammy.

Actually, Merry had slumbered so sound, that Merry felt like she hadn't even closed her eyes good when Mrs. McKeever was standing over them, shaking them awake.

Merry squinted. The kitchen was so bright, but she couldn't tell where the extra light was coming from. She swallowed the children's aspirin and orange juice, then handed Mrs. McKeever the empty strawberry mug.

"Yes, Mrs. McKeever. Much better."

Mrs. McKeever rinsed out the mug and set it face down in the kitchen sink. Brown like chocolate sauce, she was thin and tall and more than ten years junior to Reverend McKeever. No wonder Kat couldn't take the woman seriously.

"That's what you, girls, get for staying up all night. I told you to go to bed. Now look at you."

Mrs. McKeever fastened the last button of her cashmere coat and ushered the girls out before her. Merry and Kat moved sluggishly, Mrs. McKeever's frustration striking their heads like missiles.

"I tell you one thing, if you two sing as badly as you look this morning, you both are going to apologize to the choir. Everyone's worked too hard."

Mrs. McKeever was right. Everyone had worked hard and Merry tried her damnest to focus on that when she was standing in line at the back of the church, waiting with the other excited members of the choir.

I woke up this mornin' wit' my mind staaaaaaayed on Jesus! Woke up this mornin' wit' my mind staaaaaayed on the Lord, God Almighty! Woke up this mornin' wit' my mind staaaaaaayed on Jesus! Hallelu! Hallelu! Hallelujah!

Merry, her head still banging, marched down the aisle with her fellow young Christian Soldiers. Clean as the Lamb of Jesus in her new red and blue choir robe. Step. Pause. Step. Hands clapping. Back straight. Head held high. Singing hard and strong from her upset belly.

Singin' and prayin' wit' my mind staaaaaaayed on Jesus! Singin' and prayin' with my mind staaaaaaayed on the Lord, God

Almighty! Singin' and prayin' wit' my mind staaaaaaaayed on Jesus! Hallelu! Hallelu! Hallelujah!

Reverend McKeever and the church jumped to their feet, tickled to see Merry and the small choir marching and singing that old folks' hymn like they meant that thing!

Ain't no harm to keep your mind staaaaaaaayed on Jesus! Ain't no harm to keep your mind staaaaaaaayed on the Lord, God Almighty! Ain't no harm to keep your mind staaaaaaayed on Jesus! Hallelu! Hallelu! Halleluuuuuuujah.

Reverend McKeever stepped to the pulpit, so proud all he could do was shake his head.

"Praise God.   Praise God. Church, thank these young people for blessing us this morning. Hallelujah. I know there's an order to things. But I personally want to take this time to thank two special girls. As some of you may know, Sister Mavis, Susie... Kat has been asking me to let her organize a youth choir for quite some time and I, like a blessed fool, had been resisting. But God, in his infinite wisdom, brought Kat a friend, a servant to plead her case. And not only plead her case, brothers and sisters, but put me in my place. Merry and Kat, come on up here and sing your song."

Merry and Kat looked at each other, shocked. The church service was supposed to have the prayer, scripture and announcements first. Mrs. McKeever, still seated at the organ, nodded and lifted her arm. The choir rose, Merry and Kat took their places and a teenage girl slid behind the piano.

Nervous, Merry's eyes went straight to Excellent's pew. Her mother looked pleased, even a little proud. Mrs. McKeever started to play the old faithful hymn on the organ as she sang, slow and spirit-filled.

Paaaaaaass meeeeeee not, O gentle Saaaaaavior.   Heeear my humbbble cryyyyyyyy.   Whiiile on otheeeeers Thou art caaaaaaaallin', Sweet Jesus, Do not paaaaaaass meeeeeeee byyyyyyyyy.

Stomp. Stomp. Stomp. Mrs. McKeever stomped her foot on the floor like a bass drum and the girl lit into the piano like a boogie-woogie bluesman. A boy in the choir whipped out a harmonica, made it wail like a motherless child, and Kat started shaking and banging an anointed tambourine. Merry and the youth choir weren't singing a sad, mournful hymn anymore. They were leading a revival! Merry quickly tapped her foot and sang the refrain along with the choir, all the while clapping in time with the church that was back on their feet.

I'm singin'! Saaaaavior, Saaaavior, hear my humbbbbble cryyyy. While on others Thou art caaaaalling...I'm singin'! Do not paaaass meeee byyyy.

Merry was so caught up in the moment, that she didn't hear Kat sing her verse. She could even feel the rhythmic rocking of the sanctuary and was sweating from the heat only Colored folks in a Colored church create. But the only sound Merry could hear was her foot tapping and her hands clapping. Had she caught the Spirit and didn't even know it?

Merry eyed Excellent again. She looked confused. So did the rest of the church.

The sound rushed back to Merry's ears. It was her turn to sing and she couldn't for the life of her remember the words. She knew the words. Had practiced the words. But the words were gone, because deep down in her spirit, Merry didn't believe. And the Holy Ghost knew it.

Merry wiped her eyes and blew her nose. After Kat came to her rescue and sang her verse, Merry had begged Mrs. McKeever to go to the bathroom as soon as the song was over. She had every intention of spending the rest of the church service in there.

"Merry?"

Merry paused, either she was still drunk or there really was a God.

"Teenie?"

Merry opened the stall door, suspicious. Teenie, dressed in her Sunday best and matching hat, stood there, a big, tired smile on her face. Merry rushed into her arms.

"Teenie, I'm so glad to see you."

"Baby, you didn't think I'd miss your solo, did you?"

Merry pulled back.

"Excellent's gonna hate me."

"She doesn't hate you."

That was a lie and Merry knew it. Her auntie was just saying that to protect her. She looked at Teenie, wondering if her auntie would lie to protect herself.

"Why does she hate you?"

Teenie looked at Merry like she wanted to tell her. She changed her mind.

"She doesn't hate me, either."

Teenie mustered up a fake smile.

"Ready to go back to service now?"

"I can't go back out there!"

"Your choir has another song to sing."

"So!"

"So?! Merry, there's no shame in making a mistake, but there is shame in runnin' and hidin' after you make it."

Merry crossed her arms, pouted.

"Now, come on back to service and next Friday, I'll take you and Johnson to the movies when I get off of work."

Merry's face lit up.

"You promise?"

"I said I would, didn't I?"

Teenie winked and they walked out of the women's bathroom together. Excellent met them outside the door. Teenie and Excellent starred at each other. Didn't speak. Merry stood in between them, uncomfortable.

"I'm sorry..."

Excellent cut Merry off, her voice laced with disappointment.

"The choir's about to sing again, Merry. You need to get up there."

Merry heard her mother's command, but there was something she just had to know first.

"Can I go to the movies with Teenie next Friday?"

Excellent's eyes narrowed. Merry was so excited, she didn't notice.

"Teenie wants to take me and Johnson to the movies and..."

Teenie inched Merry towards the steps.

"Merry, go on and sing like your momma said."

"Will I see you Friday?"

Teenie nodded and Merry hurried up the basement steps. Damn shame. She had more faith in her auntie's words than the Lord's.

NOT GONE MAKE
THE WORLD STOP SPINNIN'

"**Don't** know why you draggin' your lip on the floor. Teenie put you down for that nigga and that's all there is to it."

Merry slid her hand off of the receiver, her eyes still glued to the hung-up telephone on the kitchen wall. She turned to face Excellent, who was cleaning red snapper and pickerel in the sink.

"She said it was an emergency."

"The only emergency is between that nigga's..."

"Excellent."

Excellent shot a devilish look to Corn, who appeared in the kitchen doorway.

Corn shook his head and walked over to the cabinet to look through the liquor bottles on the top shelf. Johnson rushed through the backdoor, his basketball underneath his arm.

"Is Teenie here?"

Merry leaned against the wall, dejected. Her brother had been missing Teenie as much as she was. She knew the bad news was going to hit him just as hard.

"She's not comin'."

"Oh."

Johnson sucked his tooth, tossed his basketball in the air.

"Can I go back to Lonnie's house, Ma?"

Johnson had to be kidding. Her brother was spending so much time over Lonnie's house, Merry knew something was going on between them. And it wasn't basketball.

Excellent threw her answer to Johnson over her shoulder.

"Go 'head."

Merry couldn't believe it. Why was she the only one that could see through her selfish brother like cellophane? She glared at Johnson. He winked back, turned around and left.

Excellent rinsed off her hands and wiped them on her apron.

"Merry, finish cleanin' this fish and fry it up. Everybody's gone be here soon."

"Why do I have to do it all the time? How come Johnson can't..."

"'Cause I told you to. Don't start wit' me, Girl."

Merry slouched over to the kitchen sink and rolled up her sleeves. Every Friday, her mother made her cook fish dinners to sell at their Tunk parties. She used to love fried pickerel and red snapper. Now, it was getting so, she couldn't stand the sight or smell of it.

Corn set a half-empty bottle of vodka down on the table.

"Baby, you been havin' parties wit'out me?"

Excellent glanced at the bottle and paused. The way Corn's question hung in the air made Merry look, too. She thought she had been careful. All week long, Merry had been sneaking a nightcap every night before bed. She only took a swallow each time and made sure she put the bottle back in the same, exact spot on the top shelf. Excellent hadn't noticed the missing liquor. Merry forgot to figure in Corn.

Excellent touched Corn's arm, like a guilty woman trying to ease her jealous man's mind.

"Honey, whatever liquor is left is left over from last week's card party. You know vodka's not my drink."

Corn eyed Excellent, suspicious at first, then playful. He smacked Excellent on her behind.

"Gotta go to the store. Won't win no money tonight if the house is dry. Merry, come make a run with me."

"Corn, she has to fry this fish. Blackie and Bernice'll be coming down the stairs any minute."

"Tell Blackie's ass to wait. Come on, Merry."

Corn left the kitchen like the matter was settled. Merry, though, looked to her mother first before she made a move. Excellent huffed.

"Don't take all night."

Merry wiped her hands and took off after Corn. He was waiting for her outside with the Ford running.

It was warm inside the car and the fancy, black leather interior smelled like cigarettes and cinnamon.

"How's school goin', Baby Girl?"

Merry knew her answer to Corn's question was going to be a lie. Because the truth was school, these days, was a blur. Mr. Sammy no longer terrorized her nights. The only sacrifice? Her days. Every morning, Merry was in a fog and couldn't focus or concentrate for half the day. If she was still in Mrs. Arnold's seventh grade class, she could fake it and coast through her studies. But now that she was in the ninth grade, the work was too challenging for her fuzzy brain. Thank God she had enough sense to use boring Felton to pick up the slack for her.

Merry shrugged.

"School's O.K."

"That's good, Merry. Real good. I'm proud of you."

Merry lit up inside. The whole time she had been living with Excellent, she hadn't once told Merry that she was proud of her. Merry was glad that Corn was proud of her. Even if what he was proud of wasn't true.

"Sorry I missed your song last Sunday. I couldn't get off work."

Merry starred out the window, embarrassed all over again. Corn glanced at Merry and chuckled.

"Oh, come on, Baby Girl, ain't nothin' to be ashamed of. I remember when I first met your momma, I was so damn nervous, I forgot my own name. So what you forgot the words in front of the whole church. Not gone make the world stop spinnin'."

Merry eyed him.

"Is that what she said?"

Corn chuckled again.

"Baby Girl, your momma barks. That's what she does. You just gotta learn to hear past that."

"How'd you learn?"

"Who says I did?"

Corn turned off the car's engine. They were parked in front of the liquor store. He grabbed the car's door handle, stopped.

"Merry, has Blackie been down to visit your momma?"

Blackie was their top flat neighbor. Dark as tar, he lived upstairs with his mousey wife, Berniece. And the only time Merry saw him lately was when he and Bernice came downstairs for Excellent and Corn's Tunk parties every Friday. Before Corn fell back into her mother's bed, Blackie used to sniff around Excellent and make nice by fixing things around the house. Excellent, from what Merry could tell, never gave Blackie the time of day. In fact, her mother called the poor man every black so and so name under the sun and treated him worst than dirt. That nonsense all stopped, though, the day Corn returned. But now, here Corn was asking Merry if she had seen Blackie, because the vodka was low.

Merry had a decision to make. She could straight up lie to Corn and tell him Blackie had been visiting Excellent or she could tell Corn the truth and tell him Blackie hadn't stepped foot in the house in months. Neither one of those options, though, would keep giving Merry what she needed. Her only choice? Merry had to tell Corn the truth laced with just enough doubt to keep peace in the house.

"I haven't seen him."

Corn looked at Merry for a split second, expecting her to say more. She didn't.

"Alright."

He opened the car door and got out. Merry watched Corn walk into the liquor store. If only she could ask him to buy her own bottle of vodka, she wouldn't have to lie. She really did hate lying. It was becoming way too easy for her to do.

*

"What took you so long?"

Merry drilled Kat as soon as she stepped onto the sidewalk. She had given her friend step-by-step instructions over the phone. What bus to catch. What clothes and makeup to wear. Kat was late and was wearing her Sunday best, a pair of Susie's black gloves, matching black pumps. And red lipstick. Too much.

Kat huffed, flustered.

"My dad was still awake. I couldn't leave."

Merry didn't have that problem at her house. Once the Tunk party winded down and her mother kicked everybody out, Excellent and Corn stumbled straight to their bedroom, did what grown folks do and fell fast asleep. She had a free pass.

And Merry wasn't afraid to use it. In fact, she thought she deserved her free pass. Teenie had disappointed her again and Merry wanted to cheer herself up. Go to the one place Teenie introduced her to that made her feel the most alive and free.

Merry peeked down the alley. King Kong was standing guard in front of Scottie's door. Right where she expected him to be. Merry looked at Kat.

"Let me do the talkin'."

Kat nodded and Merry high-stepped down the alley.

"What's your song, King Kong!"

King Kong looked at her, blankly, his beady eyes burgundy red.

"Oh, don't get brand new, Daddy. It's me, Merry. Teenie's baby."

King Kong's eyes drifted down the alley, interested.

"She wit' you?"

"She's comin'. She told me and my friend to meet her here."

On cue, Merry and Kat smiled and batted their eyelashes. King Kong took a drag of his sweet smelling cigarette.

"Slim ain't wit' you."

"Uh uh."

"She on her way."

"Right."

King Kong took another drag, the smoke seeping out the gaps between his pointy teeth.

"You don't believe me, King Kong?"

"What you think, Jailbait?"

Slyly, Merry pulled five one-dollar bills out of her purse and fanned them out in front of his small face. King Kong eyeballed the dough, ears perked up like antennas.

"I think you should believe President Washington. He can't tell a lie."

Kat's mouth dropped. King Kong, convinced, pocketed the dead presidents and coolly stepped to the side. Merry sashayed past him. Kat tripped after her.

"Merry, where'd you get that money?"

"My momma gave it to me."

Merry gave Kat a peek inside her purse, revealing a wad of cash.

"Sister Mavis gave you that?!"

"No! My real momma did."

Merry snapped close her purse and reached for the doorknob.

"Kat, now, remember what I told you."

"I know. I know. Detroit Royalty."

Merry and Kat stepped inside. Scottie's was hopping! And Merry and Kat were ready to shake her fast tail.

"Ooh, Merry, this place is better than you said! Let's dance!"

"We gotta say hi to Scottie first."

Merry and Kat, trying to look growner than their combined twenty-four years, strolled over to the bar. Scottie walked by Merry, did a double take.

"Merry, what you doin' here? I didn't know Teenie was comin' through tonight."

"Oh, she's not. I mean...she was goin' to, but couldn't make it. So...we came."

Scottie glanced at Kat, who was wiggling on the bar stool to the music next to Merry.

"Scottie, this is my friend, Kat."

"Hi!"

Kat stuck out her hand to shake Scottie's hand, excited. Scottie obliged her.

"Hi to you, too, young lady."

Kat chattered on, still shaking Scottie's right hand.

"Thank you so much for letting us come here. Merry told me all about you, the people, the jazz and your place. Your place... it's...it's..."

"Uh huh. I get that a lot."

Scottie leaned in closer to Kat, spoke in a hushed tone.

"If you want, I can let you keep my hand. You'll just have to make due wit'out a pinky."

Kat shot a quick look to Scottie's pinkie-less right hand and dropped it. Scottie chuckled and Merry tried not to join her. Kat fidgeted, embarrassed.

"Sorry, Scottie. Sorry about your pinkie."

"Don't worry about it."

Scottie headed around behind the bar. Kat shoved Merry.

"Why didn't you tell me Scottie didn't have a pinkie?"

Merry, her belly full of giggles, couldn't answer. Kat sulked.

"Where's the bathroom?"

"Around the corner."

Alone, Merry scanned the bumping joint for Silas. No sign of him. Maybe he was in the back room taking some poor joes for everything they had in a crap game or he was giving it good to a pretty young thing in the bathroom hallway. Whatever Silas was up to, Merry knew he was at Scottie's. And she didn't have to lay her eyes on him to know it.

Scottie stepped up behind the bar, eyed her.

"I just called Teenie's, Merry. She didn't answer."

Merry grumbled, not even trying to hide how angry she was.

"She's wit' Louis."

Scottie softened. The poor child looked like she had just lost her best friend.

"Listen, I'm not gone embarrass you in front of yo' friend..."

"But Scottie, you said I was welcome to come here anytime. Even wit'out Teenie."

"Merry, I know what I said and you know what I meant. How'd you get down here?"

"We caught the bus."

"Alright, I'll get Charlie the jitney to run you back home. You get one Faygo each and then you go. Understand?"

Merry understood. Scottie wasn't going to let her play grown tonight. Wasn't going to offer her a swallow of vodka and let her and Kat boogaloo the night away with the beautiful people on the dance floor. But did Scottie have to rub salt in the wound by making Merry drink some kiddie red, orange or purple soda pop, too?

"O.K., Scottie, but can we have Vernors instead? I like the bubbles."

Scottie smiled, despite herself.

"You like the bubbles. Girl, you too much."

Scottie sauntered down to the other end of the bar to pour the drinks. Merry swiveled around, looking for Kat. Maybe she had jiggled her way onto the dance floor without her. The girl was as strung out on jazz as Merry was. Neither one of them could get a hold of albums. Excellent and Reverend McKeever thought jazz was the devil's music, so they both would sneak off and listen to the best of the day on the radio -- The First Lady, Satchmo, Duke Ellington, Sarah Vaughn, Billie Eckstein, Billie Holliday -- whenever they got the chance. Merry had even taught Kat how to scat. Sometimes they spoke to each other by scatting. It was their own secret language that no one understood but them.

Merry snapped her fingers to the hopping jazz beat. She couldn't blame her friend if she was on the dance floor. Merry wanted to shake a tail-feather herself.

But Kat wasn't on the dance floor. She was in a dark corner, talking to Silas -- Little Red Riding Hood about to get swallowed whole by the big, bad wolf.

Scottie set two glasses of ginger ale down in front of Merry, her eyes going straight to the terribleness Merry was witnessing.

"You gone get her or you want me to do it?"

"I'll do it."

"Alright. I'm here if you need me."

Merry marched over, more jealous than worried about Kat. Silas never joked with her or looked at her the way he was looking at Kat. What made Kat so special?

Merry stepped up, ready to bite through nails. Kat smiled.

"Merry, I was just telling Silas about you."

Kat took Merry's hand and looked up to Silas, happy.

"Merry's my best friend."

Silas took a step toward Merry, his hand in his pockets.

"Merry, Merry quite contrary...this fly chick is yo' best friend? Damn. Kit Kat's so head to toe fine, you need to thank her for takin' pity on you."

Kat let go of Merry's hand, ready to fight.

"What did you say?"

Merry starred at Silas. No matter what she did, Silas could always make her feel so tiny. Kat stepped in between them.

"I said, what did you say?"

Silas stepped back with his hands up, mock scared. Merry managed to mumble.

"Kat, let's go."

"But, Merry, he..."

Kat turned and Merry was gone, on her way out the front door. She didn't know or care where she was going. Scottie, who had been watching the whole thing unravel, caught up with her.

"Baby, you alright? Did that nigga do somethin' to you?"

"No. I just want to go home."

Merry looked at Scottie, trying not to cry. Scottie shot an evil glare in Silas' direction. He had disappeared again.

"Go back over to the bar. I'll get Charlie."

Merry slouched back to the bar. Kat met her there.

"Merry, who is Silas anyway? Why did you let him talk to you like that?"

Merry sighed. She couldn't answer Kat's questions. Didn't know how to make her friend understand how she hated and wanted Silas.

All at the same time.

J & B.
ALRIGHT.

Felton's lips were soft. Softer than Merry expected them to be. Then again, Merry didn't have time to worry about Felton's lips when Silas was striding toward them on his way into the soda shop. Merry had to think fast and do something, anything to show Silas that somebody wanted her.

Merry could feel Silas walking towards them. Then, by them. She broke off her first kiss, abrupt. Felton teetered, his whole body about as solid as Jell-O, then he smiled. Merry turned to Silas like she was surprised.

"Oh! Silas..."

Silas stopped, nodded.

"Merry, Merry."

Merry took Felton's hand and looked up to Silas with lovey dovey eyes.

"We didn't see you. Remember my boyfriend, Felton?"

Silas glanced at Felton. The boy didn't look like he was breathing. Silas stopped himself from grinning.

"Yeah, Jack. How you doin'?"

"I'm in love."

Merry flinched. He's in what?! Silas, seeing the truth written all over Merry's face, went in for the kill.

"You hear that, Merry Merry? This cat is high. You got him stuck on you."

Merry squeezed Felton's hand and looked Silas dead in the eye.

"I love him, too."

Felton gasped. Nobody was expected Merry to say that. Not even Silas. Silas' eyes twinkled, mischievous.

"That's beautiful. 'Bout to make a nigga cry."

Merry stood strong. She couldn't let Silas see that he was getting to her.

Well, 'scuse me for interruptin'. You two lovebirds get back to peckin'. That's what main squeezes do. Right?"

Silas nodded to Merry. Another challenge. He was daring her to kiss Felton in front of him. Like she meant it this time. Merry, not about to be outdone, grabbed Felton's all-too-willing face and planted one on him. This was a real kiss.

At least, it felt more real for Merry because the man she loved was standing there. Watching. It was like she was sharing her first kiss with Silas, not Felton.

The chiming of a bell pierced Merry's fantasy like a needle in a balloon. Opening her eyes just as Silas stepped inside the soda shop, Merry pulled away from Felton, quick.

"Wowwwww. Merry, do you really love me?"

"What?"

Merry peeked through the soda shop window to see Silas taking a seat at the counter. He and the young soda jerk with dimples were talking. They gave each other some skin, exchanged something.

"Merry, do you love me?"

Merry was too distracted to hear Felton's ridiculous question. Inside the soda shop, she saw the pound cake Colored woman that was having sex with Silas at Scottie's sashay over and sit on Silas' lap. Merry stomped away from the window, upset. Felton followed.

"Merry?"

Merry didn't talk to Felton for the rest of the walk home. The boy was so not important that Merry didn't even say goodbye to him when they got to her house. She damn near slammed the door in his face before Felton fired out a quick question.

"Merry, can I use your bathroom?"

Merry held the door open, mid-swing. She and Johnson weren't supposed to have company in the house when Excellent wasn't home. Her sweet brother, of course, was her mother's golden boy and could do whatever he wanted to.

But Merry knew Excellent wouldn't hesitate to bring the wrath of God down on her if she caught someone, especially a boy, in the house with her.

Felton hopped back and forth on the porch, doing the gotta-pee dance.

"Come on, Merry, please?"

Merry opened the door. It wouldn't be Christian-like to let the boy pee on himself in the cold.

"O.K. Hurry up."

Felton scurried in.

"Where is it?"

Merry pointed down the hallway.

Felton plopped down their books and hurried down the hall. Merry hung up her coat, took off her shoes. A few seconds later, Felton emerged out of the bathroom, relieved.

"Thank you, Merry."

Merry pushed Felton to the front door.

"Uh huh. You gotta go."

"O.K. Oh, but wait, I have something for you."

Felton reached into his coat, pulled out a rectangular shaped something wrapped in comic strip newspaper and handed it to Merry.

"What is it?"

"It's your birthday gift. I'm sorry I didn't wrap it in pretty gift-wrapping paper. My auntie didn't have any."

Merry starred at Felton. All this time, she had been counting the days until she turned thirteen, but ever since she started drinking her nightcaps before bed, she had been forgetting things. It also didn't help that Excellent and Johnson hadn't said a word to Merry about it. Teenie also didn't call. And her momma? Merry brought the mail in every day after school. No card.

Merry looked down at the present, hesitated.

"Aren't you going to open it, Merry? I hope you like it."

Merry pulled away the neatly wrapped comic strip paper. Her gift was a book. Shakespeare's Romeo and Juliet.

"It's a classic. I know how much you like to read so...If you don't like it, I can take it back..."

"No, Felton. It's nice. Thank you."

Felton smiled, glad. Merry looked up at him, his thick, black eyeglasses still a little foggy from coming inside from the cold. Felton gazed back. Silent. Attracted. He didn't look so goofy to her now.

Just as they leaned in to kiss, Merry heard a car door slam outside. She peeked out the front door window and saw Corn heading up the walkway, carrying groceries. It was the middle of the week. He wasn't supposed to be off the railway tracks until Friday! Merry pushed Felton toward the kitchen as he stumbled to pick up his books.

"The back door!"

Merry and Felton skedaddled for kitchen. Merry flung open the back door and tossed Felton out. Right into the full arms of her mother. Two large jars of strawberry preserves crashed at their feet, splashing all over Felton and Excellent.

Excellent screamed. Corn rushed into the kitchen.

"Babe, you alright?"

Merry and Felton looked like two deer caught in headlights. Excellent wiped a glob of strawberries off of her cheek, fuming.

"I look alright?"

Corn laughed. Excellent bumped past Felton and Merry, and stomped over to the sink to wash off the preserves.

"Corn, ain't nobody laughin', but you. Will you find out who this big-eared boy is?"

Corn set the groceries down on the table and eyeballed him, gruff.

"What's your name, boy?"

Merry shot a look to Felton, who was so nervous, he squeaked.

"Fel...Felton White, sir."

Corn crossed his strong arms, army tough.

"What are you doin' in my house, Felton White?"

"I walk Merry home from school..."

Merry flinched. Excellent swerved around, raised eyebrow, hands on hips. Her mother couldn't know that Felton had been walking her home from school every day. What was the boy trying to do, get her killed? Merry chirped in, dousing the fire.

"...I let him use the bathroom."

Excellent paused, anger dancing in her eyes. Merry's explanation didn't put out the flame. She threw gasoline on it.

"Merry, what the hell else you let him do? You know you not supposed to have nobody in my house."

"But he really had to go."

Excellent walked up on Merry, ready to knock the hell out of her.

"I don't give a damn, Merry. I swear to God, if your fast ass brings any babies in my house..."

Corn stepped up, trying to be a voice of reason.

"Excellent, the boy had to use the bathroom. It's alright."

"Oh, it's alright? It's alright for this girl to stand here and lie to my face? See how alright it is if she gets knocked up. How alright it gone be then?"

Merry wilted. Silas made her feel small, but her mother? Excellent made Merry feel like she didn't matter at all.

Corn looked at Merry with apologetic eyes, cleared his throat.

"Felton, time for you to go."

"Yes, sir."

Felton scampered out, turned back to Merry as he closed the door.

"Happy birthday, Merry!"

Merry grimaced. Wasn't nothing happy about it.

*

Merry laid on her bed, starring up at the ceiling. Excellent beat her, then banished her to her room. No dinner. No cake. No presents. And Merry was being punished for something she didn't do. Merry decided she wasn't going to be innocent anymore.

If her mother was never going to believe her when she told the truth and make her bleed when she was doing right, she might as well lie and bleed for doing wrong.

There was a knock at Merry's bedroom door. Angry, she didn't answer. Johnson opened the door, stepped inside and looked at her. Merry turned her back to him, her butt still stinging a little.

"Leave me 'lone, Johnson."

"Time tuh eat."

"She said I couldn't."

"I asked Ma if you could. So c'mon."

"I ain't hungry."

"What, you still mad we forgot your birthday? Or you mad Ma caught you with yo' big eared boyfriend?"

"He ain't my boyfriend."

"So why was you slobberin' all over him? Dolores said she saw yaw outside the soda shop."

Merry flopped on her back, caught. Johnson grinned, victorious.

"Come and eat and I won't tell Ma."

Merry frowned, crossed her arms.

"I don't care. Tell her. She already think we doin' it anyway."

Johnson sighed and scooped Merry's in his arms, picking her up rough like a caveman. Merry kicked and screamed as he carried her out of the bedroom, down the hallway.

"Boy, put me down!"

"Shut up, 'fo' I drop you on yo' head."

"Let me go!"

Johnson turned the corner and plopped Merry down hard on the floor. Merry hurried to her feet, ready to knock her brother's head clean off, then she realized she wasn't in the kitchen. She was in the living room. And Corn and Excellent wasn't her only audience.

"Surprise!"

Merry faced everyone, shocked. Her mother, Corn, Dolores and Kat stood clumped together in front of her with a big German chocolate cake topped with thirteen lit candles. Merry stood there, too surprised to even smile. Johnson teased her.

"Uh huh. Thought we forgot. This was all Ma's idea. Good fo' you, Corn talked her into not callin' it off."

Corn snickered, chest stuck out.

"We got you good, Baby Girl."

"Thank you, Corn."

"I just baked the cake. I was gonna make you my famous strawberry shortcake, but..."

Excellent cut her eyes, angry all over again. Corn threw his arm around her waist and pulled her closer to him, playful.

"No, Baby Girl, the one you really need to be thankin' is yo' momma."

Merry looked to Excellent. Not even two hours ago, her mother had beaten her butt and now Excellent was throwing her a surprise birthday party. Merry didn't know what to think. How to feel.

She grinned, sheepishly.

"Thank you."

"You still on punishment."

"I know."

"Good. Now blow out these candles before they melt all over the cake."

Merry closed her eyes, sucked in a deep breath and started to blow. Then, she heard it. Thudded, smashed together notes from a piano.

Merry's eyes popped open. Excellent shot Johnson a look of death and the mistake stopped short. Corn, Dolores and Kat stepped up closer to Merry, trying to block her from seeing what was behind them. Merry craned her neck to peek around them, suspicious.

"What was that?"

Dolores and Kat fussed at Merry just like they had rehearsed it.

"Merry, you're hearing things. I didn't hear anything, Kat. Did you?"

"Just my stomach growling. Girl, would you please make your wish, so we can eat?"

Merry raised an eyebrow. She knew what she heard. Excellent huffed, her surprise ruined.

"Merry, I didn't pay all this money on this piano for all this silliness. Blow out the damn candles."

Merry obeyed, quick and in a hurry. Corn, Dolores and Kat parted like the Red Sea and she ran around the card table. A small piano with a red bow on top of it set in the corner of the living room. Merry touched the keys in disbelief.

"This is for me?!"

Excellent nodded, proud.

"Susie's going to give you lessons. She told me you like to play."

Before Merry could catch herself, she threw her arms around her mother's waist, so happy she could cry.

"Thank you!"

Excellent returned Merry's hug, more touched than she wanted everyone to see. She patted Merry's back.

Corn snapped a picture, the flashbulb startling both of them.

"Give me one mo'. Show me your teeth this time."

Still holding each other, mother and daughter smiled. The doorbell rang. Corn paused before he took the picture.

"Babe, you expectin' anybody else?"

Excellent, frozen smile, shook her head "no." Merry grinned wider. Excellent and Corn did have another surprise for her. Maybe her momma was coming! Or the surprise of all surprises! The First Lady of Jazz, herself, Ella Fitzgerald was going to come and scat with Merry while she played the birthday song on her new piano! Merry piped in, excited.

"I'll get it!"

Merry ran to open the door and came face to face with Teenie holding a bright purple box.

"Surprise, Baby!"

"Teenie!"

Merry hugged Teenie, not noticing the man entering behind her. At first.

"Sorry we're late. We got here as fast as we could."

Excellent eyed Johnson as he snuck out of the room. And Corn crossed his arms, suddenly quiet, uncomfortable. Teenie glanced past Excellent, saw the piano.

"Ooh, Merry, is this fine piano yours?"

"Excellent gave it to me! Want me to play you somethin'?!"

Merry grabbed Teenie's hand to take her over to the piano. Excellent, in their way, didn't step aside.

"Merry, you can do a concert for all of us. After you eat. Dinner's ready."

Kat and Dolores darted out for the kitchen with Corn and Excellent trailing behind them. Teenie stopped Merry at the archway in front of the man she didn't know. Teenie took his hand, lovingly.

"Merry. This is Louis."

Merry almost had to shield her eyes from Teenie's smile. So this was the married with children soldier that her auntie had put her down for? As Detroit men went, Louis was good looking, but nowhere near fine like the hip cats Merry had seen down at Scottie's or in Paradise Valley. He was paper bag brown, had a pencil thin moustache, close cropped military haircut and was shorter than Teenie. Not by much, but her auntie was making it worst, because she was wearing heels.

Louis reached out to shake Merry's hand.

"Happy Birthday, Merry. Teenie talks about you so much, I feel like I know you already."

"She told me a lot about you, too."

No, she hadn't. Teenie hadn't told Merry a thing about Louis. The little bit that Merry did know, she had overheard Scottie or Excellent say. The truth was Louis was her auntie's secret, the only secret she knew of that Teenie had ever kept from her. And Merry didn't like it.

Excellent, plate of food in hand, craned her neck to look at Teenie's hand as they joined the party in the kitchen.

"Teenie, is that what I think it is on your finger?"

"Yes, we finally did it. We got married on Friday."

Dolores and Kat squealed and crowded around to get a peek of Teenie's modest diamond wedding ring. Merry, uninterested, slipped back to fix her plate.

Corn patted Louis on the back, happy again.

"Congratulations, man! We got to celebrate! What you drinking?"

Corn skirted over to the cabinet, took out two glasses as Louis answered.

"J & B."

"J & B. Alright."

"So, Louis, did you and Teenie get married at your church?"

Merry rolled her eyes. Her mother was calling Teenie a heathen. She wouldn't blame her auntie if she responded like one.

"No, we drove over to Toledo last Friday and stayed over for our honeymoon."

Dolores, the hopeless romantic, chirped in.

"Was it a beautiful wedding?"

Teenie glanced at Louis, sideways. He chuckled.

"Oh, it was nice. The judge had to ask me twice, though, before I said 'I do.'"

Dolores leaned in, nosey.

"Did you change your mind?"

Teenie looked to Louis again. Everyone, but Merry gathered around. Louis answered, stone-faced.

"No, Teenie just wanted to get me back, because I tricked her."

Teenie pushed him, playful.

"You gave me a heart attack is what you did!"

Corn handed Louis his drink. Teenie continued the story, tipsy in love.

"One of his Army buddies called me at the shop Friday, said I needed to meet him. It was an emergency..."

"She thought I was dead..."

"So I rushed over there, expectin' the worst. And this fool..."

"I had my buddies do a full salute, uniforms, guns and all..."

"What can I say, the man had a gun in my face, I couldn't say no..."

Teenie and Louis laughed. Merry starred at the happy couple. It was official. She didn't have an auntie anymore. Teenie was Louis' wife now and it wouldn't be too long before Teenie would be one more person that Merry didn't matter to.

Merry raked her uneaten food into the garbage. Watching her auntie with Louis had made her lose her appetite. For everything. She didn't want to play the piano. And she didn't even want a piece of her German chocolate birthday cake anymore.

No, Merry wanted something else, something stronger. She wanted what Corn and Louis were having.

A drink.

KENTUCKY, 1965

Merry's throat was dry. She was sweating and her throat was dry, because she had just hurried out of the cracker diner, her life and barbeque chicken in hand.

The only problem? The bus in front of her wasn't Greyhound and it wasn't headed for Detroit. It was county and headed straight for the Kentucky State Women's Correctional Institution. The hellhole she just came from.

Merry plopped down on the bench. She had just talked all that smack with the poor white trash waitress, escaped an execution befitting a nigger, and now she couldn't go anywhere.

Merry looked down to the barbeque chicken that she was cradling in her hands like a newborn baby. She wondered how her own babies were doing.

Well, Felton, Jr. and Juliette weren't exactly babies anymore. Her skinny, handsome son, who answered to the nickname Jr. Baby, was tall, had bad eyes just like his square daddy and was 16. And light bright Juliette, who was smart as hell like Merry and looked like her mutt daddy had spit her out, was 14.

Merry hadn't seen her children for almost five years, since before she got sent up to the Big House. They probably wouldn't recognize her now. Hell, Merry had been through so much shit, she wasn't sure if she would even recognize them.

Merry ripped a drumstick off of the barbeque chicken, took a bite. It was good. If the crackers in the restaurant changed their minds and came after her with a noose, at least she'd die full. Now all she needed was something to drink. She glanced around for a water fountain and swallowed another bite of chicken. She was just going to have to be thirsty. She couldn't go back inside and ask for water. That would be like handing the honkies the rope, herself.

The doors of the prison bus opened. Merry looked, curious, and shielded her eyes as the white male driver stepped off the bus. He slid a silver flask into his pocket, the bright light of the sun bouncing off of it. And the white male guard, standing up at the front of the bus, closed the door behind him.

Merry made sure not to look at the driver as he walked past. She was so thirsty for what he had in that flask, that Merry was afraid that if she looked at the man too hard, she might knock him over the head for it.

Merry took another bite of her chicken.

Clink. Clink. Clink. The noise sounded like a shank tapping lightly on a prison bar. Merry glanced around, alert.

Clink. Clink. Clink. There the noise was again. This time, a female prisoner on the bus, a broken black woman about twenty years older, got Merry's attention. She was tapping on the bus window with her handcuffs. Merry took a closer look at the junkie, a once beautiful woman with matted hair and a fresh gash on her oblong face. She couldn't call her name, but Merry knew her from prison.

Merry shook her head. The old broad hadn't even been out of the joint for two good months and here she was back again. The woman placed her hand on the window, mouthed a question.

"Is it good?"

Merry squinted. The woman's mouth was so chapped and raggedy, Merry couldn't read her lips. The woman mouthed the silent question again and lifted her handcuffed hands to her mouth like she was eating.

"Is. It. Good?"

Merry understood this time. She grinned and started to nod just as the guard, baton drawn, stomped down the bus aisle for the woman. In one swoop, he knocked the woman upside her head, wailing on her.

Merry looked away. She didn't like what she was feeling. Defenseless like all of the other female prisoners who were also turning a blind eye on the guard beating the screaming junkie jailbird.

The muffled screams stopped. Merry looked just as the guard backed off the woman, winded, cocky. He scanned the bus like a greedy kid in a candy store. His eyes landed a few rows up on a young woman, skin and bones, sunken eyes, junkie twitch.

The young woman's dirty royal blue dress hung off of her like a fitted gown on a wire hanger. She was petite, chocolate brown skin with good hair, barely there breasts and haunting eyes. The woman was sweating, scratching and swaying side to side. Her jones coming down so hard on her, she was sick.

Merry starred. She was having a heat stroke. She had to be. There wasn't any other explanation for what she was seeing. *Who* she was seeing.

Merry was starring at herself. Her four-years ago self.

Feeling the horny guard circling his erect baton around her breasts, Merry looked at her dope fiend self eyeball to eyeball. She felt the hot window glass against her sweaty forehead as she jerked and twitched forward, unable to escape the guard's probing, thrusting fingers between her musty legs.

Merry gagged. Outside on the bench, she could feel the guard's molesting hands all over her. But on that hot prison bus? Merry's dope fiend body was crying out for smack so bad, that she didn't feel a thing.

In that moment, Merry remembered.

Merry set down her chicken on the bench and stood. Her eyes burrowing into the guard's turned face, she stepped forward and shouted. Not once moving her lips.

"Leave me alone, motherfucker! Get your goddamn hands off of me, you cracker son of a bitch!"

The guard must have heard Merry's threatening thoughts, because he stopped. The guard hit the bus window, trying to scare Merry away like she was a stray dog.

"Get 'way from here, Nigga!"

Merry kept her eyes fixed on him. The guard stomped off the bus, baton drawn. That's when Merry recognized him. He was a little younger, a hell of a lot skinnier, but still the same evil asshole that had been using her as an outhouse for the past four years. The cracker had even escorted her to the prison gate a few hours ago, but he didn't recognize Merry now. Because he didn't know her. Yet.

"Nigga, what the hell you lookin' at?!"

"Nothing."

"Damn right, nothin'. That junkie bitch is a low life, black ass piece of cunt like you."

The guard glared at Merry, took a long sniff of her.

"The air smells fresh on you, Gal. Real fresh. You homesick? I got a extra seat. Wanna join her?"

The guard circled his baton around Merry's breasts. Her first instinct was to slap him, pull away. She did neither.

"No. My bus is coming."

The guard chuckled like a spider toying with a fly caught in his web. He ran his baton down Merry's chest, past her stomach.

"What if I told you, your bus is my bus."

Merry stopped his baton, starred at him.

"You can't do that."

The guard, his eyes flashing with anger, shoved the baton hard into her stomach. Merry dropped to one knee. He gloated over her.

"I can do whatever I want, nigga. Remember that."

The bus driver scrambled out of the diner, Alice and Aileen right behind him.

"Delmar, this nigga givin' you trouble?"

"Naw, Alice. She ain't no trouble. Are you, Nigga?"

Merry shook her head no. The guard slipped his baton back into his hoister, eyeing her.

"Let's go, Lucius. I got a date with a pretty lady. Can't keep her waitin'."

Merry struggled to her feet as the prison bus pulled off, taking Delmar and Merry's four years ago self with it. Alice and Aileen went back into the diner, but Merry could still feel all of the cracker customers' eyes on her.

She scooped up her barbecue chicken. To hell with waiting on that slow Greyhound bus and risking another forgotten memory biting her on the ass.

She was better off walking.

DETROIT, 1948

"**Did** it feel good, Merry?"

Merry pulled up her panties and sat up. She and Felton were in her basement, a piece of Excellent's wool material underneath their still dressed bodies. Hearing voices, Merry looked up through the basement window and saw two pairs of snow dusted, sneakered feet run up the back porch stairs and into the house. It was Johnson and Lonnie. Her brother couldn't do anything without that boy these days.

Merry stood up to fold up the wool material. Felton, zipping his pants, touched her hand, vulnerable.

"Merry?"

Merry paused.   Something about the way Felton touched her made Merry's body remember that she wasn't a virgin.

Merry pulled back her hand.

"I have piano lessons."

"Now?"

"Yeah, Mrs. McKeever's comin'."

"Oh."

Merry tugged on wool. Felton hopped off, disappointed. Neatly, she folded up the material and placed it in the clothesbasket next to her mother's sewing machine.

Upstairs, the doorbell rang. Merry pushed Felton up the basement stairs as he scrambled to grab his coat and hat.

"That's Mrs. McKeever."

"But, Merry, what about your homework?"

"Bring it to school tomorrow. And get some wrong this time. Mrs. Barton's not stupid."

Before Felton could say anything else, Merry tossed him out the side door like trash. Then, she bolted up the stairs to let Mrs. McKeever in. But Corinthian's First Lady was already in the front hallway with Lonnie. The ultimate gentleman, he was helping her take off her coat.

"Oh, there you are Merry. This handsome young man was kind enough to let me in out of the cold."

Lonnie smiled and hung up Mrs. McKeever's coat. Tall, lean and the color of pecan pie, Lonnie, fifteen, was in the ninth grade and on Deggin Junior High School's varsity basketball team. Broad in the chest with a voice deeper than a well, there was no trace of fairy on him.

Merry eyed Lonnie, unimpressed.

"Where's Johnson?"

"In the bathroom. Where were you?"

Merry looked at Lonnie, wanting to smack him. He knew Merry had been in the basement doing what grown folks do with Felton. Just like Merry knew Lonnie had been in her brother's room doing what fairy folks do with Johnson.

"I was hangin' up clothes."

Mrs. McKeever clapped her hands and headed into the living room.

"Good, Merry. Then, your fingers should be nice and limber for our lessons. Lonnie, do you play?"

"No, Mrs. McKeever. I just play ball. Johnson says Merry's good."

"You a lie! I said she ain't bad!"

Johnson bounced up next to Lonnie in the doorway, fussing. Lonnie slid over to the other side of the doorway, fussed back at him.

"That's what I said."

"No, it ain't. You said I said she was good."

"Boy, that's the same thing."

"No, it ain't!"

Mrs. McKeever, amused by Merry's brother and his boyfriend bickering like an old married couple, stepped in, correcting Johnson.

"No, it isn't, Johnson."

Johnson nudged Lonnie.

"Told you, Fool! Even Mrs. McKeever said it ain't the same!"

Everybody fell out laughing. Merry hated to admit it, but her brother could be funny sometimes. Especially when he was in a good mood. And these days, no one put him in a better mood than Lonnie.

Anybody else would think that the brightness in his eyes was because of Dolores. He had started going with the poor girl to cover up that he was really sniffing behind Lonnie. Lonnie had a girlfriend, too. Nina. A pretty high yella eighth grade girl with long hair, Nina was popular, a cheerleader and was always strutting around in Lonnie's letterman jacket. And everyone gobbled it up like caramel corn. The teachers shamefully favored them. The boys envied and worshipped them. And the girls lusted and chased after them. The whole school was blind to what Merry could plainly see. Johnson and Lonnie were sweet. And transparent. Like vodka.

Merry covered her mouth and coughed. She wouldn't mind a drink right now. It had gotten so that Merry was sneaking a taste of vodka in the morning when she woke up. Not a full nightcap. Just enough to stop her head from pounding. And sometimes, if Merry got the yearning, she would sneak another taste when she got home from school. Truth was, that's what Merry really wanted to be doing right now.

She wanted to be tipsy and bopping to jazz in her bedroom. Not learning to read sheet music and playing *Twinkle, Twinkle, Little Star* on the piano with Mrs. McKeever.

"Well, that was pitiful. No form. Limp fingers. Maybe I should just give your mother her money back. Is that what you want, Merry?"

The answer was yes. But Merry knew better than to tell Mrs. McKeever the truth.

"No."

"No? Then what's the problem, young lady?"

"I'm tired of playin' the same borin' thing over and over. Can I play somethin' else?"

"What would you suggest?"

"I don't know."

"Oh, I think you do."

Mrs. McKeever tickled the ivories lightly, her fingers fluid, gliding.

"There's the classical genius of Mozart. The gospel blues of Dorsey. Or I can do you one better. How about this?"

Like a piano man hopping at Scottie's, Mrs. McKeever lit into the keys and pounded out a swinging jazz tune. Merry couldn't believe it. Her First Lady, sanctified, blessed, still had the face of a Christian missionary, but her fingers were flying, possessed like Duke Ellington and Count Basey center stage at The Cotton Club.

"Mrs. McKeever, how did you..."

"I wasn't always a First Lady, Merry."

"But Reverend McKeever.."

"He wasn't always a Reverend, either."

Merry touched the keys, mimicking a few notes of Mrs. McKeever's swinging tune. Mrs. McKeever watched her.

"Merry, can I ask you something?"

"Yes, ma'am."

"Is Kat alright? Is she having problems in school or with a boy?"

Merry stopped fooling with the piano, guilty. Kat was drinking nightcaps, too. And ever since the white boy that she liked humped and dumped her, Kat had been carrying a thermos of vodka in her lunchbox everyday. It wasn't a problem, though. Kat was in the seventh grade. The work wasn't as hard as Merry's. The only problem that Merry could see her best friend having was the same problem she was having. She missed her momma. Still.

Merry turned to Mrs. McKeever.

"There's nothin' wrong, Mrs. McKeever."

"Merry, I need to know. She talks to you."

"Really, Mrs. McKeever. Nothin's wrong."

Mrs. McKeever looked at Merry, trying to read the lie that was hidden in plain sight on her face. Then, she smiled.

"Thank you. Coming from you, Merry, that makes me feel better. I trust you."

Merry smiled back. Mrs. McKeever was right to trust her. Merry would never let anything happen to Kat. She was her best friend, her sister.

Kat was the back of Merry's hand.

BABY,
WHAT YOU DOIN'
WIT THAT PISTOL?

Three A.M. And Merry wasn't dreaming. She wasn't dreaming, because she wasn't sleeping. She wasn't sleeping, because Corn and Excellent were fighting. And they were fighting, because Merry lied. And Merry's lie about Blackie? It was eating at Corn, chewing him up from the inside out like a cancer. And Corn's cancer was now his and her mother's cancer. And their cancer was bleeding through Merry's bedroom walls.

"Woman, you must think I'm a goddamn fool!"

"Corn, you drunk."

"No, I ain't! Ain't enough liquor in this damn house for me to get drunk on! You just had to rub the shit in my face, didn't you, Excellent? Not good enough the nigga's lips been sloppin' up all my liquor. You just had to let me know Blackie's crusty ass been sloppin' you up, too!"

"Nigga, I told you I don't want no goddamn Blackie!"

"You want the nigga so bad, you won't leave!"

"Nigga, please."

"I saw your ass, Woman!"

"You ain't seen shit."

"I saw the way you was lookin' at Blackie at the card party! Eyeballin' him up and down like a ho in the street."

"I wasn't lookin' at Blackie no more than you was lookin' at Teenie at Merry's party. She still got that mole on her ass?"

Merry sat up in her bed. Corn and Teenie? She figured Corn had left her mother the first time, because he had been fooling with some woman. But she never once thought that that home-wrecker heifer was her auntie.

Now it all made sense. That's why Excellent threw Teenie out of her house. And that's why things were so tense between them.

"This ain't about Teenie, Excellent."

"Well, it sure as hell ain't about me and my kids followin' your triflin' ass to Chicago. How long this good job at the hotel gone last, Corn? How long it's gone be before I'm carryin' your sorry ass again?"

Merry pressed her ear to the cold wall. She wanted to know the answer to that, too. Corn had been let go from his baking job with the train company two months ago and her mother had been carrying him, working weekends for another white family. Excellent had been riding the man hard to get a factory job at one of the auto plants. But Corn resisted. Said, yes, his hands were meant to be covered in oil. Crisco. Not STP. For the past couple weeks, he had been hustling pies and cakes out the trunk of his car. Starting to build his own business.

"Godamnit, Excellent! Can't you see I'm tryin' to do somethin'?"

"Nigga, you ain't trying to do shit, because you ain't shit."

Merry winced. If her mother's words stung her, then they must have sliced through Corn like a hot knife through butter.

"Motherfucka!"

Merry heard Corn yell before she felt the heavy pound through the wall. Then, Merry heard a crash, stomping, tussling. Her mother screamed.

Merry jumped out of bed, ran into the hallway. Johnson, scared shitless, was already there. Merry yelled at him.

"He's beatin' her!"

"They jus' fightin', Merry."

Merry took a step for Excellent's bedroom door. Johnson stopped her.

"What you gone do?

Merry shook loose her arm. Her brother was taller than Corn, had a chest broader than most grown men, but he was still a pussy. Merry glared at him.

"What *you* gone do?"

A banging on the back door answered their question. It was their upstairs neighbor, Mr. Blackie.

He bolted in, a superhero in red long johns and a bathrobe, his cape.

"I heard screamin'. Everything alright?"

"They fightin'."

"Fight my ass. Where is he?!"

"In the bedroom."

Mr. Blackie stomped out of the kitchen. Top heavy, he was a muscular man in his arms and his neck. But he had little, skinny legs and was shorter than Corn.

Merry and Johnson followed Mr. Blackie out into the hallway. Just then, Excellent's bedroom door yanked opened and Corn jetted out with an armful of clothes.

"Get the hell out, Nigga! Get out!"

Excellent, blood dripping from her lip and nose, ran out and hurled a lamp at him. Just missing Corn's head. Corn turned around, furious. Then, he saw Blackie.

"Nigga, what the hell you doin' in my house?!"

Mr. Blackie walked past Excellent, got in Corn's face.

"Sounded like there was a problem."

"I'm gone show you a goddamn problem."

Corn shoved Blackie hard in his chest, his armful of clothes going flying. Blackie took a swing at Corn and Corn, like the Brown Bomber, Joe Louis, himself, sidestepped Blackie's wild roundhouse, socked him in the gut with an uppercut. No wind left in him, Blackie dropped to one knee.

Corn starred down at him, then looked to Excellent, his eyes woeful. He turned to round up his clothes and Blackie, low to the floor like a plantation wrestler, grabbed Corn around his thick legs and completely lifted him off his wide feet. They came crashing down hard on the coffee table.

Excellent charged back down the hall to her bedroom. Then charged back out. With a pistol. Merry and Johnson lost it.

"Corn! Mr. Blackie! Stop!"

But Corn and Mr. Blackie were too far gone to hear them. Like two niggas in the street, they kept thrashing each other around the living room, tumbling over Excellent's good furniture, stomping on her valuables, heirlooms and whatnot. Hand steady, Excellent pointed the gun at them, cocked it. Corn and Blackie froze, turned, starred at her.

Corn, his eyes focused on Excellent's, stood slowly. He swallowed, spoke quiet and calm.

"Baby, what you doin' wit' that pistol?"

Excellent answered matter-of-factly, just as if she was holding a Bible.

"I ain't gone have you niggas tearin' up my house. I worked too hard for it."

Mr. Blackie, jumped in, nervous.

"Excellent, I was just tryin' to help you. Corn the one..."

Excellent shifted the pistol to him.

"Blackie, I don't need your black ass to protect me from my husband. Go back upstairs. To your wife."

Blackie, not sure if he should move or not, hesitated. A pounding at the front door startled everybody.

"Excellent! You alright in there! Excellent!"

The shrill voice shrieking on the other side of the front door belonged to their nosey, old neighbor, Ms. Ruthie. Blind as Ray Charles, the woman could hear a cricket peeing on cotton.

Excellent lowered her pistol. Corn was so disappointed, he didn't even blink. She handed the pistol, handle first, to Johnson.

"Johnson, put this in my underwear drawer at the bottom."

Johnson, the first time he ever held a gun, carried it out in both hands, careful. Merry watched her brother tiptoe out, steered clear of him. Ms. Ruthie pounded again.

"Excellent! I can hear you in there! Open the door!"

Excellent pulled back the curtain and peeked out the living room window. Corn bent down to gather his clothes. She glanced at him, ran her hands over her ruffled hair, wiped the drying blood from her lip.

"Merry, open the door."

Merry obeyed. But she didn't expect to find there what she did. Half the block was out on the sidewalk and standing on the porch with Ms. Ruthie were two white cops -one old, one young.

Ms. Ruthie reached over Merry's head thinking it was Excellent.

"Excellent?!"

"I'm alright, Ms. Ruthie."

Ms. Ruthie followed Excellent's voice and barged in with the cops. Excellent, always the Christian hostess, stepped up.

"Officers, my husband and Mr. Blackie, here - he lives upstairs - were playing cards. They got to arguing about who won and..."

The older white cop, who actually reminded Merry of Santa Claus in a police uniform, stopped Excellent.

"Were you a part of that argument, Ma'am? Is that what happened to your nose and lip?"

"No, sir. I don't play cards. I don't gamble at all."

Merry knew this was a serious moment, but she wanted to laugh. The cops had no idea they were standing in the most popular Tunk House on Dequindre and Davison. Her mother was the go-to person every other Friday for the block club's card parties. And Excellent could play cards with the best of them.

"Excellent, what I heard didn't sound like no card game gone wrong. Did Corn put his hands on you?"

For the first time, Corn spoke up for himself, careful not to bring attention to the anger hiding in his voice.

"Officer, I didn't touch my wife. Never have, since the first day I met her."

The younger officer - his black hair slicked back with grease, and brown eyes peering - snooped around the living room with his hand on his holster.

"Well, now that can't be true. Judging by this boy and girl, you must have touched your wife at least twice. Then again, you are a little yellow to have such chocolate children."

Corn flinched, the love he had for her and Johnson was written all over his sweating face. Excellent came to his rescue.

"Officers, Ms. Ruthie got it all wrong. I heard my husband and Mr. Blackie tusslin' out here and I was in such a rush to see what was goin' on, I tripped over my husband's shoes."

The younger officer stood next to Corn and eyed him, threatening.

"You busted your lip and nose on his shoes?"

"No, the bed frame. At the bottom of the bed."

The older officer, not in the mood to have another dead nigger on his shift, eyed his trigger-happy partner. He looked straight to Merry, sympathetic.

"What's your name, Honey?"

"Merry."

"Hi, Merry. I'm Officer Petosky and that young man over there by your father is my partner, Officer Gerald."

Merry's eyes darted over to Officer Gerald. He nodded, hand still on the holster.

"Now, Merry, I need you to answer a question for me. Answer truthfully. Is that how this happened? The way your mother said?"

Merry paused. All she had to do was say yes. She didn't have time to feel guilty about that all of this was her fault.

That just because she didn't want to give up her nightcap, her mother's lip and nose were bleeding and the police were ready to shoot Corn in the back of the head.

Merry looked to her mother, then to Corn, trying to apologize with her eyes.

"Yes, Officer Petosky. Just like my mother said."

"Alright. Let's go, Gerald."

Officer Gerald, content that he had scared the shit out of yet another nigger, backed away. Ms. Ruthie started spitting, she was so mad.

"That's it! You just gone go like that?! The man was..."

Officer Petosky tried to calm her down.

"Ms. Ruthie, we appreciate your concern but this misunderstanding is simply a matter of a card game and of a husband that needs to learn to pick up his shoes. Isn't that right, Mrs..."

Officer Petosky's eyes fell onto Excellent. She crossed her arms, finished his sentence.

"Mavis. And yes it is."

Ms. Ruthie followed the sound of Excellent's lie, peered at her with worried clouded over gray eyes.

"Excellent, you sure?"

Excellent stepped up, took Ms. Ruthie's frail hand, then handed it to Officer Petosky.

"Officer, could you please make sure Ms. Ruthie makes it back home safe?"

Officer Petosky nodded, more than cordial.

"Yes, Ma'am."

Officer Gerald opened the front door and Officer Petosky tipped the bill of his hat to Merry as he headed out with Ms. Ruthie.

"Thank you for your help, Merry."

Merry nodded. That's all she could do. After all the shit that was swirling in the air because of her, it would have been wrong to tell Officer Petosky, "You're welcome."

Too wrong.

GUESS GOD
HEARD ME

Merry had a hole in her the size of Georgia. She missed Corn. Missed his laughter. Missed the way he made her mother smile. And missed the way he made the house smell. Like cigarettes, cake and cinnamon.

Johnson didn't notice the change. He was too busy fooling with Lonnie to pay attention to anybody else. But Merry saw the difference in Excellent right away. She hadn't sewn a stitch since Corn left. And that wasn't like her mother. Excellent always finished what she started.

And that's how Merry knew her mother was burning in Hades when she saw Excellent's beloved sewing machine for sale. They had to be hurting for money pretty bad for Excellent to give that up. That sewing machine was her refuge, the closest thing to a dream that Excellent had and now it was laid up in a dingy pawnshop window with a sloppy hand-written price tag slapped on it.

Merry squinted to read the chicken scratch on the price tag, but couldn't make heads or tails of it. She went inside. There was no one at the counter.

"Hello?"

Merry walked further in, cautious. Outside, it was daytime, but the pawnshop, which smelled like stale pistachios and looked like a junkyard exploded inside of it, was dimly lit.

"Hello? Is anybody here?"

"Yeah, yeah, yeah. Keep your pants on."

A round man, Jewish, in his forties, with a head as smooth as a egg, got up from a pallet on the floor behind the counter. His stubby fingertips burgundy red, he dug into a half-empty plastic bowl of pistachios, grabbed a handful.

"What do ya want?"

"How much is that sewin' machine in the window?"

"It's on the tag."

"I can't read the tag."

"What do ya mean you can't read the tag? Can't you read?"

Merry's eyes narrowed. This raggedy, red mouth Jew lived behind the counter on the dirty floor of his musty pawnshop and he was calling her dumb?

"I can read. You jus' can't write."

The pawnshop owner spat out the half-eaten pistachios on the floor and lunged over the counter, pissed.

"You talkin' about my penmanship?"

"Chick. En. Scratch."

Merry glared at him. The pawnshop owner growled.

"Ninety bucks."

"Sixty."

"Eighty."

"Seventy."

"Seventy-five, Girlie. Take it or leave it."

Merry left it.

She only had enough money on her to pay Tito, the wetback wino, to buy her and him each a pint. She was going to have to return tomorrow and pray that she could still buy back Excellent's sewing machine. It would take a big chunk out of the money she had left from her momma, but after all of the mess she had started, Merry at least owed Excellent that much.

*

"You're... my friend, Princess."

Merry, standing in the alley behind the liquor store with Tito, the wetback wino, slid the fifth of vodka into her book bag, said nothing.

Friends? Nigga please. The only friends Merry had were Kat, Teenie and the toilet bowl. For the past two weeks, she found herself running to the bathroom to throw up. Merry figured it had something to do with her nightcaps. She was drinking more, more often and sometimes it made her stomach too uneasy to keep anything down.

"Merry, you sure you don't want some dinner? I made enough."

Louis' food sure did look good. Tender beef roast, creamy mashed potatoes, string beans and buttermilk corn muffins. But the heavenly smell that under normal circumstances would make Merry's taste buds shout hallelujah was making Merry gag. She swallowed the acid gurgling up from her stomach to answer him.

"I'm sure."

Louis picked up a tray with a plate of food and glass of fresh made lemonade setting on it.

"O.K. More for your auntie, then."

"Can I take it to her?"

Merry reached for the tray. Louis hesitated. She could tell by the way he was holding on to it, that he didn't want her to take it. Teenie was his wife, his responsibility, and he didn't want Merry's help.

Merry looked at Louis, her hands still outstretched. The truth was, she didn't want to help him. Merry had shown up on their doorstop unannounced after school, because she needed to lay eyes on Teenie and get her to make sense of everything. But the moment Merry arrived, she knew something was wrong. Louis, normally clean-cut, looked like he hadn't shaved in days. And the only woman's voice she heard in her auntie's newly-wed top flat home was Sarah's Vaughn's.

A failed soldier relinquishing his post, Louis sighed and handed Merry the tray.

"Maybe she'll eat for you."

Merry nodded, then headed down the short hallway to Teenie's and Louis' bedroom, careful to stay on the runner.

The door was already open.

"Teenie? You awake?"

The room - just large enough for a bed, two mahogany dressers - one tall, the other, shorter with a vanity mirror on the back wall - was dreary inside. Gray light from the grey winter sky shone in through the lone bedroom window. Teenie was lying on her side, eyes open, starring silently at a pistachio ice cream colored wall.

"Louis made you dinner."

Again, no response. Merry set the tray down on the dresser and sat down on the bed next to Teenie, touched her shoulder.

"Teenie?"

Teenie blinked back to life, turned slowly to the sound of Merry's voice, smiled.

"Merry? How long you been sitting there?

"Just now. Louis cooked for you."

Teenie's eyes floated over Merry's shoulder to see the tray of food on the dresser.

"It's time for breakfast already?"

"No, Teenie. Dinner."

"Oh. Oh, right."

Merry brought the tray over to Teenie. Teenie sat up in the bed, her back against the mahogany headboard. She took a sip of lemonade. Didn't touch her food. Merry watched her auntie, sad.

Teenie wasn't herself. Beautiful. Vibrant. Confident. Instead, she was withdrawn, lost and gray. As gray as the winter sky pouring through her bedroom window. And Merry didn't know why. All Louis had told her was that Teenie had been to the hospital for two whole, mysterious days. And now she was back home recuperating from something that was too painful for her or Louis to talk about.

"Where's Louis?"

"Eatin'. He's about to leave for work."

Teenie took another sip of lemonade, touched the side of the bed next to her. It was still neatly made, not a sheet out of place. Louis hadn't slept there last night. And by the looks of the blanket and pillow Merry saw folded up on the couch in the living room, Merry could tell her new uncle hadn't slept with her auntie since at least the last time he shaved.

Teenie rubbed the side of the bed, lost in a memory.

"Merry, I ever tell you about the time I almost got married?"

"To Louis?"

"No. Before him."

Merry perked up. Teenie was about to answer the unasked question rolling around in her head since the night Corn left. Merry just found out about Corn, and all of Detroit from the North End to Black Bottom knew Teenie had stolen Louis from his wife and two kids. No question. Teenie was a jezebel. But Merry didn't see her auntie that way. Teenie was everything she wanted to be.

Merry leaned in, listened to Teenie's tale of lost love.

"I was seventeen and his name was Ernest, Ernest Webster. He was my teacher. Ernest had these big brown eyes that had this way of looking right through you. And once he set those big, brown eyes on me..."

Teenie chuckled like a schoolgirl, the grayness momentarily lifted from her face.

"In the beginnin', we had to keep our romance a secret, because he was engaged to a young woman from a good family with lots of money. But Ernest didn't want her. He wanted to marry me and have lots of babies..."

Teenie trailed off. Merry wasn't letting her auntie off that easy. She wanted to hear the rest of the story.

"What happened?"

Teenie looked at Merry, a smile in her weary eyes.

"You happened."

"What?"

"You, Merry. You happened."

Merry looked at Teenie, not able to hide the confusion on her face. She stood.

"I'll ask Louis if it's time for your medicine."

Teenie turned on her, stern.

"Merry, you lucky I'm talkin' to you at all instead of beatin' your tail for that mess you pulled sneakin' down to Scottie's."

Merry looked at Teenie, busted.

"Yes, I know. I always know. Now. When I need my pills, I'll tell you. Sit."

Merry sat. Teenie continued.

"I don't know what started it all. Your momma and daddy got into a fight -- They were always fightin' -- and he left her over momma's house. Excellent had to have been thirteen months pregnant, as big as she was. I didn't think she was ever going to have you. But sure enough, the night I was supposed to run off with Ernest, your momma's water broke."

Teenie laughed from the memory.

"Excellent was hysterical, cryin' like a baby and everybody, Stella, Rosemary, all of them were runnin' around like chickens wit' their heads chopped off. But momma knew exactly what to do. Guess who had to help her?"

"You?"

Teenie shook her head, a sincere chuckle escaping from the side of her mouth.

"All those fools in that house that I helped raise and momma made me help bring you into the world...As soon as I saw your little head pop out from between your momma's legs, I knew."

Merry glowed, the obvious question they both knew the answer to on her lips.

"What did you know, Teenie?"

Teenie smiled, mischievous.

"I knew I never, ever wanted anythin' poppin' out from between my legs! That night, I told that man I couldn't marry him. No way! I didn't want children. Never! Ever!"

Teenie fell out laughing. Merry, unable to resist her auntie's contagious laughter, gave in. They grabbed hands, and Merry gently wiped at a lone tear rolling down Teenie's cheek. Neither laughing anymore.

"Baby, I guess God heard me."

TEENIE DIDN'T
HAVE HERS

Merry didn't miss her period. Not one bit. She didn't mind trading the monthly bloody visitor between her legs for the daily swelling of her belly or the nauseating sickness that snuck in through her nose and vaulted out through her mouth. But now the bottom of her back was vexing her. The fire in her legs, that Merry hadn't suffered since she last set foot on Locust Grove soil had returned with a vengeance. And the clothes Excellent had bought too large for her to grow into, Merry was one day shy of growing out of.

"When are you going to tell her, Merry?"

Merry examined her spreading hips in Kat's bathroom mirror, rubbed her small pudge belly. She looked like she had swallowed a grapefruit, whole.

"Maybe I won't."

"What do you mean, you won't? You have to tell her, Merry. You're only going to get bigger before you have it."

"Then, I won't have it. Teenie didn't have hers."

That's true. Teenie didn't have her baby. But what Merry should have told Kat was that Teenie lost it. At least that's the way the doctor described it. The way Teenie described it? God took her baby. He took it, because she didn't want it.

"Merry, what do you mean? Are you going to get rid of it?"

"No. Not that way."

"Then, how are you not going to have it?"

"Because I said I wasn't. That's how."

Kat eyed Merry, frustrated. Merry knew she sounded crazy. But she didn't care. Her mind was set and she didn't feel like arguing about it. Merry flopped down her dress and grabbed Kat's paper cup right out of her hand. She downed the taste of vodka in one quick gulp. It burned. Still.

Merry coughed.

"Got some more?"

Kat swiveled around on the flower print toilet seat cover, took the top off of the back of the toilet and pulled out her father's stash - a cool, wet fifth of vodka.

"Do you think I can do that, Merry?"

"Do what?"

"Think Susie away. My grades went down just a little bit. And her nosey butt has been talking to my teachers, asking me questions about boys. Now she's got my daddy all worried."

Merry took a sip. Her friend was serious, but all she could do was smile.

"Nope, Kat. You can't."

"Why not?"

"Because then who's gonna teach me how to play the piano? I'm gonna be a star, girl. A star!"

Merry struck a Lena Horne pose and Kat gave Merry the finger. Their laughter was interrupted by Reverend McKeever's impatient knock at the bathroom door.

"Kat, what are you and Merry doing in there?"

"Just getting ready, Daddy."

Kat and Merry scrambled to toss out their paper cups and put the vodka bottle back in its hiding place.

"Well, hurry up. I'm needed earlier at church than I thought. You and Merry need to come on if you want me to drop you off at the show."

Merry loved going to the show. Especially Paradise Valley Theater. Now that Teenie was married and not feeling herself because she lost the baby, she hadn't taken Merry to see Ella or Billie or Louie perform there in a long while. And because Mrs. McKeever was suspicious about how wild Kat really was and Corn wasn't around anymore to distract Excellent, Merry couldn't sneak out with Kat to see the shows. Instead, Merry just had to make due by listening to her favorites on the radio or Mrs. McKeever would turn a blind eye and let her and Kat sneak listens to her and the Reverend's coveted jazz albums.

Still, though, Merry missed seeing The First Lady, Lady Day and Satchmo in living color. The next best thing?

Catching a matinee and seeing the Duke, Lean Horne, the Nicholas Brothers, Cab Calloway and Bojangles sing and dance on the silver screen. Merry had patted her foot and snapped her fingers to just about all of the Colored and White musicals, even the short ones just featuring Colored entertainers performing a song or two. And she knew *Cabin in the Sky* and *Stormy Weather* backwards and forwards.

Merry stepped up with Kat to the ticket booth, too excited to wait. Too bad, she was going to have to.

"What you mean the movie's not playin'?"

Merry peered up at the young man in the ticket booth. He sighed, not wanting to explain himself again.

"Look, the movie's not here. Like I said. Now, do you want to see *Pinky* or not?"

Merry and the young man starred each other down like two kids about to fight after school on the playground. Kat peeked over her shoulder at the line of impatient folks behind her, stepped in.

"We'll take two tickets."

Merry glared at the poster of Ethel Waters cradling a white woman in her arms, nearly shook her head off.

"No. Kat, I'm not seein' that stupid movie."

"But, Merry..."

"She's right. You don't want to see it. A white girl plays the part of a Colored woman passin'."

Kat and Merry swerved around to see who was butting in their business. It was the soda jerk with dimples from the shop, looking good enough to eat in his street clothes.

An older man and woman behind them grew restless.

"Well, if none of yaw want to see it, get out the damn line!"

Kat stepped out. The soda jerk greeted the young ticket seller outside the booth with a handshake Merry had seen before, then started sweet talking Kat. Merry, uninterested and frustrated, spotted Mr. Yancy, on his way inside the theater. She made a beeline right for him.

"Mr. Yancy!"

"Merry! What brings you down to Paradise?"

"I thought I was coming to see Lena Horne, but he said that you don't have the movie."

"Right. Right. Some nonsense about her looking too white. Anybody can look at that woman and tell she's Colored. White folks."

"So, you really don't have the movie?"

"No, Baby, we don't. Why don't you see *Pinky* instead? Lena was supposed to play the part, but it's still good. I'll treat."

Merry sighed. She had her mind all set for Colored folks singing and dancing, not watching a white woman playing a Colored woman pretending to be white. She looked over her shoulder to Kat, who was giggling all up in the soda jerk's face.

"Thank you, Mr. Yancy. Can my friend see it, too?"

"Sure. I'll wait right here."

Merry slouched back over to Kat and the soda jerk, a frown on her face and in her voice.

"Alright, Kat, we can see the stupid movie. Mr. Yancy said he'll pay for us."

Kat smiled at Merry, her nose wide open.

"That's O.K. Raymond wanted to know if we would like to get something to eat with him and his friend."

Raymond grinned like no girl had ever turned down his dimples. Merry wasn't impressed and she definitely wanted no parts of Raymond's rude friend from the ticket booth. Kat took Merry's hand and swung it back and forth, a playful plead.

"Come on, Merry. It'll be fun."

Merry rolled her eyes. Kat didn't know this boy five minutes and already wanted to run off with him. Merry had to go just to make sure the girl didn't do anything stupid.

Merry walked back over to Mr. Yancy. Raymond and Kat followed a few steps behind. Mr. Yancy's eyes landed on Raymond.

"We're not going to see the movie, Mr. Yancy."

"Are you sure, Merry? I can get you all good seats."

"No, thanks. We're hungry. We're gonna get something to eat."

Mr. Yancy, despite his better judgment, nodded. He laid his hand on Merry's shoulder, gentle.

"O.K., Merry. Give Teenie my love?"

Merry told Mr. Yancy she would. And she meant it. But at that moment, she had a more pressing issue. She, Kat and Raymond were walking away from the theater and his rude ticket booth friend was nowhere to be found. Merry, in no mood to be the third wheel, grilled Raymond.

"Isn't your friend comin'?"

"Oh, Allen ain't my friend. He's my cousin."

Merry glared at Kat. They didn't know Raymond from a can of paint and now there was no friend. Hell, how did they even know if the boy had some money?

They rounded the corner and Merry saw a car she couldn't help but recognize. A new maroon Chevrolet Fleetmaster coupe. Raymond nodded to the familiar driver behind the wheel.

"That's my friend."

Merry's heart dropped. Out of all the fools on the North End to break bread with, she was going to have a double date with Silas? Silas rolled down the driver's window, aggravated.

"Nigga, what took you so long?"

Raymond draped his arm around Kat's shoulders, cool.

"Thought we could get somethin' to eat. While we wait."

Silas' eyes flashed, like he wanted to slap Raymond, but then thought better of it. He looked to Merry, his hands tied.

***

Merry sat in the front seat of Silas' Fleetmaster, picking at greasy pieces of red snapper, cold French fries and thick slices of soggy white bread in her cardboard take-out box. The inside of the Silas' car was as maroon as the outside. Not a speck of lint or dirt was on the seats or the floor, the car even still had that new car smell.

Merry could tell Silas loved his Fleetmaster, took care of it. And she would have been impressed if she wasn't so bored. Patting her foot to Satchmo's wailing horn on the radio, she glanced in the passenger side's mirror, saw Kat and Raymond swapping spit in the backseat. Silas doused more hot sauce on his fish, sucked his fingers.

"What's the matter, Merry Merry? You don't like red snapper?"

Merry snapped, disgusted.

"Yeah. When it's good."

Silas looked at Merry's sour face, busted out laughing. The sound of his happiness was so big, so warm, Merry felt herself smiling. All this time she had loved Silas, he was always making fun of her, laughing at her. But now, he was sitting in front of her, looking right at her, laughing with her.

Silas leaned back on the headrest, exhausted from busting his gut.

"Merry, Merry, you right. This does taste like shit."

Silas grabbed Merry's box of food off her lap and tossed it out the driver's side window into the dirty snow covered street with his. He rolled the window back up, shivered from the cold. The rear window was starting to fog now, thanks to Kat and Raymond's horizontal dance in the backseat. Merry pretended not to notice. Silas took a flask out of his inside coat pocket, turned it up.

Merry eyed him, thirsty.

"Can I have some?"

Silas stopped mid-swig and looked at Merry surprised at first, then curious. He handed her the flask. Merry swallowed the hot taste of liquor like a pro. Silas watched, impressed.

"Hmm, hmm, hmm. Merry, Merry, I see fuckin' ain't the only thing you been doin'."

Merry, guilty, handed him back the flask. Silas screwed the top on the flask, slid it back into his pocket.

"Guess Felton ain't as square as I thought, the way he got your hips spreadin'. Lay it on me, Merry Merry. Does my man hang to the left or the right?"

Merry looked at him, didn't miss a beat.

"To the right. It's crooked."

Silas laughed. Again.

"Damn, that's fucked up. Cat with a crooked stick got a hard way to go. Shit."

Silas pulled a reefer cigarette and a book of matches out of his inside coat pocket. Coolly, he lit the reefer, inhaled deep and long. Merry watched the smoke trail past his full lips, attracted. Silas eyed her.

"Guess you want some of this, too?"

"Yeah."

Silas took a puff and leaned back on the headrest, oh so mellow.

"Merry, Merry, this shit's too good to waste on you."

Merry leaned back in the passenger's seat, just as cool. Maybe it was the liquid courage or the baby growing inside of her giving her extra strength, but Merry didn't feel small like she usually did with Silas. She flung her question at him like a Frisbee.

"Who are you savin' it for? Your girlfriend?"

"I'm a grown man. I don't have girlfriends."

"What you have, then?"

Silas looked at Merry sideways. He reached for her chin, gently pulled it toward him and leaned in for a kiss. Merry, quivering from anticipation, slightly parted her lips, closed her eyes. Tenderly, she felt his lips brush against hers. Then, a thin, paper pointed tip slid in between her lips and a strong stream of sweet smoke filled her mouth, her lungs.

Merry gagged. Kat's head popped up over the front seat, worried.

"Merry, you O.K.?!"

Silas took the lit reefer butt first out of his mouth and passed it over Kat's head to Raymond.

"She's just zooted."

"Zooted? What's zooted?"

Raymond pulled Kat back by her hips, rough.

"Bring that fine ass back here and let me show you."

Kat fell back on Raymond's hardness, all giggles. Merry swallowed, able to breath again. She gazed up to Silas, who was peering over her head out the window. Merry turned to see what he was starring at and saw Silas' pound cake colored woman in a Ford on the other side of the park, tongue kissing a young Colored man goodbye. She then got of the car and sashayed into her apartment building.

Silas hit the back of the front seat, hard, startling Raymond before he could give Kat a puff. They both jumped.

"Hey, man, what the hell..."

"Raymond, take 'em home and come back to get me in a hour."

Raymond, still horny and always the jokester, rubbed Kat's butt.

"Lizzy's home now, Silas. Why don't you give me five mo' minutes?"

Silas glared at Raymond, death in his eyes. Raymond hopped to it.

"O.K., Silas. Back in a hour."

Silas got out of the car, too calm to be up to any good. Her high kicking in, Merry watched him walk in slow motion across the snow covered park toward the pound cake Colored woman's apartment building.

Kat and Raymond slid in the front seat next to her. Raymond checked the side view mirror, pulled away from the curb.

"So, Merry, where you live?"

Merry thought, then giggled. She couldn't remember.

Merry looked back out the window to get one last glimpse of Silas. He was gone.

**

"Merry, get back into the car."

It was snowing again. Beautiful flakes large enough to catch on the tip of your tongue. And Merry, blissful, was outside in front of the pawnshop getting covered in them.

Forehead and hands pressed against the pawnshop's filthy glass door, Merry teetered around. She had a big dirt spot on her forehead, her coat was undone and she was only wearing one mitten. On her left hand. Kat, shivering behind Merry, glanced over her shoulder through the open passenger side door to an impatient Raymond waiting in Silas' car.

Merry slowly lifted her arm and pointed to the pawnshop display window. She slurred, her words sticking between her tongue and the roof of her dry mouth.

"Kat, we made...a deal. And he's been...gone. I've been...comin'...back and the...Jew man's...been gone, but he still...has it...see? He still...has Excellent's sewin'... machine."

Merry dug in her pocket, pulled out a wad of money.

"I'm...gonna...buy it...back."

Kat shoved the wad back into Merry's pocket before Raymond could see it.

"Merry, there's nobody in there."

"Yes, he is! The Jew man's...sleepin'...on the floor...behind the counter..."

Merry pushed Kat out of the way, started banging on the door. In slow motion.

"Hey, Jew...man! Give me...my sewin'...machine. Wake...up! Wake... up!"

Raymond nervously glanced at his watch and lunged over to close the passenger side door. Kat darted from Merry's side, stopped the door.

"Hey! Where are you going?"

"You heard Silas."

"But you just can't leave us!"

Raymond yanked the car door hard and slammed it shut, nearly chopping off Kat's fingers. Took off. Behind her, Merry, frozen mid-knock, admired her mitten less right hand like she was seeing it for the first time. A slow giggle dripped from her lips.

Kat turned around, so not in a laughing mood.

"What?"

Merry smiled at her, glassy eyed.

"I lost...my...mitten."

*

"We there yet?"

Merry gripped Kat's warm hand. They were side by side, sharing a mitten, their hands shoved in Kat's coat pocket and walking against a snowstorm.

Merry, nose running, was nowhere near high anymore. Kat mumbled through her chattering teeth.

"One more block, Merry."

Merry leaned into her friend, kept marching. She was soaking wet and in pain. But she wasn't about to complain to Kat about it. This whole thing was her fault. Raymond left them, because her high tail took too long banging on the doors of an abandoned pawnshop. And Kat was real salty with Raymond for running out on them. But Merry? She couldn't even be mad at the boy. She saw the way Silas looked at him. Hell, Merry would have left herself, too.

Merry lifted her head. One block to go was now three houses until. Through the blinding snow, she saw two figures on the front porch knocking on the door.

Merry and Kat paused at the walkway, curious. Before he could turn, Merry recognized Louis. And bundled up next to him? Was her momma. Dora.

"Momma?!"

"Merry!"

Merry ran up the steps into Dora's open arms.

"Baby, whut you doin' out here in all dis snow?"

Merry opened her frostbitten mouth to lie without thinking twice about it.

"Me and Kat went to the show and had to walk back, because the bus didn't come."

Merry expected her momma to say "uh huh" or "O.K.," but instead she felt Dora's willowy body shift. Dora slightly pulled back from Merry, lifted her chin, looked at her face, into her eyes.

She knew.

SO,
YOU SAY

"**Excellent,** you can jus' look at duh girl and tell! Whut duh hell you mean, you didn't know?!"

Merry and Kat, out of their wet clothes and wrapped in two warm blankets, were gobbling up oxtail soup at the kitchen table.

Excellent, still dressed in her housekeeping uniform and sitting at the end of the table, buried her face in her hands, spent.

"What are you doin' here, Momma?"

Dora plopped her red-bone, spotted hand on her slender hip, angry that Excellent was changing the subject.

"I came tuh see 'bout Teenie. I'm gone stay wit' her and Louis fo' awhile."

Excellent chuckled to herself, bitter.

"You act like she the only one ever lost a baby."

Dora stepped up to Excellent ready to beat her ass to the white meat.

"Gurl, you really gone make dis 'bout Teenie losin' her baby or Merry havin' hers?"

Merry looked to Excellent, anxious to hear her answer. Excellent pulled her hands away from her face, slow, calm. Not looking at Dora on purpose, she eyed Merry instead.

"Merry, you and Kat go to your room."

Merry and Kat got up to leave. Dora stopped Merry.

"No, you don't, Merry. Dis is yo' business. And you gone handle yo' business. Ain't dat right, Excellent?"

Excellent slammed her hand down on the kitchen table.

"Momma. What. Do. You. Want. Me. To. Do?"

"It ain't 'bout whut you gone do. It's 'bout whut she gone do."

"The hell it ain't! Who you think gone take care of this baby? Teenie? You? Or you think Merry's wild ass gone keep this bastard child clothed and fed?"

Merry dropped her spoon in her empty bowl and wiped her mouth with her napkin. All this hooping and hollering over a baby she wasn't going to have? It was time to tell her momma and Excellent how she was going to make everything right.

"Momma, yaw don't have to worry 'bout it, I'm not gonna have it."

Excellent and Dora looked at Merry like she was crazy. Her momma exploded first.

"Excellent, what duh hell mess you been puttin' in this chile head?"

"Nothin'! I didn't even know she was pregnant. Remember?!"

"Den where she get dis, Excellent? Where she get dis talk 'bout gettin' rid of her baby?"

"Not. From. Me. Maybe from that big eared boy."

Merry stood up, frustrated, but Dora and Excellent's eyes were already focused on Kat, Felton and his Aunt Florise in the kitchen doorway.

Felton looked scared to death, standing there next to his old maid auntie. The color of homemade beef gravy, Florise was a big and tall lady with a square chin and large hands and feet. If she didn't have such a soft voice and didn't wear her fine hair so long, anybody would have been hard pressed not mistake her for a man in drag.

Kat stumbled, apologetic.

"I'm sorry, Mrs. Mavis. I thought it was my daddy."

"That's alright, Kat. They right on time."

Excellent stood, smoothing out the wrinkles in the lap of her housekeeping uniform.

"Thank you for comin' out on such a bad night, Mrs. White. Is it still snowing?"

"No, it stopped. And it's Ms., not Mrs."

Excellent nodded, put off a bit by her standoffishness. Dora stepped up, not pressed about Florise's attitude.

"Miz White, I'm Merry's grandmotha, Dora. Want somethin' to warm you up? Coffee? Tea? Whiskey?"

"No, thank you. I'd just like to get to the business at hand."

Merry and Felton glanced at each other. A few weeks ago, they were two kids doing what grown folks do in her mother's basement. In secret. Now, their business was all out in the open.

Excellent ushered Felton and his aunt out into the living room to talk. At least, that was the plan. Wasn't long before Merry and Felton were watching words fly around the room like daggers.

"You callin' my daughter a liar, Ms. White?"

"All I know, Mrs. Mavis, is that my Felton is a good boy, an honor student with a bright future. In all of the years he's been in my care, he has never fallen victim to any bad elements..."

Dora damn near lept out of her chair.

"Merry ain't no bad el'ment. Neitha is dis boy's chile growin' in her belly."

Florise looked right at Dora, didn't raise her voice above a whisper.

"I don't believe this to be Felton's child."

Merry spoke up before Felton, defending herself.

"But, Ms. White, I haven't been wit' anybody else."

Florise looked at Merry, a slight smile forming at the corners of her thin lips.

"So, you say."

"Aunt Flo!"

"Stay out of this, Felton."

"Oh, no. It's too late for Felton to stay out of it."

Excellent clasped her hands together across her lap, her calmness amplifying how angry she was.

"Whether you want to believe it or not, Ms. White, your nephew's got a baby on the way."

Dora nodded in agreement. Florise looked at Excellent with condescending eyes.

"Now, the question is, is he gonna step up, be responsible and help provide for this child or not?"

Florise stood.

"Not. Let's go, Felton."

Felton grabbed Merry's hand, pleading.

"Merry, I know it's mine and I..."

"Felton. Now!"

Felton jumped and followed his aunt out. Merry watched them leave through the living room window. Dora put her hand on Merry's shoulder.

"Dat's alright. Colored women don't need niggas to raise they babies no way. 'Specially not some big eared boy like dat."

Merry gazed up to her momma, glad that she was there. She started to smile, but then saw Excellent, disgusted, leave the room.

PROMISE.

Merry was a star.

She knew it in her mind, heart and soul everyday as she practiced boogie-woogie licks on the piano or danced in front of her mirror, singing and scatting into a hairbrush.

She didn't care if nobody else knew that they were in the presence of greatness. Merry liked it better that way, actually. She didn't have to worry about giving folks autographs or taking pictures with them. Instead, Merry could have a regular life out of the spotlight.

That all changed, though, the day Merry came face to face with her reality. No longer was she the snazzy dressing, smart, country girl that had gotten double promoted. She was the pregnant girl. And the whole school knew it.

"Merry, is it true?!"

Dolores ran up on Merry in the hallway, the only one brave enough to ask Merry the question that all of the other kids were muttering under their breaths as she waddled by.

Merry opened up her coat. Her belly poking out, her answer. Dolores touched it with both hands.

"Wow! I didn't believe it when Johnson told me. Is it Felton's?"

Damn, did the stupid girl have to say the boy's name loud enough for everybody in the world to hear? Merry starred at her, hard. Dolores looked around to the students and teachers pretending not to listen. She whispered.

"Oh, right, right. Sorry."

Merry snatched her coat closed, saw Felton walking into their ninth grade classroom up ahead. He glanced at Merry, guilty.

"Felton didn't walk you to school?"

"His auntie won't let him."

Merry didn't mean to sound as bitter as she did. But the truth was, she had gotten used to Felton walking her back and forth to school every day. And she was angry with him for not standing up to his he-she auntie and putting her down.

The final bell signaling the start of class rang. Dolores took a step to leave, stopped.

"I'll see you later, Merry?"

Merry paused. For some reason, the way Dolores said that sounded like she was saying good-bye. Merry turned around, saw Principal Bennett waiting and understood why.

***

"I have to leave?"

"Just until you have the baby, Merry. It's for the best."

Merry sat in Principal Bennett's office, not sure what to think. Just a few months ago, he had sat in that very seat, singing her praises about how bright she was and how proud he was to have her as a student at Deggin. And now he was kicking her out, because she was a virus in danger of infecting the entire school.

Merry lashed out.

"What about Felton? Are you makin' him leave school, too?"

Principal Bennett stammered.

"Uh, no. I'm not."

"Why not? This is his baby, too."

Merry starred at Principal Bennett, waiting for an answer. He didn't have one.

"That's not fair, Principal Bennett."

Merry crossed her arms across her belly, tearful. Principal Bennett cleared his throat.

"Well. I understand that's how you feel, Merry. But as I said, it's my job to protect the students of this school and I'm going to do everything in my power to do that."

Principal Bennett set a piece of paper on the desk in front of Merry. She didn't look at it.

"This is an agreement form between the school board and the City's Truant Department for your mother to sign. It states that I have given approval to your teacher to send your assignments home everyday with your brother, Johnson, so you won't fall behind."

Merry wiped at her unwanted tears trailing down her face.

"Will I be able to graduate and go to the tenth grade?"

Principal Bennett looked at Merry, sincere.

"Stay on top of your studies, Merry, and it'll be just like this never happened."

Merry sniffled and dabbed at her eyes with the tissue Principal Bennett gave her. This never happened. If only that were true.

**

"Very good, Merry. You've been practicing."

Merry smiled at Mrs. McKeever, proud of herself. She maneuvered her belly as close as she could to the piano, excited to pound out another tune.

"Can you teach me another one? Somethin' harder?"

Mrs. McKeever shifted, disappointed.

"Actually, Merry, this is your last lesson. Your mother thought the money could go to better use."

Mrs. McKeever, her eyes floating to Merry's belly, got up to gather her things.

"It's a shame, too. You're the most natural talent I've seen in a long time."

Merry followed her out into the front hallway to get her coat.

"Well, maybe you can still give me some pointers on Saturday. You know, ones you don't mind givin' away for free?"

Mrs. McKeever paused, choosing her words carefully as she buttoned up her coat.

"Merry, Rev. McKeever and I talked about this and we think it'd be better if you take a break from the choir for awhile. And you shouldn't spend nights away from home either. It's safer for you and the baby."

"Oh."

For a split second, Merry thought Mrs. McKeever was putting her down like everybody else, but what she said did make some sense. Even if Merry didn't like it.

Merry brightened. She had another idea.

"Can Kat come over here, then?"

Mrs. McKeever flung her fluffy pink scarf around her neck.

"No, Merry."

"Why not? I'll be safe at home, like you said. Then, we can go to church from here with my mother, just like we do at your house..."

"Merry. Reverend McKeever and I don't think you should be spending so much time with Kat anymore. She needs to focus more on her studies, her duties at the church..."

Merry held open the front door for Mrs. McKeever, too sad to cry.

"But Kat's my best friend."

"No, Merry. That baby is your best friend."

Merry closed the door, Mrs. McKeever words eating through her like rock salt through winter ice. This baby she wasn't going to have was taking everything she loved away from her. She had to come up with a faster way to think this child away.

Merry opened her book bag, found just want she needed.

*

Merry was supposed to be thinking. But she was sleeping. And she was sleeping? Because she snuck a taste of vodka. And vodka was known for making folks do a lot of things. But thinking wasn't one of them.

Merry turned over on her side, shirking off the familiar hand on her shoulder. She grumbled.

"Johnson's lyin'."

Teenie sat down on the bed, upset, shook Merry harder.

"You ought to know. Wake up."

Merry opened her eyes, slow, and rolled on her back. Teenie didn't look happy.

"Louis and I just went to the movies. Guess who we saw?"

"Did you see Lena Horne's new movie? The one with The Duke and Satchmo?"

Teenie pinched Merry's arm, twisted hard.

"I said who, girl. Not what."

Merry yelped and jumped up, sobered. Teenie glared at her.

"Answer me, Merry."

"I...I...don't know."

"Yes. You. Do."

Merry looked into Teenie's angry eyes, decided she better come up with something fast. She threw out the obvious.

"You mean Mr. Yancy?"

"Yes, Mr. Yancy. He saw you and your friend with Raymond. Do you know what Raymond does?"

Merry paused. This had to be a trick question. The boy was a soda jerk at the soda shop. Everybody knew that.

Teenie jumped in, answering her own question.

"He's a junkman, Merry. He peddles dope out of the soda shop."

Dope. The word sounded so heavy and foreign to Merry. Teenie hadn't spoken to her about dope - doing it or not doing it - so Merry really had no idea what it was. From the way her auntie was acting, though, Merry could tell that dope had to be low down, something worst than playing numbers, drinking or smoking -- all the things Merry had seen Teenie do.

Teenie grabbed Merry's arm, hard.

"Are you doin' junk, Merry? Are you buyin' dope from Raymond?"

"No! He's Kat's friend."

"Is she?!"

"No, Teenie. We just got somethin' to eat. One time. I swear!"

Teenie peered into Merry's eyes, searching them for the slightest hint of a lie. Merry tried to not think of Silas. If her auntie damn near tore her arm off for hanging out with Raymond, Teenie would surely kill her if she knew Silas had been along for the ride.

Teenie let go of Merry's arm, sat back.

"Stay away from Raymond, Merry. You hear me?"

Merry rubbed her arm.

"O.K."

Teenie touched Merry's face, tender.

"Promise?"

Merry looked at Teenie. She didn't understand what all the fuss was about, but there was no denying the concern seeping through her auntie's pores. She nodded, a child promising her mother not to touch a stovetop's enticing, hot flame.

"Promise."

HOP, BANK, HOLE.

Johnson was late with Merry's homework. And she was losing her mind.

More than once, Merry had told her brother how important her homework was to her. Here she was pregnant. Still. Four months or so later, and Merry had finally come to grips with the truth --- she could no more think that baby growing in her stomach away, than Johnson could think himself into liking girls. Nope. She was stuck with this baby. And, as long as she was stuck and locked away from the outside world like a bad ass harlot, Merry thought she might as well throw herself into her studies and finish the ninth grade at the top of her class.

After all, all Merry had was time. Not only was she not allowed to go to school, but Excellent, too angry and ashamed of Merry to look at her, had padlocked the piano. And Kat? Merry, who had stopped going to church altogether, hadn't seen or talked to Kat in a couple of months.

On top of that, the only thing that could make Merry forget that she was a thirteen-year-old girl pregnant with a bastard child, she was out of. Her plan was to go to Tito and pay him to buy some more, but she couldn't, because her momma, still in town visiting Teenie, split every day between the two houses.

It was almost unbearable at first. Dora, always a hustler, had struck a deal with a boarding house on Dequindre and Davison to wash and iron all of the single men's laundry. Word soon spread about how right her price was and before long, men were coming out of the woodwork like roaches, dropping off their dirty drawers, shirts and slacks to Excellent's house.

Business was so good, Dora didn't hesitate to put Merry to work. Yes, she was just as disappointed about Merry having a baby so young, but she didn't look at Merry like she was the woman at the well like everyone else did. Dora, herself, had had Excellent when she was the ripe old age of 21, but that was only because she had learned a lesson from her own mother, Delilah, who had birthed Dora into the world when she was just fifteen.

In those days, there was nothing strange about having babies young. In fact, it was expected. And nobody ever thought about sending pregnant Colored girls away to hide in shame. Just the opposite, Delilah worked all the way up until she delivered Dora in the cotton field.

Dora expected the same of Merry. For her to work and not hide away in the house until nature took its course.

But Merry didn't want to work. She wanted a taste.

When she first ran out of her stash, that - not the pain that her premature body was going through to shift, stretch and make room for the baby - was all she could think about. Mr. Sammy had even started haunting her dreams again. Defenseless, Merry turned back to the first thing that helped her. Books.

That's why her studies were so important to her now. Other than washing and ironing strangers' skid-marked drawers and waiting for the baby she didn't want to come, Merry had nothing else in her prison of a life.

"Merry, get yo' big belly 'way from dat screen do' and finish ironin' these pocket squares. We gotta stay on schedule."

Merry took another peek out the door, wiped her sweaty forehead with the back of her hand and stepped back into the living room. It was a hotbox thanks to the steaming iron and the separated stacks of neatly folded men's clothes lined up on the couch and piano.

Dora patted her foot as she packed the clothes into laundry bags, pleased.

"I tol' e'erybody tuh come by and pick up they clothes 'fo' I leave, but in case some man straggles through here afta I'm gone, take duh money and mark his name in duh book like you always do. I'll git duh money from you on Sunday."

Merry peeled one of the last pocket squares off the pile, started ironing. Didn't respond.

"Merry, you hear me?"

"Yes, Momma."

"What you got yo' lip poked out fo'?"

"Nothin', Momma."

"Uh huh..."

Dora eyed Merry, a slight knock at the front screen door stopping her from getting all in Merry's business. She got up, grabbed a packed laundry bag, double-checked it.

"Dat must Orin Townsend. Said he'd be by here early tuh pick up his clothes. Let him in."

Merry frowned. Orin Townsend was fat, sloppy and slow. Wouldn't be so bad if the man wasn't so lonely. All of the other men picking up their laundry would be in and out of the house in five minutes. But Orin Townsend always managed to stretch his visit to thirty minutes by running his mouth about nothing.

Merry slouched over to the door. She so didn't want to see that man. Lucky for her, she didn't have to.

"Merry!"

"Kat!"

Merry bolted out the door, and they tackled each other with a huge bear hug. Excited, they looked at each other, screamed.

Dora came flying up to the screen door.

"Merry, what duh hell..."

"Momma! It's Kat!"

"Lawd, you almost gave me a heart 'tack. Yo' momma and daddy know you here, Kat?"

"Yes, ma'am. We had a half-day at school today and my daddy said I could come to visit Merry."

Merry swung Kat's hand back and forth, beaming.

"Can I visit out here with Kat for awhile, Momma? Please?"

"Alright. I'm gone rest my eyes fo' a minute. Wake me up when Orin comes."

"O.K. Momma."

Merry and Kat scurried to sit down on the top porch step. Kat touched Merry's belly.

"Wow. Look how big you got. Does it hurt?"

"My back and legs sometimes. I don't throw up anymore."

"Does it kick?"

"All the time."

"Really?!"

Kat plopped her ear down to Merry's belly. Merry rested her hand on Kat's shoulder, saw Silas' car parked a few doors down the street.

"Is that Raymond?"

Kat popped up, smiled, mischievous.

"Yeah."

"Thought you hated him."

"I did. But then he came to church..."

"What?"

"Yeah, he showed up at church to apologize. And when I wouldn't talk to him, the fool came to my school!"

"What did you do? When you saw him?"

Kat smacked her lips, exaggerating.

"After what that boy did? I wasn't going to talk to him. I didn't care how many times he came up to my school."

"How many times did he come?"

"Every day for a week."

Kat smiled. Giddy, she fiddled with a gold charm bracelet dangling on her wrist. Merry touched it, yearning.

"Raymond gave it to me."

"Is it real?"

"Uh huh. Fourteen karat gold. Raymond gave me some earrings, too. I hid them in my toy chest with Mr. Snuggles."

Merry pulled her hand away from Kat's bracelet, a little jealous. Kat noticed.

"Hey, want to take a ride, Merry? Me and Raymond have a little time before he has to take me back to school in time for Susie to pick me up."

"Thought you said there was a half-day at your school."

"Yeah, it was. For me. Everybody else just had to stay."

Kat and Merry laughed. Just like they used to every Saturday night in Kat's bedroom. Merry felt a tiny kick in her belly, remembered.

"Kat, you sure you wanna be seen wit' me?"

"Merry, please. I'm still mad at daddy and Susie because of what they did to you. I don't care..."

"What about Raymond? Does he know?"

"No. But he won't care, either. Don't you want to go?"

Merry did want to go. But there was still one thing holding her back. The promise she made to Teenie.

"Did you know Raymond was a junkman, Kat?"

"A what?"

"Teenie says Raymond sells dope out of the soda shop."

"What's dope?"

"I don't know."

"Me, neither."

Merry and Kat looked at each other, silent, both of them trying to wrap their naive, curious minds around the heaviness of the word. Merry wobbled to her feet.

"Let's ask him."

**

Merry didn't want to risk not going with Kat by waking her momma up to ask her, so she left a note instead. But as loud as Raymond was laughing, a rolling, high pitch squeal like a rat caught in a trap, he was surely going to wake her.

Raymond wiped the corner of his eye, still choking back chuckles.

"What's...What's your auntie's name, Merry?"

Merry, sitting in the back seat, crossed her arms, defensive.

"Everybody calls her Teenie."

"Teenie...Teenie...Don't she run numbers and boost outta Jew woman's shop downtown? Lichenberg's, some shit like that?"

"Lowenstein's."

"Yeah, Lowenstein's. That your auntie?"

Merry nodded. She knew Teenie ran numbers, and the boosting, even though no one ever outright told her, wasn't news to her, either. Raymond shook his head.

"Ain't that some shit."

Raymond laughed and Kat joined him. Merry didn't see what was so funny.

"So, is it true or not?"

Raymond eyed Merry, reached in his shirt pocket and pulled out a reefer cigarette, sniffed it.

"Old heads think anythin' that ain't booze or cigarettes is dope."

Kat took the reefer cigarette from Raymond, curious.

"This is what Silas was smoking."

"Lucky for me, Bright Eyes, Silas ain't the only one lightin' it up. Ain't that right, Merry?"

Kat passed the reefer cigarette back to Merry. She looked at it, the frozen memory of her first high starting to thaw.

"What is it?"

"That's the Northend's finest. The best reefer in town."

Merry and Kat looked at Raymond, clueless. He continued.

"Muggles? Gage? Golden Leaf? Gunja? Mez? I know you heard of mez!"

Merry and Kat shook their heads, no. Raymond grabbed the reefer cigarette, tossed it back into his shirt pocket, explained.

"It's all reefer, ladies. Mellow. Natural."

Kat chirped in.

"And it gets you zooted? Like it did Merry?"

"If the price is right. And the price, Bright Eyes, is always right."

Raymond ran his finger underneath Kat's chin, playful. She giggled. Merry had more questions.

"You make a lot of money sellin' reefer, Raymond?"

Raymond held up Kat's wrist, showed off her bracelet.

"Fourteen karat. Walked right into J.L. Hudson's myself, paid cash for it."

"Then why don't you open up a store?"

Raymond broke out into a large grin, his dimples the size of saucers.

"You mean, like a reefer store?"

Merry looked at Raymond, serious. He laughed.

"Merry, you know liquor wasn't always sold in stores? Durin' Prohibition, the man could throw you up under the jail just for tossin' back a drink! Then, they saw how much dough they could pocket from booze, so they made it legal. Now, every time a nigga buy a bottle of sauce, the man get a cut. Hell, the only reason a nigga drink is to forget how much he hates white folks! We gettin' tore down and white folks sittin' back, rollin' in dough, takin' baths in tubs full of nigga's tax dollars! Ain't that some shit?"

Raymond laughed again, but this time, there was anger in his eyes. Merry recognized that look. Every Colored man she had ever met or known from sharecroppers to ministers to city slickers had that ability. The ability to keep white folks at ease by making their mouths smile, even when their eyes had deadlier intentions.

Raymond ranted on more about the man, taxes and what Colored people ought to be doing, but Merry wasn't listening. Orin Townsend was bouncing up the street to her house, about to pass the car. She slid down in the seat, damn near to the floor.

Raymond stuttered to a stop, eyed Orin as he passed.

"Oh, so you put the young boy down for a workin' man, huh, Merry? Why don't I holla at him?"

Raymond reached to blow the car horn. Kat grabbed his hand. Merry pleaded.

"Can we just go 'fore my momma kills me?"

Raymond chuckled, started the car.

"Alright. Only 'cause it's a matter of life and death."

Kat scrunched down in the front seat and Raymond pulled off, passed the house. Merry peeked over the backseat, through the rear window and saw a just woken Dora greet Orin at the front door.

As she slid back down the seat, Merry heard her momma call out her name.

*

Solace, smoke and pork skins.

Merry smelled all three the first moment she stepped foot into the pool hall. It was the middle of the day, yet the joint on Dexter and Davison was bustling with working Colored men in uniform. Factory slaves on their way to or just getting off of work lined the bar chomping on pork skins and slopping down beers and something harder. And the rest, cigarettes dangling from their full lips, laughed and joked and played pool for money. The amount, like a Colored man's opinion, didn't matter. Bets could range from a nickel to a fool's whole paycheck and nobody cared either way. Because the game wasn't about winning or losing. It was about the fact that they were Colored men, it was 1949 and they could play pool with each other. In peace.

Merry looked behind the bar to a framed black and white photo not calling much attention to itself. Joe "The Brown Bomber" Louis smiled back at her. Sweaty and wearing his signature trunks, he was standing just outside a boxing ring with his tree trunk of an arm draped around the shoulders of a dark skinned, grinning boxer, who looked a little older and worn for wear. They were both still wearing boxing gloves and the grinning slugger's left eye was puffy enough to show up on a black and white photo.

Merry eyed the grinning boxer's face again. If the pool hall was owned by The Brown Bomber, Raymond's bragging self would have definitely told them. So, the man in the picture had to be the cigar smoking, loud talking, stocky man behind the bar.

"Naw, naw, man. Don't be bringin' up that depressin' shit in my place. Niggas don't come to J.T. Carter's Plan B to get mad. They come to J.T. Carter's Plan B to have a good time!"

J.T. slapped hands with a nodding customers at the bar. Muscular with broad shoulders, still, J.T. was the color of dark chocolate and looked to be a couple of years past forty. His hands were large and his neck less head was as square as a block of melting ice.

J.T. flicked the huge ash off of his chewed over cigar, snickered.

"'Sideswhich, if you gone tell the story, tell it right. The '43 riot ain't start 'cuz white men threw a Colored woman and her baby off the Belle Isle Bridge. It started 'cuz the man caught some niggas bangin' some pink pussy. And yaw know we lose our damn mind over some pink pussy!"

The entire bar exploded in laughter.

Raymond stepped up, slapped hands with J.T.

"Ain't pink pussy sweet?"

"Pretty and sweet, Junior. Pretty and sweet."

J.T. and Raymond laughed together, but this time, the men at the bar lassoed their lips before the laughs could escape from their mouths. Merry and Kat glanced at each other, a little uncomfortable.

J.T. noticed the girls and glared at Raymond.

"Junior, why didn't you tell me there were angels in my pool hall?"

Raymond shrugged. J.T. leaned against the bar, flirting.

"Angels, please tell the man upstairs I'm sorry for the foul words you just heard. I ain't been myself."

J.T. grinned again, edged on by the men chuckling. Merry and Kat smiled, at ease. Raymond laughed.

"Nigga, please. You been yourself for too damn long. My table open?"

"Ain't it always?"

Raymond strolled to the back of the pool hall with Merry and Kat in tow. Merry couldn't help but notice the men sneaking glances at her belly as she passed. She whispered to Kat to take her mind off all of the eyes on her.

"Did you know Raymond was a junior?"

"Uh uh. He never said anything to me about his daddy."

"Well, who is J.T. to him, then?"

Kat shrugged.

"All I know is J.T. used to box with Joe Louis. Raymond said the champ gave J.T. the money to open the pool hall."

Merry nodded to herself. That explained the picture over the bar. It was pretty much common knowledge in the Colored community that if money grew on trees, that tree was Joe Louis. Just about every restaurant, bar, nightclub, pool hall and dry cleaners from Detroit's North End to Harlem had been bankrolled by the champ in some form or fashion.

Merry followed one step behind Kat, surprised that grown men were actually parting like the Red Sea for Raymond. The boy had his own pool table? And J.T., who was old now, but had made a living sparring with Joe Louis, could obviously take him. So why was the man jumping through hoops like Lassie?

Merry started to ask Kat, but then realized that they had stopped walking. Raymond stood in front of his pool table, watching two thirty-something men - one short, the other a hair taller - in the heat of a game. The short one, the color of a wet brown paper bag with a mole for a face, was on the verge of winning. The taller one, the hue of a peach with the fuzz on his face to match, screwed chalk onto the tip of his cue stick and called out his impossible shot.

"Hop, bank, hole."

"Bullshit."

"I got five more where that come from. You don't believe me?"

"Aw, nigga, you ain't said nothin' but a word!"

The mole-faced man dug in his pocket, but stopped short when he noticed Raymond standing there.

"Know what, Terry, man? Let's take the money and get a drank instead."

"Damn, Gil. Shirley got you that scared of losin' your money?"

"Naw, my man here just needs to use the table. That's all."

Terry looked to Raymond, saw no threat. He aimed his cue stick on the table.

"Watch and learn, youngster. You can have the table in a minute."

Raymond chuckled. Gil gripped on the pool table, afraid. The men in the pool hall kept drinking and chattering in the background, but even Merry knew that they were really paying attention.

The only man not fazed by the tension building in the room was Terry. Cool, calm, and collected, he eyeballed his shot and rolled his cue stick twice in his neat hands. Merry could tell by looking at them that his hands were soft from not slaving day-in and day-out in a car or military factory. Terry was wearing a mailman's uniform. Had to be the only Colored mailman on the entire North End.

Gil stammered.

"Terry, man, I could really use that drank. I'm thirsty as hell."

Terry looked up from his amazing shot, annoyed that his friend was peeing his pants over baby-faced Raymond.

"Man, what the hell is wrong with you?"

Raymond answered for him.

"Gil said he was thirsty."

Terry straightened up, looked right at Raymond.

"Well, Gil can get a drink after I'm done."

Raymond and Terry starred at each other. All the chattering in the pool hall stopped.

Merry and her belly slid around Kat to get a better look.

Raymond smiled. Again. Gil croaked a plea.

"Terry."

Terry, hearing the weakness in his friend's voice, shot a look to Gil, then glanced around the pool hall. They had an audience of grown ass men watching him about to fight a boy they were all afraid of.

Terry starred back at Raymond, spoke to Gil.

"You paying for that drink, man?"

Gil sighed, relieved.

"Yeah, man. I'll buy you two."

Raymond, ever the gentlemen, stepped sideways to let Terry pass. As he did, he brushed past Merry's belly. Merry looked up into Terry's light eyes as they landed on her. The peach fuzz on his face - reddish brown just like his close-cropped good hair - was neatly trimmed into a beard and he smelled good. Like talcum powder.

Merry took a whiff of him, watched him walk away. Raymond grabbed the pool stick and started gathering the balls into the triangle.

"Bright Eyes, get the rest of those balls for me. I'm goin' to teach you how to play pool."

Kat hopped to it, excited to be with the baddest nigga on the North End.   Merry's curiosity was burning a hole through her tongue.

"So who are you anyway, Raymond? Why was that man so scared of you?"

"Was he scared?"

"Yeah, him and everybody else up in here."

Raymond laughed, a boisterous squeal from his gut. He shouted to Kat.

"Hey! Hey! Baby! Watch your step over there. Don't slip in that ugly nigga's pee."

Raymond slapped hands with the guffawing men at the other pool tables.   Merry turned just in time to see a still angry Terry and frightened Gil walk out. Then, she heard glass shattering. J.T., who was jockeying with men for position at the window, called out to Raymond.

"Hey, Junior. You got trouble out here!"

Raymond, who was no more bit concerned about anything but the ass in front of him, grinded against Kat and kissed her on her neck.

"Whatever it is, man, can wait."

"Not this, Junior. It's Silas' car."

Raymond bolted away from Kat and out the front door.

"Lizzy! What the hell you doin'?!"

Lizzy, Silas' common-law wife, didn't answer. Fired up from throwing a brick through Silas' Fleetmaster's driver's side window, she was possessed, slicing through the car's white wall tires like Vienna sausages. Raymond ran over to her. Lizzy flashed her shiny switchblade, stopped the boy dead in his tracks in the middle of the narrow street.

That's when Merry waddled up and got a good look at her. Lizzy wasn't as pretty as Merry remembered. She was skinny. Too skinny. And she had a black and blue eye. Her right one.

"Fuck you, Raymond. I'm sick and tired of Silas screwin' every young bitch he see. Tell his limp dick ass to come out here himself and deal wit' me."

"He ain't here, Lizzy."

"You a damn lie, Raymond. Silas! Brin' your ass out here!"

Raymond inched closer to her.

"Lizzy, I swear, he ain't here. I'm just drivin' his car."

Lizzy's switchblade arm wavered a little and for the first time, she glanced around to all of the nosey men from Plan B on the sidewalk gawking at her.

Raymond whispered.

"Come on, Lizzy. Gimme the knife, so we can talk this out. I got somethin' to make you feel real good."

Lizzy licked her lips, her dope fiend body aching for the goodness Raymond was offering. Merry and Kat, prompted by the sudden silence, pushed their way onto the curb to get a better look. Lizzy zoned in on Merry's belly, went off.

"Is that the lil bitch Silas got pregnant?"

Raymond stammered.

"Wha...What?"

Lizzy waved her switchblade in Merry's direction, wild. Merry stood helpless, her heart beating out of her chest, as everybody but Kat stepped away from her.

"That li'l pregnant bitch over there, Raymond! Her! Right there!"

Raymond looked at Merry, didn't answer fast enough. Lizzy took off running right for Merry, her switchblade raised over her head like a sword. And Merry just stood there. She should have bolted away from that curb, but her eyes were deadlocked with Lizzy's and she couldn't pull away. Not even with Kat tugging on her arm so hard, it was about to pop out of the socket.

Raymond tackled Lizzy to the street and slammed her hand gripping the knife against the asphalt so hard, he drew blood.

Police sirens blared in the just around the corner distance. Everyone hurried back into Plan B faster than roaches scurrying from light. And Lizzy, still laid out in the street, slapped her hands over her eyes and Raymond emptied out his pockets into the gutter.

Kat headed across the street to Raymond. Merry yanked her back.

"Kat, we gotta get outta here."

Kat nodded. The police car screeched up, stopped just short of hitting Lizzy. Two cops Merry recognized, Officers Petosky and Gerald got out of the car. Merry and Kat darted quick looks to each other, walked away. Kat in one direction. Merry the other.

Merry hurried. Her house on Dequindre was a 15-minute straight shot on the Russell bus. That was plenty of time for her to get her lie straight before she got home.

KENTUCKY,
1965

Home. At this rate, she was never going to make it home.

Merry winced. The fire in her bones was melting her legs and her flat feet were throbbing so bad, she wanted to plop down on the side of the road and saw them off.

Merry peered uphill ahead of her, the sun beaming down on her so hot, it made the heat rising off of the empty dirt road look like a pool of cool water. She stopped, looked downhill behind her. Lush fields. Trees. Same empty dirt road.

Merry wiped her brow. She needed to find some shade and rest a spell. Deeper into the field, she saw a tree on a hill surrounded by a cluster of bushes. The grass, tall and thick like carpet, Merry reached the tree, sat down and peeled off her shoes.

She leaned her head back against the tree trunk and closed her eyes. Just a few seconds of shut-eye was all she needed. Merry had been so excited to finally be getting out of that hellhole, she hadn't slept at all last night. Now was the perfect time to snag a few winks while she was waiting for her bus.

Merry yawned, just as a familiar scent trailed past her nose. It was the same kind of tobacco that the men back home rolled their homemade cigarettes with. Merry peeked around. No sign of man, woman or child. But that smoke! It was close enough for her to snatch the unseen cigarette from the invisible puffing stranger and take a drag.

Merry stood up, walked around the tree, stopped. A few hops down the hill was a creek. And in that creek was a Black man in a white robe holding a young Black girl in a white dress under clear water while a congregation of Black women - Christian Soldiers, smoothed faced to wrinkled, donning white dresses, white gloves and matching wide-brimmed white hats - watched, silent. The Good Reverend Dr. pulled the little girl up out of the water and everyone clapped. The little girl, so full with the spirit, started to cry.

Merry's face twitched. Some place buried deep inside was a little girl who still loved Jesus. But 30-year-old, ex-con Merry wasn't about to let the spiritual sight she was witnessing resurrect that long dead emotion from the tomb. She had a bus to catch.

"Beautiful isn't it?"

Merry spun around, didn't see anyone.

"Up here."

Merry looked up. In the tree was a boy. He looked to be about 17, 19 at the oldest. As black as Nat King Cole with a Sidney Poitier clipped tongue and Harry Belafonte chiseled chest, he held his camera in his left hand and butted out what was left of his cigarette on the tree trunk with his right.

"The baptism. Beautiful, right?"

Merry didn't answer. The boy, his afro perfectly round with not even a shadow of hair on his face, smiled.

"What, you never seen a Black man in a tree before?"

Merry chuckled, walked away. The boy jumped out of the tree, called after her.

"Allow me to introduce myself, Queen. R.B. Eddie. Pleased to meet you."

Merry kept walking, her shoes and response flung over her shoulder.

"You always go around climbing trees like a monkey, R.B.?"

"Only when I'm taking pictures."

R.B. caught up to Merry, fell in stride with her.

"You not from around here, are you, Queen?"

"From the way you talk, neither are you."

"Education at it's finest. Finished Kentucky State College just last week. I'm headed to Chicago to be a reporter. Got a job waiting for me at The Chicago Defender."

"That right?"

"More than right, Queen. It's true. Where you headed?"

Merry, back on the side of the dirt road, looked both ways. Still no signs of a bus. She dropped her shoes on the ground, stepped into them.

"Not to Chicago."

"Oh. Well, maybe you should. Consider going to Chicago, I mean."

R.B. looked at Merry, smiled. It had been a while since a man had looked at her that way. Before she landed in the joint, Silas had long stopped looking at her at all. He would just swing at Merry, knowing she was and would always be there. And in the joint? Those bastards couldn't see anything except their pink limp dicks that they forced into Merry day in and day out. Like sun on her face after weeks of being locked away in the hole, it felt nice to have a man flirting with her.

Merry shifted her hips, flirted back.

"I thought the place to be was up in that tree, R.B."

"Oh, yeah, I saw that tree and couldn't help but climb it. I was up there over an hour, waiting."

"Waiting for what?"

"To capture something interesting. And you know what? The whole time I was up there, I saw a humming bird, an angry squirrel and that little girl's baptism. But I didn't see one bus."

Merry looked at him, not able to stop the sides of her mouth from turning up into a grin.

"Monkey Boy, how old are you?"

"Old enough to know better."

"Well, then you know you better go back up in your tree. My old man's waiting on me."

R.B. placed his hand over his heart, sincere, dramatic.

"Queen, if you were mine, I would have picked you up and carried you home on my back before I had you out here waiting for a bus that's not coming."

Merry listened, too cool to show she was impressed. R.B. shrugged.

"Now, I don't know where you're headed. But I can take you as far as Chicago. A brother could use the company."

Merry paused. Truth be told, she was the one that could really use the company. The company of a stranger she met on the side of a Kentucky dirt road. The company of a boy just barely a man.

To make her feel like a woman. Again.

I REMEMBER
MORE THAN YOU KNOW

"Mommaaaaa!!"

Merry grabbed her belly and screamed. Soaked and lying in a liquid pool of her insides, her gown was plastered to her contracting body like wet toilet paper to a shoe.

Excellent ran into the bedroom, saw Merry rolling on the floor and hurried to her side. Johnson flicked on the light, scared to death.

"Ma, is it the baby?!"

Excellent, armed with the unexplainable strength of a mother whose child was in danger, scooped Merry up into her arms and carried her over to the bed.

"Johnson, get me some clean towels and hot water. Then, call Teenie and momma, tell them the baby's coming."

Johnson hesitated, confused.

"Don't you want me to get Mr. Blackie to drive you to the hospital?"

Excellent scurried around the twin bed, propped up pillows underneath Merry's sweaty head.

"Too late for that. Gone now. Do what I told you!"

Merry screamed, her body springing forth like a possessed jack-in-the-box. Johnson shot out of the room. Merry grabbed for Excellent, wild.

"Don't make me have it, Momma. Please don't. I don't want to..."

Excellent gently pushed Merry back down on the bed.

"This baby's comin', Merry. Whether we want it to or not."

"But. I. Don't. Want. It."

Excellent squeezed Merry's hand tight, her words quick, but calm.

"Merry, listen to me. This baby is ready and I need you to get ready. You hear me?"

Merry gritted her teeth, the tail end of the contraction passing over her like a wave.

"Uh huh."

"Alright. Breath like this."

Excellent drew in a deep breath through her nostrils and exhaled, slow. Merry copied as best she could.

"Good. Now prop up your legs and push like you goin' to the bathroom when I tell you."

Merry propped up her quivering legs and Excellent sat down on the end of the bed in front of her.

Johnson bolted back into the room, carrying every towel that they owned in the house. Seeing Merry's legs propped up, he dropped the mountain of towels, covered his eyes.

"Ma, I didn't know how many you needed. This enough?"

Merry and Excellent chuckled, the seriousness momentarily broken by Johnson's silliness. Excellent teased.

"Boy, how many babies you think she havin'?"

Merry grabbed her stomach and lunged forward. Excellent grabbed some towels, sprang into action.

"Johnson, wait outside!"

Johnson obeyed. And Merry fell back hard onto her pillows like she was having a seizure. Excellent stuck her hands in between Merry's trembling legs, ready to catch her first grandchild.

"Push, Merry! Push!"

Merry grunted and pushed.

"Come on, Merry. I see the head. You almost there. Push."

Merry, exhausted and scared, started to cry.

"I can't. I can't. I can't do it."

Excellent gripped Merry's knees, forceful.

"Yes. You. Can. Merry. Push!"

Merry took a deep breath, then exhaled. The next sound she heard was a whimper. Then, a screeching cry. Merry strained to see the wailing child Excellent was pulling from between her bloody legs. She panted.

"What is it? Is it alright?"

Excellent stared at the red velvet newborn in her hands, didn't answer. Merry panicked.

"What's wrong? What's wrong wit' my baby?!"

***

"Merry, he sho' do look like dat big eared daddy o' his. Guess you had no choice, but tuh give him his name. I still like Charles betta, tho'."

Dora was sitting on the edge of Merry's bed, her great-grandson Felton, Jr. asleep in her arms. Teenie was standing, proud and excited, and Excellent - seated in a chair on the bed - looked about as run over as Merry did.

Excellent shook her head.

"Momma, every boy child born in this family is not Charles."

Teenie tensed. Dora snapped.

"I ain't say it wuz. I jus' always liked the name, dat's all."

Dora eyed Excellent, upset, and Teenie stepped up to take the baby.

"Stop bein' so greedy with my grand nephew, Momma. It's my turn."

Dora smiled and handed Felton Jr. to Teenie, as sweet as pie. But Merry could look at her momma's face and tell she had no sweetness right now for Excellent. She had to know why.

"Who's Charles, Momma?"

Merry was talking to Dora, but an answer from Excellent would have been fine, too. Teenie spoke up.

"Your uncle. He died a long time ago when he was a baby. It was an accident."

"What kind of accident?"

Again, Merry was talking to Dora. This time Excellent answered.

"An accident that killed him 'stead of me."

Dora hopped up, riled.

"Goddamnit, Excellent. You always gotta make everythin' 'bout your ass."

"Momma, you the one dug up Charles' name."

Teenie jumped in.

"That's right, Excellent, his name. There's nothin' wrong with saying his name."

Dora crossed her arms, justified and Teenie and Excellent starred at each other. Favored child versus first-born.

Felton, Jr. stirred awake in Teenie's arms, belted out a shrilling cry. Teenie felt the bottom of the blanket, then handed him to Merry.

"I think Jr. Baby's hungry."

"Already? I just fed him."

Dora chuckled as Merry adjusted Jr. Baby Felton to her.

"You might as well git useta niggas hangin' off yo' titties now, baby. You know whut you doin'?"

Merry started to answer, but Jr. Baby sucked the wind out of her when he clamped down hard on her left breast. Hell, no, she didn't know what she was doing. But her baby boy? Merry looked down at him as he hungrily sucked her nipple dry. Her son knew exactly what to do.

**

Merry had heard stories about her uncle Warren. About how he punched a white man silly for spitting in his face and left Locust Grove in the dead of night to escape a charbroiled lynching. He was long gone by the time Merry was born and the only way she really knew him at all was from pictures. The same coffee and cream complexion as Excellent, Uncle Warren was sturdy in the chest and was always laughing or smiling. Merry couldn't imagine then that the young man in the black and white photos was the same crazy nigga that had beaten a white man. And she still couldn't imagine it today, surrounded by a living room full of migrated relatives and looking at Uncle Warren with her baby boy in the palm of his large hand.

"...Whut you say, the baby ain't have no balls when he first came out."

Excellent sipped on her lemonade.

"Fool, he had balls. Just not the..."

Excellent glanced at Johnson, trailed off. Johnson pouted, crossed his arms.

"Might as well say it, Momma."

Merry and everybody busted out laughing. Uncle Warren louder than all of them. Auntie Stella, Teenie and Uncle Warren's wife, Lois, trailed into the living room, nosey.

"What's so funny?"

Somehow Aunt Lois managed to ask the question with a mouthful of food. Dark as smoke, short and round, Lois looked like a black circle with feet.

Uncle Warren sat back down.

"Excellent wuz tellin' me 'bout the baby."

Auntie Stella clapped her hands, excited. The slow one of the bunch, she was the complexion of ground white pepper thanks to Dora bedding a cracker traveling bible salesman in between husbands.

"Oh, you mean how he look like Charles! Jr. Baby look jus' like him, don't he, Excellent?"

Teenie said nothing, uncomfortable. And Excellent exhaled through her flaring nostrils. Uncle Warren laughed it off.

"Aw, you was just a baby yourself, Stella. You don't even remember what Charles looked like."

"Yes, I do, Warren! I remember more than you know."

Merry heard the conviction in her Aunt Stella's whiny voice and searched her face for the reason why. Uncle Warren stepped over and kissed Merry's on the forehead.

"Don't you pay Stella no mind, Merry. You take care of uh..uh..What's his real name?"

"Felton, Jr."

"It is?"

Uncle Warren's mouth was open, but the voice that flew out of it was Felton's. He was standing, nervous, in the living room archway. Uncle Warren waved him in.

"It's alright, boy. Come over here and meet yo' son."

Felton walked over to Merry as everyone else left the room.

"Did you really name him Felton, Merry?"

"Yeah."

Felton gazed at their tiny, sleeping son, scared to death and full of awe. Merry snarled.

"Where's your auntie?"

Felton's shoulders drooped, apologetic.

"I left her at home. She told me if I came here not to come back..."

"So why did you come, then?"

"Because this is my baby, Merry, and I want to take care of it."

"Yeah, right. Like you took care of me?"

Felton grabbed her hand, pleading.

"Merry, I'm sorry. But look..."

Felton dug in his pocket, pulled out a small rubber-banded wad of bills, placed it in her hand.

"I've been saving this for the baby and I'll get more. I swear."

Merry looked at the money, then to Felton. He meant it.

Excellent stepped back into the room, carrying a baby blue crochet blanket. She cleared her throat and handed the blanket to Felton.

"This is for the baby. Wrap him up tight in it and follow me outside."

Merry held on tighter to Jr. Baby, protested.

"But it's cold out there."

"Merry's right, Mrs. Mavis. I don't understand..."

Excellent gritted her teeth, her last nerve frayed.

"Just. Do. What. I. Said."

Felton, knowing better than to disobey Excellent, reached for his son with shaky hands. Merry hesitated.

Excellent zipped up her coat, headed for the front door.

"The boy won't drop the baby, Merry. Hurry up. Everybody's waiting."

Merry looked to Felton, still not sure. She instructed.

"Put your arms right and you got to be careful with his head."

"O.K."

Felton nodded and adjusted his arms. Merry passed their slumbering baby to him, clumsy, like a selfish child with a new toy.

Bundled up, Felton, Merry and son stepped out onto the porch into the brisk November air. Excellent and the whole family was waiting.

"Alright, Felton, walk Jr. Baby around the house one time. For good luck."

Merry had to butt in. Up until 15-minutes ago, Felton was missing in action. She didn't care what the boy was promising now and it didn't matter that Merry was too young to have a baby and had absolutely no idea what she was doing. Jr. Baby was her baby, not his.

"I can walk wit' him."

Excellent dismissed Merry just as easy breathing.

"No, Merry. This is a man thing."

Merry silenced. Felton's voice quivered.

"Mrs. Mavis, do I have to do anything else, anything special?"

"No, just put one foot in front of the other."

Uncle Warren chuckled loud from his belly.

"And hurry up, boy. It's cold!"

*

Merry didn't know what else to do.

She tried feeding him, rocking him, burping him, changing him, and nothing was working.

Jr. Baby was still screaming at the top of his powerful lungs, his small, round face red and wet with tears.

Johnson yelled out from his room.

"Merry, shut that boy up!"

"I'm tryin'!"

Merry looked down at Jr. Baby, frustrated. He wasn't a cute doll to her anymore. Weeks of not sleeping, nasty diapers, and sore titties had taken their toll. She was tired of the yelping bundle of a son in her arms and she just wanted him to be quiet. No, gone. Merry wanted Jr. Baby gone.

Excellent opened the door, exhausted.

"Is he wet?"

"No."

"Hungry?"

"I tried. He won't take it."

"Where's his blanket?"

"Uh..."

Merry searched around the bed as Excellent walked over to the bed. She found it on the floor. Excellent took it from her.

"Merry, I made this for him for a reason. Now, pour some J & B in a glass. Bring it to me."

Merry hurried out of the room to the kitchen. She scooted a chair up to the cabinet and climbed up. On the top shelf, she found a half-full bottle of J & B and a newly opened bottle of vodka. Merry paused. She was expecting the J & B, but the vodka was a surprise. Since Corn had been gone, the only vodka in the house were the hidden bottles in her book bag that she used to pay Tito to buy for her.

After she got pregnant and was made a prisoner of her house, though, she was forced to go dry. But now, faced with her favorite nightcap, the drought was over. And she wanted a taste.

Merry reached for the Vodka bottle, then stopped. Something was different. The house was quiet. Her baby boy wasn't shrieking anymore. She grabbed the J & B bottle instead.

"What you do?"

Merry rushed into her bedroom, carrying a short tumbler glass of J & B. Excellent put her finger to her lips and laid her sleeping grandson down into his wooden crib.

They tiptoed out of the room.

"How'd you get him to stop cryin'? He likes you better, doesn't he?"

Excellent plopped down on her bed, ignored Merry's frustrated question.

"When he cries like that, swaddle him tight in the blanket. Makes him feel like he's safe, back in your belly."

"And what's this for?"

Excellent took the glass from her.

"Gas. Put a drop of this on your finger and wipe it on his gums. He'll pass it and fall right to sleep next time."

Excellent tossed back the liquor in one gulp, handed the glass back to Merry.

"He got that screamin' from you."

"He did?"

Excellent climbed in the bed and laid down on her side. She half-chuckled.

"Guess you didn't like me, either."

Merry stood there in the dark holding the empty tumbler glass, not sure if she should laugh or leave. She left.

Back in the kitchen, Merry rinsed out the glass, set it face down in the sink. Then, she climbed back up on the chair and hungrily grabbed the vodka bottle off the top shelf.

All she needed was one taste. She unscrewed the top, knocked back a quick swallow. It was so sweet, it didn't even burn.

DETROIT,
1949

Virtue itself turns vice, being misapplied. And vice sometime's by action dignified.

Merry underlined the stanza from Romeo and Juliet with her red ink pen, read it to herself again. She liked how the poetic words danced in her mouth, heavy as wet snow, but light as autumn leaves. It made her think. She couldn't just zoom through it like one of Excellent's hidden romance novels or get lost it in like one of Kat's fantasy adventure books. She had to be ever-present, thinking, to decode exactly what the old guy, William Shakespeare, was saying.

Now virtue, Merry knew what that meant, but she had to look up vice in the dictionary.

She learned that vice - just like dark and light, black and white - was the opposite of the same coin of virtue. It meant evil, bad, wrong. And she had been taught all of life that nothing good could come from bad. But the stanza, which she had now read to herself three times, was saying something all together different.

Sometimes folks could poison their good intentions, because they were trying to do right, but they go about it all wrong. And other times, they could have nothing but bad intentions and they set out to do nothing but wrong and it turns out good anyway. Merry figured that was why folks were always saying they had good intentions, or the ends justified the means. It was their way of apologizing for the pain they were sure to cause you on the front or the back end.

Merry cut her eyes over to her padlocked piano in the corner. After months of not being used, her birthday gift had become just another piece of furniture. A plant stand, more specifically. Like a wild creature from the Amazon, Excellent's spider plant's long, dangling limbs had the poor piano entangled.

That was for the best anyway. Merry had long since given up trying to pick her piano's padlock so she could make sweet music on it again. And Excellent, her warden, had made it clear she would never let her play again. Merry was being punished and keeping the piano in the living room, so Merry would have to see it everyday was Excellent pouring rock salt in the wound.

"He sleepin' good now. I'm goin' nex' door to sit wit' Ms. Ruthie fo' a while."

Merry laid down her book and looked at Dora who was putting on her sweater as she stepped back into the living room.

"You gonna pick through her dreams for a number again?!"

"I jus' played dat numba one time!"

"And you won fifty dollars."

Dora fussed, guilty.

"Hell! Ain't my fault her blind ass ain't play it. I'm gone!"

Merry laughed as Dora swooped out of the house. That woman was a hot mess. But Merry had to admit, it was nice having her around. True to his word, Principal Bennett graduated her from the ninth grade after she kept up with her studies. She wasn't able to walk across the stage for their junior high school promotion ceremony, though, because she was good and pregnant with Jr. Baby at the time. But the school did at least send her certificate of promotion by Johnson, so she got proof that she finished.

That following fall, Merry was hoping to start classes at Northern High School, but she still had two months to go before Jr. Baby was due. Then after he came, there wasn't time for anything else.

Now that Merry had a mouth to feed, Dora made her a partner of sorts in the laundry business, giving her a cut of the profits in exchange for her service. And yes, Merry still hated the work, but she thought of it as a way to supplement the money Felton was giving her.

Then, there was the money she was getting every month from the government. Not soon after Merry had Jr. Baby, Excellent took her downtown and signed her up for welfare. A check came in the mail on the first of the month and Merry would sign it. Then, Excellent would take it to the bank and deposit it in an account she opened for her and give her an allowance.

Merry heard the slot on the front door squeak open and mail drop to wooden floor. She was already out of her seat and at the door before the slot squeaked closed. She flipped through the mail, yanked open the door.

"Hey!"

The mailman stopped, turned around.

"Yeah?"

Merry recognized him right away. It was Terry, the peach fuzzed face man from the pool hall that nearly rumbled with Raymond. He was still handsome, maybe even handsomer now, but that didn't matter. Terry wasn't their regular, dependable white mailman and the man needed to be set straight.

Merry stepped out on the porch, held up the letters.

"This isn't our mail."

"It's not?"

"No. This is 13443 Dequindre, not 13346. The Smallwoods are across the street."

"Sorry. I'm still learnin' the route..."

Terry trailed off as he searched his government satchel for Merry's mail. The man's hands were still neat, but this time there was something different about them. He was wearing a wedding band. A dingy, gold wedding band.

Merry, still a child, in years at least, usually never noticed things like that, but she couldn't help but pay attention this time. Terry's beat up wedding band looked totally out of place on his neat hand.

Terry flipped through some envelopes, double-checking the addresses, then pulled out Merry's mail. They switched stacks. Terry shrugged.

"Sorry 'bout that."

Merry quickly shuffled through the mail. Her welfare check was at the bottom of the stack. She turned back to head and caught Terry eyeing her. The way a man eyes a woman. Merry paused, her hand holding open the door. She wasn't old enough to be a woman, that's for sure. But thanks to Jr. Baby, she certainly did look more like one these days.

Terry smiled.

"You got everythin', right?"

"Uh huh."

Terry tapped an envelope on his satchel, stalling.

"And you said The Smallwoods are..."

"Across the street."

"Right."

Terry looked at Merry with grown man's eyes. Merry smiled, flirting with her look-like-a-woman butt, all the while knowing she was wrong for doing it. The man was married, probably had a fat wife and house full of bad ass kids. And worst than that, her momma was right next-door at Ms. Ruthie's. Nosey as hell, they both might even be on the top porch listening.

Inside, she heard Jr. Baby whimpering awake. Wouldn't be long before he was wailing like a cat getting skinned alive. Merry gripped the door to close it. Terry stepped up.

"Listen, don't I know you?"

Merry paused. Terry couldn't remember her from Plan B, could he? That was months ago. He had been eyeball to eyeball with Raymond and barely even looked at her. Besides, Merry didn't want Terry to recognize her. Because, right around the corner would be the not-so-distant memory of her being pregnant when he first saw her. Then, he'd figure out that the baby crying in the house was hers.

Merry opened her mouth. Out flew a lie.

"No. I just moved here."

"You sure? 'Cause you look real familiar."

Merry shook her head 'no.' Terry kept sweet-talking.

"Come on now, I'm real good with faces and I swear..."

Jr. Baby shrieked, taking Terry completely out of his game. He looked at Merry, alarmed.

"Is your baby alright?"

"He's not mine."

Merry wanted to bite her tongue off. She had denied her child faster than Peter did Jesus. She tried again, calmer this time.

"I'm the babysitter."

Terry smiled. He had nice teeth.

"Well, what's your name, babysitter?"

Merry formed her lips, all set to say her name. Then, stopped herself. She just got a welfare check in the mail. Terry was the new mailman. Didn't take Sherlock Holmes to figure out that only single mothers got welfare checks from the government.

"Dora. Everybody calls me Dora."

"Well, Dora, everybody calls me Terry. Except my momma. She calls me Terrance."

Terrance. Merry liked the ring of the name. Jr. Baby must have liked it, too, because suddenly, he wasn't wailing from inside the house anymore. Merry and Terry looked at each other, glad for the silence. Terry backed away from the screen door to keep himself from opening it.

"Nice to meet you, too, Dora. See you tomorrow."

Merry nodded, watched him walk away, closed the door. Johnson, who had been eavesdropping from the kitchen archway pretty much the whole time, fell out on the hallway floor.

"Dora. Everybody calls me Dora."

Merry stomped over him to her bedroom. Johnson gasped to catch his breath.

"I'm the babysitter and I wanna hang all on yo' mailman sack."

"Boy, if anybody know about hanging on balls, it's you."

Merry turned into her bedroom and saw Lonnie tossing a giggling Jr. Baby in the air and catching him in his long, large hands. She would have been mad that his fairy ass was manhandling her son like a basketball, if she hadn't been so surprised to see him. A tenth grader at Northern High School now, Lonnie had no time for her brother these days. He caught Jr. Baby for the last time, handed him over to her.

"He's wet."

Merry grabbed a clean cloth diaper off her dresser, started to change him.

Johnson plopped his hand down on Lonnie's broad shoulder. Just as big and tall as his boyfriend, Johnson looked older. He giggled.

"Lonnie, did you know that Merry's real name is Dora and she's really the babysitter?"

"Johnson, why don't you mind your own business?!"

"Wait, wait, who's talkin'? Merry or Dora? I can't tell."

Merry and Johnson started bickering. Jr. Baby, his tiny nature naked and exposed, gazed up at them, entertained. Lonnie headed out of the room, shaking his head.

"Yaw go 'head and work that out. I gotta go."

Johnson hurried out after Lonnie.

"Go? Lonnie, wait..."

Seconds later, Merry heard Johnson's bedroom door close. Merry finished putting on Jr. Baby's diaper and got herself situated to feed him. As her son hungrily tugged on her hardened nipples with his gums, Merry, bored, shuffled through the mail again. Her welfare check was still there. So were the bills. And there was a letter. A returned one.

The letter was addressed to Corn and it was written in her mother's handwriting. Excellent's penmanship was neat, controlled, yet flowing. It reminded Merry of the way actors in old black and white movies wrote letters by dipping the tip of a feather in ink. She held up the envelope to see if she could see through it. Shifting Jr. Baby to her other titty, Merry weighed her options. As far as Excellent was concerned, Corn had gotten the letter, but just hadn't responded back yet. Merry tore open the letter.

Dear Corn,

I pray that you're doing well in the Windy City. I got your address from Cassius. He said he was calling to tell me that he and Evelyn were grandparents again, but I know he was really calling, because you asked him to.

Honey, I don't blame you for not talking to me. I didn't expect for things to go so far and things to get so bad between us. Seems we can only get along for so long. That's always been our problem, hasn't it?

Well, I didn't finally write you to talk about all the things we both know we can't fix. I just thought you should know that Merry had a baby. A beautiful baby boy named Felton, Jr. that we all call Jr. Baby. You remember that big-eared boy you told me not to worry about? Well, Merry messed around and got pregnant by him. Jr. Baby is five months old and spoiled as he want to be. Momma thinks he's Charles come back again. I told her she was crazy, but I only half meant it. Sometimes when I look at him just the right way and he looks back at me with those big, old man eyes, I feel like he knows who I am.

Who's the touched one, now? I know.

Johnson's fine. All he cares about is basketball and that loud mouth Dolores. I wish he did better in school, but he's not like Merry. The principal made her leave school and do her studies from home and she still finished 9th grade at the top of her class. That's my girl! Next year, when Jr. Baby is older, I'm going to make sure she goes to high school.

Remember that nightmare I used to have? The one where Charles is crying for me in the fire and no matter what I do, I can't get to him? I'm having it again. Every time I close my eyes, I hear him screaming for me and...I know it's too late to save him. I know it is. But I can still help Merry. I swear, I'm going to do everything I can to make sure my girl goes all the way. I don't care how many toilets I have to clean.

Speaking of cleaning toilets, I better get back to it before Mr. Benson's no good ass comes nosing around for me.

Take care of yourself, Honey. And if the spirit leads you, give the kids a call. They miss you.

Yours always,

Excellent.

Merry re-read the letter three times before she put it down. This love letter to Corn that she was never supposed to see told Merry more about how her mother felt about her than Excellent ever had. Her mother cared and was worried about her. But most of all, for the first time in her life Merry knew Excellent was proud to call her daughter.

Merry heard the front door open and close and smiled, wickedly. Johnson and Lonnie were in his bedroom doing what grown folks do. And Dora was back from Ms. Ruthie's!

Merry eased Jr. Baby down out of her arms onto her bed and went searching for her momma. She found Dora in the kitchen fussing on the phone.

"...Whut you mean, I'm not 'spose tuh call you at work wit' dis, Teenie? I'm puttin' too much on dis number tuh forget. Now whut I say? Uh huh, right, right. 2498, Detroit and Toledo. Put five on it... Alright. See you tonight."

Dora hung up the phone and Merry crossed her arms in mock disapproval.

"I jus' thought of dat numba on my own."

Merry eyed the thin pocketsize, paperback numbers book crumpled in Dora's right hand.

"Oh, you go to hell!"

Dora tapped Merry on the nose with the book and darn near skipped over to the refrigerator.

"How 'bout chicken salad fo' lunch?"

"O.K., but Johnson probably won't want any."

Dora stopped.

"Johnson? Whut he doin' home from school dis early? Somethin' wrong?"

Merry shrugged off Dora's concern, trying hard not to let out the laughter bubbling up in her throat.

"Don't know. He just came home and got in the bed."

Dora hurried out of the kitchen with Merry right on her heels. Dora reached for the knob, opened the door without knocking.

"Johnson..."

Merry slid on the side of her momma, ready to get an eyeful. Johnson and Lonnie, dressed and appearing ever innocent, sat at the foot of Johnson's unmade, rumpled bed, playing dominoes.

Johnson smiled up to Dora.

"Hey, Momma."

Johnson and Lonnie stood up, pecked Dora on both of her cheeks. Merry wrinkled up her nose, disgusted. What were their nasty lips doing to each other just a second ago?

Dora looked from Merry to Johnson, curious.

"Whut you doin' home from school? Merry said you was sick."

Johnson grinned at Merry, sticking it to her.

"I was, but I feel better now."

Lonnie threw his arm around Johnson's shoulder, joking.

"Yeah. That's 'cause I beat him so bad in dominoes, Momma Dora, he too whipped to be sick!"

Dora laughed and Johnson and Lonnie fell right in line with her. Merry didn't find nothing funny. Here her sweet ass brother was standing right in front of Dora in his boyfriend's arms in a bedroom that smelled like a queer whorehouse and her momma still couldn't see the truth.

"You boys hungry? I'm makin' chicken salad."

"Thanks, Momma Dora, but I gotta get to practice."

Lonnie opened the back door. Johnson stood ready to walk him out.

"Alright. Come back soon, so I can feed you. I ain't seen you 'round here much lately."

"Yes, Ma'am."

Lonnie pecked Dora on the cheek again and she swiped at his broad chest like a schoolgirl. He looked at Merry with a confidant smirk.

"Bye, Merry."

Dora chuckled after they left.

"I dink he sweet on you."

Merry rolled her eyes, grabbed the cutting board and a knife.

"Yeah, he sweet alright."

Dora started pulling the meat off the chicken bones, lost in a memory.

"Your granddaddy hadda voice deep as well jus' like dat. He could be hummin' clear 'cross duh field and somethin' would start rumblin' up inside of me..."

"Momma, please."

"Uh uh, too late to git 'barrassed 'bout rumblin', gurl. I know you know. You got dat baby in deer as proof."

Dora laughed, tickling her self. Merry looked at her momma with a sour face. What did she know about proof? Dora had all the proof she needed to find Johnson guilty of sweetness, but she didn't. And she had the nerve to call Merry out about rumblings?

Merry chopped up the green pepper, silent. The only thing rumbling on her body right now was her stomach. She just wanted to eat lunch and be left alone.

SING IT
FOR ME

Merry kept her eyes closed as she used the toilet. She had gotten pretty good at sleep peeing. So good that she could keep dreaming and successfully sleep walk to and from the bathroom without ever waking up.

Merry wiped herself and flushed the toilet. Aside from the swish of the water draining down the toilet and the faint whirr of a running electric sewing machine drifting up through the clothes shaft that led to the basement, the house was quiet.

Merry shuffled out of the bathroom, past Excellent's open bedroom door, back to her room. She was just about to slouch over to her bed when she heard something that she hadn't heard in so long, she almost didn't recognize it. Excellent was humming.

Merry opened her eyes to make sure she wasn't dreaming. Sleepy, she followed the sound of her mother's voice to the closed basement door and pressed her ear against it. She turned the knob and crept down the stairs.

Excellent sat with her back to Merry, slightly hunched over her sewing machine. A small radio played a gospel tune on a card table to the right of her and a light bulb, a few watts shy of illumination, threw dim light over everything, making everything look washed out like an old water color painting in a white folks museum. Merry leaned against the banister and watched her mother as she sewed and hummed her tune. Gone was any trace of the tired aggravation Excellent had had when she gotten home that evening. Armed with new information from Corn's love letter, Merry had made a special dinner of fried pork chops, smothered potatoes, lima beans and crackling cornbread, hoping to make Excellent say out loud what she had admitted in writing. Merry's thinking was that if she could get her mother to say that she really was proud of her, then she could get Excellent to loosen her grip on her government check and let her handle her own business from now on.

That was the plan anyway. But Excellent was in such a don't-mess-with-me mood at dinner that Merry decided to wait for a better time to bring the subject up. Now was her chance.

She headed down the stairs, making more noise than she needed to, to get her mother's attention. Excellent looked over her shoulder, a little alarmed.

"Merry? What are you doing up?"

"I heard you."

Merry walked toward Excellent, rubbing her eyes. Excellent was making a new dress. The three dresses Excellent never finished were still hanging up on the clothesline, untouched.

"You got your sewing machine back."

Excellent chuckled, amused.

"Eberhardt finally gave it back. Had the nerve to get an attitude 'bout it, too."

Merry eyed Excellent's sewing machine again. Yep, it was the same one she had tried to buy back from the abandoned pawnshop. Her mother was lying on her best friend Mrs. Jewel Eberhardt to cover up the secret that she didn't know Merry knew. But why?

Merry, noticing the silky pink material moving through the sewing machine, changed the subject.

"What you making?"

"A dress. For Amy."

Merry's face wrinkled up, annoyed. Why did Excellent have to sound so happy about making a dress in the dead of night for that rich white girl? She already did too much for The Bensons. Hattie McDaniel in the flesh, Excellent worked her fingers to the bone day and night for them. Wasn't it enough that her mother spent more time caring for The Benson family and their spoiled kids than she did for her own? Did Excellent have to love those white bastards, too?

Merry's face turned from annoyed to mad.

"Why?"

"Why what?"

"Why you making Amy a dress?"

Excellent stopped the machine, looked at Merry.

"I'm making it, 'cause she asked me to."

"Well, I asked you if I could be in charge of my own money and you told me no."

Excellent stared at her, said nothing. Merry pouted.

"That's not fair. It's my money."

"That money's for the baby, Merry, not for you. That's exactly why I won't let you get your hands on it."

Excellent started the machine again, tired of Merry. Merry, though, wasn't done back talking.

"But it's alright for you to spend it on your sewing machine? Mrs. Eberhardt didn't have your sewing machine. The pawnshop did. I saw it."

Excellent's eyes flashed and she moved her hands from the sewing machine. Merry jerked back out of reflex. Excellent spoke, too calm.

"Go to bed, Merry."

"But..."

Excellent turned on Merry, her hands balled into fists to keep from slapping her.

"Go. To. Bed. Now."

Merry tripped backwards away from Excellent and shuffled out of the room, upset. She must have read Corn's love letter all wrong. Whoever that proud woman was that wrote to Corn wasn't the same evil woman in the basement.

Merry heard the sewing machine whir back on before her foot hit the bottom basement step and by the time she got to the top of the stairs, Excellent was humming again. Soft. Just like before. As if Merry hadn't even been down there.

****

The front door barely had a chance to close before Merry was in her mother's bedroom, snooping all through Excellent's dresser drawers, trying to find the key to her piano's padlock. It was too late to do anything about her government check. Excellent had used her money to get her sewing machine out of the pawnshop. No telling what else she was using her money for. Next month, Merry decided she'd go down to the bank and handle her money herself. But right now, playing her piano was the only way Merry could think of to get back at Excellent. Disobedience was her only weapon.

Merry opened the dresser's bottom drawer, moved some clothes. Underneath them, she found Excellent's pistol.

"What you lookin' for?"

Merry closed the drawer, quick.

"Nothing."

Merry stood and sifted through Excellent's jewelry box. She wasn't in the mood for Johnson's mess today.

"You lookin' for this?"

Johnson tossed a key in the air, cocky. Merry tried to grab it from him.

"Boy! Give it to me!"

Johnson laughed.

"How bad you want it?"

"What?"

"How bad you want it? I know you got money. Felton just gave you some."

Merry starred at Johnson. No, this boy wasn't shaking her down. Merry slammed the jewelry box closed.

"I'm not giving you nothing."

Johnson followed her back into her bedroom, scheming.

"Don't be stupid, girl. I wanna get Lonnie somethin' nice fo' his birthday. This way, we both get what we want."

"No."

"C'mon, Merry!"

"Ask momma. She always gives you what you want."

"I can't."

Merry scooped up Jr. Baby out of his crib right before he started crying. He cooed, happy.

"Why not?"

"'Cause she gone wanna know what I need it fo'."

"Then, tell her."

Merry starred at her brother, her drooling son on her hip. Johnson broke into a toothy smile, shook his finger at her.

"You think you slick. Momma bargin' all up in my room on me and Lonnie, 'cause you told her I was sick...I know you bored as hell, cooped up in this house with momma and the baby, washing and ironing men's dirty drawers all day. You wanna play your piano. I know you do. Why you actin' like you don't?"

Merry looked at Johnson, catching a whiff of Jr. Baby's breakfast already waiting for her in his diaper.

"Five dollars."

"Oops, guess you really don't wanna play."

Johnson started out of the room. Merry called out.

"Ten."

Johnson stopped, turned around, dramatic.

"Twenty."

Merry shifted her neck and raised her eyebrow. Johnson changed his tune fast and in a hurry.

"Alright, ten's good."

***

Merry paid her brother a ten spot and ten minutes later she was sitting in front of her unlocked piano. Dora would be walking through the front door any minute, but Merry couldn't wait.

As soon as her fingers touched the piano, her whole body came to life. Hands flying. Feet taping. Shoulders, neck, head and torso moving in time, in rhythm to the impromptu tune flowing out from her fingers to the keys.

Jr. Baby, just as caught up as Merry was, crawled underneath the piano bench and through her legs to touch the shiny pedals. He giggled and looked up at her. Merry, truly happy for the first time in months, giggled back.

"My Lawd."

Merry looked up, busted. Dora was standing in the hallway. Merry pulled her hands away from the piano like she was caught stealing something.

"Momma..."

"Merry, I didn't know you could play like dat."

Dora hung up her light overcoat on the hook, slipped off her shoes.

"I thought it wuz wrong how Excellent stopped yo' lessons wit' Reveren' McKeever's wife and locked dat piano up from you. I'm glad she changed her mind."

Merry, guilty and desperate, started rambling.

"She didn't, Momma. She didn't change her mind. I've been asking her, begging her to let me play again, but she just wanted to keep on punishing me. So, I found the key and..."

Dora held up her hand to stop Merry's mouth from running.

"She ever hear you play?"

"No."

Merry's eyes fell on Jr. Baby, clamoring at Dora's feet. Dora picked him up and he smiled at her, exposing two little teeth poking out through the juicy, red gums. She rested her hand on Merry's shoulder, proud.

"I'll work on yo' momma. You keep playin'."

So Merry did.

She was amazed how much she remembered. She couldn't really read music. Her lessons with Mrs. McKeever hadn't gotten that far. But Merry could hear a song or riff one time and she could play it completely by ear just like she had created the music herself.

In her mind's ear, she heard Ella Fitzgerald singing *A Tisket, A Tasket*. Her fingers fell right in line and before long she was singing along.

A tisket. A tasket. A green and yellow basket. I bought a basket for my mommie. On the way, I dropped it. I dropped it. I dropped it. Yes, on the way I dropped it. A little girlie picked it up and took it to the market...

Merry, loose now, swinging, pictured herself on the Paradise Valley Theater stage next to the First Lady, pounding on the keys, scatting together in sweet harmony.

Schooby doobie doo bop bop tweetie tweet tweet dee dee boop boop doobie do schoop doobie do schoop booday beep booday beep doo doo doo tweet tweet tweet tweet tweet tweeday biddy bop biddy bop...

Revving up for her big finish, Merry raked her hand all the way up the ivories, then plucked the final high key like The Duke, himself! Jr. Baby, totally delighted, clapped his fat, little hands.

Outside the window, she heard more applause. Merry looked over her shoulder, embarrassed.

"You take requests?"

Terry handed Merry the mail, his eyes lingering on her. Merry pretended not to enjoy his attention.

"I can only play a few songs."

"From the sounds of that, Dora, you can play anythin' you want."

Merry smiled and Jr. Baby crawled up to Merry's feet, tugged on her. Merry ignored him, her mind set on Terry.

"What's the song?"

"The *Fat Man* by Fats Domino."

"How's it go?"

"You never heard The Fat Man?"

Merry shook her head 'no.' She didn't know who Fats Domino was either. Whenever she could, Merry would sneak and listen to the radio, but if the song wasn't jazz or gospel, it might as well never have been recorded as far as she was concerned.

Merry looked dead into Terry's eyes, shifted her body slightly.

"Sing it for me."

Terry grinned, using his lips for singing the last thing on his mind right now. Jr. Baby looked up at both of them, content for the moment to just sit there and enjoy the show. Terry whispered, almost bashful.

"Dora, if I sing, everybody's ears on this whole block'll start bleedin'."

Merry plopped her hands on her hips, playful.

"Then, how you expect to me to play it if you can't sing it, Terry?"

Terry laughed.

"Guess I gotta do somethin' about that."

The next day, he did.

Merry took the single rose from Terry's soft, neat hand, charmed. No one - boy, man or otherwise - had ever given her flowers before. Terry dug in his satchel. Instead of pulling out mail, he pulled out a gift. Small, square and wrapped in shiny pink paper, Terry handed it to Merry. She looked at it, excited.

"What is it?"

"A special delivery just for you."

Merry tore through the wrapping like it was Christmas. It was a 45-vinyl record. Fats Dominoe's *The Fat Man*. Terry stepped closer to her.

"Now you'll be able to play one more song."

Merry smiled, grateful, attracted.

"Thank you."

"Anytime, sweet Dora. Anytime."

Every time, actually, would have been more accurate. Because from that day on, every time Merry saw Terry, he no longer just delivered her mail. The man came bearing gifts! A box of chocolates one day. Cookies, a stuffed animal, the next. Flowers. Perfume. A different rock-and-roll or blues 45 for every day of the week. And Merry, like any woman would, accepted all of Terry's gifts hungrily. She also kept the fact that the handsome married mailman was soon going to want something more than a Fats Domino tune played by ear on her piano in return for all his presents locked up in the back of her mind, instead of allowing her common sense to roam free.

Merry popped one of Terry's chocolates into her mouth and moaned as it squished around on her tongue. Cherry. She loved picking a chocolate and biting into it, not knowing what to expect. It was a surprise for herself. Just like Terry.

Merry put the top back on the box of chocolates and slid it under the bed with all of her other hidden goodies. Then she shuffled through the Saturday mail that Terry had given her. Bills. Water. Light. Gas. And her government check. It was the first of the month already?

Merry tore open the envelope and looked at her check. Jr. Baby stirred in his sleep. It was just the two of them alone in the house. Excellent had to work yet another Saturday for The Bensons. Johnson was out running behind Lonnie like a lap dog and Dora, who spent nights and weekends at Teenie's, was somewhere playing Kino.

Merry put on her shoes. Her son wouldn't be waking up any time soon.

She had just fed him and with a full belly, he could nap for more than an hour, two, easy. That was plenty of time for her to get down to the bank and back.

**

"May I help you?"

The red headed white woman behind the bank counter peered over her glasses at Merry, aggravated. The first of the month at a bank in a Colored neighborhood was always too much to handle, especially for a white woman who deep down thought it wasn't fair that the government was giving handouts to trifling, lazy Colored people no way.

Merry stepped up to the counter, too excited about her money to pay attention to the white woman's sourness. Merry slid her signed check over to her, proud.

"I came to cash my check."

The bank clerk snatched the check, flipped it over, pen in hand. She mumbled.

"Account number."

Merry mumbled back, confused.

"Account what?"

The woman slapped down the pen, peered over her glasses at Merry again.

"Young lady, I can't cash this check for you if you don't have an account with our bank. You have one, don't you?"

"I do. I just don't know what it is. My mother..."

"What's her name?"

"Excellent. Excellent Mavis."

The bank clerk huffed and walked over to the file cabinets lining the back wall. A middle-aged mulatto looking man waiting in line behind Merry grumbled. Merry glanced over her shoulder at him. That pasty look-like-a-white man could grumble all he wanted to. He was just going to have to wait his turn like she did.

The grumpy woman bank clerk stepped back up to the counter, slid the check back to Merry. Merry didn't pick it up.

"What's wrong? Didn't you find the account?"

"Yes. You're listed on a savings account with your mother, but I can't help you."

"Why not?"

"Because of your age. Only your mother is allowed to cash or deposit your government check."

"But it's my money. Money for me and my baby."

The woman shrugged, her disdain for Merry's welfare teenaged mother self showing all over her pale face. She waved Merry away and the mulatto man forward both at the same time.

"Without your mother's permission, young lady, there's nothing I can do."

Merry stuffed the check into her purse and stomped out of the bank. Without Excellent's permission, her ass! She picked up her pace, her mind in such a furious haze, that she didn't even hear Terry calling out for her. He caught up with her, grasped her arm.

"Dora."

Merry swerved around, ready to fight. Terry raised his hands in mock surrender.

"Hey, whatever it is, I didn't do it."

Terry looked silly. A grown man, one hundred sixty pounds and four inches shy of six feet tall, frightened of the wrath that all of Merry's five foot two, 100 pounds could bring. Merry grinned, her anger dissolving like sugar cubes in hot water. Terry smiled.

"They run out of money or somethin'?"

"What?"

"The bank. Are those fools out of dollars?"

Merry laughed. Terry was corny, but that didn't stop her lips from curling up into a smile. She answered mid-chuckle.

"No."

Terry strolled next to her, not about to let her go.

"Oh. Then what's the problem, sweet Dora?"

Merry glanced down the street for the Russell bus that wasn't coming. She didn't need to look at the way the sun was hanging in the sky or ask Terry what time his watch had to know that she had been gone from the house longer than she expected.

What was her problem? Merry's problem was she could never tell the man the truth. Instead, she would just have to tell Terry what she needed. Another gift. A ride.

*

Merry gripped the leather seat. She had never been in a truck before. Let alone a mail truck. The ride was bumpy and jerky, nowhere near as smooth as riding in Silas' or Corn's car. Didn't help that Terry was a lead foot on the brakes and the gas, either.

"Terry, the car!"

Terry swerved just in time to miss a man opening his driver's side car door. He looked at her, cool.

"Sweet Dora, I've been drivin' since before I could walk, you don't have to worry about a thin'."

"You right. Can't be worried when you're dead."

Terry laughed, stopped at a red light.

"Damn, girl. You think my drivin's that bad?"

Merry eyed him. Terry chuckled.

"Hmph. My wife says the same thing."

His wife. Merry knew Terry was married. Couldn't deny the out-of-place looking wedding band on his hand. But in the whole month Terry had been wooing her, he had never once mentioned his ball and chain. Merry hadn't brought her up either. They were having too much fun, playing with fire.

The light turned green. Terry stepped lightly on the gas, drove slower. Merry peeked out her rolled down window.

"Are the police behind us?"

"Why you say that?"

"You're not trying to kill me anymore."

"Come on now, Dora. If I kill you, who's going to go out dancing with me on Tuesday night?"

Merry crossed her legs, coy.

"Who says I want to go out with you on Tuesday night?"

Terry grinned, sweet talk dripping from his lips.

"There's this new spot I want to take you to, show you off. What size you wear?"

Merry uncrossed her legs, told him. She also told her married mailman to let her out a few doors down from her house, just in case any of her nosey neighbors were looking.

Terry beeped the horn as he drove past Merry heading up her walkway. She could hear Jr. Baby's loud screeches and wailing from inside the house. Everyone could. Especially, Felton who was waiting, angry, on the porch.

Merry walked up the steps, took out her keys. Felton stood up, a rise in his usual timid voice.

"Where have you been? He's been crying for a half hour."

"I had something to do."

"With the mailman? Since when did the mailman start giving rides?"

Merry ignored Felton's question, opened the door. He hurried inside behind her, toward the stomach curdling cries of Jr. Baby back in her bedroom. Merry hung up her jacket in the hallway, stepped out of her shoes.

Felton came back out of the room, bouncing their relieved, still teary-eyed son in his used to be skinny arms. No longer skinny as telephone wire, Felton's arms were bigger from loading and tossing back breaking bundles of newspapers off a truck every day before dawn and working part-time making screws for army tanks in a factory. He was taller, too. And older. In the face, especially. Gone was the naive bookworm Merry met and bedded over a year ago. Felton was now a workingman that provided for his family.

The day after Jr. Baby was born, Felton had promised Merry that he would help take care of their son. And he had.

Homeless, because his Aunt Florise had put him out, Felton begged the lady that owned the boarding house on Dequindre and Davison to let him stay there rent free in exchange of him doing odds and ends around the place until he found a job. Instead of one job, he found two. And school? Felton walked away from the honor roll without looking back.

Without question, her baby's daddy had sacrificed. And any other day, Merry was glad to have Felton and his extra change around to help out with the baby. But right now, Merry just didn't feel like being bothered with him. And she definitely didn't want the boy all up in her business.

Merry headed into the kitchen. Felton, on her heels, grilled her.

"Why didn't you take him with you?"

"He was asleep."

"So, you just left him?"

Merry took the leftover meatloaf out of the refrigerator and got a knife out of the drawer.

"I wasn't gone that long."

"You're not supposed to leave him at all, Merry. What if something had happened?"

Merry gripped the handle of the knife as she sliced through the cold meatloaf, visions of stabbing Felton and his talking- down-to-her-attitude right between his four eyes.

"Damn, boy, if you care so much, why don't you change his nasty ass diaper!"

Merry starred at Felton, knife in hand, looking and sounding every bit like her momma. Both of them.

Felton stepped back, deflated, threatened. Jr. Baby reached out for Merry. Felton grabbed their son's hand, pulled it close to his chest.

"Don't leave him again, Merry. He's just a baby."

Felton turned and left, leaving Merry feeling caged in. What did the boy think she was, stupid? Hell yes, Merry knew Jr. Baby was just a baby. Her baby. She didn't need to be reminded of it any more than a killer in Sing Sing needed to be reminded of his life sentence.

SAY. IT. AGAIN.

Merry tossed and turned. Excellent was downstairs in the basement again, humming and sewing on the machine Merry's money paid to get out of the pawn shop and Merry could hear it whirring, faint, from underneath the closed basement door, through her thin bedroom walls.

Merry popped open her eyes, heard Jr. Baby snoring in his crib ahead of her. She sat up, clicked on the lamp by her bed, aggravated. She wanted to go down in the basement and tell her mother that she was going to turn her in for stealing her government check to buy sewing machines and Lord knows what else. But what Merry wanted to do and what she had the balls to do were two different things.

Merry grabbed her *Romeo and Juliet* book, fell back on the bed, defeated. She opened it and out fell Corn's returned letter.

After Excellent had treated her worst than roach snot in the basement that night, Merry had forgotten all about the letter. She figured that her mother's words professing how proud she was must have just been something Excellent felt she had to say to make herself look better. But it was all just a lie to hide what Merry knew to be true. Her mother didn't give a damn.

Merry unfolded the letter. She didn't want to read it again, but there was something she did want to see. Her mother's handwriting. Just like she remembered, Excellent's penmanship was neat, yet controlled and flowing at the same time. It would be hard to copy, but not impossible.

Merry held the letter up to the lamp. No one had ever questioned when she made her momma's letters and she had even fooled Excellent into coming all the way down to Locust Grove with the note she had written in Dora's handwriting. So, the white folks at the bank? They'd be so busy thinking that Colored folks were beneath them, Merry had no reason to worry about them examining her handwriting with a fine toothcomb. She grabbed a piece of paper and a pencil stub off of her dresser, placed the paper over the letter, started tracing.

Confident that she had the flow of her mother's signature, Merry wrote Excellent's name out without tracing, held them side-by-side. Not bad.

Out in the hallway, she heard a thump. Merry shoved her handwriting samples underneath the covers, expecting Excellent to stick her head into the room to tell her to go back to sleep. But Excellent was still in the basement sewing. Merry started to write again. Another thump. She got up and poked her head out of her room, just in time to see Johnson's bedroom door push close.

Something was going on. Merry had been awake for a little while mastering her mother's handwriting and her brother hadn't once shuffled by her bedroom to go to the bathroom. Why was his door closing all of a sudden?

Merry swung open Johnson's bedroom door, scaring him half to death. He was dressed and sitting on the edge of his bed, taking off of his sneakers. New sneakers that Excellent probably bought for him with her money, Merry thought. Johnson yelled at her in a loud whisper.

"Girl, what's wrong wit' you?"

Merry crossed her arms, ready to exact revenge.

"Where you been?"

"Where you think?"

Merry rolled her eyes. Laying up under Lonnie was written all over Johnson's grinning face. Merry turned to leave. Johnson fumbled for something under his bed.

"Wait, I wanna show you somethin'."

Johnson pulled out a long, thin rectangular jewelry box and opened it. Inside was a nice watch trimmed in gold and with a shiny, black leather strap. Johnson beamed.

"Think Lonnie'll like it? The man at the pawnshop said it used to belong to some rich white man. I'm gone give it to Lonnie tomorrow for his birthday."

Johnson admired the watch, too proud of himself. Merry eyed the short sleeve, striped shirt he was wearing and a fluffy, round pillow on his bed.

"Didn't Delores give you that shirt and make you that ugly pillow for your birthday?"

Johnson snapped the jewelry box closed, slid it back under his bed.

"You and the old mailman do it yet?"

"No. And I don't have to play the fool and buy him stuff neither."

"Stupid, that ain't nothin' but sloppy seconds from his wife."

Johnson cackled. Merry felt the heat in her bones before her eyes rimmed over with it. She pounced him before he knew what hit him.

"Say. It. Again."

Johnson pulled at Merry's arms and gasped a laugh to hide the unexpected strength of her grip around his neck.

"Stupid...you got...sloppy...seconds."

Merry gripped tighter. Johnson flopped around - A wild mustang bucking to throw a cowboy off of his back. Merry held on, determined to get an apology out of her much bigger brother or strangle him. Whichever came first.

"Say. It. Again."

"Get..off...me!"

Johnson grunted. For air or for strength, Merry wasn't sure. Only thing she knew for sure was that they were rolling right off the bed. Merry, on her back with the wind momentarily knocked out of her, loosened her hold on her brother's neck. Johnson flipped around on her, reached out to grab her arms and pin her to the floor. Merry swung and pushed him. Then, she pounced him again. Like a wrestler.

Excellent couldn't turn on the light and get in the room good for them thrashing around, trying to kill each other.

"Merry! Johnson!"

Johnson heard Excellent, but Merry didn't. This was an ass whupping long overdue and nothing or nobody was going to stop her from kicking Johnson's selfish, sissy ass.

Excellent pulled Merry up by her gown collar, her arms still swinging.

"What the hell is wrong wit' you two?!"

Like tattletales, Merry and Johnson tried to outtalk each other. Excellent waved her right hand to quiet them, rubbed her throbbing head with the other.

"Shut up. Not another word."

"But Johnson deserved..."

"Naw, Ma! Merry, she..."

"I said shut up!"

Merry and Johnson silenced, glared at each other. Johnson definitely looked the worst for wear. His left eye was a little puffy. But Merry didn't have a scratch on her. Excellent growled.

"I don't care who started what, you both on punishment."

"But Ma! Merry hit me first!"

"So! You were sneaking in!"

Excellent, another shut up on the tip of her tongue, snapped her head to Johnson, finally noticed he was wearing pants.

"Where you comin' from Johnson?"

Johnson hesitated. Merry grinned. Her brother was trying to come up with a lie and her mother would see right through him. Finally.

Johnson lowered his head, mumbled.

"Lonnie's."

"What?"

Johnson looked up, started rambling.

"Lonnie really needed help with a project for school tomorrow and you were in the basement sewing and I know how much you like your sewing, Ma, so I didn't want to bother you..."

Excellent crossed her arms, listening. Merry couldn't believe it. Her mother was actually buying Johnson's load of crap. Johnson continued, growing more charming and confident with each word.

"...I thought I could just run over Lonnie's right quick, help him and get back home wit'out botherin' you. I'm sorry."

Johnson gazed at Excellent with puppy dog eyes. Just the thing that Merry had seen melt her mother's heart too many times to mention.

Excellent lifted Johnson's chin and looked at his puffy eye.

"Why you hit him, Merry?"

Excellent turned to Merry, expecting an answer. Merry croaked.

"'Cause..."

"'Cause what, Merry?"

Merry looked at Johnson poking out his tongue at her behind Excellent's back. Excellent glanced back at him. Johnson switched his face back to pitiful. The boy was good. Merry scowled. Excellent turned back in time just to see it.

"Merry, it's too damn late for this. Why did you hit your brother?"

"'Cause...he woke me up."

"He woke you up?"

"Yeah, I heard him coming in the window."

It was a weak lie and Merry knew it. All she needed was her mother to buy it. Excellent looked to both of them, everything making sense to her now.

"And that's why you two were rollin' 'round on the floor, tryin' to kill each other?"

Merry and Johnson nodded as pitifully as they could. Excellent looked at them, so not fooled.

"And I was gonna let you start playin' the piano again, but since you want to play me for a fool...One week, Merry. No visitin', no company, no phone."

Merry whined.

"But you said I could go to the movies with Kat tomorrow."

"Well, now I'm unsayin' it."

"That's not fair! What about Johnson?!"

Johnson grabbed Excellent's hand before she could answer.

"Ma, I'm sorry. I was just tryin' to help Lonnie. You always said a good Christian is 'sposed to be a friend to those in need."

"Uh huh. Make that two for you, Christian Soldier."

"Two?! Why?!"

"Boy, I already have one grandbaby. I don't need two."

"But, Ma!"

"And the next time you think you gone lie about being over that fast girl Dolores' house, wash up first. I can smell her on you."

Merry snickered. Excellent gave her the evil eye, pointed to the door. Merry swallowed her chuckles, shuffled out, laughter tickling her belly like butterflies.

By morning, those fluttering butterflies had turned into concrete caterpillars. As usual, Johnson had ruined everything. Because she couldn't control the justified urge to kick his ass, now she was stuck in the house and wouldn't be able to use Kat as an alibi to go out with Terry. Merry woke up so salty, she wanted to sock him in his other eye. Good thing Johnson was gone before breakfast.

Merry was still simmering when Excellent called to say that Mrs. Benson needed her to work late for an important dinner party. Mrs. Benson didn't work and Merry had no idea how Mr. Benson made his money, but those white folks were always having important dinner parties. Why they always waited to tell Excellent they needed her at the last minute, Merry didn't know. Right now, though, she didn't care. Excellent wouldn't be home tonight to play warden. Johnson, who she had absolutely no intention of telling the good news, would be come back home and report for lockdown. But Merry was going to go out with Terry as planned and be back in the house before her mother was the wiser.

Merry hung up the phone, dialed the boarding house for Felton, who was at work. She left a message and already had her jacket and shoes on when Dora arrived.

"Where you goin'?"

"Felton needs some more Cream of Wheat. I'll be right back."

"I talked to your momma 'bout the piano. She talk to you?"

Merry paused at the front door. She had gotten pretty good at lying since she moved to Detroit, but her momma could still read her like a book.

"No, what she say?"

"She said she was gone let you play. She ain't tell you?"

The same question twice. Merry knew that was a sure sign that her momma was on to her lying, or was at least suspicious. Merry opened the front door. She had to get out of there before Dora looked right through her and saw that she was on punishment, too.

"Maybe she forgot, Momma. You need anything from the store?"

Dora thought, then nodded her head no. Merry high-stepped out of there with the quickness. Her government check and forged permission letter from Excellent burning a hole in purse, she needed to get to the bank before the line got too long.

*

Merry was nervous. No, excited and nervous. She stood in front of the same sour teller from before, trying to play it cool. She had gone over the letter too many times to count.

It was too good for the still aggravated teller to be eyeballing it like she was. The woman looked up at Merry, her red hair clashing with her jet-black eyebrows.

"I have to show this to my manager."

Merry nodded. The woman could show her letter to President Truman for all she cared. Merry had set everything up perfectly. Her poor, God-fearing, widowed Colored mother was raising her and her sickly, younger brother with no help from anybody. And because she was slaving so hard cleaning homes day and night, it was impossible for her to make it to the bank herself. So, she wrote this letter of permission instead and told Merry to bring it to the bank.

Merry looked at the teller, talking to the balding white male manager and pointing in her direction. He said something Merry couldn't hear and the teller walked back over to the counter in a clipped pace. Without saying a word, the teller pulled open her money drawer and laid out the bills in front of Merry.

By the time Merry got outside the bank, she was damn near hopping up and down. She had beaten Excellent by her own game with her mother's own handwriting and conned the white folks into giving her her money! Merry strolled past the bus stop, in such a good mood that she wanted to take her sweet old time and walk home instead.

Merry hummed out loud, swung her purse. She had half the mind to stop at the soda shop for a scoop of strawberry ice cream. As she stopped to mull it over, Merry saw a stout Colored woman striding out the side door of Mrs. Coffee's house, carrying two bulging brown paper bags.

Merry walked up the narrow driveway, stepped up to the side door. It was closed and the screen door was locked.

She started to knock, but rang the bell instead. Within seconds, she heard a pair of little feet tripping to the door. Then, silence. A small brown face peeked out through the side windowpane. It was Mrs. Coffee's grandson, Desmond. Cute, but odd looking, the lopsided boy was six going on thirty, had a big bubblehead and his nose was always running. He hiccupped, looking dead at her.

"Who is it?"

"Merry, Desmond. Mrs. Coffee here?"

Desmond opened the door and wiped his snotty nose with the back of his hand. He eyed Merry sideways.

"You got a big bootie. Let me squeeze it."

Before Merry could cuss the boy out almost transparent, blue-veined hand came out of nowhere and snatched him back by the collar. Mrs. Coffee, the neighborhood's booster and numbers runner, appeared in the doorway. The color of vanilla ice cream, she was a handsome albino woman with a wide nose, thin lips, no eyebrows and medium length snow-white hair. She unlocked the screen door for Merry with one hand, smacked Desmond with the other.

"Boy, I told you 'bout your nasty mouth. Go out back and get a switch."

Desmond hobbled around, trying to get away.

"But Granny!"

"Granny, nothin'!"

Mrs. Coffee grabbed and tossed Desmond outside next to Merry like a bag of trash. She smiled.

"Good to see you, Merry. Excellent sent you wit' her number?"

"No, Mrs. Coffee. I came for myself. I need a new pair of shoes. Heels."

"I see..."

Mrs. Coffee headed down to the basement.

"Come on down. See if there's somethin' you like."

The sounds of Nat King Cole's *Mona Lisa* floated up from the basement as Merry followed Mrs. Coffee downstairs. Two ladies -one older with big, thick glasses and the other pigeon-toed and in her 30s - were already rifling through the stolen racks of clothes just like there were shopping downtown at Hudson's. In the corner at a card table, Mrs. Coffee's loud talking, still pimpled-face 24-year-old daughter, Phylicia, was playing solitaire, popping gum and blabbing on the telephone. Taller than Merry, but thin as a child, Merry had no idea how she gave birth to Desmond, as big as that boy's head was. Mrs. Coffee starred at her daughter - a chocolate, nearly identical copy of herself - cleared her throat. Phylicia smacked her lips, hissed into the phone.

"Gurl, let me call you back."

Phylicia hung up the phone, handed her mother a bank deposit slip, defensive.

"I was only on for a minute."

Mrs. Coffee, always the businesswoman and not the type to air her dirty drawers in front of company, folded the slip in half and got back to the task at hand.

"Phylicia, this is Merry, Mrs. Mavis' daughter."

"Uh huh. You got a baby, right?"

Phylicia looked at Merry, not caring about her one way or the other. Too bad Merry couldn't say the same. She didn't like Phylicia. As classy and professional as Mrs. Coffee was, her only daughter was rude and crude. Despite that, Mrs. Coffee still employed Phylicia in her boosting enterprise. And everybody knew the reason - Phylicia was a master, but reckless lifter. And whenever the police caught her stealing, Mrs. Coffee would bail her out and make Phylicia work in the basement until she learned her lesson. But sure enough, no more than a month or two of back working the stores, she'd get busted. And the cycle would start all over again.

Mrs. Coffee laid her hand on Merry's shoulder.

"Show Merry the new shoes we got in last night. If we don't have what she wants, let me know."

Mrs. Coffee checked on her other customers while Merry followed Phylicia behind a curtain to a closet. Phylicia pulled on the chain to turn on the light, exposing about thirty-five pairs of women's shoes of all brands and sizes still in shiny, new boxes. Then, she walked away. Merry called after her.

"Hey, which ones are the heels?"

Phylicia popped her gum, loud, kept walking.

"I look like I sell shoes?"

Merry rolled her eyes, looked at the boxes. She needed a pair of sharp heels, red ones, to go with the sexy red dress that Terry had bought for her. Low-cut, short and tight, the dress was too grown for Merry, but she liked it.

The only thing she needed now to complete her red-hot look was a pair of heels. The church girl pumps and patent leather flats Excellent made her wear weren't going to cut it. Not tonight.

Merry started searching where her eyes first landed, then worked her way down to the bottom. Would have been too much like right for the shoes to be organized by size. Merry pulled over a folding chair, climbed on top of it to get a better look at the higher stacked shoe boxes in the closet. Nothing.

"I'm sorry, Merry. Listen, I have a girl shoppin' this afternoon. I'll have her pick you up a pair a nice heels and you can come get 'em tomorrow."

"Actually, Mrs. Coffee, I need the shoes for tonight."

"Oh. And you sure we don't have anythin' for you?"

"No, no size six at all."

"Size six?"

Merry nodded. Mrs. Coffee cut her eyes to an eavesdropping Phylicia, who was pretending to play solitaire.

"Phylicia."

"What I do now?"

Mrs. Coffee said nothing. Phylicia huffed and got up from the card table, grumbling.

"Don't know why I can't keep 'em. Everybody else be keepin' stuff."

Phylicia stomped around the bar, starred at Merry.

"What color?"

"Red."

"Red?! But it's only one pair..."

Mrs. Coffee cleared her throat. Phylicia dropped underneath the bar, bolted back up with a box and thrust it out to Merry. Merry took the box, lifted off the lid. Inside was a pair of size six red heels.

Just what she needed.

SEE WHAT HAPPENS
WHEN YOU DON'T SPEAK?

"**What** movie are you and Kat going to see, again?"

Merry sat down on her bed, slipped on her heels. Felton, jealous, was lurching around her bedroom doorway, bouncing Jr. Baby in his arms. She rolled her eyes.

"Last time I checked my daddy was dead."

Merry, her red dress snug in all the right places, put on her lipstick in the mirror, careful, deliberate. Felton watched her.

"Just doesn't look like you're going to the movies. That's all."

Merry cut her eyes to Felton, her tongue razor sharp enough to slice him. Terry's car horn honked outside before she could.

Merry smiled, brushed past Felton to get her sweater.

"I'll be back before Excellent gets home, Felton. If I'm not, tell her I'm in the bathroom."

"The bathroom? Merry, your mother's not going to..."

Merry winked.

"I'm just playing."

Truth was, Merry was dead serious. She knew Felton was scared to death of Excellent. To make sure that the boy wouldn't even have to think about lying, Merry knew she needed to be back in her pajamas and Felton had to be good and gone before her mother got home.

Merry could feel Felton's eyes watching her from the house as she sashayed down the walkway to her married mailman. Terry, handsome in a chocolate brown suit, hat and tie, was eating Merry up with his eyes, too. He opened the door for her and whispered into her ear as she got into the car.

"Dora, you look good enough to eat."

Good enough to eat? Hell, Merry felt good enough to be slopped up with a biscuit! And she was ready. Riding in her married man's car, his hand on her leg, his mind already in her panties, Merry was ready to give it to him.

High and floating from Terry's attention, Merry took her time walking down the steps. Down in the pit of the Black Bottom warehouse, the house band -a growling piano man, drummer, bass player and skinny horn player - boogie woogied through a rocking blues tune while a big, bosom, hippy high yella woman wailed on the microphone.

Outlining the packed, shellacked dance floor were a spattering of green velvet cushioned booths and dozens of small, round white table clothed tables. Most of them full. And the air - blue from cigarette smoke and anticipation - smelled of cologne, the Detroit river and fried shrimp.

The hostess escorted Merry and Terry over to a table close to the front. Terry held the chair out for Merry and she grinned at him, her mind flopping like a hog in cool mud.

"You like it?"

Merry shrugged, pretending to not be impressed.

"What's to like? Just a joint in a basement."

"Just a joint in a basement? You see that line outside?"

"Yeah. Saw you give the man a twenty, too."

Terry smiled. He reached across the table, held her hand.

"Nothin' gets by you. Does it, sweet Dora?"

Merry pulled back her hand, playful.

"Let's dance."

Merry was up out of her seat before Terry had a chance to argue. The music was fast, frantic, the rocking rhythm and blues stuff that Terry liked. Merry checked out the woman throwing down next to her, got a mental picture of the steps and went for it. Terry took her hand, spun her around fast like a top and Merry fell right into him, her body following his without thinking. The man could move.

Both panting and sweating when the song was over, Terry wanted to dance one more again, but Merry's feet were throbbing so tough thanks to her virgin dance in heels, she needed to sit down. Merry headed off the dance floor, then stopped dead in her tracks. Silas, looking as cool as ice water, was on the sidelines talking to King Kong.

It took a second for Merry to catch her breath. She hadn't seen Silas since that day he got her zooted in the car. And she had been too scared shitless to think of him after his baby momma, Lizzy, tried to cut a smile in her neck outside

Plan B's. But now that he was in front of her, all of the feelings Merry had for him rushed back up to the surface.

Silas looked at her, his eyes taking in the new curves of her body. Merry glanced over her shoulder at Terry hooping it up with some man at a table and stepped up to Silas, confidant. She looked good. And they both knew it. She could see the grin playing dead at the corner of Silas' lips.

Merry's shifted her eyes to King Kong, cutting off Silas' singsong greeting before he could get it out of his mouth.

"Hey, King Kong. Remember me?"

King Kong, beady eyes already bloodshot red, eyeballed Merry and grinned.

"You all grown up, Jailbait. All grown up. How you like my place?"

"This your place, King Kong?"

King Kong's toothpick grin turned into a switchblade scowl.

"You think Scottie's cheap ass the only one can have a place, Jailbait?"

Silas snorted a sarcastic chuckle. Merry shot him a helpless look.

"No, King Kong...I was..."

Silas placed his hand on King Kong's shoulder.

"King, man, look like yo' ole lady's huntin' for you. Gone see what she want befo' she shut the place down."

King Kong, chest puffed out like an orangutan ready to fling shit, stomped away. Silas leaned in close to Merry, his lips brushing her ear.

"See what happens when you don't speak?"

Merry, her sweet spot boiling over, didn't answer. Then again, her silence was always all the answer Silas ever did need.

"Dora, everythin' alright?"

Merry felt Terry behind her before she heard him. The dry heat of his jealousy wasn't just peppering his speech, it was oozing through his pores. Silas looked at Terry, stepped back, unthreatened.

"Dora, huh?"

Merry spun around and faced Terry, her hands on his chest.

"Everything's fine, baby. He was just asking me where the bathroom was."

Terry eyed Silas again, suspicious. Silas stared right back at him, his cold, indifferent gaze hovering somewhere between I don't give a damn and I already had her. Merry touched Terry's face, trying too hard to be seductive.

"Baby, I like this song. Let's dance."

It was a slow number, something they could bump and grind to. Merry led Terry by the hand to the dance floor, all the while knowing that Silas was watching. He might have been acting like he didn't care. But Merry knew that he did. Because for the first time, Silas had competition. And whether he would admit it or not, Merry knew that a grown fine man salivating all over her had to be a knife in Silas' side that made him want to taste her for himself.

Terry's soft hands fit around Merry's hips like they belonged there. With one eye on Silas, Merry slid his hands down to cup her plump behind and rolled her hips like a grown woman who knew where babies came from. Terry moaned into her ear.

"Girl, what you tryin' to do to me?"

Merry eyed Silas again. He was looking right at her. Like there was no other woman in the room. Then a woman's thin, gloved arms embraced Silas' chest from behind and she kissed him on his neck. It was Lizzy.

Silas turned to face Lizzy and Merry lost a step. Like a puppet cut from a string, she felt like she was falling and the only thing keeping her from hitting the ground was Terry. Terry, so horny, didn't notice.

Merry pulled away. Silas and Lizzy were on the dance floor not far from them now and Merry couldn't breathe. Terry looked at Merry, confused.

"What's wrong, Baby?"

"I need to sit down."

No, what Merry needed to do was to stomp over to Lizzy and take her man. But she was too afraid to do it. Merry fought the urge to make a run for the door. And when she and Terry got back to their table, she immediately regretted not following her first mind.

"Merry!"

Kat, zooted and sloppy drunk, jumped up and wrapped her arms around Merry's neck. Raymond and Allen, his cousin from the movie theater, sat with her and Terry's table, both just as glassy eyed as Kat. She snuggled up to Merry, tight, and slurred, loud.

"Girl, you were...right. He...IS...handsome."

Kat turned her head to Terry, giggled. Merry pried herself away, thinking fast. She hadn't had a chance to tell Kat that she told Terry her name was Dora. All Kat knew was that Terry was her handsome, sugar daddy, who spoiled her with attention, gifts and money.

Merry glanced at an agitated Terry, whispered to Kat with a crooked smile.

"Kat, what you doing here?"

Kat swung around, pointed to Allen, proud.

"We're ce...le..brating! Al...len's go...ing to kill...Koreans!"

Terry shook his head, disapproving. Merry looked surprised. She had no way of proving it, but she had always sensed something slight about Allen. A fragileness that only comes from boys who love men.

"You joined the Army, Allen?!"

Allen rocked up to his feet, saluted.

"Yes, Ma'am! I ship out first thing in the mornin'..."

He and Raymond laughed and slapped hands. Terry chuckled. Raymond focused his glassy eyes on him.

"What's so funny, Old Man?"

Terry shrugged, took his hands out of his pockets.

"Youngster dumb enough to sign up to die, that's his problem. This is our table."

Raymond smiled. Merry tensed. She hated that smile.

"This table?"

"Right."

"It's a good table. I had my pick of any table in here. And this is the one I picked."

Terry took a step forward, the ass whupping he needed to give Raymond tattooed all over his face.

"Well, unpick it."

Merry glanced at Kat, nervous. Kat and Allen, high and wanting to be entertained, oohed and aahed. Raymond stood up, still smiling.

"Or what, Old Man? You gone make me? Or you gone bitch up like you did last time?"

Raymond puckered his lips, made a smooch kiss sound. Terry swung. Raymond reeled back, threw a vicious uppercut that should of killed Terry, but just made him madder. Three minutes and two overturned tables later, it took four men to separate them.

"She coming or not?"

Raymond snatched away the napkin that Kat was dabbing his busted, bloody lip with, angry. Merry, corner man to a body bruised Terry, overheard him. She handed Terry a shot of calm down. Kat, high blown, tapped Merry on the shoulder.

"Merry, you ready?"

Merry looked from Terry to Kat, stepped off to side with her friend.

"Why don't you come with us? Terry can take you home."

"You're choosing that old man over us?!"

"No, it's just..."

Merry's eyes floated over Kat's shoulder to Silas huddled with Raymond. They both eyed Terry and Terry, unafraid and alone, starred right back. This wasn't over. Merry still didn't know who Raymond was, why grown men trembled from the very sight of him. But she knew exactly who Silas was. Terry was marked, a target. And at least, if she left with the man now, Merry hoped she could save his life tonight.

Kat tugged on Merry, serious.

"Merry, I'm telling you, you need to come with us."

"What's Raymond gonna do?"

"Why do you care?"

"I don't!"

"Then come with us."

Merry hesitated, almost swayed by the pleading in her friend's voice.

"I can't, Kat."

Merry would have been better off slapping Kat in the face. It wouldn't have hurt her so much.

"Merry, I'm tellin' you, it's alright. You can go wit' your friends."

"No, that's O.K, I came with you and...What'd you call me?"

Terry grinned, kept walking. Merry grilled him in the car.

"How do you know my name?"

"How do you know mine?"

Terry took a swig from his flask. Merry crossed her arms, guilty. He handed her the flask and she took a swig. Terry watched, amused.

"I don't forget a face, Merry. Hard to ignore those welfare checks you get every first of the month, too."

Terry chuckled, cutting short Merry's drink.

"You lied to me!"

"I lied to you? You lied to me!"

"Yeah! But not on purpose! I just did it 'cause I thought...I thought..."

"You thought if I knew that baby was yours and that boy starring me down tonight from the doorway was your baby's daddy, I wouldn't like you."

Merry nodded. Terry touched her face, tender.

"Merry, if I didn't like you 'cause you had a baby, that's like me not likin' my wife for havin' my kids."

Merry threw the flask down on the car floor, her heart in her throat and hand on the doorknob.

"Well, gone be with your wife then!"

Terry caught Merry by her arm, desperate.

"Merry, I'm sorry."

Terry stumbled and Merry, still mad, wanted him to beg for her sweetness some more. She tugged her arm, ready to bolt out of the car for him to chase. But Terry stopped her cold. With a kiss. And as her married mailman trailed his apology up her tingling arm to her moist lips, Merry was the one who was sorry.

Sorry she hadn't kissed his fine ass sooner.

HE'S GONE,
MERRY

Tomorrow. Noon. Merry's foot wasn't even out of Terry's car good and already she was smiling about when she was going to kiss him again. If she was lucky, her momma would be out running errands or visiting Ms. Ruthie and Terry would be able to put down his mailbag just long enough to come inside and give her a special delivery.

Smelling like hungry backseat loving and booze, Merry strolled down the street. She came crashing back down to earth when she saw her Uncle Warren hop out of his car, on a mission. Merry ducked behind a tree just in time to see him head into her house. The front door was wide open and every light was on inside. Something was going on. What, Merry didn't know. All she knew was that Excellent was home early. Felton with his scared butt had for sure sold her down the river. And Johnson, without question, was talking about her so bad, throwing gasoline on the fire.

Merry ran down the side of a neighbor's house through the backyard to the alley. Tip toeing to the back of her house, Merry ran the lie she was about to tell Excellent through her head like an Easter speech. Her plan was to go in through the back door and be changed and in her room before Excellent was the wiser. The only problem? Mr. Blackie was all up in the kitchen talking to somebody Merry couldn't make out.

What was Mr. Blackie doing up in her house tonight? Since Corn left, he had taken to sniffing back around her mother, fixing little things around the house and running errands just to get close to Excellent's sweetness. But Mr. Blackie usually only came around on the weekends when his mousey wife Berniece was away playing nursemaid to his sick mother. For him to be downstairs buzzing around Excellent when his wife was home, something had to be going on.

Whatever it was, Merry didn't care. She just needed to get inside the house someway, somehow. She waited for Mr. Blackie to turn his head, then jetted through the fence's gate for the basement door. More than once, Excellent had slapped Johnson upside the head for forgetting to lock it. More dependable than kitchen roaches in the dark, Merry could always count on her brother to be irresponsible.

Except tonight. Merry had no choice now but to walk into the lion's den, so her mother could beat her down. Merry took a deep breath and headed around the side of the house to the front. It was bad enough she smelled of liquor and loving. She didn't need to make it any worse by staggering in through the back door.

Merry passed underneath Johnson's bedroom window and looked up. Just her luck his trifling tail was in his room looking out for her, so he could run and tell Excellent. No sign of him. Merry stepped back to double-check. The window was cracked open just enough for her to slip inside his room.

Johnson's room was a mess as usual. But at least it was empty. Merry pulled off her dress and threw on one of Johnson's dirty shirts from a pile on the floor. Now all she needed to do was make it to the bathroom where she could brush her teeth and wash the smell of Terry off of her. Merry stuffed her dress under Johnson's junky bed, crept to the door and listened. She could hear Excellent talking with Uncle Warren. If they were pow wowing upfront in the living room, Merry could hug the wall of the hallway and maybe make it to the bathroom without anyone spotting her. But if they were in the kitchen, next door to Johnson's bedroom, she was trapped.

Merry cracked open the door, craned her neck to listen. They were in the living room. She could make it to the bathroom easy. Merry took a timid step just as the bathroom door swung open. She hopped back inside and closed the door back, praying that whoever that was didn't see her. No such luck.

The doorknob was turning and Merry had no time to hide.

Dolores stuck her head inside, worried.

"Johnson? Is that you?"

Merry yanked Dolores into the room and pushed the door shut. Before the girl could say another word, Merry plopped her hand over her mouth.

"Dolores, I'm gonna move my hand, O.K.? But you gotta be quiet. You promise to be quiet?"

Dolores, wanting to talk so bad, nodded her head, fast, like an anxious dog wagging his tail. Merry removed her hand and Dolores threw her arms around her neck, frantic.

"Oh, Merry! It's terrible!"

"What's terrible?"

Dolores sniffed and pulled back, her face scrunched up. She looked at Merry, suspicious.

"Where have you been?"

"The movies. With Kat."

Dolores peered at Merry, insulted, then angry.

"You didn't go to the movies. Your momma's worried sick about you and Johnson and you didn't even go..."

"Johnson? What's wrong with him?"

"He's gone, Merry."

"Gone where?"

"We don't know! I called to see if he was O.K., because he didn't come to summer school today. Your momma answered the phone and didn't know what I was talking about. So, she called Coach Williams to see if Johnson had just played hookie from school, but showed up for summer league practice..."

"That boy's probably over Lonnie's."

"He's not, Merry. Lonnie hasn't seen him, either."

Merry paused. Johnson was up and gone when she got up this morning. Him not making it to summer school or regular school for that matter was not out of the ordinary, but him not seeing Lonnie? That was cause for alarm. Johnson was always up under Lonnie just for general principle. But today was special. Today was Lonnie's birthday and Johnson was so excited to give him the watch. Nothing, not even Jesus, Himself, would have stopped him from doing that.

Merry looked at Dolores, neither one of them wanting to say out loud what they were thinking. Down South, Colored boys coming up missing only meant one thing. The good white folks in white sheets and white hoods who would never be found guilty by a white judge or white jury of murdering a nigger were to blame. It didn't happened up

North much. White city folks, in general, pointed their nose down at their barbaric country cousins solving their problems by lynching, burning, dragging and drowning Colored boys and men.

But lately, there was a hot wind of tension blowing in Detroit that had everybody - Colored and white - on edge. The other day, a young Colored man suspected of stealing a pack of cigarettes was damn near beaten to death by a group of white men making a "citizens' arrest." Turns out, no surprise to Colored folks, of course, the man was innocent.

The territorial honkies really beat his uppity ass, because he was fool enough to believe that he deserved to be on the other side of Woodward after dark.

Then, a few weeks ago, yet another Colored family barely escaped with their lives from their burning home while their neighbors - God fearing, cross burning white folks - watched, delighted. And there were all the little incidents that happened every day in between. The looks, the stares, the things that added up day after day that brought the memory of the 1943 race riots closer to the surface. The air between white and Colored folks was so brittle, so dry, that it felt like Detroit was one spark away from a Colored man being killed for "raping" a white woman, or white men throwing a Colored woman and her child over the Belle Isle Bridge. Didn't matter that neither lie wasn't true. The fear that either could happen was truth enough to spark violence. Truth enough to claim her brother as a victim.

Merry's throat went dry. Suddenly, the ass whupping she was trying to avoid didn't matter anymore. Dolores handed Merry a piece of hard candy out of her pocket and picked the shirt she gave Johnson for his birthday up off the floor.

"Suck on this and wipe your face. I'll get you some more clothes."

If somehow between the long dead-man-walking path from her brother's room to the living room Merry forgot how serious the situation was, all she had to do was look at Excellent's face to get set straight.

"Where you been, Merry? And think twice 'fore you answer. Warren went by the theater, you wasn't there."

Excellent peered at Merry, hands at her side, ready to slap her. Uncle Warren and Mr. Blackie looked at her, too, waiting for an answer. Dolores, the only one that had smelled Merry's truth on her breath, starred at the floor, her eyes glued to a rip opening up on a worn patch of the carpet. Merry started lying, trying not to ramble.

"We went to the show earlier, then me and Kat got some ice cream after and..."

Excellent slapped Merry so lightening fast, she didn't even see her mother's hand before she felt the hot sting of it.

"Johnson could be out there hangin' from a tree and you still gone lie to me?!"

Merry mumbled, her eyes welling up with tears.

"I'm sorry."

"Damn right, you sorry. Go to your room. I'll deal with you when I'm done."

"But..."

Excellent lunged toward Merry, hand raised.

"Merry, swear to God, you don't get out my sight..."

Merry jumped, her words her only protection.

"But I can help!"

Merry cowered, hands up to shield herself. She opened her eyes to the sound of Mr. Blackie's voice.

"Maybe she can, Excellent. Merry was the last person to see Johnson. Maybe she can tell the police somethin'."

Uncle Warren grunted.

"Tell 'em what?"

"I don't know...What kind of clothes he was wearin'..."

"How you know they don't already know that?"

"How could they?"

"How could they?! Man, nine times out of ten, the cracker police the ones behind it!"

Excellent peered at Warren, furious.

"Warren, don't start this shit..."

"Excellent, I'm sorry. But I still say you don't need to be goin' to the damn police..."

"Then what do you say I do, Warren? Nothing?! While my baby's out there hang..."

Excellent stopped the word in her throat, too pained to speak it aloud. Merry looked at her mother, the same word Excellent couldn't say turning to salt on her own tongue. Uncle Warren shook his head, upset, and Dolores' mouth, for the first time in her short life, wasn't running. Mr. Blackie picked up his hat, stepped towards Excellent.

"C'mon, Excellent, I'll carry you down to the police station."

Uncle Warren barked.

"Johnson's my damn blood, Blackie. I'll take her."

Mr. Blackie darted a look to Uncle Warren, then back to Excellent.

"Excellent, you sure?"

"What the hell you mean, she sure?"

Uncle Warren stepped up to Mr. Blackie, aggravated. He had been out half the night searching the streets for a nephew that deep down in his bones he believed was hanging from a Belle Isle tree or sleeping at the bottom of Lake Michigan with a charbroiled tire around his neck, and he couldn't do anything about it. But he could crack open Blackie's head for meddling in family business. At least that would make him feel less powerless.

Excellent slipped on her sweater, ignoring the heat exchanging between Uncle Warren and Mr. Blackie.

"Gone to work, Warren. I don't need to hear Lois' mouth 'bout you losing pay."

"Lois don't run me, Excellent."

"Uh huh. Dolores..."

"I'll watch the baby and I can stay as long as you need me, Mrs. Mavis. My daddy said so."

"Thank you. Blackie, Merry, let's go."

*

As much as Uncle Warren hated the police, Merry was sure she was going to find white cross burning police officers protecting and serving in white sheets and white hoods. Truth was, Merry was actually surprised to find an entire station filled with white police officers in starched, dark blue uniforms and spit shined black shoes. Judging from the fast way the smile on the Officer Friendly's face disappeared when she, Excellent and Mr. Blackie walked into the station, though, Merry could tell that her uncle really wasn't that far off the mark.

Excellent cleared her throat.

"Excuse me, Officer. Is Officer Petosky available?"

"Who's asking."

"Mrs. Mavis. Excellent Mavis."

"What do you want with him, Excellent Mavis."

"It's my son. He..."

"You pay bail here with me. What's your boy's name."

"Officer, my son's not in jail. I'm afraid something's happened..."

"How old is your boy."

"He's thirteen."

Officer Friendly folded down his newspaper, smirked.

"*Something* didn't happen to your boy. Some black tail did."

Officer Friendly snorted a sarcastic chuckle and his fellow officers joined in. Merry glared at all of the police officers' laughing pink faces, wanting to pop them all in their snarling white mouths. She snapped instead.

"You're wrong, Officer. My brother wouldn't worry us like that. He doesn't even like..."

Officer Friendly, Mr. Blackie and Excellent zeroed in on Merry, ripping the words out of her mouth before she could swallow them. Officer Friendly smiled wider, spoke loud enough for the whole precinct to hear him.

"Put out a APB, Boys! We got a nigga fairy on the loose!"

All of the officers roared. Merry, Excellent and Mr. Blackie stood silent, angry. Excellent took a step toward Officer Friendly, placed her hand, calm, on the top of his help desk.

"Officer, that sign above your head says you're in the business of protecting and serving. You, all of you took an oath to do that, didn't you?"

The police officers, like bad schoolboys getting scolded by their teacher, stopped laughing. And Officer Friendly's smile evaporated from his thin lips faster than steam from his hot cup of coffee. Excellent looked right at him.

"My son knows better than to stay away from home, Officer. He needs protecting."

Merry kept her eyes trained on Officer Friendly. Cronies on each side of him, he was starring back at her mother, cold, like he wanted to jump over the desk and beat her head in with his baton. Excellent, an angry momma bear searching for her missing cub, stood her ground, damn near daring him to do it. Mr. Blackie, scared, reached for her arm.

"Excellent, maybe Warren was right. We can handle this on our own..."

"No, Blackie. I came here to get help for Johnson and I'm not leaving until I get it."

Officer Friendly still peered at Excellent. Silent. Merry, so nervous, would have swallowed her saliva if her mouth wasn't dry as dirt. She understood what her mother was doing, how Excellent was trying to make the police do their job and go out there and find Johnson. But even Merry could tell that Officer Friendly and his brothers in blue weren't about to be shamed into serving and protecting a nigga boy. Her mother was going to have to be content in leaving the police station without their help or end up not leaving the police station at all.

Merry peeked around the corner into the bullpen. If she could just find Officer Petosky, he could help.

She had only met him that night at the house, but he seemed different than that white wolf in sheep's clothing about to tear her mother to pieces in the police station lobby.

Merry darted around, asking the white police officers if they had seen Officer Petosky. They told her no and before they could her ask what her black tail was doing there, she'd bolt off to the next cop. Where was he?

Merry smelled the answer to her question as a strong whiff of smoke and urine trailed past her as a young officer exited the bathroom. That's where Petosky was. She was sure of it.

"Officer Petosky? You in there?"

No answer. Merry glanced around, fearful. The entire squad was watching her. Petosky's trigger-happy partner, Officer Gerald, pointed in her direction, started toward her.

Merry rapped on the bathroom door, panicking.

"Officer Petosky! Officer Petosky!"

Officer Petosky, fumbling with his belt and pants, yanked open the door.

"What?! What's the problem?"

Merry looked up at him, the unmistakable whiff of booze on his breath and the vacant look in his yellowing eyes. He didn't recognize her. She pleaded.

"My mother, Officer Petosky. She needs your help!"

"Your mother?"

Officer Petosky glanced around the station at everyone looking at them, just as his partner reached his side. Merry darted behind him. Officer Gerald grabbed her arm.

"Alright, girl. You've caused enough trouble. Time to go."

Merry tried to wiggle loose.

"But something's wrong with my brother. He didn't come home..."

"Yeah? I haven't been home in a week, you don't see my wife boo hooing about it. Let's go."

Officer Petosky stepped out of the way as Officer Gerald dragged her by. Merry reached out for him, begged one last time.

"Officer Petosky, you gotta help me. Please!"

Merry looked dead into his eyes. This time, she saw them flicker with recognition.

"Gerald, let her go."

Officer Gerald shook his head and let go of Merry's arm. Merry rubbed it, justified. Officer Petosky was different than other white men. Just like she remembered.

"What happened to your brother?"

Merry should have been the one to answer Petosky's question, but instead she let her mother take the lead. What they did know - Dolores and Lonnie hadn't seen Johnson all day and he hadn't made it to summer school or basketball practice. What they didn't know? Johnson had bought Lonnie a birthday gift. And he was supposed to give it to him today. Merry knew something terrible had to have happened to Johnson for him not to do that. Maybe some hood had knocked him out cold and stole it or worst yet, sliced him with a knife because he wouldn't give it up and her stupid brother was bleeding to death somewhere in an alley.

She blurted out, interrupting her mother.

"Johnson bought Lonnie a watch for his birthday."

"A watch? What kind of watch?"

"A nice one. Johnson was going to give it to Lonnie today."

Excellent shook her head, frustrated.

"Merry, that doesn't have anythin' to do with anythin'. Lonnie said he didn't see him."

"I know, but maybe..."

Officer Petosky finished Merry's sentence, on the same bloody page she was.

"Maybe someone robbed him for it."

Merry nodded.

"What kind of watch was it, Merry?"

Excellent shifted in her seat, attentive. Merry, not used to her mother paying her any mind, paused, uncomfortable.

"It was expensive. A watch a grown man would wear."

Officer Petosky pulled back his uniform shirtsleeve, showed Merry his workingman watch. The timepiece tick tock forgot, it had a dull, plain face and the tan leather band was worn and cracking.

"What did it look like? Did it look like mine?"

"No, it was nicer...I mean..."

Merry shot Excellent a nervous glance, stammered.

"I mean, it was different. It had a gold face and a shiny, black leather strap."

Officer Petosky scribbled in his notepad, a grin hiding behind his thin lips.

"Where'd Johnson get the watch, Merry?"

"He said he got it from the pawn shop on Dequindre."

"I know the one. If the watch was expensive like you say, the thief might of taken it back there to see how much money he could get for it. Me and my partner'll follow up on this. If we find the watch..."

"You'll find my son?"

Officer Petosky looked at Excellent, hesitated. Merry wasn't a mind reader, but she was pretty sure why the kind white man's tongue was reluctant. He didn't want to be held to a promise that all of them wanted him to keep. But none of them, not even Merry, herself, was sure that he could.

DETROIT,
1965

He promised. Silas' lying, junkie ass promised. Merry called from Chicago, told him she was getting on the 3:35 a.m. Greyhound bus to Detroit and he promised to meet Merry at the bus station. Said he was going meet her there looking good and smelling fine. Was going to have a dozen red roses and pocket full of bread to take her out on the town and drink Dom Perion, he said. They were going to party and celebrate that his Merry Merry was out. That his Merry Merry was free. That his Merry Merry was back in his life, his arms, his world.

Merry stood outside the bus station, feeling stupid. No doubt, Silas was high at their Brewster Project apartment, limp in between some dope fiend woman's legs, laughing about how Merry was waiting for him.

Hell, it'd be funny to Merry, too, if it wasn't so damn pitiful. Before Merry had gotten arrested and sent down South to the women's prison in Kentucky, she had destroyed just about every tie she had with her family in Detroit. Merry couldn't even remember how many times she had taken food out of her babies' mouths and stolen from Excellent. Merry had even robbed Teenie of some of her numbers running profits. And last she heard, Kat and Raymond had gone underground again. For all she knew, they weren't even in Detroit anymore. Sad, but true, Merry had nowhere else to go.

Merry knocked on the door, her keys in hand, clinking rhythmically against the worn wood. There was no jazz bleeding through the other side of the door. No sounds of people laughing, talking. Only silence and still, stale air.

Merry knocked again.

"Scottie? You in there?"

When Merry walked away from the bus station, she had had a plan to go to her and Silas' hole-in-the-wall apartment at Brewster Projects. She had no intention on stopping at

Scottie's. But when Merry walked by the alley leading to the place where she first met herself, the place where she was baptized in jazz and introduced to truth, she had to stop. And knock. And knock. And knock.

Merry pulled back her hand. Scottie's had no downstairs windows anyone could see from the alley, so Merry couldn't depend on boarded up windows as a clue that Scottie's had gone under. All she had to hold on to was the hope that Scottie's had survived. Jazz was dead. Paradise Valley had been mowed down by the city and Motown, led by that pretty green-eyed negro Smokey and that uppity project bitch Diana had Detroit singing and dancing to their sweet groove so tough, that anyone that had sweated, bled and breathed jazz, had died from suffocation.

Merry stepped back from the door, decided to come back to Scottie's tonight when it was supposed to be jumping. If the joint was still dark and silent then, then she would know.

Merry turned to walk away, stepped on a key. She checked her hand. She was still holding her own keys. Merry looked up. There were three small windows on the second floor. Painted shut, it looked like. Merry looked at Scottie's door. She didn't remember a key when she walked up to the door and she hadn't heard anything drop to the ground behind her the whole time she was knocking. If she had any sense, she'd leave the damn key right where they were and keep walking. Merry picked up the key.

The door opened, easy. To darkness. The only light on inside was coming from the other side of the swinging doors behind the bar.

"Scottie?"

"Back here, baby. In the kitchen."

Scottie's kitchen was nothing more than a small storage room with a stove, a refrigerator and crusty white chest freezer in it. The rickety wooden shelves were lined with boxes and cans of this and that, containers of used fish and chicken grease and seasonings. Scottie, grayer and wider than Merry remembered, was sitting in a green folding chair at her makeshift kitchen table, sipping coffee out of a teacup when Merry entered through the swinging doors.

"Damn, took you long enough! Come on over here and give me a hug, young lady!"

Scottie, too fat to rise, enveloped Merry in a bear hug and she sunk into her embrace. It felt good being. Merry hadn't really been hugged by someone that she loved and that loved her back, in years.

"You lookin' good, Merry! Real good."

"You, too, Scottie."

"If by good, you mean, fat, then you right. Merry, my ass is so damn wide, I can't get around like I used to. But you know I still handle my business."

Scottie held out her palm to be slapped. Merry gladly slid her a cool five.

"I know you do, Scottie. I know you do."

Merry sat down across from Scottie, laid her key down in between them on the table. Scottie glanced at it, took a sip from her teacup.

"Want some coffee, Merry?"

"Too early for coffee, Scottie. Got something stronger?"

Merry half-smiled. Scottie chuckled.

"Young lady, if you wanted somethin' stronger, you wouldn't of brought your ass to see me. When you get out?"

"Yesterday. Just got into town this morning."

"And here you are, sittin' across from me. I know Teenie glad you back."

Merry shook her head.

"She doesn't know. Nobody does."

Scottie set down her teacup, looked at Merry with compassionate eyes. She held her hand out to the side.

"Merry, help me up. My foot's swoll up like a grapefruit and..."

Merry hopped up.

"You need to go to the doctor, Scottie? I could drive..."

"Hell, naw. Those turkeys don't do nothin' but make it worse. Every time."

Merry got a hold underneath Scottie's large arm, helped her to her feet. Scottie's left foot was more than swollen; it was bloated.

"That looks bad, Scottie. If you won't let me take you to the doctor, let me help you upstairs, so you can get off it, lay down..."

Merry helped hold Scottie up as she took labored steps towards the swinging doors, her left foot almost dragging like a dead weight. Scottie fussed.

"I'm tired of layin' down, Merry. That's all I do. I gotta get you somethin' stronger."

"That's alright, Scottie. I can..."

"Naw, naw, Merry, you asked me for it. I'm gone get it."

They pushed through the swinging doors. Scottie steadied herself against the bar, pointed for Merry to go around and sit down. She flicked on the light.

The joint looked just like Merry remembered it. Tables and chairs in the same spots. The stage for the band up front -- although it was smaller and lower than the tall, big one from her memory. And the wall length mirror behind the bar. Merry swiveled around on her stool.

"Scottie, what the hell you doing with a jukebox?"

"Musicians hard to book these days. Half of them too high to play. The rest of them on contract with Motown, dead, gone or can't whistle in tune."

Scottie set a drink down behind Merry. She took one look at it, laughed. It was a glass of Vernors. Scottie winked.

"You still like bubbles, Merry?"

Merry toasted to Scottie.

"I love them."

Merry took a gulp. Scottie patted the bar, happy.

"How many cakes you want?"

"Scottie, you don't have to cook for me..."

"Merry, please I still burn some cakes now. Two or three?"

Scottie, moving easy and pain free on her own somehow, was already through the swinging doors and in the kitchen. Merry shook her head. No use in arguing with the old broad. She answered loud enough for Scottie to hear.

"Burn three for me, Scottie!"

"You got it, Baby!"

Merry took another sip of her Vernors, coughed. It was strong and the bubbles tickled her nose. She stood up to stretch her legs and her eyes landed on the piano upfront on the stage.

Merry sat down on the piano bench, lifted the dusty lid, touched a key. It was in tune. Just barely. She placed both hands on the piano keys, unsure. She didn't have a particular song in her head. The only thing she could think of were the bell chimes from some church she never saw when she was kicking a monkey off of her back in a hot-box prison hole in Kentucky.

Merry closed her eyes, started to play, unaware and unconcerned with how bad she sounded. Because in that moment? It didn't matter. It didn't matter that her children didn't know and love her or that her mother knew and didn't love her. Didn't matter that the only man she ever loved treated her worst than the cracker, rapist guards in prison ever could, yet she continued to love him anyway. Or that Merry, deep down, didn't love herself, couldn't love herself, because she had done so much wrong that she didn't feel worthy of it. The only thing that mattered to Merry? She wasn't an animal anymore. She wasn't trapped and caged in that Kentucky prison hot box, sweating and crying, shaking and shivering, hovering between life and death.

Merry was clean. Merry was free. And Scottie was making her pancakes.

DETROIT,
1949

Merry raked a half-eaten pancake into the garbage.

Eight days and counting. Johnson had been missing for over a week now and no one had been able to find one hair or strand of him. Merry coming clean on Lonnie's birthday watch turned out to be a dead end, too. If a thug had harmed her brother to get it, he had palmed the fine trinket for himself or peddled it to someone on his own instead of selling it back to the pawnshop.

Merry washed and dried the last plate of the breakfast dishes. Her momma, who had been holding a prayer vigil day and night, was upfront in the living room flinging blame at Excellent. Again.

"I nevah shoulda let my baby come up here wit' you..."

"From the way you told it, you didn't have a choice."

"Dat's right. I was tryin' tuh save Johnson. But looks like dey got him anyway. Danks to you."

Now Merry wasn't exactly the president of her mother's fan club, but even she knew that Johnson being gone wasn't Excellent's fault. Her momma just needed someone to blame. Someone she could lay hands on and make responsible for the disappearance of her favorite one.

But Excellent wasn't the one in the wrong. Lonnie was.

Something about Lonnie and that watch wouldn't stop gnawing at Merry. Everybody and their momma had been by the house twice since Johnson had come up missing, but Lonnie hadn't been by once. Dolores said he was just so torn up without his best friend. And Excellent seconded it. But Merry wasn't buying it. The boy was hiding something. And today, she was going to find out what it was.

Merry got the milk out of the refrigerator and filled up Jr. Baby's bottle. He had such a big appetite, Merry's titties were never ever really able to make enough milk to satisfy him. And the boy only got greedier once he started teething.

He would clamp down so tight on what little of a tittie Merry had, that he would draw milk and blood. Lucky for Jr. Baby, he was old enough now to drink primarily from the bottle, because Merry had already made it up in her mind that she wasn't going to give her son her precious titties to gnaw on anymore.

Merry screwed the nipple top back onto Jr. Baby's bottle and surveyed what was left of the milk. There was more than enough to fill another bottle. She poured the milk down the sink.

"We're out of milk."

Merry knelt down next to her son, who was lying on his back in the living room, playing and slobbering, his left foot in his mouth. Excellent and her momma stopped arguing long enough to turn their attention to her.

"I just bought some. He went through it already?"

"Whut you mean, already, Excellent? When Johnson wuz a baby he ate twice as much. Not dat you would know."

Merry set the bottle down on the coffee table, jumping in before her mother and momma could go for each other's throats again.

"This should hold him until I get back. Need anything?"

Merry looked at Excellent, not really interested in the answer. Excellent sat down, the thought about how Merry was going to pay for Jr. Baby's milk and anything else she might need not on her mind. It had been almost two weeks now since Merry forged Excellent's handwriting for the letter to the bank and cashed her government check, but Excellent had been so worried and distracted with Johnson being missing, she hadn't noticed. Excellent snapped.

"No. Just hurry back. Or should I go with her, Momma? Take Merry by the hand, so they don't get her, too?"

Excellent eyeballed Dora. Dora plopped her hand down on her hip. And Merry left, her momma's cussing for her mother whizzing by her ears. Poor Excellent. Merry was on the porch and down the steps before she was even able to get a word in edgewise.

**

Merry pushed her way through the crowd to get a spot up front. Lonnie's skins vs. shirts basketball games at the park were becoming the place everybody in the neighborhood - church folks, bookies and gamblers alike - wanted to be every Saturday. Despite how Merry felt about the boy, she had to admit he was too good putting that ball through the hoop. Just a sophomore in high school, Lonnie was faster than lightning, could dribble circles around players bigger than him and could jump higher than any and everyone on the court. He was a star. No doubt. But Merry didn't come to the park to blow up his sissy head any bigger than it already was. She came to look Lonnie in the eye and find out what he did to her brother.

"Good game, Lonnie."

Lonnie, shirtless and sweating, turned around, expecting to find one of his adoring girlfriends. Instead he found Merry. He glanced away, not able to look her in the eye.

"Merry...Sorry I ain't been by...I been meaning to, but..."

"Yeah, Dolores said you was real torn up about Johnson."

"Yeah. Yaw heard anythin' from the police or anybody?"

"No. You?"

Merry crossed her arms. Lonnie stumbled, trying to play it cool for his fans that were watching.

"Naw, how could I?"

"Come on, Lonnie..."

"Come on, what, Merry? What you talking 'bout, girl?"

"I'm talking about that watch, Lonnie. The one my brother gave you for your birthday."

Lonnie's posse looked at him, nosey, curious. Lonnie stepped up to Merry. He had a healing cut over his left eye. He grabbed Merry's arm, pulled her out of earshot.

"Johnson didn't give me nothin'. Alright, Merry?"

"Yeah, he did. You know he did."

"No, he didn't. I told your momma I ain't seen him. I ain't seen him."

A grin crept to Merry's face. Lonnie started back over to his friends. Merry spoke up, loud enough for everyone to hear.

"Johnson saved all his money up to buy the watch special for you, Lonnie. What's the matter, you didn't like it?"

Merry fluttered her eyes and smiled. Lonnie's eavesdropping fans chuckled and his crew looked on, embarrassed. Lonnie, not about to let Merry out him in front of his loyal followers, exploded.

"Merry, your faggot brother didn't give me shit! Oh, but the nigga tried. Oh, yeah, he wanted to.   Following me around and shit with his sissy ass."

Lonnie's audience hollered. He slapped hands with one of his boys, puffed out his chest. Merry shot back.

"You ought to know. It takes one to know one."

Lonnie's fans oohed. He laughed.

"Hold on, you think I'm a sissy? Naw, Merry, I ain't no sissy. Johnson got a black eye to prove it. Don't he, man?"

Lonnie glanced back to his crony. Short and muscular for a ball player, the boy answered.

"Yeah, Lonnie. A busted sweet lip, too."

Lonnie winked at Merry, puckered his lips. Merry lost it, fists first.

"What'd you do to my brother?!"

Lonnie, laughed, dodged Merry's flailing arms.

Angry, desperate, Merry scratched at the air, clawing for Lonnie's face. He grabbed her hands.

"I ain't do shit to Johnson, Merry. Last time I saw him, he was curled up crying on the ground like a little bitch."

Lonnie's eyes locked with Merry's. She had always known the boy was no good and was only using her brother. But the look of truth Merry wasn't prepared for.

The short ball player behind Lonnie started whimpering. The rest of the crew and fans snickered.

"Boo hoo, man. Come on, you gone give these fools a chance to win they money back or not?"

Merry and Lonnie still stared at each other, both armed with the key to unlock their shared gaze, but neither one making the move. Lonnie let go of Merry's hands.

"Yeah, man. Round 'em back up. I still got room for some more bills in my pockets."

Merry didn't stick around to see Lonnie line his pockets. She bought her son some milk. No doubt Jr. Baby was crying for it now. She had been gone longer than she expected. And it was taking her even longer still, thanks to the pink faced Uncle Sam in front of her, chatting it up with the store owner's wife at the counter.

Dark brown hair with lips thinner than thread, the white man was immaculate in Army uniform. His cracker tail needed to be overseas with the rest of America, killing

Koreans instead of holding up the damn store line. Merry sighed. The store owner's harlot of a wife raised a slight eyebrow to Merry, handed him his change.

"You have a good day recruitin', Sergeant Baxter."

"Oh, my day's more than good now, Willa. More than good."

Sergeant Baxter smiled, he and Willa taking longer than they needed to pass off his change. Merry rolled her eyes, then caught a glimpse of something lassoed around Sergeant's Baxter's hairy pink wrist - Lonnie's birthday watch.

*

"Mrs. Mavis, calm down."

"Calm down?! He jus' a boy!"

Merry had solved the mystery. The Klan hadn't hung her brother on the limb of some unfound tree or thrown a tire around his neck and sunk him to the bottom of the Detroit River. Johnson was in the Army. Bootcamp. Being brainwashed by Uncle Sam to kill yellow skinned, slanted eyed Koreans. And Sergeant Baxter felt justified about it.

Smug, he turned his attention to Excellent, the watch a heartbroken Johnson had bought for Lonnie then abandoned on his recruiting desk fastened around his hairy pink wrist.

"Mrs. Mavis, as I said before, the Army is not at fault here. Your son took an oath, represented himself falsely as eighteen..."

"So, you're gonna make him pay for it? You're gonna send my son over there to get killed?"

Excellent, like Dora, was standing now, eyes fixed on Sergeant Baxter, waiting for his answer. Merry watched him, suddenly noticing the flush redness of his once cool pink face and the beads of sweat popping out of the deep wrinkles in his forehead. Sergeant Baxter looked at both of them. He had been to war and back, but taking on two angry Colored woman demanding to get their son back was one battle hadn't prepared him for.

"Mrs. Mavis, I contacted my superior at headquarters personally and..."

"And?"

Excellent and Dora echoed each other. Sergeant Baxter looked from both of them, not sure which mother to respond to. He chose Excellent.

"And we're going to release your son."

"Thank ya, Jesus! Hallelujah!"

Dora, every bit the Christian warrior, cut a holy ghost step. And Excellent looked up to the heavens, clasped her hands, relieved. Merry smiled, her eyes still on the sergeant. He was the only one not celebrating. Excellent pulled back from her embrace with Dora, returned her focus to Sergeant Baxter.

"When?"

Sergeant Baxter paused. It wasn't a hard question. He had already done the heavy lifting and told them that the Army was sending her brother back home. Why couldn't he tell them when?

Sergeant Baxter cleared his throat, forcing a smile into his voice.

"The doctors assured me it'd be soon. As soon as this week."

"Doctors?"

"Yes, Mrs. Mavis. There's been an accident."

What kind of accident, Sergeant Baxter wouldn't say. In fact, no one would. Excellent called the Army every hour every day, trying to get anyone to tell her what happened to Johnson. Ignored and avoided, she got passed around from person to person, department to department, no one willing to cut through the red tape and tell her anything. With only silence to feed her worry, Merry couldn't help but think the worst. The Army was sending her brother home, but would he be in his right mind? Or had something so terrible happened to him in boot camp, that the Army was scurrying to wash their hands of the blame?

Wasn't long before folks from the neighborhood and church started asking the same thing. Even The Michigan Chronicle, the local Colored newspaper, had assigned a reporter to "investigate" the story. This was serious. And Merry knew that for sure when Teenie and two Colored men in suits and matching hats showed up on their doorstep.

They were from the Detroit branch of the National Association for the Advancement of Colored People, a brown paper bag civil rights organization that had been around 40 years almost, but was still irrelevant to average Northend Colored folks. How Teenie fell in line with them, she didn't say. All Teenie did say was that they wanted to get behind Excellent and pressure the Army into releasing Johnson quick and in a hurry.

Excellent wanted no parts of it.

"Listen to what they're sayin', Excellent..."

"I heard enough, Teenie. They just want to make more trouble for Johnson, turn him into a cause to make them look good. No. Johnson's not a damn cause. He's my son."

"Your son? I changed that boy's dirty diapers and was there for him each and every time he cried. You think I would bring them here to hurt him?"

"I said no."

Excellent and Teenie starred at each other, both right, both wrong. Dora, surprisingly silent, looked on, sick with worry and Merry, who wanted her brother home by any means possible, really wanted to stand and take Teenie's side.

One of the NAACP suits - the shorter, balding one - finally spoke up.

"Henrietta, perhaps we should..."

Teenie raised her hand, not once breaking her gaze with Excellent. Her voice, oiled with tears, cracked.

"Excellent, Johnson's nothing but a lying nigga to the Army. We want him back safe, in one piece? *We need their help.*"

A plea. Who raised or abandoned Johnson, loved or deserved to love him didn't matter. The only thing that mattered to Merry and everyone else in that living room was getting her brother back home and if her auntie had to get down on bended knee and beg her mother to work with the NAACP to save Johnson, she would.

Excellent, defenses down, looked away, wrung her hands.

"What are we gone do?"

Teenie, relieved, patted Excellent on the hand. The NAACP suits, already on their edge of their seats, began to re-explain.

Merry inched closer to hear all of the details. Outside, she heard a car door slam. She had had enough drama for the day, who could it be now? Merry looked out the window. A black sedan was parked in front of the house, a white man in Army uniform opening up the car's back door. Curious, she stepped out on the porch to get a better look.

One wooden crutch, then another exited the car first. Then, a Colored soldier, his Army dress uniform rigidly starched, wobbly lifted himself out of the sedan onto the crutches. Merry screamed.

"Johnson!!!"

Merry - Dora, Teenie and Excellent right behind her - bolted down the walkway and tackled her brother with a huge hug. One of his crutches went flying and his cap fell off his head. Johnson, barely able to keep his balance, laughed.

"Dag, girl, what you tryin' to do, break my other leg?"

Merry held on tight.

"I missed you, fool!"

Johnson hugged back, tight.

"I missed you, too."

DETROIT, 1950

"What you doin'?"

Merry was busted. Standing barefoot in her underwear in front of Terry and his wife's bedroom closet, she was rummaging through Terry's wife's clothes and shoes, trying to figure out what her man's ball-and-chain was all about. By the looks of her threads - long skirts that hid ankles, white buttoned up blouses with ruffles and flat dress shoes that even her momma wouldn't wear - Merry understood why Terry didn't love his teacher wife anymore. The woman had no fire in her. Wouldn't be long before she replaced her dull ass and took Terry as her husband instead of sneaking quickies with him during his lunch breaks.

Merry winked over her shoulder at Terry, mischievous.

"Nothing."

Terry, wet from the shower, got some clean, ironed boxers out of the dresser.

"Leave her things alone. Don't I give you enough? Damn."

Terry, annoyed, pulled on his boxers. Merry, slid up to him and ran her fingers through his soft chest hairs.

"Don't. I. Give. YOU. Enough?"

Terry looked down at Merry, anger dissolving into arousal.

"Merry. I gotta get back to work."

Merry smiled. Her man was going to be late coming back from lunch. Again. She giggled as Terry picked up her up, threw her down on the made-up bed. Merry wiggled out of her panties and Terry yanked her closer to him, his touch and kiss, rough.

She heard the sound of the front door opening down the hall one second before he did. Terry's wife, one of the few Colored teachers in the Detroit Public School system and actually a teacher at Merry's old Deggin Junior High was supposed to be down at their church teaching Vacation Bible School. But she wasn't. She was home. Merry dug her nails into Terry's back, kissed him harder.

Terry, hearing the jingle of his wife's keys, hopped off of Merry, grabbed his robe. Concerned by the unexpected sound of stumbling coming through the open door of their bedroom, Terry's wife called out.

"Terry?"

Merry sat up on her elbows, legs still propped open. Terry, in silent panic, threatened her to get her ass in the closet. Merry shook her head, no.

"Terry, is that you?"

Terry's wife's voice sounded nicer than Merry thought it would. Closer, too. No more time for games, Terry grabbed Merry up hard by her arm, shoved her toward the closet. Merry plopped her hands on her hips, jealous. Terry darted out of the room and pulled the door halfway closed behind him, his voice and face dripping with fake happiness.

"Baby?! What you doin' home?"

Merry pulled their bedroom door to a crack, peeked through it. Terry, careful not to get close enough for his wife to smell Merry on him, had her hemmed up in the hallway. Merry looked at the profile of her cocoa brown face. Medium length black hair, plump and tired looking from years of chasing behind Terry and their three children, his bore of a wife really wasn't that bad looking.

She eyed Terry, suspicious.

"I forgot the kids' cupcakes. What are you doing here?"

"I wasn't feelin' good, so..."

"Did you hear me calling you?"

"No, I mean, yes. I was...I was in the bathroom..."

Merry snickered under her breath. Terry's wife's eyes darted in the bedroom's direction. Terry coughed hard, stepped in front of his wife to distract her. Her wary eyes settled on him, worried. She touched his forehead.

"Oh, Baby, you really are sick."

"Yeah. I took a hot shower to help me...help me...breath better."

Terry coughed hard again and tossed in some sniffles for effect. A good wife, she draped her arm around his waist.

"C'mon on, Baby, I'll make you some tea."

"Your tea always works it out, Baby."

With Terry's wife occupied in the kitchen, Merry, vindictive, stuffed her underwear underneath one of the pillows on the bed, then snuck out the back door.

So proud of how smart and sneaky she was, Merry was still gloating about it when she got back home. Dora noticed the shine in her face, but figured Merry was giddy because she had just visited her favorite place - the library. That's the excuse Merry gave to her momma to get out of the house and lay up under Terry. And Dora, who had only seen the inside of the schoolhouse through the third grade, was glad to hold down the fort for the laundry business and look after Jr. Baby for a spell so that Merry could educate herself.

Deep down, Merry knew she should have felt bad for deceiving her momma, deceiving her. But she didn't. She was having too much fun. And besides, after all the drama that fool Johnson had put the family through, Merry felt she deserved the attention. Now that her fake hero of a brother was back from the Army, he was the sun. Merry, Excellent, Teenie and Dora, the planets revolving around him. And Dolores, clueless, was his Milky Way.

"Tell me again, Johnson."

"Girl, I already tol' you a hundred times."

"Please...I love to hear you tell it."

Merry, with one foot in Johnson's bedroom about to say hello, quickly pivoted back around to leave. She didn't want to hear this boy's tall tale again. To let Johnson tell it, he lied about his age and joined the Army, because he had heard poor Excellent boo hooing about money one night. That's when he knew he had to step up as the man of the house and do something just so that his single mother, harlot sister and bastard nephew could be taken care of.

Johnson had served everyone in the family, folks from church and people from the neighborhood that stinking load of mess on a silver platter and they swallowed it whole without chewing. No one knew that Johnson had joined the Army, because he didn't want to live anymore after Lonnie rejected him, beat him up and broke his heart. Or that as soon as Johnson got to boot camp in Kentucky, he knew he had made a terrible mistake and begged a fellow recruit - Raymond's sweet cousin, Allen, as fate would have it - to break his leg with a scrub brush, so the Army would release him. Or that Allen had to whack the back of Johnson's leg so many times that gangrene set in and that the Army stalled so long in releasing him, because the doctors weren't sure at first if they'd be able to send the boy back home to his mother with one leg or two. No one knew any of this.

And Merry knew, because Johnson had told her. He told her and begged her not to tell anybody. And like a fool, Merry promised to not tell a soul. What she didn't promise to do? To stand there and listen to him lie his fairy tail off.

Dolores jumped up, pulled Merry by the hand over to the bed.

"Wait, Merry! You gotta hear Johnson tell it! Go 'head, Hero!"

Merry rolled her eyes. Johnson laughed.

"I don't think Merry wanna hear it."

"No! It's a great story! Isn't it, Merry?"

"It's a story, alright."

"See! Come on, Johnson!"

Johnson eyed Merry.

"Naw...I'm tired. I'll tell it next time."

"Awwwww, Johnson, please!"

"Nope."

Dolores stuck out her lip, pouted, looked from Johnson to Merry.

"Fine. See you tomorrow."

She pecked Johnson on the cheek, cut her eyes at Merry. Merry watched her leave, unfazed.

"How long you gonna keep telling this lie?"

Johnson smiled wide, leaned back into his pillows, cocky.

"I can't help that it's a good story, Merry."

"You can help by not telling it so damn much. I'm tired of hearing it."

"Then don't listen then. And you can't say nothin', either. Or you want momma and ma to know 'bout you and the library?"

Merry glared at her brother, cornered. Even with a broken leg, the boy was still standing on steadier ground than she was.

Johnson, gloating, switched gears to his favorite subject. Still.

"So. You see Lonnie?"

"No."

"Why not? Merry, I tol' you to go find him."

"And I told you I'm not Dolores. You can't just be telling me what to do."

"Girl, you had to go by the park anyway! Why didn't you just do what I tol' you?"

"Fool, Lonnie don't care nothing about you!"

"Yeah, he does. He's just..."

"He beat you up!"

"Naw, see, we both was fightin'..."

"And he hasn't called or been over here to see you since you got back."

Johnson, eyes watering, fell silent. Wasn't no arguing with the truth. Merry, sorry for her brother, got up to leave.

"Merry?"

"Yeah?"

"You still think 'bout James?"

Merry paused. She was this close to snagging Terry as her husband, had bore a beautiful baby boy with Felton and still got tingles up her spine whenever she saw Silas.

Merry nodded. Wasn't no arguing with the truth.

LIKE A NIGGA
ON THE STREET

Merry was hungry.

But suddenly, the sweet, smokey smell of the ham steak she was frying up on the stove was too much for her. The acid insides of her stomach erupting fast up her throat, she clamped her hand over her mouth and ran over to the kitchen sink. Just in time.

"Merry!"

Merry jumped up in a panic. She hadn't heard her mother return home. She flicked the water on in the sink, quickly rinsed out her mouth, then used her hands to swipe what was left of her insides down the drain. A little dizzy, she turned the fire off on the stove, hurried out into the hallway.

"Yes?"

No answer. Merry wiped her wet hands on her housedress and shuffled toward the living room. When she turned the corner, Excellent was standing by the couch. Waiting. Merry hung by the door.

"You called me?"

"Come here, Merry."

Merry took baby steps up to her mother. Furious, Excellent smashed a carbon copy of a letter into her face.

"You think I wasn't gone find out 'bout this?"

Merry pulled back to get a better look at the letter attached to her face, but she already knew what it was.

"Answer me."

"I don't know..."

Excellent slapped her. Merry, shocked, rubbed her face. Excellent paced.

"Those white folks at the welfare office called me a thief, said I cashed Jr. Baby's check, was tryin' to trick 'em into givin' me more money. They threatened to close my bank account, cut off his assistance..."

Excellent glared at Merry, her anger so hot, it was cold.

"I had to ask Mrs. Benson for a loan just to keep a roof over your goddamn head and you had the money all along? Give it to me, Merry."

Merry looked at her mother's open palm, shook her head.

"I can't."

"What you mean, you can't?"

"I spent it."

"On what? 'Cause I don't remember you payin' a bill or bringin' any groceries up in this house."

Merry didn't answer. Excellent did it for her.

"Selfish ass. So busy worried about what I was buyin'..."

"It's my money."

"No! It's Jr. Baby's! Did I ever let the boy run out of clothes or diapers? Was he ever hungry, laid up sick in the bed wit'out his medicine?"

Merry mumbled, low, barely loud enough for Excellent to hear her.

"No."

Excellent took a step toward her, threatening.

"What?"

"No!"

Merry flinched, expecting to get smacked. Excellent starred at her, hard, shook her head.

"You want to be so damn grown. Now I'm gone let you."

"Wha...What?"

"I been a customer at that bank for ten years. I wasn't 'bout to let you embarrass me and let those white folks know I didn't write that letter. So, I'm gone keep things just the way you left 'em at the bank. But you hear me and hear me good. From now on, any and everythin' you or Jr. Baby eat, drink or wipe your ass with, you pay for. The only time I ever want to hear or talk to your selfish ass 'bout your money is at the first of the month."

"Why? What happens then?"

"You pay me room and board. $20."

"A month?"

"Each and every."

"But that's not fair. I can't..."

"You don't, I'll kick your ass out like a nigga on the street."

Merry didn't argue. Besides talking back to her mother would have made her and Jr. Baby homeless sooner rather than later. What she really needed was time so she could set things up with to Terry, tell him the good news.

"...And then she told me I had to give her money every month. My money! Just 'cause she was mad I stopped her from spending it! Ain't that some mess?!"

"Yeah, babe. Some mess."

Terry's halfway listening words fell out of the side of his mouth in between gulps of hungry kisses. Pants unzipped, in the back of his truck, the horny married mailman only had one thing on his mind. He flung up Merry's skirt, grabbed at her panties. Merry, on her back against sacks of mail, ranted on.

"I can't wait to see Excellent's face when I tell her you're going to be taking care of us. She can kiss my twenty dollars a month goodbye."

Merry tugged at Terry's pants, trying to pull them down the rest of the way past his no longer moving hips. Terry hesitated.

"Hold on, what you mean..."

"I mean, we can finally be together, Terry. Just like we said. Me, you, Jr. Baby, the baby..."

Terry pulled away.

"Merry, I already got a wife and kids. I'm not 'bout to...What'd you say?"

"I said me, you, Jr. Baby..."

"After that."

Merry grinned, rubbed his arm, guilty.

"You mean, the baby? Baby?"

"Goddamn it, Merry!"

Terry lunged up, ready to bolt. Merry scrambled to stop him.

"Baby, what's wrong? This is what you wanted."

"I didn't want no damn baby, Merry."

"But you said..."

"I didn't say shit 'bout wantin' no more babies and I damn sure didn't say nothin' about leavin' my wife. Get rid of it."

Merry, knowing she heard Terry right, asked anyway.

"What?"

"I said, get rid of it. Then, things can go back to normal."

Merry heard Terry right this time, too. But she didn't have to ask him to clarify. Normal meant they would continue sneaking around, doing what grown folks do without his wife knowing about it. Normal meant Merry would do what was not, kill the baby in her belly and continue to bed a man who had no intention to wed her or love her the way she deserved to be loved.

That's what normal meant. The sad thing? For Merry, that was enough.

"That's all he gave you?"

"Uh huh. Is it enough?"

Merry looked at Kat, helpless. She shook her head.

"Wait a minute."

Kat - too skinny with scarred arms - shuffled away from Raymond's grandmother's cluttered dining room table and disappeared through the doorway. Merry glanced around, anxious. She hadn't really seen Kat in a long time. Wild and strung out, Reverend and Mrs. McKeever had given up on her. Church was no longer her home. Her home, no longer her sanctuary. And Kat's father? Raymond would have to do.

Merry leaned back in the chair, tried to relax. If anyone used to make her feel at ease, it was Kat. But something was awkward between them now. She had felt it when Kat came by the house to give her respects to Excellent when Johnson came up missing. It was like they were still back at that night Terry and Raymond got into it at the club. Kat had begged Merry to leave with them, but Merry didn't because she wanted to make sure Raymond didn't double back later that night and kill Terry. It wasn't about her choosing her man over her best friend. She was just trying to save Terry's life. But that night, Kat didn't understand that. She felt kicked to the curb. And today - the wounded look in Kat's eyes a dead giveaway - she still did.

Kat shuffled back into the living room, slipped on her shoes. She was dressed now, wearing a fitted sleeveless red dress that looked like it was stripped off the back of a mannequin from one of those expensive downtown department stores. Hotter than July outside, Kat slipped on her sweater.

"Come on. I'll take you."

"What about the money?"

"Don't worry about it."

Merry didn't ask Kat why she didn't need the money or where they were going. She trusted that her best friend was taking her to fix her problem. But as soon as she and Kat turned into the alley, heading for the back door of Slauson's Funeral Parlor, Merry's trust went bust.

"Where we going, Kat?"

Kat kept walking. Merry stopped.

"Thought you were taking me to a doctor."

"You know any doctors that do this, Merry, you tell me."

Kat stepped up to the back door, knocked. Merry panicked.

"Wait, wait, Kat, I don't wanna..."

"You want to keep it?"

"No...but..."

Kat knocked again. Merry, scared and confused, couldn't figure out whether to stay or run. Behind the door, they heard a man's voice. Cautious. Deep.

"Who is it?"

"Clyde, it's Kat."

"Raymond send you?"

"No. I need a favor."

Clyde opened the door. Tall, willowy and twentyish, he didn't look to Merry like he sounded. He was high yellow and had good hair like Billy Eckstein. Fine, except for his pimple of a face, the man had so many dots on his mug, Merry could have connected the dots with the toothpick in his mouth if she wanted to. She didn't want to.

Clyde stuck his hands in the pockets of his used-to-be-white blood spotted butcher's jacket, smirked.

"Damn, girl, you knocked up again?"

"No. She is."

Clyde's eyes shifted to Merry, who must have looked like she was in shock, because she was. Kat being pregnant was news to her. Kat being unpregnant and not telling her? Merry couldn't even wrap her mind around. Clyde frowned.

"Who's this?"

"My best friend, Merry. I told her you'd take care of her."

"Damn, Kat, I'm workin'...How long you gone hold this shit over my head?"

Kat starred at Clyde, the dirt she had on him tightening around his neck like a noose.

"What?"

Clyde stammered.

"Nothin', Kat. Nothin'."

Kat pushed past Clyde, walked inside. Merry followed, a damp air smacking her in the face as soon as she crossed the threshold. It was cold inside. Quiet. And everything - the worn leather furniture, faded fake flowers and paint-by-numbers portraits on the wood-paneled walls - smelled like old mothballs. They walked up the back steps to a small coffin showroom. Kat took a seat. Merry stood a moment, apprehensive, glanced around. She had never been in a funeral home before and had never seen a dead person. When the only dead person Merry knew, her great-grandmother, Delilah, passed on, she and Johnson were both too young to go to the funeral.

Merry looked back at the door. Kat huffed.

"Are you going to sit down or what?"

Merry sat. Kat flipped through a copy of Ebony. Merry turned to her friend.

"Why didn't you tell me?"

"Tell you what?"

"That you were pregnant."

Kat shrugged, turned a page.

"I tried."

"When?"

"Don't you remember?"

Merry racked her brain for a phone call or visit with Kat in the last few months. Kat flipped another page, didn't look at her.

"You don't, do you?"

Merry, too embarrassed to nod, looked at Kat, guilty. Kat plopped down the magazine and walked over to admire a pearl pink coffin.

"My mother was buried in a coffin like this. Pink, rose pink, her favorite color. Had flowers on the handle just like this..."

Merry stepped up to Kat, touched her hand, apologetic.

"Kat, why didn't you just tell me?"

Kat shrugged Merry off, moved her hand.

"Jr. Baby was crying and you were fussing, complaining about Johnson, Excellent, somebody and...Ooh, look..."

Kat headed over to white coffin on the other side of the room, excited.

"Look at this one, Merry. This is the one I want. When I die, tell Raymond to bury me in this one. This one here. Doesn't it look like heaven?"

"Kat, I don't want to talk about no damn coffins."

"Then what do you want to talk about, huh? That baby's dead and gone. Now we're here for you."

"How do you know about this place?"

"Clyde's mother's been fixing women for years. After she died, he took over the family business."

"And what's going on between you and Clyde?"

"Please, Clyde works for Raymond."

"Was the baby...his?"

"Girl, you really think I would tip out on Raymond with Clyde's pizza face ass?!"

"No, but..."

"Merry, the baby was Raymond's. He's always talking about how he's going to knock me up, make me pop out his babies. But after what I saw you go through, I don't ever want to have a baby."

"So Raymond doesn't know."

"No, he doesn't know about Clyde's sticky ass fingers either. Clyde thought he was slick, got a little greedy on one of the jobs. I found out about it..."

"And you didn't tell Raymond."

Kat ran her hand across the coffin lid, nodded. Merry eyed her.

Clyde appeared in the doorway.

"I'm ready."

Merry, hand-in-hand with Kat, followed Clyde as he took long strides down the narrow hallway, passing three open parlors. The inn was full today - Mother Lilly Beales in the main parlor off the hallway. An old Christian soldier, she had a garden of flowers. Robert Holloway in the next parlor to the right. A mean looking bastard, he only had one lonely wreath from his wife to keep him company. And Sylvia Gray in the small back room. More like a walk-in closet, really. Looking no older than twenty, the dead woman had no flowers at all. Merry glanced at her visitors book. No signatures either. She was alone.

"You're not keeping that in here, are you?!"

Merry froze in the doorway of Clyde's small, but functional preparation room. There was an empty stainless steel gurney waiting for her in the middle of the room, but her eyes were glued on covered dead body on top of another gurney against the wall.

"'Course not, Merry. I was just waiting on you and Kat to help me roll him out into the alley."

Clyde took a sloppy bite of his half-eaten corn beef sandwich, grinned. Merry lost it.

"Hell, no! Kat, I'm not doing it with that dead body..."

"Merry, it's O.K. I had two dead people in here with me. It won't..."

Clyde, mouth full of sandwich, mumbled a correction.

"He."

"What?"

Clyde nodded toward the dead body on the gurney.

"It's a *he*."

Kat rolled her eyes, calmly took Merry by both hands.

"It's alright, Merry. *He* won't hurt you."

Merry shook her head, her eyes floating back over to the dead body.

"I can't do it like you, Kat. I can't do it with that in here."

Clyde sighed, frustrated.

"Damn, Kat. Just give the girl some shit to nod her out. I'm runnin' behind..."

"She doesn't do shit."

"You said she was your girl. I just thought..."

"Well, you thought wrong, Clyde. Pour her a drink."

"I look like a bartender to you?"

"I said, pour her a drink."

Clyde stomped over to a cabinet, grabbed a half-empty bottle of J & B and poured a swallow into coffee mug already on the counter. Kat snatched the mug from him, handed it to Merry.

"Merry, drink this down. It'll calm your nerves..."

Merry looked to her friend, frightened.

"Is it going to hurt, Kat?"

Kat moved the mug up to Merry's mouth.

"It'll be over before you know it."

Merry, obedient, drank. Then, over Kat's shoulder, she saw Clyde preparing to fix her. In his hand was the biggest, longest knife she had ever seen. Merry's fingers fell limp, the dirty coffee mug slipped and the room - spinning, soundless - went dark.

CALL HER
A BITCH AGAIN

"No! Don't!"

Merry bolted up in the dark, clutching her stomach. She was still in one piece from what she could feel and wearing the same clothes she went to Slauson's Funeral Home in, but this bed she was lying in? Merry didn't recognize.

Merry looked around the small room, her eyes adjusting to the blackness around her. Two mahogany dressers - one tall, the other, shorter with a vanity mirror on the back wall. She peered at the wall. Pistachio ice cream. She was at Teenie's.

Merry swung her feet around the side of the bed, stood up. Her legs were much steadier now than they were a few hours ago in Clyde's cold preparation room.

Merry may have been a little fuzzy about the details of what happened after she fainted, but one thing she knew for sure. She was still pregnant. After she came to, she had been too scared to go through with it. But Merry was even more afraid of going home to face Excellent. That's why she had asked Kat to bring her to Teenie's. To buy herself some time.

Merry shuffled down the hallway where Teenie and Louis were watching *The Long Ranger* on television in the living room. Louis, noticing her in the archway first, nudged Teenie.

"I was just 'bout to tell you to go slide a mirror under the girl's nose to make sure she was still breathin'. You sleep good, Lazarus?"

Merry nodded. Teenie looked at her with heavy eyes.

"How you feel?"

"Better."

A lie. They both knew it. Merry changed the subject.

"Where's Kat?"

"She left. With Raymond."

Teenie spit out Raymond's name like it was a piece of shit on her tongue. He was a dope peddler she had warned

Merry to stay away from. And now Teenie considered her guilty by association. So did Louis.

"Teenie, you checked that girl's purse before she left here, didn't you?"

Teenie looked at him, said nothing.

"Don't look at me like that. That girl's a dope fiend. Anybody can look at her and tell it."

Louis' words sprayed the room like mist, settled on Merry. Teenie lunged up, angry.

"Put your shoes on, Merry. Time to take you home."

Louis leaned back into the couch, not pressed.

"After my show."

"I said, *it's time to take her home, Louis.*"

"And I said, *after my show.*"

Teenie snatched the keys off of the coffee table, headed for the front door.

"What you doin'?"

"I was drivin' when I met you, Louis. I'll be drivin' after you're gone."

"What the hell you mean by that?"

"Come on, Merry."

Merry hurried out with Teenie right behind her. Louis caught the front door before it closed.

"Woman, what the hell you mean by that?!"

****

Merry tapped her foot, uneasy. If only Teenie would just talk to her. Then, Merry could ask her to turn the radio back on, so she'd have some music to break the silence of Teenie's disappointment riding shotgun between them.

Teenie stopped at a red light, starred straight ahead. Merry couldn't take it anymore.

"Teenie, please talk to me. I know I messed up. But if you don't talk to me, I don't know what I'm going to do."

The light turned green. Teenie stepped on the gas, said nothing.

"Teenie, please. I'm begging you. Don't do me like this."

"Do you like this? Merry, you did this to yourself. Why do you insist on being so goddamn stupid?"

Merry stumbled, Teenie's true words backhand slapping her heart.

"Teenie, I didn't mean..."

"You didn't mean what? Didn't mean to be runnin' wild, havin' sex wit' that no good married man?"

Stubborn tears fell from Merry's eyes.

"Terry loves me."

"The nigga sent you to get butchered on, Merry. You really think he's gonna leave his wife and babies?"

"Louis did."

Teenie gripped the steering wheel and snapped back, defiant.

"That's different."

"Why?"

"Because that's my business, Merry! I'm grown. You are fifteen years old. You have one baby, another one on the way. How are you gonna better yourself now?"

"Terry didn't mean it. He's going to take care of us."

Teenie, furious, swerved the car over to the side of the road. Merry, not wearing a seatbelt, fell into her. Teenie twisted Merry's arms around, looked for needle marks.

"Teenie! What are you..."

"Are you doing junk, Merry?"

"No!"

"You're talking out of your head. You must be doing junk!"

"I'm not, Teenie! I swear! I swear..."

Teenie starred at Merry and fell limp back against the seat. Merry, whimpering, looked at her. Teenie wiped at tears about to drop from her eyes.

"Merry. If you never hear anything I ever say again, hear this. Nobody's ever gonna take care of you. Hear me?"

Merry nodded. Not hearing her auntie. At all.

***

"But why? Why I have to tell her?"

Merry asked Excellent the burning question one more again. Her last chance before she would be standing face-to-face with Terry's unsuspecting, bore-of-a-wife. Excellent wasn't trying to hear it.

"Oh, so your fast ass grown enough to get pregnant by her husband, but not grown enough to tell her?"

"I just don't see why..."

"Ring the bell."

"But Terry said..."

"Ring the damn bell, Merry."

Merry rang the bell. She wanted to run, but Excellent was right behind her. Seconds ticking by, Merry re-read the name, The Baileys, written in macaroni shells on a child-made construction paper sign hanging from the porch light. Nervous, she turned around to leave.

"Nobody's home."

"Ring it again."

"But..."

Just then, the front door swung opened. And Terry's wife, barbecued stained apron around her waist, was standing there.

"...Tina, everyone's in the backyard...Oh? You're not Tina. Are you here to pick up one of the kids?"

Merry, frightened, suddenly couldn't get her tongue to wag. Excellent nudged her hard in the back.

"No. My name is Merry. This is my mother, Excellent."

"Nice to meet you both. How can I help you?"

Terry's wife smiled, polite, curious. Her eyes floated from Merry to Excellent. Excellent didn't say a word.

"May we come inside?"

Terry's wife's smile quivered slightly. She looked to Merry, knowing.

"Sure."

Merry had used Terry's house as a motel with him many times before, but for some reason it seemed more like a home today. Could have been the sounds of his children playing in the backyard, or maybe it was the sight of his wife sitting across from her on the loveseat, waiting to hear the news from Merry that she already knew deep down.

Terry's wife spoke first.

"Would you like something to drink? Water? Lemonade?"

Excellent and Merry both shook their heads 'no.' Terry's wife folded her hands on her lap.

"Well, let's just cut to the chase then. How long have you been sleeping with my husband?"

Terry's wife's eyes, zeroed in on Merry. Merry answered, busted.

"A few months."

"Come on now, Merry, more than a few. Be honest."

"I am being honest. That's why I'm here."

Terry's wife paused, Merry's reason for barging in her happy home crystal clear.

"You're pregnant."

Merry nodded.

"I just thought you should know."

I thought you should know before Terry leaves you for me was what Merry was really saying. Guilty feelings or not, she still wanted the man. And Terry's wife, no dummy, heard Merry's cloaked threat loud and clear. They starred at each other. Excellent spoke up, slicing through the tension.

"Mrs. Bailey, Merry came here out of respect. A wife should know 'bout her husband's responsibilities..."

"You mean, his mistakes, don't you?"

Terry's wife stood.

"I'd like both of you to leave my house now."

Merry cut her eyes to Excellent - I told you so. Terry's wife walked over the door, calm.

"Right now."

**

"Merry! Open this goddamn door!"

Merry tripped over Jr. Baby's toy truck in the middle of the hallway and tumbled over to living room window. She recognized the voice yelling for her. She just couldn't believe that his crazy, drunk ass was outside on her porch, banging on her front door like a stone cold fool.

Merry yanked back the curtain, looking dead-on into the furious face of Terry. He punched at the window, cracking it. Merry screamed, fell backwards away from him.

"Bitch! She left me!"

Excellent, pistol in her housecoat pocket, headed for the front door. Johnson stepped in front of her, yanked the door open.

"What's your damn problem, man?!"

Terry, not expecting a man to be a part of the equation, stutter-stepped up to Johnson, pissed.

"I need to talk to Merry."

"Naw, what you need to do is get the hell off my Momma's porch."

"Merry, you motherfuckin' bitch!"

Enraged, Terry rushed Johnson, tried to get inside the house. Johnson pushed him back, hard, in his chest. Terry skidded back, dropped to his knee. He looked up and saw Merry peering at him, her face sliced in two by the splintering crack in the living room window. Johnson stepped in front of him with balled fists. Terry shook his head.

"I ain't got no problem wit' you, man."

"You gotta problem wit' my sister, you gotta problem wit' me. Call her a bitch again."

Johnson took a step closer, threatening, the audience of nosey neighbors jeering him on. Terry raised his hand, deflated.

"Alright, alright. I'm leavin'. I'm gone."

Merry - heart hurting - moved the curtain out of the way to get a clearer view of Terry as he stumbled down the porch steps. Teenie was right. Terry didn't love her. And yes, the man was leaving. But he surely wasn't gone. Come tomorrow, he'd be back on her front porch again, mail in hand, his unwanted child growing in her belly.

*

Dora took a sip of her second cup of coffee, eyes focused through the cracked living room window. Merry entered the room, Jr. Baby on her hip.

"The mail come?"

"Oh, don't e'en wurry 'bout it...I'm waitin' on the nigga."

Dora took another sip. Merry set Jr. Baby down to crawl to his toys. Merry sat down, depressed.

"No need gettin' sad 'bout it now, Merry. You need tuh be figurin' out how you gone take care of dat new baby."

"The government'll give me more money."

"I didn't raise you tuh sit on yo' ass, waitin' fo' free money, Merry. Whut you gone do?"

"There's always the laundry business."

Dora snorted.

"Yo' work's so half-ass, Orin's duh only one that'll let you touch his clothes. And dat's only 'cuz I'm still here."

"What you mean, still here, Momma? Where you going?"

"Rosemary's drinkin' again. She needs me."

Merry's heart dropped. Rosemary was her drunk of an auntie in Atlanta. The baby of family, she was known for disappearing on binges weeks at a time and no one else - not her fat husband or her brain dead kids - could ever or talk any sense into her.

Merry fell to her knees.

"Momma, you can't go!"

"I'm already gone. Right afta I kick yo' mailman's ass."

"But I need you. And Johnson..."

Dora waved her off.

"Yaw don't need me. Yaw gone do whut you gone do whetha I'm here or not."

Merry buried her face in her momma's lap. Dora lifted up her chin and brushed at tears rolling down Merry's cheek.

"Stop that cryin'. You don't care nuthin' 'bout me.

"Yes, I do, Momma. I love you. Please don't go."

Merry threw her arms around Dora, hugged her. Dora returned the hug, patted her on the back.

"Wipe yo' face, Merry. You got company."

Merry looked out the window. Kat was stepping up on the front porch. She met her outside.

"Hey."

"Hey."

Merry wiped at her eyes. Kat looked, concerned.

"You O.K?"

"Yeah..."

"Bet I can make you feel better."

Merry grinned. She was pregnant with a baby she didn't want, her man didn't love her and her momma was leaving her. Merry loved the girl, but there was nothing Kat could do to make her feel better right now.

Kat took Merry a few houses down the block to Silas' parked car. Silas and Raymond got out of the car as they walked up.

"Merry, Merry, you alright?"

"Yeah."

"Good. 'Cuz, we heard 'bout what happened wit' that baby killin' nigga of yours last night."

Silas tossed Raymond the car keys and they strolled back to trunk. Raymond laughed.

"Yeah, Merry, we heard he was out here callin' you and yo' momma all kinds of bitches."

Raymond popped the trunk. Bound and gagged inside was Terry. He was beaten up, but alive. Kat nudged Merry, pleased.

"Told you."

Terry grunted at Merry, begging for mercy with his eyes. A side of Merry, the hurt side that wanted to get back at him for treating her lower than a whore, wanted Terry dead. The other side that still loved him? Wanted to let him live.

Silas, eyeing a police car creeping up the street, tapped the side of the car. Raymond closed the trunk. Merry reached out to Silas.

"Silas, wait...What you gonna do to him?"

Silas leaned against the car, said nothing. Merry pleaded.

"Don't hurt him."

Silas looked at Merry, unmoved. The police car eased up on the side of them.

"How you doin', Raymond?"

Merry stiffened. It was Officer Petosky. And Raymond was grinning at him.

"Just fine, Officer Petosky. Officer Gerald, nice to see you."

Raymond draped his arm around Kat and Merry turned around, busted. Officer Petosky squinted up at them from the passenger's side, unpleased.

"Didn't know you and Merry were friendly, Raymond."

"Well, you know me, Officer Petosky, I'm friendly wit' everybody."

Officer Petosky eyed a silent Silas, looked back to Merry.

"Heard you had a disturbance last night, Merry. Is everything alright now?"

No. The answer was no. If Merry could only save Terry's life and not land Silas, Kat and Raymond up under the jail in the process, she'd gladly spill the beans. But that wasn't possible. Merry was trapped. With no other choice but to lie.

"Yes, everything's fine."

Officer Petosky looked at her, trying to read her. He tapped the side of the car, satisfied.

"Alright. Tell your mother I said hello."

Merry nodded and Officer Petosky and his partner drove off. Raymond, Silas and Kat got back into the car. Merry begged one last time.

"Silas, see! I didn't say nothing! I'm not going to say nothing! Just don't hurt him!"

Silas started the car, didn't say one word. Powerless, Merry watched him pull away from the curb.

DETROIT, 1965

Merry touched the hood of Silas' car. Cold as Mother Mary's titty.

Merry wasn't surprised. She had heard it in Silas' raspy voice when she called him from Chicago. She knew then that he was lying, that he wasn't coming to pick her up from the bus station. But she didn't want believe the truth slapping her in the face. Again.

Merry tried her key in the lock. It still worked. She opened the door. The apartment was just the way she left it. Nasty. The plywood floors so dusty, they were gray. Greasy take out bags, dirty clothes, garbage, cigarette butts and used needles piled up on the card table, blanketing the ratty furniture and strewn about the junkyard box of a room.

Merry carved out a path to open a living room window. She looked around, coughing as the mustiness and mugginess escaped out the holes in the mesh screen. What the hell was she doing back here? This apartment Merry called home with Silas for too many damn years was worst than jail. At least in jail, she was kept there against her own will. But here, Merry voluntarily shackled her mind, body and soul to Silas. Without question.

Merry swiped a pair of red panties and ripped stockings off a folding chair. A ring of keys hit the floor. She picked them up, looked at them, then sat down, weary. The bedroom door creaked open. Silas, hair all over his face and head, and scratching himself shuffled past the living room to the bathroom. He doubled back.

"Merry Merry?"

Merry looked at him, too tired of his shit to give a damn anymore. Silas chuckled.

"Damn, girl. You got here quick."

"Thought you were gonna meet me at the bus station."

"I was...Just lost track of time."

A doped up voice slurred out from the bedroom.

"Who the fuck is that, Silas?"

"Nobody, bitch. Mind yo' business."

Silas pulled the bedroom door closed, walked toward Merry.

"You lookin' good, Merry Merry."

Merry, unfazed, starred him dead in the eye.

"You look like shit."

Silas smiled.

"See, that's the shit I'm talkin' 'bout! I miss that shit! Wanna drink?"

"No."

"A bump?"

"No."

"Damn, Merry Merry! What the fuck those crackers do to you in there? You done found Jesus?"

Merry eyed him, said nothing. His trifling junkie ass didn't deserve an explanation. Silas snorted sarcastically, slouched over to the bathroom and pissed on Merry's self esteem through the open door.

"Merry Merry gone go straight! Shiiiit. You gone be high as hell by tomorrow."

Silas laughed. Merry looked to the floor. Damn him. As much as she had survived, he could still make her feel smaller than flea shit. Silas paused in the bedroom doorway, tossed an insult over his bony shoulder.

"Bed's big enough for three. You comin'? Or you gave up dick, too?"

Silas strolled into the bedroom, left the door open. Merry starred after him, flashes of slicing that sarcastic smirk off of his face with a switchblade.

**

Merry slammed the apartment door closed behind her, mind made up to never see Silas' evil ass again. She didn't know where she was going or how long it would take her to get there, but she did know she wasn't going to be walking to her mystery destination. Merry was going to be driving. In style.

Merry opened the door of Silas' Fleetmaster and slid into the driver's seat, real easy like. She grinned to herself. Silas was so high, it would take him awhile to notice that his precious baby was gone. And when he finally did sober up and take notice, his arrogant ass wouldn't believe that Merry took it. Merry lit a cigarette, clicked on the radio and turned the corner. Blending into the traffic on Davison, she knew what her first stop would be.

"Merry!"

Johnson picked Merry up off the front porch, hugging her so tight, she couldn't catch her breath.

"Girl, you look good!"

Merry patted Johnson's stomach. No longer washboard, he had a slight pudge.

"You got fat."

"That's 'Lores' fault. She cook too damn much."

Johnson and Merry smiled, looked at each other, uncomfortable. Merry, sorry for all of the things she stole from them to feed the monkey on her back and Johnson, guilty for not coming to visit her when she was locked up in Kentucky. Johnson's eyes floated over Merry's shoulder, saw Silas' car.

"Damn, Merry. That you?"

"Silas'. I borrowed it."

Johnson shook his head, tickled.

"Merry, you ain't never gone change. Come in here and say 'hi' to everybody."

Merry followed Johnson into his and Dolores' bungalow home as he yelled out for his tribe to come to the front room.

"'Lores! Boys! Get up here."

Merry stood by the door, took in the sight of her queer brother playing family man. When Johnson and Dolores got married after he first knocked her up ten years ago, Merry just knew it wouldn't last. By day, he was the straight-laced, devoted boyfriend and workingman. But by night? Johnson was knee deep in his double life, the last to leave the faggot party, prowling Palmer Park all hours of the night for anonymous, one-night stands from men who wanted and needed the same.

Merry looked at Johnson. Marrying Dolores out of a sense of responsibility and to keep up appearances was one thing. But bringing three knuckleheaded boys into a union built on a lie? Merry knew her brother was selfish, but he couldn't be that selfish, could he?

One son, then another and another tumbled into the room. Stair steps in height, the oldest son was Johnson, Jr. or J.J., as everybody called him. The spitting image of Johnson with the light skin coloring of Dolores, he was nine and as tall as a twelve year old. Right behind him was his almond hued, middle brother, Jackson. Eight years old with Dolores body features and Johnson's good hair, he didn't speak much. And bringing up the rear was the baby, Julian. The darkest of the bunch, he was also the smallest, sassiest and smartest.

They all grinned up at Merry, polite, like they would any other stranger. Dolores trailed in behind them.

"What's all the fuss about, Johnson. You know I'm cooking..."

Dolores stopped when she saw Merry, surprised. Johnson chirped up.

"Baby, look what the wind blew in."

Dolores blinked, plastered on a smile.

"Merry! You're back."

Dolores hugged Merry - enough space between them to plow a truck through - patted her back. Bless her heart. Dolores still followed old school rules. Either say something nice or don't say anything at all. Dolores' compromise was stating the obvious. But what she really wanted to know was when Merry got back and why she was standing in her living room. Merry decided to answer Dolores' first unasked question.

"Yeah. Just got back today."

J.J.'s eyes lit up, excited.

"Auntie Merry, did you bring us something?"

Johnson and Dolores exchanged an embarrassed glance. J.J. was what the old folks called slow. Baby boy, Julian slapped his forehead with his hand, dramatic.

"Naw, fool! She was in jail."

Johnson smacked Julian upside the back of his peanut head.

"Boy, shut the hell up. Yaw gone to yo' room."

The boys tumbled out the living room. Johnson and Dolores turned their attention back to Merry.

"Want somethin' to drink, Merry? Don't think we have much, but I'm sure I can squeeze out enough for a taste..."

"Give me some water, Dolores."

"Water?"

"Yeah. Lots of ice."

Dolores left and Merry and Johnson sat down. Both still uncomfortable, they looked at each other. Johnson spoke first.

"You seen Ma and the kids?"

"Uh uh, came here first. I saw Scottie."

"Oh, yeah? How she doin'?"

"Not good."

"Damn. I gotta get by to see her."

Merry nodded, settled into the silence her brother had waiting for her. Dolores called out for Johnson from the kitchen, saving him. He returned with two tall glasses of lemonade.

"'Lores just made this fresh. I keep tellin' her we need to bottle it up and sell it. Bring some more money up in here."

Johnson gulped down the entire glass, wiped his mouth with the back of his hand. Merry drank, too. Johnson eyed her.

"That all you got, Merry? The clothes on yo' back?"

Merry couldn't drink for chuckling. Her baby brother knew her too damn well. Still. She set down her glass.

"Me and Silas...It's not gone work, Johnson."

"It ain't never worked, Merry. Shit. If it was up to me, I'd sleep on the floor, give you the bed. But after you stole the television that last time..."

Merry nodded.

"...The silverware, J.J.'s bike,'Lores' momma's weddin' ring...And what you did to Ma..."

"I know. I know...."

Merry took another sip of lemonade, stood. Johnson looked up at her, not ready for her to go.

"You leavin'?"

"Silas gone be missing his car soon. If he comes looking for me..."

"Ain't seen you since I don't know when."

Johnson walked Merry out onto the porch, crunched some bills into her hand.

"I don't get paid 'til Friday, so..."

"No, Johnson, you need it."

"Use it to put yourself up somewhere for a couple of days, Merry. Get your head straight."

Merry kissed Johnson on the cheek and took the money, grateful for it. But more grateful that her brother still cared.

*

Merry told herself she was just cruising, taking in the sights of what she hadn't seen, what she had been locked away from for so long. Downtown Detroit and Belle Isle were as vibrant as ever. But Paradise Valley and Hastings Street? The stomping grounds that - for good and bad - shaped the woman that was Merry? Gone. And the homes and neighborhoods of the hardworking folks from the Northend? Bulldozed and replaced by the Davison Freeway.

Merry glanced at the gas gauge. Damn near at E. She had Johnson's money in her bra. She could fill up the tank now and keep going to Toledo or Chicago if she wanted to. Her man never loved her, her son and daughter were better off without her and her past, the only thing she knew and depended on like a cripple does a crutch, had been wiped away. Why not hit the open road and find a fresh place to begin again?

Merry turned the car around. She owed her children a word first.

Goodbye.

DETROIT,
1951

"Julie-what?"

"Juliette. It's famous from Romeo and Juliette. By William Shakespeare."

Excellent huffed.

"Hmph...It's too different a name for a child to carry."

Merry cut her eyes. And Excellent ain't? She cradled her light bright, sleeping, newborn baby girl closer to her.

"Well, I like it."

"I'm gonna call her Julia."

"That's gonna confuse her."

Excellent plopped down in the chair by the side of Merry's Herman Keefer Hospital bed, tired.

"Didn't confuse you."

"What?"

"When I had you, I named you Mary. M-a-r-y. But Momma, she wanted to name you Delilah, after my grandmomma. I told her I wasn't gonna shackle you with some old, ugly, heavy name like she did me. She got so mad at me, she called you it anyway just to spite me."

"Why'd she stop?"

Excellent chuckled from the memory.

"'Cause you told her you liked your other name better."

"I don't remember that."

"You couldn't have been more than two years old, Merry. You were just a baby."

Juliette cooed and stirred in her sleep. Merry looked down at her daughter. She was so beautiful. She had a headful of brownish red hair - the fine texture of Merry's and the color of Terry's, full pink lips, no eyebrows and a button nose with nostrils almost too big for her tiny face.

A thought skipped across Merry's mind.

"Wait, didn't you say, M-a-r-y?"

"Uh huh."

"Well, then why do I spell it..."

"Teenie. After she found out you liked Mary better, she taught you to spell it that way, 'cause you were such a happy child. I just never changed it."

You never changed it, because you weren't around to, Merry thought. Before she was three, her mother had already ran off with Corn to Detroit and Merry knew that was the real reason why her name was spelled like the adjective and not the virgin mother.

But saying that out loud to her mother? That would have been too much like right.

**

Finally. Merry was snoring. Excellent was gone. Teenie, Louis, Johnson, Dolores and the last of her country people had rolled through the hospital to lay their eyes on Juliette, the new addition to the family. And Merry had even been able to speak to her momma, who was calling from Atlanta, on the phone. Now, like her baby, the only thing on Merry's mind was sleep. And lots of it.

Merry rolled over, her eyes slitting open just enough to get a slanted glance of Juliette sleeping in the bassinet on wheels by her bed. She slid her hand over to lay hands on her baby. It was empty.

Merry jumped up, startled. Terry's wife, standing at the foot of her bed rocking an alert Juliette in her arms, smiled at her.

"Good. You're awake."

Merry sat up straight.

"What are you doing here?"

"I just had to see for myself."

Terry's wife looked down at Juliette, pleasant.

"She has his eyes."

Merry slid out of the bed, reached out for Juliette.

"Give me my baby."

Terry's wife stepped away. Playful, she touched Juliette's button nose, spoke baby talk.

"Your mother's friends beat my husband half to death. Yes, they did, Juliette. He was afraid to press charges."

Juliette gurgled a gummy, drooling smile. Terry's wife rubbed noses with her, giggled. Merry walked up on her.

"I said, give me my baby."

Terry's wife looked to Merry, her smile gone and eyes cold as death.

"I'm not my husband, Merry. I'm not afraid of you or your goddamn friends. Come near my husband or my family again and I'll kill you. Understand?"

Merry nodded. Terry's wife took one last pleasant look at Juliette, then placed her back into Merry's arms. Merry kept her eyes peeled on her as she left.

*

Merry was exhausted. Tired as hell, actually. But she couldn't close her eyes not for one second for fear that Terry's crazy wife was going to come back and smother her with a pillow and snatch her baby right out of her sixteen-year-old arms.

Merry's eyes popped open. She didn't even remember falling asleep. But that didn't matter now, because there was a man leaving her room.

"Silas?"

Silas turned around, disheveled.

"Oh, Merry Merry, didn't mean to wake you."

"What are you doing here?"

"Was in the neighborhood, heard you had the baby, so..."

Silas motioned to the nightstand by her bed. A fluffy, stuffed teddy bear grinned back at her. Merry smiled.

"Thank you."

"Ain't nothin'."

Silas stepped closer to Merry's bed, peeked at Juliette purring in her arms.

"She looks like you."

"Think so?"

"Yeah. Light as hell, but yeah...You can tell she's yours."

Silas grinned, weary. Merry looked at him. The man needed a shave, a haircut and his eyes were bloodshot red. From crying, not from boozing.

"Well, I'll let you get back to sleep."

"You can stay, Silas..."

"Naw, Merry Merry, the way you were callin' the hogs home just now, I know you tired."

Silas started to leave. Merry spoke up, afraid.

"Silas."

"Yeah?"

"Could you stay just until I fall asleep? Terry's wife came by and she..."

Silas smiled.

"The mailman's wife paid you a visit, huh?"
"Yeah."

Merry cradled Juliette in her arms, peered up at Silas, pitiful. He looked at his watch, scratched his head.

"Alright. Guess I can stay a minute."

Silas pulled the chair over, sat down. Merry starred at him, unconvinced he was staying. Silas nodded.

"It's alright, Merry Merry. Close your eyes."

NOT
BY YOURSELF

"**Alright,** Merry. You can look now!"

Merry pulled her hand away from her eyes. A bunch of wrapped presents were piled on top of the coffee table like Christmas. Kat, sitting across from Merry with baby Juliette in her arms, beamed.

"Surprise!"

"Aw, Kat, you didn't have to do all this."

"What?! Merry, nothing's too good for my god baby. I got her some really pretty things from Crowleys, Federals. Even picked up some clothes for Jr. Baby..."

Jr. Baby, curious, wobbled up to the table, yanked down a box.

"Kat, really, Raymond spent too much money."

"Raymond! You hear that?"

Raymond stuttered stepped out of their kitchen, his eyes glassy and mouth moving slow.

"Wh--at?"

"Merry said you spent too much money."

"Shiiiiit."

Kat and Raymond laughed. Merry didn't get the joke.

"What's so funny?"

"You. If you think Raymond came out of his pocket."

Merry gasped.

"You stole these?"

Kat shrugged, proud of herself. Raymond boasted.

"Your girl's pretty good, Merry. Mrs. Coffee was even sniffin' 'round her."

"For real, Kat?"

"Yeah, but, Mrs. Coffee takes too much off the top. Besides, I'm not trying to make a job out of lifting. Open something!"

Merry started tearing off wrapping. Pretty lace and velvet dresses, bonnets, underwear, sweaters, snowsuits, tiny socks and soft-soled shoes, blankets, sparkling glass bottles, bright white diapers. Kat only lifted the best.

Jr. Baby bopped his new brown and white teddy bear upside the head, laughed. Raymond got down on the floor next to him.

"What you got there, man? A bear?"

Jr. Baby handed it to him. Merry smiled.

"That looks like the bear Silas got for Juliette. I tell yaw Silas came to visit me in the hospital?"

Raymond scooped Jr. Baby into his lap.

"He did?"

"Yeah. He said he was in the neighborhood, but I think he just came to see me."

Merry grinned, delusional. Raymond glanced to Kat to speak. She did.

"Merry, you didn't hear?"

"Hear what?"

"Lizzy killed herself. Two weeks ago."

"What?"

"Yeah, she slit her wrist that night you had Juliette, but Silas caught her and got her down to Herman Keefer in time. The next week she tried, Silas couldn't stop her."

"What happened?"

"She shot herself in the head. Right in front of him."

Merry plopped back into the couch cushion, winded.

"How's Silas doing?"

Raymond put Jr. Baby back down on the floor and stood up, pissed.

"The nigga's gone crazy, Merry. He came over here, wavin' a pistol, sayin' my shit killed Lizzy. My shit didn't have nothin' to do wit' it! The most my shit'll ever do is nod you out. Niggas don't be killin' themselves and shit. Right, Baby?"

Kat nodded, cradled Juliette.

"Right."

Raymond paced, getting angrier.

"Silas been goin' around, bad mouthin' me on the street, tellin' niggas my shit ain't good, messin' with my money."

Merry followed him back and forth with her eyes.

"You talk to him?"

"Talk to him? Merry, I'm stayin' away from his ass, so I don't kill him."

Merry stood up, appealed to Raymond. He was ranting now, but she knew the boy loved Silas even more than she did.

"Take me to see him, Raymond."

"Merry, did you hear what I just said?"

"Yeah, but I need to see him. Take me over to his place."

Raymond shook his head.

"He took his kids over to his momma's house since Lizzy tried to off herself the first time. And no one's seen the nigga since the funeral. He's probably in there dead."

"Even more reason to take me over there, Raymond. C'mon, don't you want to know if he's alright?"

Merry starred at Raymond, hoping that she got through to him. He looked back at her, hurt and anger etched all over his face. Merry turned to Kat.

"Kat. Where does Silas stay?"

"I'm not going to tell you, Merry. You don't need to go..."

"Alright. I'll find out for myself."

Merry grabbed her coat and purse, headed for the front door. Raymond spoke up.

"What you gone do, Merry? Walk 'round in the snow 'til you find him?"

"Eveybody knows Silas, Raymond. Somebody'll know where he is."

Kat threw a mean look at Raymond.

"Fuck that, Kat. Merry wants to go. Let her fucking go!"

Merry reached for the doorknob. Raymond called out.

"Shit! Alright, alright, Merry. I'll take you."

**

Brewster-Douglas Projects. Merry had heard about Detroit's Negro Only complex. Even after the deadly race riot that broke out in 1943 with white folks after Colored families tried to move into the Sojourner Truth Homes on the Eastside, Brewster-Douglas was still the only project that crooked Mayor Albert Cobo allowed negroes to live in. Trendsetting for its time, the project was comprised of six 15-story high-rise apartment buildings and had Negros from Detroit to Cleveland waiting on a long list to get in. Silas had been one of the lucky ones. His good job at the Chrysler plant basically made him a shoo-in for the unit. Then, throw in the fact that he was a family man, too, and those white folks couldn't wait to hand over the keys.

Merry looked out the window as Raymond drove through the complex. It looked nice, clean. And that just wasn't because of the fresh snow falling. Maybe it was the fact that the sky rise buildings were so tall. Colored folks who lived that high up in the sky must not be interested in starting mess on the ground. At least that's what the outside looked like to Merry. Inside Silas' place? A whole different story.

Merry, stumbling over trash and clothes on the floor, stood in between a heated Silas and Raymond.

"Nigga...your daddy was gurglin'. Gurglin'! The back of his head blown out and you know what he asked me?"

"Oh, here we go..."

"He asked me to look after you, take care of you and Momma Printup like you was my own and you do this shit to me! You snot nose, motherfucka!"

Silas, drunk, stepped threateningly toward Raymond. Raymond starred at him, unafraid. Silas picked at a scab.

"What, you gone do, Nigga? You afraid? Nigga, you afraid?"

Raymond stood his ground.

"Silas, swear to God, you put yo' hands on me..."

Merry tried to get back in between them.

"Raymond! Wait in the car."

Silas sneered, slicing through Raymond's manhood.

"Yeah, listen to Merry Merry, Nigga. She tryin' to save yo' ass."

Raymond didn't move. Silas teetered right in front of him, close enough for the boy to lay him out flat if he wanted to. Merry called out the obvious, trying to stop the inevitable one last time.

"Raymond, don't! He's drunk."

Raymond blinked. Merry was right. Silas was more than drunk; he was pathetic. And kicking his ass now when he was at his lowest would mean Raymond was a coward taking advantage. Raymond eyed Silas, whatever respect he had left for his hero gone.

"C'mon, Merry. Let's go."

Raymond turned to leave. Silas yanked his cigarettes out of his shirt pocket and plopped down on a chair, disappointed it seemed that he couldn't egg Raymond into beating his ass. Merry followed Raymond to the door.

"Raymond, wait for me in the car. I need a minute."

"I ain't waitin', Merry, I'm leavin'."

Merry peeked over her shoulder to Silas, hunched down in the chair, broken, alone.

"I'll get Silas to bring me back."

"Merry, that motherfucka can't pee straight right now..."

"I'll get back to the house, Raymond, alright?"

Raymond shook his head.

"That nigga ain't worth it, Merry. I'm tellin' you."

Raymond left. Merry turned to face Silas. He looked up at her, a demon wanting to be left alone.

"What'd you stay fo'?"

"To help you..."

"I don't need yo' help."

Merry started for Silas' kitchen, unfazed.

"When's the last time you ate?"

"I said, I don't need yo' goddamn help, Merry Merry!"

"Silas, I can smell your breath over here. Brush your teeth, so your food don't taste funny. And take a shower. You smell like spoiled shit."

Merry walked into the kitchen. Silas looked after her, shocked. Then, obedient, he got up from the chair.

*

Merry fluffed the last pillow on the couch, then stood back to admire her work. While Silas was in the shower, she had put a quick hurting on the pigsty apartment he called home. The kitchen was spotless. The dining room was ready for dining and the living room was actually livable now. She'd hit his bathroom and bedroom after they were finished eating.

Merry placed the hot plates of food down on the dining room table. Silas had been in the bathroom long enough for two showers. Merry heard the bathroom door open behind her.

"Hope you like corn beef hash. You only had one good egg so..."

Merry turned to realize she was talking to herself. She headed for the bedroom.

"Silas?"

Silas called out through the open door.

"I'll be right out, Merry Merry. Smells real good."

Merry, not taking the hint, stepped into Silas' bedroom. She found him sitting naked on his bed, a needle gripped between his lips and a rubber hose tied around his right arm. She stopped, starred. Silas looked back at her. She could either accept him or leave him. Her choice.

Merry's sat down next to him. Silas stuck the needle into his hungry vein, looked at Merry, grinned lopsided.

"Merry Merry, I ain't copped...by my...self in years."

Merry took his trembling hand.

"You're not by yourself."

WHAT THE POLICE
WANT WIT YOU?

Smack and Silas.

Merry was in love with both of them. And the best thing about it? She didn't have to sneak around and hide one from the other. The situation, as far as she was concerned, was heavenly. Merry got to get high with the man she had always loved and she didn't give a damn that she was turning herself into a dope fiend. She didn't even feel guilty that Lizzie was hardly dead and cold in the ground and she had already burrowed her way into the open, bleeding wound Silas still had for the woman in his heart. The only important thing? Was how wide open her nose was for Silas. How wide open her heart. How wide open her veins.

Merry peeked through the men clothes rack, saw Old Man Luther listening to the baseball game on the radio and reading his daily newspaper at his makeshift check out counter. Today was promotion day for Merry. For weeks, she had been apprenticing under Kat, lifting a little bit of this and that from Colored stores along Dexter and Davison and in Paradise Valley. But today was the first day Merry was lifting by herself. Whether she was ready to go at it alone or not really wasn't the point. The love of her life, had such a bigger appetite for junk than she did, that there was less and less left in the needle for her share these days. If Merry wanted to continue to get high and she didn't want to taste the palm of Silas' hand any more, she needed to contribute to the house kitty.

Merry puttered around the store, the lie that she was looking to get her father a birthday gift buying her some time. She lifted her used-to-be-pregnant blouse and fastened another alligator leather belt around her now small waist. She had three of them. She could sell two of them and give one to Silas as a present. Slick as shit, Merry then pocketed a pair of cufflinks, picked up two silk ties and walked up to the counter, smiling.

"I like these. How much are they?"

Old Man Luther, eyes clouding over from glaucoma, squinted at the ties, sputtered.

"More than what you got."

Merry plopped her hands on her waist, flirting.

"How you know what I got?"

"He don't. But I do."

Merry turned to see Old Man Luther's fat daughter, Thelma, blocking the store doorway.   Merry grinned, busted.

"Thelma! Looking good, girl. Is that a new dress?"

"New dress my ass. Put the shit on the counter, Merry."

"What?"

Thelma unfolded her arms, cracked her rusty knuckles.

"I said, put the shit on the counter."

Before Thelma could take a step, Merry plopped the cufflinks and alligator belts down on the counter, quick. Then with insincere sorries spilling out of her mouth, she tried to back her way out of the door, but Thelma's giant tattle-tail ass had other plans for her.

"Officer Petosky, you got this all wrong..."

"Really. So Thelma didn't catch you liftin' in her store?"

Merry, trying to think of the right answer that would abracadabra her way out of the backseat of Officer Petosky's patrol car, squirmed and starred at the back of his pale, white neck. He glanced at her over his shoulder. Officer Gerald, driving, looked straight ahead. Merry mumbled.

"I was buying..."

"...Your father a gift. Right, that's what Old Man Luther said. But your father left for St. Louis, was it?"

Merry didn't want to correct him. Petosky was wrong about the who and the where. The least she could do was point him in the right direction.

"Chicago."

"That's it. Chicago. You ever been, Gerald?"

Officer Gerald shook his head, no. Officer Petosky smiled.

"Me neither. I heard it's nice, tho'. Real nice. Has your mother ever been to Chicago, Merry?"

Merry paused. Was this white man trying to sniff around Excellent? Or was he just toying with her like a cat who has a mouse cornered? Whichever it was, Merry didn't give a damn. They weren't arresting her. Thelma had wanted them to throw her up under the jail, but Officer Petosky decided a warning would do. The only problem? He was hell bent on talking to Excellent.

Officer Petosky, responding to Merry's silence, eyed her again.

"You don't know? Well, I'll ask her myself."

Officer Gerald turned the corner, chimed in.

"You should also ask her mother about Silas and Raymond..."

"...And the mailman. Right, I forgot about that. How's the baby, Merry? A girl, was it?"

Merry answered, but she really barely heard Officer Petosky's throwaway question about her baby girl. Her mind was stuck like a shoe in used bubble gum. Officer Petosky knew what Silas and Raymond had done to Terry. He wasn't able to prove it, because Terry was too afraid to say who beat him breaths shy of death. But he knew. And that's why he wanted to talk to Excellent. Not only to scare Merry straight about shoplifting, but because he also wanted to put the fear of God in Merry about hanging around Silas and Raymond, the devil's foot soldiers. Little did Officer Petosky know, though, Merry had already laced up her boots and was now a foot soldier for Satan, too.

Merry, leg shaking, spoke fast.

"Officer Petosky, you don't have to wait, you know. Sometimes my mother has to work late and..."

"I got no place to be. You, Gerald?"

"Nope."

Merry sunk down in the backseat. Excellent was probably stepping off the Russell bus and it wouldn't be long before she would be trudging her way home, only to be greeted by the cops and Merry's trifling, 'I'm-not-arrested-but-I'm-in-trouble' ass. Merry had to get rid of these white men with the quickness. But how? She opened her mouth, not sure what was about to fly out. The squad car radio crackled on.

"Calling all cars. Shots fired at Davison and Joseph Campau. White male wounded. Calling all cars."

Officer Gerald started the car. Officer Petosky hopped out, opened the door for Merry.

"Today's your lucky day, Merry. But if I even hear about you liftin' or find out you're passin' time with Silas and Raymond again, it won't be a warnin' next time, understand?"

Merry, glad to be free from that stinky backseat, nodded. And she didn't even wait for them to drive off before she started up the steps.

"Merry! What you do? What the police want wit' you?"

Merry took the steps two at a time, didn't look up. Ms. Ruthie's nosey self had been sitting on her top porch, eavesdropping the whole time. She wasn't going to tell her own mother anything about her escapades today. She, for sure, didn't owe that blind, old woman an explanation.

"Merry! I know you hear me! You oughta be ashamed of yourself! The police know 'bout you leavin' those babies alone everyday? I oughta tell them!"

Merry slammed the door behind her. Ms. Ruthie made her ass itch. Wasn't any business of her's what Merry did or didn't do with her kids. Besides all was quiet in the house now. Juliette, still a little baby, slept all the time and Jr. Baby, used to being left alone by now, was most likely playing with his toys in her room.

Merry dipped into the bathroom, locked the door. That close call with Officer Petosky had her wanting a taste. She took her favorite spoon, a book of matches, needle, rubber hose and a pinch of smack out of her purse. After this, she would check on... Would check on... Her babies.

"Merry!"

Merry jumped up with a start. She was slobbering with a rubber hose tied around her arm and still seated on the toilet in the bathroom. She had nodded out longer than she planned and Excellent was banging on the bathroom door.

"Merry! What the hell you doin' in there?!"

Merry, scrambling to gather her stuff, tossed everything in her purse and threw it behind the bathtub. Then, she yanked open the door, stopping her mother in mid-knock. Excellent starred at her.

"Merry, you better not be pregnant. Swear to God..."

"I'm..not pregnant..."

Excellent eyed Merry, suspicious.

"Where's Jr. Baby?"

"What?"

"Julia's cryin' in there in a shitty diaper and I can't find Jr. Baby. Where is he?"

Merry hesitated. When she dipped into the bathroom without checking on her kids, she just knew where they both were. Locked in her room. If Jr. Baby somehow got out, he could have fallen down the basement steps and broken his neck for all Merry knew. Still a little high, Merry said what she was thinking.

"I don't know."

"You don't know? What the hell you mean, you don't know?!"

"I locked...the door...for a minute."

"Godamnit, Merry! I told you, not even for a minute! I'm gonna call upstairs, see if Blackie's seen him. Check the basement."

Merry headed toward the basement door, her legs a little slower than the rest of her. Juliette's attention deficit whimpers floated out into the hallway as she turned the doorknob. Then, like a belch reminding Merry what she had had for lunch earlier, she remembered.

"He's over Ms. Florises'."

Excellent, phone still in hand, looked at Merry, blinked.

"You just now remembered that?"

Merry nodded, what had happened coming back to her now. Felton, long convinced that Merry wasn't responsible enough to watch after his baby boy, had come by that morning to take Jr. Baby over to his aunt's for safekeeping.

And Merry, who had no plans to be stuck in the house watching her unwanted crumb snatchers anyway, was more than happy to hand her son over. So what, taking Juliette wasn't part of the deal. Jr. Baby was her favorite anyway. Could have been because Juliette looked so much like her lying, cheating, peach-faced daddy or the fact that Merry really only had room in her small heart to love smack and Silas. But whatsoever it was, Merry didn't give a damn. She just wanted to get high.

And getting rid of one child for the day - even her favorite - was better than nothing.

DETROIT,
1953

"**Kat,** I thought you said Clyde was here to do business?"

Merry plopped Clyde's pocket change on top of her piano. A precious gift from her mother four birthdays ago, it was now outside in the alley about to be lifted into Clyde's hearse. That is, until the negro's money came up short.

"Merry..."

"Merry, nothing, Kat. A deal's a deal and your boy is light."

Clyde, hands still in his pockets, shifted a toothpick in his mouth.

"You don't want my money, Merry?"

"I just said I didn't, didn't I?"

Merry barked at Clyde, failing to camouflage the dope-fiend in her willing to take whatever pennies he coughed up. Kat tapped Merry on the shoulder.

"Merry, look..."

"Look my ass, Kat. Clyde said he would pay $90 and he only brought $25."

Clyde picked up his money one bill at a time, just slow enough for Merry to recount it.

"Shit, that's more than anybody else'll pay. Old as dirt, out of tune. I got half the mind to take it from you anyway and use it for firewood."

"Use it for what?"

Merry stepped up, angry. Her selling Excellent's piano to cop smack was one thing, but Clyde's embalming fluid sniffing ass talking about chopping it up and roasting dead bodies over it? That was blasphemy.

Kat spoke up.

"Merry, Juliette..."

"Kat, I'm taking care of business now..."

"But Juliette's dancing!"

Merry turned just soon enough to see her little girl twirling like a beautiful ballet dancer inside a jewelry box. She giggled, took a bow.

"Momma! Auntie Kat! Did you see me? You see me?!"

Kat, proud of her little student, clapped.

"That was beautiful, baby! Beautiful!"

Merry, no urge to go to her child at all, watched as Kat hurried up to Juliette and smothered her with kisses.

Clyde sucked his tooth.

"Your little girl turned out cute. Good thing you kept her."

Merry cut her eyes. Clyde was an ass. But the man had something that she wanted. Hell, who was she kidding. Something she needed.

"Hold on, Clyde."

Clyde eyed her. The nigga knew before he came that Merry was going to take that twenty-five dollars. She was a junkie, stone cold. And nothing else mattered. Not her little girl's dancing. Not her selling the only birthday present her mother ever gave her. Not one single thing. Merry palmed the money.

"You cheap muthafucka. Give me and Kat a ride. Downtown."

**

Kat whined, her head in her hands.

"I told you this was a bad idea."

Kat was right. Merry should have known better than to go shopping when she was hungry. But twenty-five dollars wasn't enough to buy a good taste for her and Silas, let alone Kat, too. And Kat asking Raymond for an extra taste was a waste of time, because to him, getting Merry high was the same as getting Silas high. In fact, the boy had called himself catching a 'tude, because Kat and Merry kept hanging out with each other. But Kat and Merry weren't just best friends; they were sisters.

And cellmates. On lockdown at City Jail, they were starring at the back of the head of the woman responsible for putting them there - Mrs. Lowenstein.

"Now, Ma'am, you say you know the girls?"

The officer loaded some paper into the typewriter as Mrs. Lowenstein nodded her head.

"Just the brown one. She's the niece of my employee, Henrietta."

Merry, leg twitching, slumped further down on the bench. She should have just taken the twenty-five dollars from Clyde three hours ago and copped a taste instead of getting greedy. But no, she had to go and lift from Mrs. Lowenstein's husband's jewelry store.

Mrs. Lowenstein looked back at Merry, shook her head.

"It's a shame. Henrietta's the most honest person I know. This is going to break her heart."

The officer took a slurp of coffee, double-checked.

"And you're pressin' shoplifting charges on both of them?"

Mrs. Lowenstein's face turned cold, back to business.

"Absolutely."

Merry eyed the officer, trying to make out what Mrs. Lowenstein was saying to him as he henpecked her answers onto the typewriter's keys. Truth was, Merry and Kat hadn't gotten a chance to lift much of anything before Kat got careless.

Kat leaned on Merry, heavy.

"Where is he, Merry? Where's Raymond?"

"I don't know. He should of been here by now."

Actually, Raymond should have been there long before now. Silas was at work. No reaching him until tonight. If then. And Merry didn't want to nor did she have to call Teenie or Excellent. Just as soon as Mrs. Lowenstein got back to her clothing store, she was going to tell Teenie, who would tell Excellent. The only thing Merry had to do was to get gone before either one of them showed up to retrieve her.

Merry stood up. Mrs. Lowenstein was leaving.

"Mrs. Lowenstein?"

No answer. The woman was just going to walk by her and leave her under the jail to rot. Merry had to stop her.

"Mrs. Lowenstein, please!"

Mrs. Lowenstein snapped.

"What, Merry."

"I can work it off."

"You can work it off?"

"Yeah, everything we took. I can work in your store..."

Mrs. Lowenstein looked at her like she was crazy. Merry stammered.

"O.K., not your store. Wherever you want me to. I'll do anything, clean your house, take out your trash. Whatever you want for however long you want, Mrs. Lowenstein, until I pay you back."

Mrs. Lowenstein peered at her.

"You think you can pay me back, Merry? I'm not the one you owe. Henrietta, that's who you owe."

Merry swallowed. Mrs. Lowenstein was right. She did owe Teenie an apology, but what Merry really wanted to give her favorite aunt was something more valuable. The gift of ignorance.

*

Merry and Kat held onto each other like two fever-ravaged, shivering babies. Sickness, Merry knew, but this illness she couldn't comprehend. She was freezing and boiling. And her stomach was cramping so bad, she kept checking to see if blood was dripping down her legs.

Kat leaned over the side of the bench again, her mouth agape and gagging.

Merry squeezed her friend's clammy hand. As bad as she was feeling, Kat was worse. She had been throwing up her insides for an hour now, and shaking and sweating like the devil gave her the flu.

Merry looked around the jail cell for help. An old, used up whore was snoring loudly in the corner. And a woman, not as young as Merry, but not as old as Teenie, was starring right through her.

Merry got up, banged on the bars.

"Officer, we need help! Officer!"

A fresh faced, fat bodied police officer stepped inside.

"What's the problem?"

Merry, dizzy, leaned against the bars.

"My friend is sick."

The officer's brown eyes darted over to Kat. Then, he unsnapped the key-chain from his belt, found the right key.

"Her boyfriend's here. He can take her to get her medicine."

"What about me?"

The officer shrugged. Kat struggled to her feet, fussed.

"But, Officer...that's a mistake. Raymond's bailing out... both us."

"That's not what he said. Now, if you don't want to go..."

Kat looked to Merry, her heart not wanting to leave, but her fiending body desperately needing to. Merry took Kat by her quivering arm, helped her to the open cell door.

"It's O.K. Just keep trying Silas. He'll come get me."

Merry grinned. She actually believed what she was saying. Kat grinned back.

"O.K., Merry. O.K."

*

This was the longest. The longest that Merry had gone without a drink or a taste in she couldn't remember when. She didn't care anymore. Didn't care who she disappointed. Cared less than a damn who knew she was a screw-up and talked about her. Silas. Teenie. Excellent. Her momma. Hell, even Jesus' trifling self could come to Merry's rescue for all she cared. Merry just knew that whomsomever was coming to bail her out, she needed to be up out of that jail cell yesterday.

"Officer! Officer!"

The broke-down whore chuckled.

"Finally ready to call yo' momma, huh?"

Merry ignored her, pounded on the jail cell bars again, weak. The whore laughed, lit a cigarette.

"How old are you, 'Lil Bit?"

Merry called out for the officer and banged on the bars again. The whore blew a thick ring of smoke in the air.

"Fuck you, too. I was jus' tryin' to keep your mind off that monkey humpin' your back."

Merry's legs buckled. In her head, Merry was cussing that used up whore out, but in reality? All Merry had left in her to do was to hold onto the bars. She yelled out for help again.

"Officer!"

Excellent, still dressed ever the part of the maid that she was, hurried through the door, her gaze locked on a wild-eyed Merry. She rushed to the bars.

"Merry, you alright?"

Merry grabbed her mother's hands. Excellent's were warm. Hers, cold and clammy.

"Oh, Momma, I'm so sorry. I didn't mean it..."

Excellent turned on the police officer.

"What's wrong wit' my daughter?"

The police officer looked at Excellent. The answer was past obvious.

"I'm not a doctor, ma'am."

"Well, she needs one. My daughter needs a doctor right now."

Merry, desperate, gripped Excellent's hands.

"Please, Momma, I'm sick. Real sick."

"Where's it hurt, Merry?"

"Everywhere...Just get me out of here and I'll get back the piano. I promise."

The police officer, eager to shackle another charge to Merry's ankle, perked up.

"What's she talkin' about?"

"Nothin'. My daughter's just talkin' out her head. She needs a doctor."

"Lady, this is a police station, not a hospital. You wanted to see your daughter. Now you have..."

Merry held onto Excellent, panicking.

"Momma! Don't leave me. Don't leave me here!"

Excellent, every ounce of her wanting to stop her pain, looked Merry square in the eye.

"I'm not leavin' you, Merry. You comin' wit' me."

The police officer hissed.

"Lady, you just said you couldn't post bail."

"Well, now I can. I'm not leavin' my daughter here."

Daughter. Merry hadn't heard her mother call her daughter in forever. And if her twisted mind hadn't been flooded with thoughts of getting high, the milestone might have meant something. Instead, the word went in one ear and out the other. So did Excellent's talk of Ms. Ruthie dropping a dime on her to the police and telling them that she was "witnessing" a robbery in progress. The blind bat had heard the whole thing, but by the time the cops finally showed up to arrest Merry, she was long gone. And her babies were the only ones left there to greet them.

Merry eyed the car door. Mr. Blackie was in the driver's seat, her mother riding next to him and the street light, a temporary mint green, waited up ahead.

Excellent rested her hand on her purse, indebted.

"I'll pay you back, Blackie. Just as soon as I get my next check."

"That's alright, Excellent. Just glad I could help. Where we gone take her?"

"To the hospital. Maybe they'll keep her 'til she has to go to court..."

"What if they don't? You can't take her home. The judge said..."

"I know what he said, Blackie."

Merry glanced over her shoulder at Merry, blind to what everyone, even Blackie could see.

"How you feelin', Merry?"

Merry glared at Excellent, growled.

"I'm sick. I told you I was sick. Why do you keep asking me that?"

Blackie stopped at the red light, looked at Merry through the rear-view mirror. Excellent wrung her hands.

"I know you sick, Merry. That's why we're takin' you to the hospital."

"Just take me home."

"I can't take you home."

"Why not?!"

"'Cause you left those babies alone one too many times, Merry. I had to leave work today and claim Jr. Baby and Julia as mine, so the state wouldn't take 'em. The judge said if I let you anywhere near them, they'll take 'em again. This time for good."

The threat of losing her children not enough to douse the jones gnawing away at her, Merry snapped.

"Then take me over Teenie's. I can stay with her."

Excellent sat back in her seat.

"Teenie don't want you. She knew you were in jail before I did, but she wouldn't come. Wouldn't even give me any money to bail you out, 'cause Louis wouldn't let her. But you gone 'head, run to her if you want to."

"You lying!"

"I'm lyin'?! I'm here, Merry! I'm here!"

Merry yanked opened the back door, shot out. Excellent called after her, as Mr. Blackie, his foot about to press down on the gas, slammed on the brakes. Excellent scrambled out of the car, too slow, too late.

Merry was faster. Merry was quicker. Merry was gone.

DETROIT,
1965

Served the nigga right.

Silas should have given her a key and then she wouldn't have had to break the lock to get into the apartment.

Merry headed straight for the bedroom, opened the top nightstand drawer, found Silas' stash.

Merry slumped against the bed, the smack swimming upstream through her system. A crooked grin crept onto her face.

"What the fuck!"

Merry's head jerked back mid-nod. Silas was home and the man sounded none too happy. Merry stumbled to her feet, just in time to come nose to nose with Silas and his pistol. She chuckled.

"Hey, Baby."

Silas pulled back his pistol, pissed.

"Goddamn it, Merry! What the hell you doin' here?"

"I had...to use...the bath...room. I let...my...self in."

Merry slithered past Silas into the hallway and saw that her man wasn't alone. His daughters, LaTonya and Lenora, were standing by the front door with their jackets still on. Merry smiled. They didn't. Silas grabbed her arm.

"You take my shit?"

Merry, feeling too good to be scared, came clean.

"Yeah...and it was goooooood."

Silas slapped her. The pain was delayed, but it was pain just the same. Merry fell backward to the floor, tried to scamper away.

"Silas, wa..it! I can ex..plain... I was in jail...I kept call...ing..."

Silas stomped toward her, his hands balled into fists. Merry flipped over, scurried on her knees. LaTonya and Lenora looked on, numb. Silas yanked Merry back by her hair, wrapped his big hand around her small throat.

"What I tell you 'bout takin' my shit, Merry? What I tell you?"

Merry, eyes watering, no air left in her, croaked.

"I'm...sor...ry."

Silas broke his grip. Merry dropped to the floor, gasping.

"Damn right, you sorry. Get your jailbird ass the hell out my house."

Silas stepped over Merry as she reached for him, missed. She looked up, locking sights with LaTonya and Lenora. Their eyes were cold. And distant.

LaTonya took Lenora by the hand, left the room.

**

"When are you going get tired of this, Merry? When are you going to get tired of Silas beating on you?"

Kat dabbed at Merry's swollen face with a cool cloth and alcohol. Merry grimaced.

"I deserved it, Kat."

"You didn't deserve this, Merry."

Merry took the cloth from her friend and looked at herself in the bathroom mirror. The left side of her face was so black and blue, Merry could make out the outline of Silas' hand on her bruised cheek.

Raymond stepped into the bathroom.

"She finished?"

Kat, protective, stood by Merry's side.

"Not yet. Merry, are you hungry?"

Merry opened her mouth, Raymond answered.

"Fix it to go."

"Raymond, we can't just put her out."

"Yeah, we can. Her momma came by here already lookin' fo' her. Next time, they might brin' company."

Kat started to fuss back, Merry stopped her.

"He's right, Kat. I better go."

"Where are you going to go, Merry?"

Merry thought, couldn't answer. Teenie wasn't an option. At least, that's what Excellent told her. And going home? After the way Merry ran off, she knew that her mother would just as soon escort her back to jail herself before she gave her refuge against the judge's orders. Merry shrugged.

"I don't know, but I'll call you when I get there."

*

The bus station was smaller than Merry remembered. When she was a hick, just off the bus from Locust Grove, it all seemed so majestic to her. But now it was just a dirty, small bus station with splintered benches that reeked of cigarettes and broken dreams.

Merry looked up at the board. Not much left to choose from. Youngstown, Ohio and London, Kentucky. She had heard of Youngstown before. Dolores' and her high yella family hailed from there. Just Merry's luck some of the girl's big mouth kin were still struggling down there and she would bump into them. Merry plopped the money Kat gave her down on the counter.

"One ticket to..."

Merry paused, changed her mind.

"Two tickets to London, please."

The ticket clerk glanced up from his glasses, not pleased Merry was interrupting him from his crossword puzzle. He picked up the money.

"Only 'nough here for one."

"That's alright. She can buy her own."

Merry turned to face Teenie who was standing behind her. She snatched her money off the counter, started to bolt. Teenie stepped in her way.

"Where you goin', Merry?"

"You tell me. You seem to know what I'm gone do, where I'm gone be."

Teenie looked at Merry's black and blue face, softened.

"What happened? Who did this to you?"

"Mrs. Lowenstein. Yeah, we got into a fight in jail. Remember? The place you wouldn't bail me out of?"

"Merry..."

Merry pulled away.

"What?! You care about me now?"

"I'm takin' you home."

"You can't. The judge said so. How about this? How about you take me home with you, Teenie? Is Louis in the car? I'll ask him."

Teenie shook her head, her heartbreaking.

"How long, Merry?"

"How long what?!"

"How long you been doin' junk?"

Merry hesitated, the truth and a lie both perched on the tip of her tongue. She had a choice to come clean with her auntie or to deny the dope fiend reflection of herself in Teenie's sad eyes. Merry spoke. Fast.

"I don't know what you talking about. I'm not..."

"Don't lie to me, Merry."

"I ain't lying! Mrs. Lowenstein the one lying!"

Teenie grabbed Merry, yanked up her sleeve. The truth was spelled out in her collapsing veins. Merry tried to pull away, yelled.

"Let me go!"

Like an animal caught in a trap, Merry struggled, slapping at Teenie's arms, stomping on her feet, anything to loosen Teenie's hold on her. But her auntie wasn't letting go.

Merry collapsed, angry, grateful tears welling up in her eyes.

"Let me go, Teenie...Let me go."

DETROIT,
1965

As soon as Merry stepped up onto Excellent's new porch on Deering, she wanted to leave. She didn't have to say goodbye to Jr. Baby and Juliette. Or more to the point, she didn't deserve to.

Merry, turning around to flee, caught sight of a familiar pair of eyes squinting at her from inside. Juliette, a younger, brighter version of herself, strolled up to the locked screen door, munching on a bag of chips. Merry grinned, started to speak. Juliette cut her off.

"Momma! That lady's here to see you!"

That lady? Here Merry was starring her daughter in the face, and the girl had the nerve to call her "that lady"? Yes, she had been strung out on dope and in and out of jail since the day

Juliette was born 14 years ago. Yes, Excellent had told Merry that she had a police order to keep her from coming around any more after she begrudgingly became legal guardian of Juliette and Jr. Baby, so her poor grandbabies wouldn't become wards of the state. And yes, absolutely yes, Excellent didn't remind Jr. Baby or tell Juliette that Merry was their mother, so that Juliette wouldn't go blabbing her mouth to her teachers on the off chance that Merry - just like she was doing today - showed up unannounced, out of jail. Ready to make a fresh start. And Excellent, out of the guilty goodness of her heart, let Merry stay a night or two. Again.

All of it was true. To be honest, Merry even thought it best that she play the daughter of a friend role and she was relieved that she had never told Juliette who she was. But deep down, she wondered why her daughter couldn't see her and tell that she was flesh of her flesh, bone of her bone.

Juliette pushed opened the screen door and got back on the wall phone in the kitchen. Excellent stepped out into the hallway, not surprised to see Merry at all.

"Dress is snug on you."

Merry smoothed out a wrinkle running across her waist, grinned.

"Eating potatoes three times a day put the weight back on me. You gotta take it out for me now."

"Hmph, as good as you sew now, you don't need me."

Excellent and Merry chuckled, uneasy. They sat down in the living room, tense. Merry, glancing around Excellent's new digs, extended the olive branch first.

"This is nice."

"Officer Petosky's a good landlord. Thank God for him."

Merry nodded, her silence the only amen she was interested in offering. Last year, the City announced plans to extend the Davison Freeway east from Woodward to Conant. The expansion wasn't going to be complete for another four years, but that didn't keep the white man from bullying and forcing hardworking Black folks out of their homes. Excellent included. Officer Petosky, though, the great white hope that he was, came to the rescue and offered up one of his two-family flats nearby on Deering Street. And thanks to him, Excellent and the kids were one of the first families from the Northend to find a safe place to land.

No doubt, the situation was definitely something to be grateful for. But thanking God for Petosky? Merry couldn't make that leap. For some reason she just couldn't shake the feeling that all Petosky's niceness - him pulling strings and getting her sent to Kentucky State Women's Corrections to get clean and moving Excellent in to rent his house - was going to come back someday to bite her in the ass.

Excellent eyed Merry, leery.

"Johnson said you were back, Merry, but you wasted your time comin' to see me."

"I don't need money. I just came to tell you I'm leaving. Tonight."

Excellent, unimpressed and unapproving, frowned.

"Where you and Silas goin'?"

"Not Silas, just me. And I don't know, I'm thinking of Chicago. Maybe taking up sewing at a hotel or something. You know, get myself set up, so I can send money back for the kids every month. Maybe Corn..."

"Corn left Chicago years ago. He's back in Atlanta now takin' care of his momma."

"Oh. Well, you think he could put a good word in for me where he used to work?"

"Don't pull Corn into your shit, Merry."

"What shit? I'm serious."

"And what your serious ass gone do? You think you can just walk out the jailhouse into a hotel and they gone hire you? Where you gone tell them you've been for the last four years?"

"Whatever the hell I..."

Merry caught herself, gritted her teeth.

"Look, I didn't come to get your damn permission, Excellent. I just came here to tell you I'm leaving and to say goodbye to my kids."

Merry stood, frustrated.

"Felton! Juliette!"

No response. Excellent offered, matter-of-factly.

"Jr. Baby's at work."

"Well, Juliette's in there running her mouth on that damn phone. And I know she heard me."

Merry started for the kitchen. Excellent, her mother tone louder than her voice, called out.

"Julia!"

Quicker than a heartbeat, Juliette bounced into the room.

"Yes?"

"Merry wants to tell you somethin'."

Juliette looked at Merry, not wanting to be bothered. Merry started, nervous.

"I just wanted to tell you that I'm leaving. I'm going to Chicago for a new job and once I get settled, I was thinking I could send for you to visit if you want."

Merry paused, giving Juliette a chance to express how excited she was, but the girl just looked at her blankly.

"Don't you even want to know why I want you to visit?"

Juliette shrugged.

"Juliette..."

"My name is *Julia*."

"Well, I named you Juliette. It's famous for..."

"...Romeo and Juliette. I know."

"You know?"

"Yeah."

Juliette's nonchalant "yeah" lifted and dropped to the floor, the dismissal that it was. She knew Merry was her mother. Her no good, dope fiend, jailbird mother. And it didn't matter. At all.

Juliette snapped her head in Excellent's direction, quick.

"Momma, can I go? I have homework to finish."

Merry's mind raced. She had always hoped that one day her daughter would know the truth. But not like this. She had to explain.

"Juliette, wait a minute..."

Juliette ignored Merry, her eyes still fixed on Excellent.

"I have a lot of extra credit to do, Momma. Gi Gi's on the phone waiting."

Excellent nodded.

"Gone ahead. And set the table for dinner."

Merry, castrated, demanded an answer.

"When you tell her?"

"I didn't. She must have found out on her own."

Excellent stood, not pressed. She headed for the kitchen.

"I cooked some pork chops. You stayin'?"

Merry, trying to stave off the growl of her stomach and the dam of tears welling up behind her eyes, shook her head, 'no.'

DETROIT, 1953

Nine months and a day. That was Merry's sentence.

At the most, all she could of gotten, in fact, should have gotten for her first offense was a slap on the wrist - community service and parole like Kat did. But somehow the judge found out she was a terrible daughter, a horrible mother and an ungrateful, doping wretch who made a run for it and he wanted to punish her for being a menace to society.

Merry plopped down her chewed up blanket and pillow on the bottom bunk. The other three obviously had owners. Owners she hadn't met yet, because the County Jail cell was empty. Merry looked around. Four gray walls and four flat bunks with a filthy, stinking toilet between them.

In the hallway, a bell rang. Signaling what, Merry didn't know and didn't care. She sat down on the bunk. It was harder than concrete. She would have been better off squatting on the floor.

"Well, well, well, look what Santa done brought me."

Merry looked up. A woman, somewhere in the neighborhood of 30, construction paper brown and tall, was standing in the barred doorway, smiling at her. Merry knew better than to smile back. It was July, not December. And she wasn't a Christmas gift left under the tree by some fat, jolly white man. A second bell rang. The woman strolled into the cell.

"I always wanted a baby doll. Now lucky me, I got one."

The woman stood in front of Merry, damn near licking her chops like the wolf that she was. Merry gathered her blanket and pillow, nervous.

"This your bunk?"

The woman smiled, nodded. Merry stood, tossed her blanket and pillow up on the top bunk. The woman winked at her.

"That's mine, too."

Merry looked at her. She was serious. Merry rested her hand on the top bunk, intimidated.

"Both of them?"

The woman nodded. Merry sighed, trying to mask the aggravation bumbling up in her stomach.

"Then where am I supposed to sleep?"

The woman glanced over her shoulder to the toilet. Merry followed her gaze.

"You serious?!"

"As a heart attack."

"Why can't I sleep here?"

"'Cause these here bunks are mine, Baby Doll. Just like you gone be."

The woman stepped up, pinning Merry up against the bunk. A third bell rang and two laughing women sauntered into the cell. The one that Merry couldn't see flopped down on the bottom cot, but the older one with bad acne stopped.

"Damn it, 'Chell. You need to get that 'lil bitch out of here before Rudolph checks. How many times we got to tell you?"

'Chell eased up, smiled. Merry wiggled out from under her, a 'thank you' on her tongue for her hero, but the pimply faced woman slapped it back down her throat.

"Now get the hell out of here, bitch. I ain't doing shit detail for nobody."

"I'm *supposed* to be here."

"Shit, ain't nobody *sposed* to be here. You sposed to be here, 'Chell?"

"Naw, BeBe."

"Me, neitha, girl. What about you, 'Licia? You *sposed* to be here?"

BeBe moved to the side to look at her cellmate on the bottom bunk. It was Phylicia, Mrs. Coffee's mean ass daughter, acting brand new. She starred dead at Merry.

"Nope."

BeBe turned back to Merry, hands on her wide hips.

"See, bitch, we all innocent up in here. So if you *sposed* to be here, that means you ain't shit and you *sposed* to sleep on the toilet."

BeBe and 'Chell slapped hands, tickled with themselves. Merry, not impressed, wasn't giving up that easy.

"But they told me this was my cell. Phylicia, tell them..."

BeBe whipped her head back around to Phylicia, unbelieving.

"'Licia? You know this bitch?"

Phylicia looked up at Merry and tossed her an used up book of matches. Merry opened the book. There was only one match left.

"You better light that 'fore you go to sleep. 'Chell's shit stinks like hell."

****

A roach scurried across the cell, his black back glistening in the moonlight streaking though the barred, glass window. Searching for food, it paused at the toilet, then caught sight of Merry's slumbering foot.   Antennas twitching, it scampered onto Merry's Wayne county issued shoe, crawled up her leg.

Too frightened and uncomfortable to sleep, Merry jerked, her eyelids heavy as concrete and her nodding head losing out to gravity. Her eyes closed. Then like a siren announcing a four-alarm fire, her neck snapped back and her eyes sprung open. Merry yelped and jumped off the toilet, her feet stomping a Holy-Ghost-Get-This-Roach-Off-Of-Me dance. No luck. That stubborn sucker wasn't shaking loose. Frantic, Merry kicked off her shoes and socks, yanked off her pants and her unwanted guest, exposed, tried to scurry away. Merciless, she squashed it. Bare foot and all.

Phylicia flicked off Merry's sock from her pillow, pissed.

"What the hell wrong wit' you?"

Merry looked at Phylicia, half crazed, the fact that she was standing in the middle of the cell in her underwear so not important. Merry lifted her foot, revealing what was left of the crushed roach. She wiped it off with her sock. Phylicia wrinkled her face.

"Uh, that shit is nasty."

'Chell's groggy voice echoed from the top bunk.

"Hmmm. No, it ain't."

Merry didn't have to look up to know that 'Chell's dyke self was eyeballing her ass. She shook her pants, pulled them back on and laid down on the bottom bunk, defiant. To hell with 'Chell. Merry was a lot of things. But she wasn't shit and she damn sure wasn't supposed to sleep on no damn toilet.

'Chell, Merry's pillow underneath her head, sat up on her elbows.

"What you think you doin', Baby Doll?"

Merry turned on her side, right into the gaze of Phylicia. "Sleeping."

Merry heard 'Chell coming off the top bunk to get her.

"Didn't I tell you this was my bunk, Baby Doll?"

Merry looked up at her, calm.

"Well, it's mine now."

"What you say?"

Merry stood up, her eyes never unlocking from 'Chell's.

"I said, It's. Mine. Now."

'Chell starred down at Merry. 5'4 in heels and barely a hundred pounds wet, Merry looked about as dangerous as a gnat challenging a rhino. 'Chell smiled. From the top bunk, BeBe stirred awake.

"Oh, shit."

Distracted, Merry flinched and in that split second, 'Chell punched her. Hard. In her stomach. Merry dropped to her knees. 'Chell got down in her face, her hot breath singeing Merry's nose hairs.

"That bunk is mine, Baby Doll."

Merry, her womb throbbing in pain, couldn't protest. 'Chell lifted her chin, gentle.

"Say it."

Merry glared up at her, all the go-to-hells and fuck-yous she wanted to say silent. She croaked.

"That bunk is mine, Baby Doll."

'Chell started to smile, pleased. Then, stopped. Merry winked. 'Chell, furious, raised her hand. Phylicia spoke up.

"Leave her 'lone, 'Chell."

"You hear what this l'il bitch said to me?!"

"Yeah, she said what you told her to say. Now leave her 'lone and take your ass to sleep. Damn."

Phylicia flopped over on her side. 'Chell looked back at Merry, a sore loser. Merry glanced at 'Chell's skinny, ashy ankles, ready to grab them and trip her if she made a move.

Poor child didn't even see 'Chell's fist coming.

***

Merry felt at a disadvantage. Bad enough she was fresh meat in jail, but now, thanks to a left cross from 'Chell last

night, she was a wounded gazelle with only one good eye. Easy pickings for any carnivorous cheetah or hungry
hyena that laid sights on her.

Stomach churning, Merry fell in line with her other inmates at the cafeteria counter. Breakfast, whatever it was, smelled old. Damn. It looked worse.

Phylicia, next to her, agreed. Blankfaced, she looked at the scoops of green eggs and gray grits as the old lady inmate plopped them down on her tray, then scooted down. Merry, salty, did the same.

"Thanks for saying something to 'Chell, 'Licia."

Phylicia glanced at Merry. Merry's attitude was not cute and obvious. She shrugged.

"I was just tryin' to go to sleep."

"So was I. Why didn't you just tell them you know me?"

"What, you think you comin' down to my momma's basement, payin' pocket change for some shit I stole makes us best friends?"

"No, but all you had to say..."

"Say what? Vouch for yo' ass? Look, Merry, whatever you did to get in here, that's yo' business. Whatever you do while you in here, that's yo' damn business, too. I'm not your friend. In here, you don't have no friends."

No greater truth. Merry didn't like Phylicia -- this was true -- but she'd be a damn fool to stare the girl's truth in the face and not take heed to it.

**

Merry hated Tuesdays and Thursdays. Because on those two wretched days, boyfriends and girlfriends, husbands and wives, mothers and fathers, sons and daughters and friends got to lay eyes on, and if the money was right, lay hands on their locked down loved ones.

Since Merry had been in, the only visit she had to look forward to was a monthly, awkward one from Excellent. And that was only to get cigarettes. Excellent hadn't once brought Jr. Baby and Juliette to see her and Merry, who only missed her babies when she allowed herself to, never asked Excellent to bring the kids, because they were living, breathing reminders of all of the wrong Merry had done. Instead Merry held out hope for visits from Teenie, who couldn't stand seeing her caged up. And Johnson, with his selfish ass, had only blown through once or twice. Merry wondered if she would do the same to him if the shoe was on the other foot. No, the boy was still her brother. But let Kat come down on the wrong side of the law.

Merry told herself that it didn't bother her that Kat had forgotten about her. Just like she convinced herself of Silas' ignorance. The way they left things was bad, yes. But Merry had the scars to prove that they had had worst fights before. Silas just hadn't come to visit her, because he didn't *know* she was in jail. Yeah, that was it.

Merry folded back the front page of the Michigan Chronicle. The Korean War was over and the not-much-to-it Negro paper was splattered with photos of high yella, high society Negros cheesing at welcome home parties for the weary troops. Merry chuckled to herself. The men, fraternity and NAACP card-carrying member types, donned tuxedos and didn't have one strand of their conked hair out of place. And their church going, sorority-bred women, faces powdered to make them look even lighter, were dripping in jewels and dressed in expensive gowns. The soldiers looked fine, too. Uniforms starched stiff enough to slice anyone who rubbed up against them, most of the men weren't smiling.

Merry could relate. In her 18 short years, she had seen more than her fair share of shit. And these days, Merry felt beyond the opposite of her name.

A shadow slanted across the newspaper. Merry pulled it back and found Phylicia standing in front of her with a library book in her hands. It was the encyclopedia, book E. She slid it over to Merry, sat down, grabbed the newspaper. Merry glanced at the encyclopedia, suspicious. Phylicia pretended to read the front page, whispered.

"Turn to page 73."

Merry, a sly eye checking for the librarian guard, flipped to the page.

Instead of finding riveting information on the history of eels, she found a crumpled, half-written note about cigars on Wayne County Jail stationary in the warden's cursive handwriting. Phylicia asked under her breath.

"Can you do that?"

Merry scanned the note, thinking she had missed something.

"Do what?"

"Write a note from the warden. I know what you can do. I know about the bank."

Merry looked at her, confused. Only Excellent knew about Merry forging that letter to the bank. How did Phylicia know about that?

Merry shook her head, started to deny. Phylicia wasn't having it.

"I need you to write a note from the warden, tellin' the guards to let me see my son for his birthday."

"Uh uh, 'Licia. Why you want to put me all up in the middle of your mess? Just give the warden a cut."

Phylicia peered at Merry, pissed.

"A cut of what."

Merry knew the answer to the question Phylicia wasn't asking. But she wasn't supposed to know that Phylicia was running a small, members only numbers hustle in jail for her enterprising mother, Mrs. Coffee. Negro inmates, with only cigarettes or toiletries as currency, would make their picks on the inside with Phylicia and their people on the outside would pay or collect from Mrs. Coffee.

How Phylicia found out what the numbers were everyday, Merry didn't know. But one thing she did know? Phylicia's jailhouse numbers hustle was hard to pin down. And that's why the warden wanted in.

Merry closed the encyclopedia, slid it back over.

"I can't do it, 'Licia. After all, we ain't friends, right?"

Phylicia laid her hand on top of the book, calm.

"Naw, we ain't. But I know 'Chell really wants to be."

Merry looked at Phylicia, trapped. Weeks of getting her ass beat had finally earned Merry 'Chell's respect. Or so she thought. The real reason she wasn't that horny dyke's bitch? Phylicia was standing in front of Merry, and if Merry knew what was good for her, she'd do whatever she had to, so Phylicia wouldn't step out of the way.

Merry glanced at the clock on the library wall, the second hand ticking away the little time she had to pull off the job. The warden, Phylicia told her, was leaving for a three-week vacation on Friday. Two days from now. Somehow, Merry had to get the man's handwriting down, write out the note word for word from Phylicia's mouth and get it back to Phylicia on jail stationary, no less.

Merry studied the warden's half-written cursive note one more again. He wrote on a slant, almost as if he was left-handed, and he had a funny way of writing p's, f's and l's. No open loops.

Merry snatched some toilet paper off the roll, pulled out a stubby pencil. She didn't have much time. One practice tracing run, then she'd do it for real on the stationary. Why did the girl only give her one sheet?

Merry laid the toilet paper over the note, started to trace. Then she heard footsteps approaching behind her. Not the soft soled ones of an inmate, but hard soled, deliberate ones. It was a guard.

"You did what?!"

Phylicia, a winning tunk hand in front her, snarled at Merry. Merry glanced at Phylicia's pile of cigarettes on the top of the picnic table, wanted to ask for a smoke. She didn't.

"I had to 'Licia. Just get another piece."

"What, you think I can just walk up in the warden's office anytime I want and get office supplies? You jus' gonna have to make it work."

"And how am I supposed to do that?"

Phylicia scooped her winnings into her pocket and stood up to leave.

"I don't know. But the warden's leavin' tomorrow and if you know what's good for you, I better have my letter 'fore he's gone."

Merry wanted to laugh. She wasn't sure she could pass off the warden's handwriting well enough for a letter, let alone get her hands on some paper that he would he write it on. Any inmate that wanted to write a letter could get free lined paper from the library. But the warden wouldn't be caught dead writing on that. He had legitimate paper that men in power scribbled orders on. Merry knew that if she had more time, she could get hold of some. But jail payback already had her scrambling, trying to dig herself out of a hole she had no idea how to pull herself out of.

Merry spotted an unused cigarette trying to blend into the brown grass. She picked it up, started to light it, then stopped. On the other side of the yard, chain-smoking up against a wall was Merry's way out of the hole.

Merry tucked the cigarette into her pocket and sauntered over. A pair of unfriendly, untrusting sky blue eyes met her.

"Sally, can I talk to you for a minute?"

Sally, a eggshell faced mulatto with chewed up nails and muddy blonde hair, lit another cigarette with a smoldering butt, puffed. The mistake of a poor white trash momma and long gone nigger daddy, Sally never looked anybody in the eye and kept to herself.

Sally dropped her eyes, mumbled.

"What do ya want?"

"I want to do something for you."

Sally lifted her head, curious, like a child who had never gotten a Christmas present.

"For me?"

Merry smiled. If she was going to get Sally to buy this load of shit she was selling, she had to make it sound good.

"Girl, I've been watching you, how hard you work. And you deserve a vacation, Sally. Tomorrow, let me clean the warden's bathroom for you."

Sally's shoulder's slouched and she nudged a cigarette butt from the pile with her shoe.

"You think I'm stupid."

"No, Sally, I don't..."

"Yeah, you do. I swap places with you, you steal somethin' from the warden's office and I get punished for it."

"Nobody's going to get punished, Sally..."

"Yeah, stupid Sally will. Everybody thinks Sally's stupid."

Merry couldn't argue. Everybody did think that Sally she was stupid. But Sally proclaiming it out loud tugged on Merry's scabbed-over heart. She knew how it felt for everyone to think she was not worth loving or fighting for. And in the moment, even though Merry needed to take advantage of Sally's self-loathing to save her own hide, all Merry could do was feel for her.

Merry cleared her throat.

"I'm sorry."

Sally looked up, surprised.

"You're...sorry?"

Merry shrugged, her answer barely out of her mouth before she turned to leave.

"Yeah."

Sally, chewing on what was left of her gnarled fingernails, fell in step next to Merry.

"O.K...I'll do it."

Merry stopped, looked at her to be sure.

"You will?"

Sally, mumbled, kept walking.

"Yeah...but I need cigarettes for my vacation. Three packs of 'em."

*

"Where's Sally?"

The warden's secretary, a non-descript polish looking woman with a thick black eyebrows and a flat, wide behind from years of desk jockeying, starred at Merry, irritated. Merry grinned.

"They switched us. Just for today."

The secretary peered at her, suspicious, reached for the phone.

"Why? She wasn't released."

"I don't know. But I heard about the warden's problem. And you can either let me clean it up before he gets back from breakfast...Or you can explain to him why his toilet is still nasty."

The secretary, no fool, waved Merry into the warden's office. Cramped with wood paneling, the room was neat, but not anything to write home about. And the bathroom, a glorified closet with a toilet in it, was off to the side.

Merry headed in, set down her bucket. The warden would be back from breakfast soon. That didn't give her a lot of time to swipe the letterhead, wipe down the toilet and get the hell out of dodge before he got back.

The telephone rang in the warden's office. From the secretary's desk, Merry heard her answer.

"Warden Barkley's office...Yes, Mayor Cobo. Absolutely, Mayor Cobo. No, sir, he's never too busy for you. Please hold."

Merry leaned back from the toilet to catch sight of the warden's secretary hauling ass out of the office. Sure she was gone, Merry hurried over to the warden's desk, started scavenging. Side drawers, nothing. Bottom drawer, locked. Top drawer, a Wayne County Jail half-used notepad.

No time to search further, Merry heard the warden's barks vibrating through the walls. She swiped the notepad, dove under the desk.

"Damn it, Helen! Why didn't you just tell the bastard I was gone?!"

"It's the Mayor, Warden. I thought..."

"And that's your damn problem, Helen. All the work you're not doing around here, you think you have time to think? Close the door."

Helen eyes shot to the open door of the bathroom.

"But, Warden, there's..."

"Close the damn door!"

Helen obeyed. And Merry prayed the warden wouldn't sit down at his desk. As usual, God wasn't listening.

"Al! How the hell are ya? And Ethel? Give her my best, will ya? Good... Good... What can I do for ya? John Martin? Yes, I remember him. Last night at the lodge, yes. Uh huh... Well, Al, now being warden of a major metropolitan jail is more than a stepping stone, I'd say. Took me thirteen years to get here. Uh huh... But there's something to be said for experience, Al...I see...No, I've driven through Kentucky once or twice, but I've never...Kentucky State Women's Correction? No, can't say that I have...I'm sure it is. I'm just heading out the door today on vacation. Judy's been nagging me for years to take some time and...No, Mr. Mayor, I understand."

Merry, scared to death and scrunched up into a corner of the warden's desk, could hear the warden's teeth gnashing over her heart pounding.

"Oh, poor baby."

Phylicia admired Merry's forged note from the warden, sarcastic.

"When I get out, the warden can come work for me. You, too, Merry."

Merry shook her head. The warden was leaving, not just for vacation, but for good. Merry just wanted Phylicia to get out of her damn face, so she could do the rest of her own time, mind her own business.

"That's alright, 'Licia."

"What, you got other plans?"

The answer was yes, but Merry didn't offer it. She had been thinking about going to night school or maybe picking up her momma's laundry business again or asking Scottie to let her help out at the club. She didn't have all the details worked out just yet.

"I'm working on some things."

"Uh huh...Well, when you ready to make some money, I'm startin' my own thing."

"I'm not trying to come back to jail, 'Licia."

"And you think I am? Shit, Merry, I'm not talkin' stupid. I'm talkin' smart."

Smart. A smart woman would have turned around and ran her smart ass the hell away from Phylicia. But that would of been too much like right.

Merry was a fool for even listening.

DETROIT,
1955

"Merry! I know you ain't gone act like you don't see me!"

Merry rolled her eyes. That's exactly what she was going to do. That is, until BeBe put her on front street.

Merry turned to face her. Not even two years later and her old cellmate looked ten years older. Whatever BeBe had been doing out in the streets hadn't been kind to her.

Then again, what Merry had been doing out in the streets hadn't been kind to her either. She was in jail. Again.

**

Excellent told Merry she could stay. She wouldn't tell the authorities and Merry could sleep on the pullout bed in the living room until she got back on her feet. All Merry had to do was follow five simple house rules.

Number one - No junk. Number two - No more babies. Number three - No no-good niggas. Number four - No stealing. And number five - Merry couldn't tell Juliette who she was.

All of that was fine with Merry. She had been in jail for nine months, governed by batons and bells, restricted by guards and rules. She could obey her mother's overbearing commandments just long enough to get herself together if she had to. The only one that stuck in her side like a thorn was lying about who she was. Every time Juliette and Jr. Baby called Excellent "momma," Merry wanted to correct them. She didn't deserve to and truth was, the thought of raising her children made Merry wheeze and gasp for air. But she still wanted to hear them call her momma.

"Gone home to yo' babies, Merry."

Merry looked around the empty Scottie's. She picked up two glasses at the end of the bar, wiped away the wet spots they left on the counter.

"That's alright, Scottie. I don't mind staying."

"I know you don't. But this ain't about what you want, now is it?"

Scottie plopped her hands on her hips. Merry so didn't want to go home to her mother's cold couch, but she knew there was no use in arguing. Once Scottie made up her mind, Jesus, himself couldn't change it. Merry found that out first-hand when she asked Scottie to let her work at the bar. Excellent, Teenie and even Scottie, at first, thought it was a disaster waiting to happen.

But Merry, desperate not to clean white folks houses with Excellent, appealed to Scottie and somehow Scottie, her friendship with Teenie on the line, looked past the obvious and agreed.

Merry dug in her pockets for bus fare. She hadn't looked at the clock before she left, but judging by the midnight blue of the night, it was about three in the morning. If she hurried, she could make it to Excellent's and get two, maybe three hours of sleep in before her mother woke the whole house up to get the kids ready for school and go to work.

Merry sat down at the bus stop, lit a cigarette. She was alone. This time of night, she usually had the stop to herself. And Merry liked that.

Lonely, on the other hand, Merry couldn't stand. That's why she pulled the string and got off the bus when she did.

"Merry Merry...Heard you was out."

Merry looked at Silas, conflicted. They were standing in front of the gate, outside the auto plant as the second shift streamed in. Silas looked like he wasn't surprised to see her.

"What you doin' here?"

Merry shuffled her feet. Good question. She had been passing Silas' plant for weeks and thinking about him for even longer. Deep down, she knew he knew she was out. Instead of celebrating that Silas probably had another woman and she was free of him, the thought of her man not giving a damn about her was eating Merry up so tough, she had to see if he still loved her.

She didn't expect Excellent or Scottie or Teenie to understand, so she didn't tell them. But any fool paying attention could see that Merry was slow dancing with poison again. Long sleeve blouses. Makeup covered bruises. Not showing up at all or disappearing for hours at a time. Merry was hooked. Again. On smack. And on Silas.

The only person who could call Merry on her mess was in worst shape than Merry. Or so she heard. Merry hadn't seen or spoken to Kat since she got out. But Silas told her that Kat's free-tasting habit was so bad, that Raymond had cut her off and Kat, strung out, was now enslaved to a dope-peddling pimp called Peach. Merry wanted to feel happy to hear the news. At least feel as happy as Silas was to tell it. But she didn't.   She felt justified.

Merry looked through the peephole and rested her hand on the knob, debating whether to turn it.

"Come on, Merry. I know you're in there. Open the door."

Kat knocked again. Merry walked away from the door. Kat rang the bell, frantic.

"Merry, come on, please! I saw Silas leave. Let me in."

Merry stopped. Her backstabbing friend actually sounded like she needed her. Merry yanked open the door, her compassion at arms length. The sight of Kat, though, made Merry want to draw her close. She looked bad. Skinny, hair all over her head and circles as black as tar under her sunken eyes, Kat looked as if she had been chasing a high for days. And she was losing.

Kat, jittery, started to rush in, but Merry didn't move out of the way.

"Merry..."

"What you want, Kat?"

"I want to come in."

Merry, catching a whiff of her friend's stale breath, moved to the side. Kat scurried in, rambling.

"I've been looking all over for you. Your momma's, Scottie's, Teenie's..."

"What'd they say?"

"They said you went back to Georgia."

Merry and Kat looked at each other, knowing. Merry's family was trying to protect her, but they would have been better off telling Kat she moved to the moon, than saying she moved back down south to Locust Grove.

Kat, scratched at her arms, jonesing.

"I knew they were lying. All of them. I knew you were out of jail. And I knew you were over here. I just had to get over here, Merry. Get over here, so I could get right and think... I know you got some, Merry. Give me some, Merry. All I need is a taste..."

"Last time I gave you a taste, I ended up in jail."

Kat looked at Merry, guilty.

"That wasn't my fault. I told you it was a bad idea. I told you I didn't feel right."

"Like you don't feel right now, Kat, huh? Couldn't find the damn jail, but here you come to see me now."

"It's not like that, Merry...I made a mistake...I'm in trouble..."

"Uh huh, well, take your trouble to Raymond. Let him get you right. Oh. You can't, can you? That's O.K... Silas'll be back in a minute. Maybe he'll let you suck his dick. How much?"

Merry starred at Kat, cold. Kat lashed back, bleeding out from the knife in her gut that Merry was holding.

"Fuck. You."

Those two words were the last ones Merry heard from Kat. The last words she heard before her dope fiend friend went back out to the streets and picked up some john that didn't pay her and Peach, beat her to the edge of death. Merry found out about it later that night from Scottie, right before Scottie was about to fire her. Scottie hadn't said anything yet and Merry wasn't sure if she had noticed the missing liquor and money from the cash register over the weeks, but Merry knew it was coming. She could read the disappointment in Scottie's eyes.

"She alright?"

"She's down at Herman Keefer. Ain't opened her eyes yet."

"I need to go see her."

"Yeah."

"I'll be back after."

"No, you ain't. You gonna buy some junk wit' my money and get high wit' that nigga Silas."

Merry, slapped in the face with the truth, didn't argue.

And as she sat at Kat's hospital bedside, Scottie was the last thing on her mind. Merry was expecting getting fired. What she wasn't expecting was losing her best friend. She'd do anything to get Kat to open her eyes again, to get her safe. But Merry knew that even if she got Kat safe, she would never be free, because Kat owed her pimp and if Peach couldn't get his payment out of her friend's ass, he'd settle Kat's tab with her blood.

One thing at a time, Merry thought. First, she had to get Kat safe. Dropping the dime into the payphone, she knew just who to call.

"Hello?"

Rev. McKeever's voice sounded groggy, but alert, the result of a shepherd accustomed to getting late night calls from members of his flock in need. Merry cleared her throat, choking back tears.

"Rev. McKeever...it's Merry."

She told him his baby was in trouble, that he should come right away. Merry knew she wouldn't be there when he came.

"You lost, Angel?"

Merry looked at J.T., in no mood for games. He knew she wasn't lost and he knew who she was after.

"Where's Raymond?"

Merry meant that specifically. Was Raymond holding court at his pool table or handling business in the back room? Whichever it was, she knew he was at Plan B.

J.T.'s leaned on the bar, his mouth smiling.

"Raymond who, Angel?"

Merry rolled her eyes. She would find him herself. Two men stepped in her path. Merry bitched.

"I don't have time for this, J.T. I need to talk to Raymond."

"Wish I could help you, Angel, but ain't no Raymond here."

J.T. shrugged. Merry tried to push through the henchmen and one of those fools grabbed her, ready to toss her out like trash.

"Let her through."

Merry walked up to Raymond. Some hussy she didn't know was hanging all over him, and Clyde, Allen and the rest of Raymond's ass kissing crew were drinking and playing pool.

"Merry, you learned how to fight in jail, huh? Arm and legs swinging all over the place, my man could hardly get a hold of you..."

"Can I talk to you for a minute?"

"We talkin'."

"I mean, alone."

Raymond glanced around to his posse.

"We all family, Merry. Whatever you gotta say to me, you can say to them."

Merry glanced at Clyde, pissed, continued.

"Kat's in the hospital. Peach beat her up pretty bad... The doctor said he's not sure when she'll wake up..."

Merry paused deliberately to give Raymond a chance to say something. He didn't.

"Did you hear me, Raymond?"

"Yeah."

"Kat's in trouble..."

"I heard you. What that gotta do wit' me?"

Raymond looked at Merry, calm, pleasant even, as if he was asking Merry for directions. Merry starred back at him, angry.

"What you mean, what that gotta do with you? You gotta help her."

Raymond paused. And Merry didn't look around her, but she could feel his groupie's collective temperature drop. Even the bitch on Raymond's arm was feeling the chill.

Raymond chuckled, looked to Clyde.

"You hear that, Clyde? Merry walked up into my place of business to tell me what I should do...No, no, that I have to help Kat. You believe that shit?"

Clyde shook his head.

"Naw, man."

Raymond looked back to Merry, his stare stone cold.

"Kat is a lyin', stealin', junkie, whorin', baby killer."

Merry swallowed, trying to keep her face from reacting. But Raymond already knew the truth. He didn't need her to second it.

"That bitch killed my baby. Not once, but twice. And you come here to tell me...I need to help her, Merry?"

"Look, Raymond, whatever Clyde told you..."

"This don't have shit to do wit' Clyde, Merry..."

"But, let me explain..."

Merry started to argue, but Raymond eyed his goons and they stepped up, silencing her protest. She looked to Raymond. His heart broken. His mind made up. If Kat was going to be saved, Merry was going to have to pick up the cross and don the crown of thorns herself.

*

"I gotta tell you, Merry, that was alright what you did. Cops ridin' you to give up 'Licia, but you didn't. That was alright."

No matter where Merry thought she was hiding in the joint, BeBe always found her. And this time around, the woman was Friendly Fanny. Always happy to help.

BeBe nudged her.

"'Licia's not gone forget that. When you get out, she'll take care of you."

Merry didn't know about all that. True, she hadn't told the police anything about Phylicia's business. But in reality, they had never asked. When the cops picked Merry up with a pocket full of hundreds and a shoplifted fifth of vodka, they just assumed that she was peddling dope. Thoughts of Merry stealing mail and forging checks with Phylicia's crew weren't even a part of the equation.

Merry also hadn't calculated getting caught lifting. Again. She had a pocket full of money, but didn't want to touch it, because with it she finally had a little over $500. Enough to pay off Kat's debt and buy her friend's freedom. Merry only lifted the booze to celebrate. She didn't need it. She didn't need that damn off-duty cop to spotting her, either.

BeBe offered Merry a cigarette. She took it. BeBe struck a match, lit Merry's cigarette first.

"You smart, Merry. Washing' checks is real smart. My ass went back to the streets. Fuckin's all I know."

Merry exhaled, the smoke rising, evaporating up into the free, blue sky. Fucking wasn't a bad thing to know. In fact, it was actually a smart thing to do, as long as you were the one doing the fucking.

Merry took another drag of her cigarette, snubbed it out in the dead grass with her shoe. She was already up on her feet before the lunch bell rang.

DETROIT,
1956

One year of jail behind her, this time Merry didn't bother with the charade of going straight. Inside, BeBe had hooked her up to the pipeline that pumped smack straight from the streets into her fiending veins. And after 12 months of being on lockdown with a new warden who built a career on looking the other way, Merry was more strung out on dope now than she was when she went in.

Street smarter and motivated to keep feeding her jones, Merry went back to business as usual. Her key still worked at Silas', her job was still waiting at Phylicia's and the couch was still open at Excellent's.

Merry hardly recognized Jr. Baby and Juliette anymore. Her son, chocolate brown like her and the spitting image of his father, was seven and wearing glasses now. Spoiled and chunky from eating Excellent's cooking, he had some size and weight on him. Just the opposite of his daddy who weighed fifty pounds wet. And Juliette, five and smart, had a mouth that ran a mile a minute.

Merry didn't see Juliette and Jr. Baby too much these days. She rolled through Excellent's every now and again, but hadn't stayed there in she couldn't remember when. But then again, it's not like she got an invitation. Johnson, married to Dolores now, was about to drop their second brat and they had set up house in Johnson's room. Even if Merry wanted to stay and Excellent wanted her there, there wouldn't have been any room.

Merry didn't give a shit anyway. She had business to take care of. And with Kat gone, she didn't have to worry about using the money she earned from washing and forging checks on anything but taking care of her and Silas. She did miss her best friend, though. A while back, Kat wrote her from California, told her that her daddy sent her to stay with her aunt and uncle, so she could get right with Jesus. She was happy, she said.

"You ready, Merry?"

Merry eyed a postbox on the corner through the glass of the telephone booth. It was perfect. Located at a popular intersection, it was close to grocery stores and banks and everybody on the North End used it. On any given day, Merry could find checks to pay bills for insurance, house notes, utilities or checks sending hard earned money down south to relatives in need.

The best day to go fishing, though, was Sunday, because Negros never paid their bills on time and always wanted to get their money in the mail on the Lord's day, so it would go out first thing Monday morning. Lucky for Merry, the post office stopped picking up mail every Saturday after three, so between then and Monday morning, the post office box would get full all the way to the top. Easy pickings for Merry to just stick her hand inside and scoop up a handful of easy money. The fact that she was stealing from neighbors and forging the signatures of people that she knew - Orin Townsend, Mr. Yancy, just to name a few - didn't bother Merry at all. To feed her habit, she had stolen from her kinfolk, so stealing from her skin folk wasn't something she was going to toss and turn over.

Merry took a drag of her cigarette. It was time to do this thing.

"Yeah, 'Licia. I know what I'm doing."

Merry hung up and walked over to open the slot to the post office box. It looked just like Christmas. She shoved a handful of mail into her purse and was going back for more when she heard a pair of brakes squeaking behind her. Merry glanced up, expecting the car with bad brakes to pass her. It didn't.

Officer Petosky and Officer Gerald pulled up to the curb. Merry nervous, played it cool. They got out of the car, walked up to her.

"A little late to be mailin' a letter, isn't it Merry?"

Merry looked at Officer Petosky, the stolen mail burning a hole in her purse.

"Just paying a bill, Officer Petosky. I want it to get there on time."

Officer Petosky, sad, glanced at his partner.

"How's your mother doin'? How's Johnson?"

Merry paused. Officer Petosky wasn't fooling anybody. The man wasn't making conversation and he didn't give a damn about Johnson. All he wanted to know was how Excellent was doing.

"Fine. Johnson got married."

"I heard. Already had one little boy and got another one on the way. Your mother's got a pretty full house over there now, huh?"

Merry didn't answer. Officer Petosky was tap dancing on a sore spot and they both knew it.

"Yeah, well, we're not gonna hold you, Merry. Just wanted to ask you a question...About Raymond. Have you heard anythin' about him? Seen him?"

"Raymond? No..."

For once, Merry wasn't lying. She hadn't talked or seen Raymond since she had been back.

Last she heard, he had gotten that hussy she saw him with pregnant and he was still peddling dope. Whatever Officer Petosky was talking about was something that must have just happened. Or maybe he and his partner were trying to trap her, get her to say something.

Officer Gerald cleared his throat, not buying it. Merry expanded her answer.

"Really, I haven't heard anything...Haven't seen Raymond."

Officer Petosky eyed Merry. Every time she ran into him, he always looked at her that way. Smack time approaching, she wondered what the hell the man was looking for. Officer Petosky explained.

"A pimp turned hustler, Vernon Walker, was murdered. Everybody calls him Peach. Heard of him?"

Merry nodded. If Petosky was asking her about Peach, then he also knew that her best friend Kat used to be one of the man's sex slaves. Wasn't no use in denying that she knew him.

"Raymond killed him. We know he killed him. We just need to find him. Now, Merry, when you see him, I need you to be responsible, understand?"

Officer Petosky, close enough for Merry to smell the liquor on his breath, starred at her, expecting only one answer.

Merry nodded. Again.

DETROIT,
1961

Merry's head bounced into a nod. A nod hard enough to snap her neck. With Raymond long gone and Peach dead, it had taken no time for another nigga, a stone-cold gangster known as Main Man, to step up to replace them.

Merry leaned back into her high, mellow, sweaty. All of the windows were closed in the apartment, and the living room was hot, sticky. Outside, Merry could see the project kids in the middle of the street running in and out of water streaming out of a fire hydrant and the grown folks that should have been watching them tossing back liquor hidden in paper bags, blasting music and talking shit in the front walkway.

Merry hummed to herself. She liked that song bouncing up against her apartment window. The man's smooth voice wasn't the best, but it was light and crisp. Like buttered popcorn. Didn't hurt that Smokey's fine green-eyed ass wasn't hard to look at either. Merry sang.

"My momma told me..."

Merry stumbled up to her feet, dropping her hose and used needle to the floor.

"You better shop around...Shop, shop around now...You betterrr shop around...Shop, shop, shop..."

Merry clapped her hands, laughed out loud. Fuck Silas and Kat. To hell with Excellent and her kids. She didn't need nobody to have a good time. She could party all by herself.

There was a knock at the door. Merry, so happy, picked up the phone.

"Hello?"

A dial tone answered her. Merry looked at the phone, confused. The knock came again. Merry chuckled, danced over to open the door. In mid-step, she stopped.

"Hi, Merry."

He was older, taller, handsome. And Merry couldn't even hear a trace of stutter in his grown man voice. But those eyes. Those piercing hazel eyes were the same.

"James?!"

They hugged, tight. In that moment, innocent, pure, forgiven.

Merry closed the door. She knew James was looking at her, taking in the sight of how torn down she looked, how bad she was living. Merry tugged at the collar of her flimsy short-sleeved blouse. She wasn't wearing a bra and her needle-tracked arms were exposed. She felt naked in front of him.

Merry grabbed one of Silas' shirts off the couch, pulled it on. James watched her.

"How you doin', Honey Bee?"

Merry, eyeing her copping kit by the window, moved some stuff over on the couch, made room for James to sit down.

"Oh, you know me. I'm good."

Merry smiled. Just one look at Merry's hair all over her head, sunken eyes, skin and bones, she looked every bit the dope fiend that she was. Merry tossed some clothes over her kit, opened a window, nervous.

"Have a seat. Sorry, the house is a mess and it's hot as hell in here, but I can get you something...something to drink...What do you..."

James sat down, his rolled up white dress shirt wrinkled and his black suit pants creased.

"That's O.K., Merry. I can't stay long."

Merry ran her hand over her wild hair, disappointed, crossed her arms.

"Oh. O.K."

Merry sat down, noticed James' wedding ring. A tinge of jealousy pricked up like a thorn underneath her tough skin.

"So...What you doing here, James? How'd you find me?"

James took a breath, clasped his hands.

"You not gone believe this, but Johnson told me."

"Johnson? How the hell that happen?"

"I ran into him in Chicago at a card game."

Merry shook her head, unbelieving.

"Johnson hates losing his money too much to play cards..."

"Yeah? Well, I looked up and there he was. Him and some nigga named Allen."

James looked at Merry and she returned the gaze, filling in the blanks of what he wasn't saying. Allen, despite doing a full tour in Korea, was a flaming queer. And her married brother with kids partying and traveling with him said more than the obvious.

Merry hung a left, asked another question.

"Yeah? Johnson driving all the way to Chicago, had to be a lot of bread in the pot. Did he win?"

"Naw, nigga lost everythang. I gave him his money back, tho'."

"Why'd you do that?"

"'Cause, that's what brothers do, Merry."

James looked at her, serious. Merry laughed.

"James, what the hell you talking about?"

"Johnson's my brother, Merry. That means you..."

"My daddy died on the railroad tracks..."

"Naw, he didn't..."

"My momma...Excellent said he got hit by a train..."

"They lied, Merry. Your momma, my momma, all of them. Our daddy just died. I buried him yesterday in Chicago."

The rest of it, Merry hardly heard. Her daddy was a no good, drinking, gambling, womanizing rolling stone that had dropped seed in Philadelphia and Georgia, had families in Chicago and Cleveland and had even fucked his way out west to California and Texas before making a pit stop in Florida.

A God-fearing man, John Henry married all of his baby mommas, even if he didn't stay with them long enough for the child to be born. All of the children somehow, except Merry and Johnson, showed up at the funeral. And with everybody from an old maid from Philadelphia to a toddler boy from Cleveland looking at him with his daddy's eyes, James said his momma as past ready to tell him the rest of the story.

Merry and James were the second and third oldest. A handsome con man with big hands and feet, their father was playing house with both of their mothers at the same time. In fact, when their mothers were carrying them and all the way up until Merry and James started to talk and walk, Excellent and Leila used to sit across the aisle from each other every Sunday at church. By the time Excellent got tired of her husband catting around, John Henry already had James' family living and growing across the railroad tracks. Pregnant with Johnson, Excellent kicked him out, told everybody the man was dead to her.

Dead. Merry understood that. That's how she felt most days. But the difference between her daddy and Merry being dead? That boiled down to choice. If Merry wanted to numb herself with booze and take herself out with smack, that was her business. But killing off her daddy and having her believe that she could never know, see or touch him when the man's trifling ass was alive and breathing just across the railroad tracks? That wasn't Excellent's or hell, her momma's decision to make.

By the time James dropped Merry off at Excellent's house, she was seething.

The front door on the top porch where Johnson, Dolores and the boys now lived and Excellent's front door were open, but all the activity - children playing, grown folks chattering, gospel music and barbeque pit smoke - were floating from the backyard up to the street. Perfect. A family gathering.

A drink in her hand and the crumpled welfare check she helped herself to from Excellent's purse, Merry stepped out on the back porch. Excellent was taking the chicken and ribs off of the grill, chatting it up with Ms. Ruthie and a nursing Dolores seated in folding chairs to the side of her. Nine-year-old Juliette was by the fence playing hopscotch with GiGi, her shy little friend from across the alley. And Merry didn't see Jr. Baby or her nephews, but she knew they were probably upstairs watching television or playing toy soldiers. Merry took a swig of her drink, let the screen door slam behind her. Three pairs of eyes swung in her direction. Ms. Ruthie spoke up first.

"Excellent, is that Johnson wit' the ice?"

Merry smiled, looked right at Excellent.

"No, Ms. Ruthie. It's me. Merry."

Excellent and Dolores shifted, in no mood for drama. Ms. Ruthie reached out for Merry, insincere.

"Oh. Merry. Good to see you."

Merry rested her hand on Ms. Ruthie's shoulder, just as fake.

"You too, Ms. Ruthie."

Merry sniffed the air, nodded to her mother.

"Smells good."

Dolores looked between Merry and Excellent, apprehensive. Excellent put the last of the ribs in the roasting pan, closed the barbeque pit lid.

"Julia."

"Yes, momma?"

"Yaw take this meat in the house and start saucin' it for me."

Juliette shuffled over with GiGi. Excellent handed the tray to her.

"Dip it in the sauce and brin' it back out like I showed you. And you bet not drop it."

Merry glanced at her frowning daughter, too selfish and caught up in her own mess to wonder or feel guilty about how fast her child was growing up. Excellent wiped her hand on a towel, looked at Merry.

"How much you been drinkin', Merry."

Merry huffed.

"Not enough."

Excellent headed inside.

"Well, come in here and fix a plate, soak up some of that liquor on your stomach."

Merry, pissed, didn't follow.

"You don't tell me what to do, Excellent. You can't say shit to me."

Dolores, baby hanging off her tit, reached out for Merry.

"Merry, don't..."

"Don't what?!"

Ms. Ruthie fussed.

"You shouldn't talk to yo' mother like that, Merry."

Merry lashed out, hurting.

"Excellent ain't my mother, Ms. Ruthie! She left me and Johnson down south to chase after a nigga. And all that time, I thought my daddy was dead. All because of her. She ain't my mother, Ms. Ruthie. Excellent ain't nothing but a lying, two-faced bi..."

"I'm not gone tell you again, Merry."

Excellent starred at Merry, her eyes cutting Merry's words short.

"Come. In. Here. And. Fix. Your. Plate."

Merry peered at Excellent, all the venom she had for her mother in her heart on the tip of her tongue.

"Fuck. You."

Excellent slapped her. A mother's reflex. Merry, the familiar taste of blood in her mouth, slapped her mother back. And down.

"Momma!!!"

Juliette dropped the roasting pan of sauced meat and flew down the porch to Excellent's side.

"What'd you do to my momma?!"

Merry couldn't answer her daughter. Because in that clear, lucid moment with her mother, on the ground staring up at her, Merry was too aware.

Too aware of what she had done.

*

"You high."

Absolutely, Merry was high. After she slapped Excellent down in front of Juliette, Merry took off to out run the throbbing, aching emptiness clawing, grabbing, gnawing at her insides. She didn't like that feeling. She needed to forget it. So, Merry took her mother's money, bought some smack from Main Man and jammed it into her veins as fast as she could.

Merry looked at Phylicia, chuckled, dry.

"Mind your business, 'Licia."

"Mind my..."

Phylicia, gritted her teeth, stopped counting the money.

"Bitch, you are my business. And the next time you come fishin' high..."

"I make more money for your ass than anybody. Mind. Your. Damn. Business."

Merry glared at Phylicia, ready to slap her into next week with Excellent. Phylicia backed off, plopped a stack of bills down in front of Merry. Merry counted.

"What the hell is this?"

"Your cut."

"What the fuck you mean, 'Licia. I wrote more checks than this."

"Wasn't safe to cash them all. Things too hot right now."

"The only thing hot, 'Licia, is my check dangling around your neck."

"You calling my momma a liar?"

Merry glanced up to Phylicia's son, Desmond, who was towering in the dining room/kitchen doorway. Sixteen going on forty and over six-feet tall, the boy's nose was still running, but at least his man-child body now matched his nappy, bubble head. Merry snarled, ready to kick his ass, too.

"Need me to spell the shit out?"

Desmond took a threatening step toward Merry. Phylicia held up her hand.

"I taught Desmond better than to hit a woman, Merry. Take your shit, 'fore I change his mind."

Merry followed Phylicia's advice. Desmond was a young blood, but already had a reputation for being a gang running, street law-enforcing monster that tortured and took out snitches, rivals and folks who couldn't pay what they owed when they owed it. He was known as one of the best. But more importantly, as Main Man, Merry's dealer and Desmond's gang brother bragged, Desmond was also known for enjoying it. And as bad a day as Merry was having, she didn't want to give Desmond the gift of her ass and put a smile on his face.

One step outside of Phylicia's Linwood apartment gate, though, Merry was the one smile less when she saw Officer Petosky. She knew it. Excellent had called him, had told him that she was high, that she had slapped her down, stole her check. Merry rounded the corner, threw her smack in the bushes, Officer Gerald on her tail.

Her skinny legs were still moving, her punctured arms still flailing when he pinned her to the ground.

KENTUCKY,
1961

"**Wait** a minute...let me talk to you for a minute..."

Merry dug her heels into the gravel, thrusting her fiending body backwards, struggling against the possessed guard dragging her handcuffed to the hotbox roasting in the Kentucky sun in the middle of the prison yard. Merry pleaded.

"Please...I got money. You can have all of it...Just don't put me in there. I'll do whatever you want... Make you feel good. Let me make you feel good, Daddy..."

Merry licked her chapped lips. The guard's dead eyes landed on her, cold, horny. He smiled.

"Don't get greedy, gal. There's plenty of me tuh go 'round."

Cocky, he lifted his gnarled hand up to his nose, sniffed.

"I'll be back fo' seconds. Don't you wurry."

The guard winked. Merry lunged. And the guard rammed his baton into her stomach, dropping her to her knees. Like a caveman, he pulled Merry backwards by her hair, her kicking legs making dirt angels in the gravel. Another guard joined in the struggle, picked her up and they threw her at the hotbox. Merry, clawing, spitting, her arms pinned in the doorway felt the guard's foot in her chest before she saw it.

****

Merry gasped for air. Her chest tightening. Her ribs breaking. She was pinned in the hotbox. Being choked. And raped. By him.

Merry screamed and a dirty, long-gone hand clamped over her mouth. Her body jerked as a man that wasn't there plowed himself through her. Merry opened her tear-blinded eyes. Saw Mr. Sammy.

Merry kicked. Merry fought. Merry yelled. Her back pressed against the wooden walls of the hotbox. Her bloodcurdling screams echoing through the prison yard.

***

Merry was sweating too much, water evaporating too fast from her body like a fugitive soul, to be shivering. Yet she couldn't stop trembling.

The food door to the hotbox yanked open, slitting the sunlight across Merry's crazed, light deprived eyes. Merry shielded herself, growled, and flung the tin tray of grub and tin cup of hot water back at the food door.

"Fuck you, Motherfucker!"

Merry lunged at the sliding door, her hands wildly grabbing at the opening, trying to force herself through. The door slammed shut.

Merry kicked. Merry fought. Merry yelled. Her back pressed against the wooden walls of the hotbox. Her bloodcurdling screams echoing through the prison yard.

**

Merry's cracked lips stopped moving. She was done kicking. Done fighting. Done yelling. Her back flat, still against the wooden walls of the hotbox. Her silence echoing through the prison yard.

Two pairs of footsteps stopped outside the hotbox. The padlocked popped and dropped to the ground. The door, the morning sun casting shadows behind it, creaked open.

"She dead? Delmar, is she dead?"

"Shut up. Grab her legs."

*

Merry opened her eyes, her momma's voice her alarm clock.

"Git up, Merry. You been on yo' back long 'nuf."

Merry, obedient, sat up and swung her legs over the side of her prison cot. Every sunrise, the only thing that got Merry to face another day was the sound of her momma's gruff voice ordering her to raise up off her backside and to face what was coming at her. Without the crutch of diving into the bottom of a bottle or shooting herself up with junk to forget. To escape. To hide.

Not that Merry had any other choice in Kentucky State Women's Corrections. After she returned from the dead, everything came crashing back down on her. The police had been watching her and Phylicia fish and fraud folks out of their money for months when they finally came down on them. Because Phylicia was the mastermind, they threw the book at her and sent her to prison in upstate Michigan. And that's where Merry should have gone, too, except Officer Petosky, sweet on Excellent, called in a favor. Merry was a dope fiend, he told the judge. And Merry, the dope fiend, needed more than punishment for what she had done. Merry needed to be saved. She needed to be fixed. So, the judge, compassionate, shipped down to their sister prison in Kentucky.

The siren blared. Like a trained mouse in a wheel, Merry scuttled outside with the others and fell into line. She squinted, the sun in her eyes. Even so, Merry could still see the sky. She had never seen a sky so blue.

Delmar stepped in front of Merry. His scent was so familiar, she wanted to gag. Notepad and pencil stub in hand, he barked out her number.

"2813."

A statement. Not a question. Merry smirked. No doubt she was standing in front of Delmar's raping ass. Just like she was the day, the week and month before. She looked past Delmar.

"Here."

Delmar checked off her name, moved down the line. Merry zoned out at as her sister convicts went through the motions of roll call. Most of them were just like her. The lowest of the low. Thieving, prostituting forgotten dope fiends, who were sentenced to the House of Corrections to brand repentance onto their lost souls and to burn the monkeys off of their broken backs. And their families, just like Merry's, thought that they were doing the right thing. They thought that their daughters, sisters, wives were being saved, were being fixed. But this place? The Kentucky State Women's Corrections was destroying more than it was mending. Merry had learned a trade. Thank you, Jesus. And Merry had gotten clean. Praise the Lord. But she felt filthy from Delmar's putrid scent caked and covered all over her. And there was nothing she could do about it. Merry couldn't fight. She couldn't complain. Because if she did, that meant the hotbox. And Merry had already survived the hotbox once. She was scared to death to face it again.

Merry pressed down on the worn pedal, moved the cheap material through the sewing machine as the needle punctured through it. One more panel and she'd be done with her second pair of drapes for the morning. Under other circumstances, she'd be proud of herself. Her drapes were the best in the lot.

If she were talking to Excellent, she would have thanked her for passing something down to her other than flat feet and wide nose. But Merry hadn't spoken to Excellent since she stepped foot on prison soil. She wouldn't even see Excellent when she got Mr. Blackie to drive her all the way down there to visit. And Teenie and her momma weren't off limits, either. Merry sent every one of her auntie's letters back unopened and she hadn't even tried to reach out to her momma. They were all dead to her. Just like her daddy.

Merry turned the panel over, wiped her face. The whir of the other sewing machines in the muggy shack sounded like a swarm of worker bees making honey. It was almost peaceful, the sound.

A guard called out Merry's number, snapping her out of it.

"2813."

"Yeah?"

"You gotta visitor."

Merry wanted to ask who, but thought better of it. Besides, she wanted to stretch her legs anyway. And if the unexpected visitor turned out to be none other than her lying mother or two-faced auntie, then she'd be happy to send both those heifers packing.

"Momma?!"

Dora looked small, old. She smiled.

"Baby!"

Dora halfway rose from her seat, wobbly, reached out for Merry's hands. Merry held on, happy, surprised, despite herself. She sat down, her hands landing across the white line on the metal table, her eyes soaking up every wrinkle and freckle on her momma's weary face.

"Momma...what you doing here?"

"Since when I need a 'scuse to see you, gurl?"

They laughed and the visiting room guard cleared his throat. Merry pulled back her hands. Dora looked over her shoulder at the guard, understood. She clasped her hands together, worried.

"They treatin' you alright in here?"

"Yeah. They feed me, keep a roof over my head..."

Dora cut her off, stressed again.

"You alright?"

Merry stopped. She knew what her momma was asking. And she also knew from the way her momma was starring through her, that Dora could smell Delmar on her, too.

"Yeah, Momma. I'm alright. I'm clean."

Dora nodded, accepting Merry's half-truth.

Merry, uncomfortable, changed the subject.

"How you, Momma?"

"Merry, you know I ain't come all duh way down here tuh talk 'bout me."

"Something wrong with the kids?"

"No, Julia and Jr. Baby fine. Not dat you'd know."

Merry rolled her eyes. Here we go.

"Merry, why you turn Excellent 'way when she came all duh way down here tuh see you? And Teenie said you sent all her letters back. Didn't even read 'em."

"They lied to me."

"Merry, you done tol' too many lies yo' damn sef tuh be ridin' a high horse."

"After what happened with James, Momma, why didn't you just tell me?"

"Yo' daddy wuz dead tuh yo' momma, Merry. So he wuz dead tuh me. Dat's what family does. Dey stick tugetha. If you cared 'bout anybody 'sides yoursef, you'd understand dat."

"I understand yaw didn't give me a choice. I understand yaw didn't tell me the truth..."

"Yo' daddy ain't want nuthin' tuh do wit' you. He wuz a low down, mean, sefish son-of-a-bitch who beat down women and dropped babies everywhere he went. He hurt yo' momma bad. So bad, she couldn't stop cryin' or get out the bed some days. So when she tol' me the nigga wuz dead, he wuz dead. You hear me? I know you grown 'nough tuh know how dat feel, Merry."

Merry did know exactly how Excellent felt, but she was too proud and too angry right now to admit it. Dora continued.

"You need tuh forgive yo' momma. She loves you."

"Excellent don't love me. She don't give a damn about me."

Dora shook her head, disappointed, ashamed.

"All dis time, I thought you wuz duh one wit' sense. Worried 'bout Johnson when I shoulda been worryin' 'bout you."

"Momma..."

"Jus' do whut I said."

"But, Momma..."

Dora glared at Merry, stopping short her tongue. Merry, like a chastised child, lowered her eyes.

"O.K. I'll forgive her, Momma.   But you gotta do something for me when I get out."

Dora, shook her head, vehement.

"Uh uh, no..."

"Momma..."

"You can't move back wit' me, Merry."

"But I don't need to go back to what I was doing, momma. I don't need to go back there."

"I already helped you run befo', Merry. I ain't gone hep you run again."

Merry looked at her momma, tears springing to her eyes. They had never uttered a word about what happened with Mr. Sammy since she helped her and Johnson escaped to Detroit that tragic night years ago. Yet, here Merry was reaching out to her momma for help and Dora threw Mr. Sammy in her face like a pot of hot grits.

Merry lowered her head. The only salve that could soothe the burning was the truth her momma didn't want to hear.

"When you gone forgive me, momma? When you gone forgive me for trying to do the right thing?"

"Wuzn't nothin' right 'bout whut you did."

"What Sammy did, Momma. What Sammy did."

"You always been fast, Merry. Fast as hell. Dem wuz good white folks..."

"He was gone take the farm. He wasn't gone stop..."

"You laid wit' dat man."

"Not before Johnson did."

Merry eyed Dora, angry. She wanted her momma to feel what she was saying. Dora scowled.

"Don't. You. Dare."

"Why you think Sammy wanted Johnson working with him all the time, Momma? Why do you think Johnson always came home and went straight to bed?"

"Uh,uh...uh, uh...Not my baby."

"Well, I laid with Sammy, Momma. Opened up my legs and let him take me to save your damn baby. The nigga's a bigger fag now then he was then."

Dora swung on Merry, damn near taking off the whole left side of her face.

"You jus' a lie. Jus' a goddamn lie."

Merry starred at her momma, in too much pain to cry. Dora protested.

"Johnson a good man. A family man. He done made somethin' of himsef. I'm not gone let you..."

Merry scooted back her chair from the table, stood. Dora wasn't having it.

"Sit. Your. Ass. Down. And take it back."

Merry walked away. She wasn't taking shit back. Wasn't taking back that Johnson was a faggot. Wasn't taking back that she was a dope fiend, baby-dropping convict. And she wasn't taking back that Sammy's evil hand and her momma's sanctified denial was at the root of it all.

Merry nodded to the guard to open the door. Dora wobbled to her feet.

"Merry! Don't you walk 'way from me. Brin' yo' ass back here!"

Merry, one foot in front of the other, disobeyed her momma. And she didn't look back. Not even as she heard Dora's heart breaking as the prison door swung close.

DETROIT,
1967

Goddamn Orin. Mowing the lawn. Again. Why the man had to cut the lawn at the crack of dawn, Merry didn't know. She shuffled down the hallway to the community bathroom. It was empty. 'Bout time. She locked the door behind her, ran water in the tub.

This wasn't so bad. Really. Two years ago, after she parked Silas' car in the Detroit River, she walked into a boarding house on Dexter and Davison and never left. The old lady that ran the one taken by the freeway on Dequindre and Davison had passed and left her second property to Orin Townsend's slow ass to run. If Merry had had anywhere else to go, she would have. Instead, she stayed and got a job at the Chrysler Plant on Jefferson, sewing seat covers. That was her square, boring, life now. No smack. No lifting. No fishing. No man. No nothing.

And that was just fine with Merry. Every now and again, she saw Excellent and the kids, talked to Johnson and rolled through Teenie's to play a number or to find out how her momma was doing. Mostly, though, Merry stayed to herself and kept up with what was happening with her people through Scottie, who had lost her foot to Diabetes and Merry made a point of checking on on the regular.

Merry towel-dried, looked at herself in the steamed mirror. She looked tired. Thirty-two years old and she had already lived a lifetime and then some. Outside, she heard Orin's lawnmower growl off. If he was finished with the front lawn already that meant she was running late for work. Merry pulled on her robe, hauled ass.

"Mornin', Merry!"

Merry rolled her eyes. She didn't feel like being bothered with Orin's retarded friendliness today. She hurried down the walkway.

"Don't have time, Orin."

"Merry, the rent..."

"When I get back from work, Orin."

"But you already missed the bus, Merry. Right, Elgin?"

Merry snapped her neck, ready to cuss Orin out for talking to imaginary friends. A man's voice from underneath the hood of a bucket parked in front of the boarding house responded, dry.

"Yeah, 'bout five minutes ago."

Orin nodded. Merry grumbled, mad at herself.

"Shit..."

Orin floated to her side.

"You gone get in trouble, Merry?"

If by trouble, Orin meant Merry's supervisor had already warned her that if she was late again, the plant would dock her pay? Then, hell yeah, she was going to get in trouble. Merry didn't answer.

"I don't want you to get in trouble, Merry. Elgin can take you. So you won't be late."

Elgin jerked his head out from under the hood with the quickness. But Merry's tongue was faster.

"Uh uh, Orin, I can get there on my own.."

"Yeah, Unc, I gotta get back to the shop..."

Orin slapped down both of their protests.

"It's O.K., Merry. Elgin don't mind. Do you, Elgin?"

Orin smiled and Elgin, on the spot, grunted. Merry looked from Orin to Elgin, really seeing him for the first time. The color of a gingerbread cookie, Elgin was thick around the middle, but not fat like his uncle. Big-eared and needing a shave, he didn't stand that tall, either. And his fat ring-less hands and dirty fingernails were gray black with oil and dirt. He was a grease monkey. Definitely not her type. She could stand being in his piece of shit car for twenty minutes if she had to.

"So you gone pay my uncle his rent money, right?"

"What?"

Merry glared at Elgin. It wasn't a question. It was an accusation. But, eyes on the road, hands on the wheel, an unfiltered camel cigarette dangling from his half-moon lips, the nigga said it all even-toned, like he was asking her what time it was. Merry snapped.

"I pay my bills."

"May be. But people always taking' advantage of Unc. I'm just lookin' out for him."

"Well look out for him somewhere else, nigga. I handle my business."

Merry crossed her arms, pissed.

**

Merry puffed on a cigarette, still riled up over Elgin calling her out in the car. Who the hell did he think he was? If it was back in the day, she would of cussed him up one side, down the other and then had Silas whup his ass. Good thing for him, she had taken up her working stiff ways.

Merry took her place at her station, waited for the assembly line to whir back on. The air in the auto plant, teeming with ash, steel and fiber particles, was thick enough to chew, but Merry wasn't wearing a mask or protective glasses. Wasn't necessary, her foreman said. Besides, she had gotten used to the scratchiness in her throat and thickness in her chest.

The assembly line grumbled back on. Merry got to sewing. She was in a rhythm. A zone. That is, until she noticed that the car seats coming down the line to her were half done with stitching so tacky, she could see inside to the stuffing. Merry yanked her seat cover over it, yelled down the line.

"Hey! Wake the hell up down there! You fucking up!"

A frustrated voice shouted back.

"Fuck you, bitch!"

Merry leaned back, quick. She recognized that voice. And that face.

"Baby Doll!"

'Chell lifted Merry off of her feet, bear hugging her. Merry half-heartedly patted her back.

"Damn, 'Chell. I can't breathe..."

'Chell loosened her grip, set Merry back down, smiled wide.

"I'm sorry, Baby Doll. You jus' look so damn good."

Merry shrugged, memories of 'Chell's ass kickings bumping into her like the second shift folks rushing to make their way through the plant's revolving door. She turned to leave.

"Yeah, you, too."

'Chell reached out for her.

"Whoa, whoa, Baby Doll, you ain't seen me all this time and all you got is, 'yeah, you, too'?"

Merry shook her loose.

"Look, 'Chell I'm not a fresh fish no more. You put your hands on me, you gone need 'Licia's protection."

'Chell looked at Merry, hurt, confused.

"I don't know nothin' 'bout 'Licia's protection. I just wanted to buy you a drink. Damn."

Merry licked her lips. Now 'Chell's dyke departing ass was speaking her language. She stopped her.

"Make it two, and I'll teach you how to sew, so you don't lose your damn job."

'Chell hungrily agreed to Merry's terms. The joint she chose, of course, wasn't a spot Merry would have chosen. A hole in the wall full of women, Merry knew exactly where she was without 'Chell even saying it.

Merry plopped down in the booth across from 'Chell, pulled out a cigarette, reached for the matches laying on the table. 'Chell beat her to it and struck one, ever the gentleman. Merry leaned her cigarette into the flame, puffed. 'Chell smiled.

"Where you been, Baby Doll? I ain't seen or heard 'bout you in so long, I figured you went straight."

Merry shook her head.

"I tried some shit with 'Licia..."

"Oh, yeah?"

"Yeah. Then a judge relocated me for a minute. To Kentucky."

"Oh, shit. You got sent up to Kentucky Women Corrections?"

"Four years."

"Damn, Baby. I heard bitches go up in there and don't come out right! Shit, order doubles of whatever you want. We gone celebrate you makin' it out that motherfucka!"

'Chell raised her arm to get the barmaid's attention. The short, big thighed woman walked over to her, already carrying a tray of drinks. She set the drinks down in front of them. 'Chell corrected her.

"Naw, Baby. We ain't order yet."

"Well, keep yo' money in yo' pocket for these first two. It's on him."

The barmaid motioned over her shoulder to the only man in the whole joint. Merry and 'Chell looked. He raised his glass, smiled. Merry laughed. 'Chell wasn't amused.

"You know that nigga?"

"Yeah."

"Shit. Here he come."

R.B. Eddie. Damn, the boy still looked good. As black as Nat King Cole with a Sidney Poitier clipped tongue and Harry Belafonte chiseled chest, he still wore a perfectly round afro. But now, two years later, his baby face was complimented by a bushy moustache framing both sides of his top lip.

Merry looked up at him, tickled.

"Thanks for the drinks. Monkey Boy."

R.B., beer in hand, flirted.

"My pleasure. Queen."

Feeling the heat pouring off of 'Chell, he turned to her, hand outstretched.

"Hi, I'm R.B. R.B. Eddie."

'Chell, palms flat and throbbing on the table, starred at him, pissed.

"I gotta pee."

'Chell stood up, aggressive, and R.B., wise, side stepped out of her way. He looked to Merry, amused.

"I think she likes me."

"Yeah, just like every woman in here."

R.B. sat down in 'Chell's vacant seat.

"I know, right? I didn't notice at first when I walked in here, but then I saw you...Hold on, is she..."

Merry eyed him. Nigga please. R.B. held up his hands, apologetic.

"Hey, I had to ask, Queen. Two years is a long time..."

R.B. took another sip of his beer, his eyes locking with Merry's. Merry, her memory taking her places she had no business going, changed the subject.

"What you doing in Detroit, R.B.? Thought they were rolling out the red carpet for you in Chicago."

"They did. But The Defender wasn't ready for me, Queen. Corner office, secretary, I walked away from all of it."

"Uh huh."

"I'm serious, Queen. Monday, I heard The Michigan Chronicle was looking for someone to report the crime beat. Tuesday, I was in the publisher's office, signing on the dotted line."

Merry sipped on her drink. It made the bullshit R.B. was shoveling go down her throat smoother. R.B. smiled, shrugged.

"That's alright, Queen. When you read my column in the paper tomorrow, you'll be buying me a drink."

"Think so?"

"Oh, I know so. Especially when you find out what my column's about. Ever heard of the Black Panthers?"

Merry shook her head no. Sounded like a negro league baseball team.

"Yeah, well, you may know more than you think you do. What do you know about Raymond Printup?"

Merry snuffed out her cigarette in the ashtray. She hadn't heard Raymond's name in over six years when the cops were looking for him after he went on the run for killing Peach. After the way he did Kat, Merry was hoping somebody had done the same or worst to him. Merry played dumb.

"Who's that?"

R.B. slapped his hand over his heart, dramatic, like Merry had shot an arrow through it.

"Aw, c'mon, Queen! You know I know you know him!"

Merry eyed R.B., cool.

"I don't know what you know, R.B."

"You don't know what I know....Alright...Raymond was a small time dope dealer, dabbled in heroin, but his bread and butter was weed. About six years ago, he disappeared after a pimp, Peach, came up dead. The cops had been looking for him ever since..."

"Is he dead?"

"Naw. He's back. Head of the Detroit chapter of the Black Panthers. And the word is the gun toting, switch blade slicing queen by his side is Reverend McKeever's baby, your girl, Kat McKeever."

Merry laughed.

"Now I know you lying."

"I'm lying, huh? Well, I'm headed across the street to cover the recruit meeting at their headquarters. You can come see for yourself."

"How'd you manage that invitation?"

"Raymond. He thinks I believe his I'm-living-the-revolution-for-the-people-now jive dance. But I know he's still pushing heroin out of Slauson's Funeral Parlor."

Merry's eyes flashed. Not much, just enough for R.B. to notice the truth hiding there. R.B., cocky, stood.

"But you don't know anything about that either. Do you, Queen?"

Merry watched him leave, didn't answer. She didn't have to. Now she knew what R.B knew. And R.B. knew too damn much.

*

"Baby Doll, why you leave me? You know I got a bad stomach..."

Merry glanced to the side, sshed 'Chell. The Black Panther Headquarters was no bigger than a broom closet and all four walls were crowded with Negros crammed in shoulder to shoulder. At the front of the room, prowling back and forth before two other officers sitting in folding chairs, was Raymond. Donning a black beret topped afro, green army fatigues and laced up, spit-shined military boots, he was in the middle of his soul stirring recruiting speech. Merry chuckled. The fool sounded more like a country preacher than a ghetto revolutionary. R.B., leaning on the sidewall, nodded to Merry. 'Chell whispered.

"What the fuck is this?"

Merry whispered back.

"A kill whitey meeting."

'Chell, trying not to laugh, started coughing. Merry patted her on the back, shook her head as folks glanced in their direction. A girl about the age of Juliette appeared in front of them with a sign in sheet on a clipboard. Merry waved the child off before she could even open her mouth. The girl reported back to a sister member sitting in the front row, motioned back to Merry.

Before the woman with the scar on her cheek turned to look, Merry knew exactly who she was.

DON'T HAVE
A CHOICE

"**Detroit** Royalty...Jesus....Couldn't nobody tell us we weren't grown!"

Kat gazed around Scottie's, amazed. Hair styled in a curly afro and dressed like a soldier, she didn't look like the carefree Kat Merry remembered. She was still thin, but no longer dope fiend skinny and her serious face, though scarred, had a glow to it. A glow that Merry had never seen before.

"Remember how big this place used to be?"

Merry nodded her head, winked.

"Yeah, everything was bigger then, especially Scottie's pancakes."

Scottie fussed back from the kitchen.

"Watch it, Merry! Next time you come knockin', I won't let your ass in!"

Kat and Merry busted out into giggles. Just like old times. Kat sat down on the barstool next to Merry, looked at her.

"It's been too long, Merry."

"I know. I heard about your daddy's heart attack. How's he doing?"

"Alright. He just needs to stop drinking. But I'm the last person he'll listen to about that. How long you been clean?"

"Almost six years. I was locked up. Not like I had a choice."

"I hear you. My aunt and uncle didn't have bars on the windows, but they might as well had."

Kat and Merry, hard memories suddenly squatting on the stools next to them, sipped on their gingerales, silent. Merry spoke up, guilty.

"Kat...When you moved to California, I meant to write you back, but..."

"I didn't expect you to, Merry. I just wanted you to know I was alright."

"Well, are you?"

"Am I what?"

"Alright."

Kat smiled.

"What you mean?"

"C'mon, Kat, what the hell you think I mean? The Black Panthers? You?!"

"It's not what you think, Merry."

"I heard you were the Queen of Defense."

"Yeah, well, the brothers..."

"The brothers?!"

"Yeah, the brothers taught me about guns and knives, but that's not the point."

"Then what is?"

"Revolution, Merry. It's time Black people stand up, stop being afraid of and depending on the white man. We have to take charge of our own lives. Feed ourselves, educate our children, run our own business, protect ourselves and our families from the crooked pigs by any means necessary. That's what the Black Panthers are all about."

"You sound just like Raymond."

"I hope so, Merry."

"You hope so? After what that nigga did to you, you hope so?"

Kat smiled. Again. Merry starred at her, really starting to get pissed off. Kat explained.

"Merry, remember when you said, you didn't have a choice to kick dope when you were in prison? Well, I learned a long time ago, when it comes to kicking Raymond, I don't have a choice."

That was the wrong thing to say. For the past two years, at least, Merry's square, straight life had been about nothing else but choices. She had chosen to leave Silas and stay clear of smack. She had even chosen, out of guilt, to stay away from her children and to sign a piece of paper that gave Jr. Baby permission to take his father's last name. So, for Kat to look her in her face and say she didn't have a choice when it came to Raymond?

It was like kicking Merry right in her gut.

In fact, it took all that Merry had to sit there and listen to Kat tell her tale of how, one year after her daddy sent her to California, Raymond - the letter Kat had written him in his back pocket - showed up on her aunt and uncle's Los Angeles doorstep, on the run for killing her pimp, Peach. One look at Raymond, Kat said, and she knew she would go wherever he asked her to. They ended up in Oakland -- Raymond's Vietnam vet, half-brother, Donnie, lived there. He told Raymond he could stay under one condition. That he get straight. Kat seconded the motion. And with her love and support, Raymond quit cold turkey. Clean and ready to start their life together anew, they took Donnie up on his offer to join an upstart community organization, The Black Panthers.

Merry, a plate of half-eaten pancakes in front of her, interrupted.

"So you telling me, Raymond really came back here to do this Black Panthers' thing. He ain't dealing?"

"I told you, Merry. We're about uplifting the community now. Doing the right thing..."

"Right, right, but what about Peach? What about the cops?"

Kat shook her head, picked up her last piece of bacon.

"Raymond wants everybody to think he did it, Merry. Even me. But the only reason he ran was because heat was coming down on the funeral parlor. He just needed to lay low for awhile..."

"Raymond didn't kill Peach."

"No. He doesn't have the stomach for it."

Merry eyed Kat, seeing right through her best friend.

"You say that like you know who does."

Kat stopped chewing, paused.

"I haven't told Raymond about this, Merry. He would have lost his mind."

Merry, sensing the tears behind Kat's eyes, promised.

"He won't hear it from me."

Kat sighed, pushed her plate away.

"Remember that night I came to see you?"

Merry shifted, uncomfortable, guilty.

"Yeah...You said you were in trouble."

"I was. Just wasn't my trouble. Peach called himself being a hustler. He wanted to get into pushing dope, but didn't have enough money to get started on his own, so he went to Main Man and his gang to front him, to be his silent partner and protection. Things were going pretty good for awhile, but Peach...All Peach wanted to do was party. Pretty soon we were copping more smack than Peach was selling and that started messing with Main Man's money and before we knew it, Peach was so far in the hole, the only way he could make it right was to stall them or pay up in full. But Peach didn't have the money. The only thing Peach had was hoes... Merry, that night when I came to you, I had just crawled out from under six niggas and jumped out of a second story window..."

Merry grabbed Kat's hand, reliving her pain.

"Kat, I'm sorry..."

Kat looked at Merry, the tears finally falling from her eyes like raindrops.

"You didn't know. I was too fucked up to tell you..."

"But I should have known...I could have stopped..."

Merry trailed off, the truth of what happened to her best friend that horrible night hitting her like lightning.

"Peach didn't beat you, did he?"

Kat shook her head, no.

"I only said he did, 'cause he told me to."

"Main Man told you to?"

"No. A cop."

"What?!"

"Yeah, they were always hassling us, the girls...but that night, after I left you, I actually thought that they would help me. As soon as I got his attention, I knew..."

"Kat, we gotta do something about this. Who did this to you?"

Kat whispered, her anguish still so real, Merry's heart was hurting.

"I don't know, Merry. Pigs all look the same to me. All I remember is his badge."

**

For the rest of the week, Merry couldn't get Kat's badge number digits out of her head. In fact, it seemed she saw some combination of the digits everywhere she looked. Whether Merry was buying groceries at the store, reading the newspaper or slaving on the assembly line at work, someway, somehow she ran across the number as if it was reminding her that she had to do something. What that something was, though, Merry didn't know. She sure as hell couldn't march into the police station, demand to see every pigs' badge, then call them out. This was 1967 Detroit and in 1967 Detroit, the fuzz was hated. The fuzz was feared.

The fuzz was king. From tag team partners harassing and severely beating prostitutes to Tac Squad gangs of four brutalizing Black men and teenage boys for "disturbing the peace," everyone - man, woman and child - knew that the police were the enemy. They weren't to be trusted or looked to for support and the only protection their shiny law and order badges offered was the selfish shielding of themselves.

Then there was the matter of Peach. Despite Raymond's "alibi" and his I-did-it-for-love confession to Kat, Kat still didn't believe that Raymond killed Peach. The truth, though? Kat really had no solid idea who did. The same cop that beat her and laid her out at the gates of heaven could have done it. But why? It actually made more sense to Merry that Main Man had Desmond do the honors. Peach, led to believe that Desmond beat Kat to the edge of death to send him a message, could have miraculously came up with the money he owed Main Man. The fool that he was, Peach then probably found himself between the same rock and a hard place not even one year later. But this time, Main Man wasn't in the mood for bartering and the only payment he would take to make things right was Peach's life at Desmond's hand.

At least, that's what Merry thought. In theory. She, like Kat, had no proof either. To get at the truth there really was only one option. Ask Desmond. But Merry cared too much about breathing to do that.

Too bad Officer Petosky didn't feel the same way. About Merry's life, that is. Standing in the middle of her room - one too many drinks in him, unshaven and in street clothes - the man hardly looked himself. Didn't sound himself either.

"Merry, I need you to do me a favor."

Merry glanced at her closed door, the knowledge that a cop -- hell could have been Petosky --- beat Kat knocking on the other side. Suspicious, she eyed him. Merry had never seen Petosky out of his uniform or without his trigger-happy partner. Yet, here the man was, teetering in front of her, talking crazy.

Merry crossed her arms, caught. Her do him a favor? His white ass didn't do her any favors coming up to her room where everyone could see in the middle of the day. Yes, she was clean because of him. And yes, her children had a new roof over their heads because of him. But Petosky hadn't come calling to ask her to do him a favor. Petosky had come calling for Merry to return one.

"Why you need this?"

R.B. looked at Merry, twirling the book of matches between his fingers. Hoping to revisit memory lane, he had hurried down to meet her at a bar and politely listened to the little mess she had to say, no questions asked. But R.B. wasn't stupid. Merry grinned, sly.

"Get me what I need, then we'll talk."

"Aw, c'mon, Queen, you gotta give me more than that. I got out of Kentucky without swinging neck-first from a tree, make this worth my while."

"Can you do it?"

R.B. smiled.

"Queen, who you talking to? 'Course, I can do it. I wouldn't be here if I couldn't."

Merry paused. They weren't talking about sex anymore. R.B. wanted something more important. A story.

"Raymond's not pushing dope out of Slauson's."

R.B. leaned in, hungry.

"Oh, yeah? Who is?"

"Find out who that badge number belongs to and I'll tell you."

*

Merry wasn't nervous. It was opening night and she was starring in the role of Judas, but she wasn't nervous. Why? Because she had decided to lay it on the altar and tell Jesus' right hand everything.

Kat looked at the snapshot, speechless. Merry watched her best friend, thoughts of the lie she told R.B. to get the cop's identity and address justified. No doubt, R.B. was snooping around Clyde's doorstep right now, thinking he was the mastermind behind peddling smack in his coffins. He wasn't. With Raymond out of the picture, Main Man was the head nigga in charge now, and Clyde, as slimy and selfish as he was, wasn't going to give Main Man up no matter how many questions R.B. asked. It was a dead-end. But, for Merry, it was worth it to scare the sweat off of Clyde for jewing her out of Excellent's piano too many years ago.

Kat picked up the photo, vengeance lacing her words.

"This is him."

Merry nodded. Kat's eyes finally focused on Merry.

"How'd you get this?"

"Don't worry about that. What I need to know is what am I telling the cops."

If it hadn't been so damn serious, it would have been funny. Merry and Kat playing like they used to, laughing and joking in their pajamas, sleeping over at Kat's house. The only difference now? They were grown. And this game of truth or dare wasn't between themselves. It was with the pigs.

Merry fell asleep, confidant. She had fed Petosky the story just as planned. Raymond and his Black Panther Party officers were going to be meeting with some "investors" around 3 a.m. at a blind pig on 12th Street. The word was that not only would drinks be on the table, but so would money, drugs and guns. The fact that it wasn't true wasn't the point. Merry and Kat just needed the pigs to show up at the half-empty, after-hours joint, see that Raymond and the Black Panthers weren't there, then Merry could use the excuse that Raymond must have given out the misinformation on purpose, because he was suspicious that a rat was in his midst. Then, the police - worried that Merry's cover was blown - would have to pull her out.

It was foolproof, their plan. So foolproof, that Merry was dreaming. And the sirens in the nearby distance, police cars, ambulance and fire engines blaring closer and past the boarding house, the hooping and hollering collective, blanketing the streets like angry locusts, looting, fighting, setting the city ablaze didn't wake her.

At first.

"Oh my God."

Merry bunched her housecoat together in front of her, her eyes glued outside the window. The pre-dawn sky, normally navy grayish blue, was charcoal black with smoke and ash. And the buildings, homes, business stretching for blocks and blocks as far as the eye could see were glowing yellow-orangish-red from flames.

Detroit was burning. It was the 23rd of July and Detroit was burning.

Elgin rushed past her with a rifle.

"Elgin! What's going on?!"

"Yo' friends picked the wrong niggas to beat on, that's what's going on."

"My what?"

"The cops, Merry. They busted up a joint on 12th street. Niggas wasn't having it."

Merry's mind raced. Petosky and the pigs were supposed to show up, find Raymond not there and leave. Detroit was not supposed to be burning.

Elgin shoved bullets into the chamber, snapped shut his rifle. Merry looked at him, alarmed.

"What you about to do?"

"I gotta protect this place. Cop or nigga, they try to burn it, they goin' down."

Elgin ran outside. Merry raced upstairs to the hallway payphone. She needed to make sure that Juliette and Jr. Baby were alright. She yanked the phone off the hook, dropped in her dime. Nothing. The phone line was dead.

Merry threw on some clothes. The buses probably weren't running. And a jitney or cab no doubt was also out of the question. Still, Merry was determined to get over to Excellent's someway, somehow.

Orin stopped her in the hallway.

"Where you goin', Merry?"

"The phone's not working. I gotta check on my kids."

"It's too dangerous, Merry. The police are killin' people. You need to stay inside."

Merry pushed past him. Orin followed on her heels, called out for Elgin, who was standing guard on the porch as Merry charged by.

"Elgin, stop her!"

"What?!"

"Stop Merry!"

Elgin shrugged as Merry quickly disappeared down the sidewalk.

"She wanna go out there and get shot, that's her business."

Merry was already too far gone to hear Orin pleading for her. She looked both ways. No bus. No cab. And the cars that did pass by her on the crowded, riot filled streets were bustling with enterprising hustlers and newly available "fire sale" merchandise. Behind her, she heard an approaching siren. Merry ducked into a narrow alley walkway.

A police car zoomed past, siren blaring. Merry scrunched up against the wall, hid behind a garbage can. Afraid to look, she heard a car horn blow. Sharp, quick, three times. Merry peeked around the metal can. Elgin flung open the passenger side car door, waved her in.

"Merry! C'mon!"

Other than Elgin asking Merry where she needed to go, they hardly spoke the entire ride over. This was no time for small talk. This was time for dodging the cops and speeding down alleys instead of the streets without getting shot. Why Merry wasn't raising her own kids wasn't Elgin's business. And why Elgin was risking life and limb to carry her over to Excellent's wasn't Merry's. Of course, that didn't keep Merry from asking.

"Why you doing this?"

"Unc told me 'bout your kids. I got kids. Three girls."

"They in Detroit?"

"North Carolina. Their momma took 'em back down there wit' her. Where the house?"

Excellent's house was the second house from the corner. And from the looks of things, all was well. Stepping on the porch, the only thing Merry heard floating out of a cracked open living room window was the news playing on the television. Merry rapped on the door, hard. From inside, she heard someone running to the door. Excellent yanked open the door.

"Jr. Baby?! Oh, Merry..."

"Felton's not here?"

"No! He left over an hour ago!"

Excellent paced away from the door, worried sick. Merry closed the door behind her, one flick of her tongue away from asking where her daughter was when she saw Juliette watching the news, transfixed, on the black and white television.

"Jr. Baby said he was going shopping. I've been watching, but haven't seen him."

Excellent pounded her fist against her thigh.

"Lord, I told that boy not to go. If he got himself shot..."

"Excellent, he didn't. He's on his way home right now."

Merry locked eyes with her mother, the words laying in a puddle at her feet more an effort to convince herself than Excellent. Juliette reported over her shoulder. Calm. Disconnected.

"I've seen everybody but Jr. Baby. I even saw Langston from the basketball team. He had a stereo."

Excellent stormed out of the room. Merry and Juliette looked after her. Juliette turned back to the television.

"All these fools burning everything...The reporter said it started because the police broke up a welcome home party for a Vietnam vet at some bar. And now these fools are burning everything..."

Merry laid her hand on Juliette's shoulder, the closest thing to a hug she knew her daughter would allow her to give.

"It's going to be alright, Juliette. Everything's gonna be alright."

Juliette, uncomfortable, scooted over, forcing Merry's unwelcomed hand to slide off her shoulder.

"What you doing here?"

Merry swallowed, momentarily choking on her daughter's salty rejection.

"I was worried. I couldn't get through on the phone and..."

As if on cue, the phone rang. Juliette dove to pick it up just as Excellent did in the kitchen.

"Hel.."

Juliette stopped, listened. Merry pestered her.

"Is it Felton? Juliette, is it..."

Juliette shook her head, quick, annoyed.

"It's Auntie."

Juliette hung up the phone and the front door swung open. Jr. Baby stomped in, carrying a brand new television. He called out, his voice deep, too proud of himself.

"Momma! Come here. I got you something!"

Juliette hurried over to him, impressed.

"Is that a brand new Zenith color television?!"

Jr. Baby's eyes flitted to Merry, then back to Juliette.

"You know it. Momma!"

Excellent walked into the living room, looking through Jr. Baby as if he wasn't there. He showed off the television, excited.

"See what I got you, Momma?!"

Excellent gazed at him, blank, said nothing.

"Oh, come on, Momma, don't be mad at me. What's the matter? Don't you like it?"

Excellent passed the television, sat in the armchair.

"That was Teenie on the phone."

Jr. Baby picked up the television, moved it closer to its new spot in living room.

"Niggas burning up around her house, too?"

"She's down South visiting Momma."

"Teenie know she picked the right time to take a vacation... Ju, move!"

Juliette fussed back.

"You gotta move the other television first, fool! Don't put it there!"

Excellent sunk back into the armchair. Whatever was taxing her mind was heavier than Detroit burning and Jr. Baby and Juliette fighting over a stolen television. Merry couldn't help but feel it, too.

"What's wrong with Momma?"

"I heard her talkin' out her head, callin' for you. It won't be long now."

"What you talking about, won't be long? We gotta go...Call Johnson."

"I did. He said he can't leave his family. And I don't blame him. You jus' gonna have to take the bus..."

"There's not enough time to take the bus. Besides the police aren't letting anybody in or out of Detroit. Greyhound's probably not even running. I'll just take Johnson's car."

"Johnson need his car, Merry."

Merry looked at Excellent, pissed. Her momma was dying and Excellent was defending Johnson's selfish ass? Merry felt her face turn warm, then hot.

"Felton, I know you didn't carry that television all the way home on your back. Who drove you?"

Jr. Baby eyed her, suspicious.

"My boy Winston from 'cross the street. Why?"

"You need to ask him if you can borrow his car."

Jr. Baby stood, a man not about to be ordered around by a woman he didn't consider his mother.

"I don't need to ask Winston nothin'."

Jr. Baby starred at Merry, all signs of her baby boy gone. At eighteen - a quick and dirty elopement and divorce already under his belt - he was distant and cold to her now. She had seen friendlier eyes in prison.

Merry headed outside.

"Fine, I'll just knock on every door until I get him. Ask him myself."

Nobody followed her. Either Excellent, Jr. Baby and Juliette didn't believe Merry would knock on their neighbor's doors or they just didn't give a damn. Luckily for Merry it didn't come to that. As soon as she stepped out on Excellent's porch, she spotted Elgin's car pulled over to the corner with the hood up.

"What happened?"

"Pushed her too hard."

"Can you drive it?"

"After she cool down. Need a ride back?"

"I need a favor."

Elgin took a drag of his cigarette. Merry dropped the other shoe.

"My momma's sick."

Elgin motioned back to Excellent's house, confused.

"I thought that was..."

"Excellent didn't raise me. My momma's dying."

Merry looked at Elgin, desperate. Elgin, wired like any other man to come to the rescue of a damsel in distress, started to do just that.

"Where she stay?"

"Georgia."

"Aw, hell naw..."

Elgin slammed down the car hood. Merry pleaded her case.

"Come on, Elgin! Last time I saw my momma, I didn't leave things right."

"Uh huh..."

"Greyhound buses ain't running and the police are shutting the city down. I don't have anybody else I can ask..."

Elgin flicked his cigarette butt in the street, reached for his car door. Merry touched his hand.

"Please, Elgin...You told me you have kids. Don't you have a momma, too?"

Elgin looked at Merry, his heart touched, his arm twisted. Jr. Baby, on the other hand, was too busy putting his foot down.

"I ain't goin'."

Merry, embarrassed, glanced over her shoulder at Elgin, waiting at the curb. Excellent, standing on the porch with the kids, tried to talk some sense into Jr. Baby.

"Boy, it's too dangerous out there for a woman by herself. You gotta..."

"I. Ain't. Leavin'. You. Momma."

Juliette chimed in.

"Me neither, Momma."

Excellent sighed, the smoky smell of fire in the air and pop pop of gunshots nearby. She looked to Merry.

"Pack some clothes, then. We all goin'."

THE HOUSE
OF CORRECTIONS

Merry couldn't remember the last time she had spent any real time with Felton, Jr. Not Jr. Baby. She hated that name and was the only one in the family that refused to call her first born that.

Not that it mattered a damn to Jr. Baby. He was a man. Awkwardly handsome just like his father with the same bad eyes, crooked smile and self-righteous attitude. Seemed to Merry, the older her son got, the more he disregarded and disrespected her. And taking his daddy's last name didn't help any. Truth be told, Merry only signed that piece of paper giving Jr. Baby permission to legally to become his father's son, because deep down she wanted to give him a reason to love her. Again.

Juliette stirred in the backseat. Merry glanced over the shoulder at her and Excellent, dozing. They were just outside of Cincinnati, close to five hours into their trip. It was six or so in the evening, and it had taken some back alley driving, to wait out the rioters, dodge the police and get around the blocked off streets. Everybody was exhausted. Even Merry's eyelids were drooping, heavy. A losing battle, Merry felt the car swerve. Jr. Baby stifled a yawn as Merry's eyes popped open.

"Felton, maybe you should let me drive."

"I'm alright."

"I know you tired, Felton. Just let me take over."

"Merry, I said, I'm alright."

Jr. Baby gripped the wheel, case closed. From the back seat, Excellent re-opened it.

"You not 'bout to drive us into a ditch, boy. Let Merry drive."

Jr. Baby didn't argue. In fact, it wasn't even five minutes before the boy was calling the pigs home in the back seat with Juliette. Up front now with Merry, Excellent looked out the window at the passing country landscape, her arms crossed and tongue still. Merry kept her eyes on the road, just as silent. The only sound in the car between them was Aretha Franklin demanding "Respect" on the radio and Jr. Baby's snoring.

Excellent spoke to the window, irritated.

"We gone have to stop."

"You gotta use the bathroom again?"

"Wouldn't be so bad if this car wasn't so damn bumpy. How you know this Elgin again?"

"He's Orin's nephew."

"Hmph, real nice of Orin's married nephew to let you drive his car to Georgia."

"He ain't married."

"That what he told you?"

Merry started to say 'yes,' but stopped. Elgin hadn't actually told her one way or the other if he was married. All she knew was that his daughters were down in North Carolina with their mother, and Merry had just assumed that the woman and Elgin were divorced or at least separated. Then again, Merry who hadn't had anything passing for a conversation with the man until Detroit burst into flames hadn't cared enough to ask.

Merry snapped.

"Excellent, why you all up in Elgin's business? Can't a man just be nice to me?"

Excellent shrugged, pretending not to care.

"Depend on how nice you been to him."

Merry gritted her teeth. Merry had done something good and self-sacrificing, convinced a man she didn't like to help her and her family without lying horizontal. And her mother was calling her a whore. A prophecy fulfilling, loose and wild title Excellent had bestowed upon Merry from day one. It wasn't true. This time. And Merry, pissed, wanted to put her mother in her place.

Merry cut her eyes at Excellent, sarcastic.

"I ain't been no more nice to Elgin than you were to Blackie. Excellent."

Excellent darted her eyes back to Merry. Touche. She darted her finger out the window to some bushes on the side of the road.

"Pull over."

Merry obeyed, deciding this was as good a time as any to stretch her legs and take a break. Juliette and Jr. Baby woke up, pulled out the fried chicken and tuna fish sandwiches, started eating. Merry and Excellent joined them. *To Sir With Love*, a corny love song by a very white British girl named Lulu was disturbing the radio. Merry started to turn the station just as a news reporter broke in.

"This just in...President Lyndon Johnson, in efforts to stop the increasing violence caused by ongoing rioting and looting that erupted in Detroit nearly 48 hours ago, has deployed federal troops from the 82nd Airborne into the Motor City. The National Guard Troops, sent into Detroit without Michigan Governor George Romney declaring a "state of insurrection," have been deployed to quell the disorder..."

The reporter went on to say something else, but Merry didn't hear it. This was all her fault. Detroit was burning because of her. And there was nothing she could do about it. Merry clicked off the radio.

Juliette and Excellent fussed. Jr. Baby grumbled the loudest.

"What you doin'?!"

Jr. Baby lunged over the seat, clicked the radio back on. Dionne Warwick's syrupy *Alfie* was starting. Merry turned the key in the ignition. Jr. Baby, demanded an explanation.

"Damn it, Merry! Why you do that?"

Merry started the car, avoided her son's question.

"Yaw, close the doors. We gotta make it through Kentucky before dark."

*

The night air was muggy. Stifling. Thick. And if there was a cool Kentucky breeze to offer Merry any relief, it was long since gone.

Merry took a drag of her cigarette and blew the smoke out of the window. It was so damn hot that the cloud of smoke got stuck in the humid air.

Merry glanced up at the full moon as some hillbilly preacher droned on the radio. He was rambling something about throwing yourself on the altar and buying a vial of his consecrated, holy water. Looking over to Juliette sleeping in the passenger's seat, Merry considered it. Her daughter at sixteen was everything she had wanted to be. Smart. Pretty. Popular. A year ahead of herself in school, kids and teachers alike called Juliette, Red. She had gotten her daddy's coloring from the top of her head down to her toes. And she had friends. Her best friend from across the alley, Gi Gi. And boys who courted and called her on the phone. Who escorted her to school dances and church socials. Boys she wasn't having sex with.

And Merry was proud of her. Her daughter was a good girl. Juliette excelled in school, held a part-time job, baby-sat her cousins and she never missed a Sunday or Wednesday's choir rehearsal at church. Merry could even tell just by looking at her that Juliette had never smoked or drank anything.

Merry was proud about that, too. But she still wanted that vial of holy water. Because Merry needed a miracle to part the Red Sea of detached pain and lost years between her and Juliette. Merry loved her daughter, but she wanted to like her. And even though deep down she knew she didn't deserve it, Merry really wanted Juliette to love and like her back.

Merry pressed down more on the gas. Goddamn Kentucky kicking up feelings in her like the car's tires kicking up asphalt off the road. She didn't have time for this.

Juliette roused awake, the question anyone would have asked perched on her lips.

"Where are we?"

"Kentucky."

Juliette rubbed her eyes, looked out the window at the dark shadows trailing by.

"Isn't this where you were in jail?"

Merry's fingers gripped the steering wheel, too caught off guard to be ashamed.

"Yeah. You knew where I was?"

"I knew the address. We gonna pass it?"

"Pass what?"

"The House of Corrections."

Merry's jaw tightened. They were closer to the iron cage prison that held her captive for four years than she wanted to admit. In fact, she knew for sure that the newly asphalted highway that they were riding on was the same dirt road she walked like Cain when she was released from the joint.

Merry answered her daughter's question with a lie.

"I don't know. Probably."

Juliette tossed another dart at Merry.

"What was it like?"

"Some place you don't ever want to be."

It was the truth. A painful, scab pulling truth that Merry didn't want to discuss anymore. Juliette peered at her, annoyed.

"You don't want to tell me?"

Merry starred straight ahead, anger starting to boil up her throat. Why couldn't the girl just leave it alone? All that book learning and her daughter didn't have enough common sense to shut her damn mouth.

Juliette crossed her arms, a teenage girl with too much attitude.

"Alright. Don't tell me then. I don't care no way."

Merry's eyes narrowed, hurt. She knew Juliette didn't care about her. Felt Juliette didn't care about her. But this was the first time Juliette had actually said it. Out loud. To her face.

Merry bit her lip, pissed.

"What. You. Say?"

Juliette didn't hesitate to repeat.

"I said, I don't care about you being in jail...You're probably used to it anyway."

"Girl, who the hell you think you talking to?!"

Merry starred at an intimidated Juliette, her hand itching, tingling, ready to go upside her daughter's now silent mouth. From the backseat, a laughing Jr. Baby instigated.

"Ooh, Ju gone get a spanking..."

Merry and Juliette hollered back, unified if only for a second.

"Shut up, Felton!"

Excellent sat up, woken out of her fitful sleep.

"Merry, what the hell... "

Juliette turned around in her seat, tattle telling at a mile a minute.

"Momma, I asked Merry what it was like for her in jail and she got mad and starting yelling and screaming..."

"Juliette, you a lie. That's not what happened."

"Uh huh, Momma. Yes, it is. Merry..."

"Shut up, Julia. You know yo' ass quick to lie. Stop the car, Merry."

"What?! We're in the middle of nowhere. I can't..."

"I said, stop the damn car!"

Merry did as she was told and Excellent scurried out of the car into the darkness. Juliette, concerned, called after her.

"Momma, where you going!"

Merry knew the answer.

"She gotta pee."

Merry flung open her car door. Hell, so did she. She headed over where Excellent was, found the tree. Excellent, skirt lifted, was finishing on the other side. Merry pulled down her pants, squatted.

"That girl needs her ass beat, Excellent. She's got a smart mouth."

Excellent stepped around the side of the tree, in no mood to be told how to raise her child. She threw her response over her shoulder.

"You oughta know. She got it from you."

Merry looked after Excellent. Of all the things her only daughter could take from her - her intelligence, her popular personality or good looks - the very thing Merry couldn't stand about her child was the only thing her mother would give her credit for?

Merry shook, pulled up her pants and returned to the car. She found Juliette in the driver's seat.

"Momma said I could drive."

Merry looked to Excellent, tired of being bossed around like one of the kids.

"Does she have a license?"

Jr. Baby, in the passenger's seat, barked, disgruntled.

"Naw, just a stupid driver's permit. She don't even know how to drive."

"Shut-up, Stupid! I can drive better than you."

"You gone drive us in a ditch, Stupid."

"No, I'm not!"

Merry snatched open the driver's side door. Just because she worked at Chrysler didn't mean she could afford to buy one.

"Get in the back, Juliette."

"But, Merry, I know how to drive."

"Well, you can practice in your uncle's car. C'mon..."

Excellent, weary, fussed from the backseat.

"Merry, Julia passed the test. Now. You need to rest. Jr. Baby'll watch her."

Merry closed the door. She didn't like it, but Excellent was right. Merry was tired. And it was about time for Jr. Baby., who had done more sleeping on this trip than anything else, to earn his keep and watch his sister.

Besides, this was Kentucky. The same place where she had seen her fiend self shivering on a County Jail bus to hell. Merry didn't want to take a chance trying to save herself from herself again and failing. Again. She'd rather take her mother's advice and sleep her way through Kentucky.

Sleep her way away from herself.

YOU THINK
I'M A LIE, TOO

Raindrops pelted off of Elgin's car roof like pebbles skipping quickly across a pond.

Merry was sleeping. And the cool breeze that she was looking for in Kentucky had found her. It felt good and cool like the cold alcohol her momma used to rub on her young legs when she was aching.

One, two, three, Merry heard the car doors slam. She stirred awake. It was early morning. And she was home.

Merry sat up as Excellent, Juliette and Jr. Baby hurried through the rain. She wiped her mouth, swiped sleep from her eyes. Twenty-years ago, her momma's shack of a house with a patch of a lawn and her favorite magic mailbox at the end of the gravel driveway was larger than life to her.

But now? The grass needed trimming and the roof - long replaced by her eldest uncle Harris who added an indoor bathroom to the house when he couldn't convince Dora to move - needed mending.

Teenie was at the screen door, letting everybody in by the time Merry slipped up on the porch. One look into her auntie's eyes and Merry knew.

Teenie tried to hug her. Merry pulled away.

"When?"

"In her sleep."

Merry bolted into her momma's room, saw her. She was lying on her back, her eyes closed, her hands folded across her waist. Peaceful, just like she was sleeping.

Merry scrambled to her momma's side, took her hand, not once noticing that Excellent and Juliette were already in there. Hot tears streaming, her chest heaving, Merry buried her face in her momma's bosom, pleaded like a child.

"Momma, please...Please wake up...I'm here...I'm sorry...I'm so sorry..."

Merry, in denial, looked at Dora, rubbed her hair.

"I made it, Momma. All you gotta do is wake up. Just wake up..."

Desperate, Merry climbed into bed with her momma, the aching eyes of her mother following her. Unsure, Juliette took a step towards the bed. Excellent raised her quivering hand.

A baby cub inconsolable at her dead mother's side, Merry wailed.

**

The tap on Dora's bedroom door was light, almost an after thought as the door creaked open. The mouth-watering scent of breakfast - ham steak, cheese eggs, grits, potatoes and onions and buttermilk biscuits - wafted into the room. First. Teenie, a worried look on her face, followed.

"Breakfast is ready."

Merry, mumbled.

"I'm not hungry."

Teenie sighed.

"Merry, you need to eat. It's not good for you to be cooped up in here alone..."

Merry shot Teenie an angry look. She. Wasn't. Alone. How the hell could Teenie say that? Realizing what she said, Teenie allowed her sad eyes to settle on her mother. Dora was still. Still. She looked back to Merry, offered the closest thing she could to an apology.

"I'll leave a plate for you in the oven."

Teenie left the door open on purpose behind her. Merry glanced after her and then back to Dora. What was she going to do now? She never got a chance to say she was sorry. Never got a chance to tell her momma that she loved her and that she was sorry for breaking her heart with the truth that didn't mean shit to Merry now.

Merry lowered her head into her hands. She wanted to cop so bad. Her tongue, swelling, tasted like cardboard. Some booze - if her momma had some in the house - would do, take the edge off. But if Merry wanted to disappear, to stop the hot pain eating away at her insides, she needed to cop. Right now.

Sensing a presence in the room, Merry lifted her head. She found Juliette standing in the doorway, a glass of lemonade in hand.

"Thought you might be thirsty."

Merry, sniffling, wiped at tears trailing down her cheeks. Juliette set the lemonade down on the nightstand next to Merry, started back out of the room. Merry stopped her, her voice gravelly from crying.

"You drive all the way here?"

Juliette shook her head no.

"Jr. Baby starting whining so bad, Momma let him drive."

"Where is he?"

"In the bathroom."

Merry, desperate, headed next door to the bathroom. She knocked on the door just as she heard Jr. Baby running water into the bathtub.

"Felton...Felton, I need Elgin's key."

Her son heard her. Merry knew he did. But the only response she got was him belting out "Soul Man" at the top of his lungs.

Merry hurried into the living room, the sounds of Teenie and Juliette talking in the kitchen steps away.

She scanned the room, saw Excellent's purse, their bags and Juliette's and Jr. Baby's jackets. Something shiny, on top of her momma's prized radio caught her eye. Elgin's car key. She grabbed it, walked out the front door.

*

Merry had no idea where she was going. Locust Grove and smack? If there was ever any two things that didn't go together that was it. All Merry could think to do was to head on the other side of town, across the railroad tracks. Growing up, everybody and their momma knew that if you were looking for a good time - gambling, booze and hoes - that was the place to go. The same and more, Merry figured, had to be true today. And she was past ready to find out.

As a child, though, Merry had always been afraid to even venture up to the railroad tracks. The railroad tracks had killed her daddy. The railroad tracks - Dora had pounded in her head - were the gate to hell. And Merry, like a fool believed her.

Merry halted at the country road corner, looked both ways. Stopped. Up ahead was a sight she prayed she'd never see again. The sight of Mr. Sammy's house.

Merry slid the gear into park, shut off the engine. Mr. Sammy's house looked like no one had lived there in years.

She got out of the car, the sound of tall, damp grass scratching the car door and smushing under her feet. Merry stood there, her palms sweaty, her breath quickening. She could leave right now. Turn around and go.

Merry reached to open the car door, then heard the creak of the barn door. Open and close. Open and close. Merry looked back at the barn, scared to death, but knowing what she had to do.

Merry stepped inside, the moldy scent of Mr. Sammy's barn overpowering. Everything was just as she remembered it. Same old, scattered tools, a rusty plow and rotten stacks of horse feed. It was damn near empty. Except for the memory of Mr. Sammy raping her. Splitting her body, her mind, her heart, her soul in two.

Merry, anger and pain oozing out of her pores like sweat, snatched up a hoe, swung for the windows. Glass shattered all around her as she swung and screamed at the memory of Mr. Sammy clamping his hand over her mouth and plowing through her. Swung and screamed at the memory of her chest tightening, her ribs breaking, herself gasping for air. Swung and screamed at the memory of what her life had become. How her life had turned out. All of the mistakes she had made. Because of Mr. Sammy. Because. Of. Him. Because. Of... Herself.

Merry dropped the hoe and collapsed in a heap on the horse feed covered ground.

All of these years she had been blaming Mr. Sammy for her life, for her pain. But the real demon needing forgiveness for devouring her soul? Herself.

From outside, she heard the quick footsteps of someone approaching. Too exhausted to look up, she didn't. Excellent rushed inside.

"Merry..."

Her mother sounded worried, frightened. Probably from the sight of how she looked, Merry thought. But Merry didn't care.

"How'd you find me?"

Excellent stepped closer to her, her words labored.

"I know what happened wit' Sammy, Merry."

Merry glared up at her.

"You think I'm a lie, too."

Excellent shook her head as tears - the first tears Merry had seen her mother shed in twenty years - welled up in her eyes.

"Don't matter what I think, Merry. Only what I know. And I know Sammy."

Merry heaved. *Excellent knew Sammy.* Her mother knew Sammy like she knew Sammy. Like Johnson knew Sammy.

Excellent knelt down in front of Merry, touched her face.

"You know why Momma was callin' out for you, Merry? She was callin' out for you, because she wanted to tell you...She wanted to tell you...She was sorry, Merry..."

Excellent's voice quivered.

"I'm sorry, Merry."

Merry, the two words she had always needed to hear from her mother, fell into Excellent's arms, weeping. Her mother was sorry for leaving her behind as a child and killing off her daddy. Sorry for not believing her. For not knowing how to love her, for judging her and not forgiving her. Sorry for not protecting her. From men. From the world. From herself.

In the middle of Sammy's barn, surrounded by broken glass, decayed horse feed and horrid memories, Excellent was sorry for it all.

And Merry and Excellent cried. Mother and daughter. Bound by more than blood. Bound by more than tears.

Bound by more than love.

More
Monice Mitchell Simms!

Please turn this page
for a preview of

THE MAILMAN'S
DAUGHTER

coming soon
from flower girl publishing

SHE GONE,
1994

"Ju...lia, I...real..ly...need...to..go..."

"Uh huh..."

"Please."

Julia stopped tucking her mother in, looked down at her. Small, weak, her oxygen mask gripped in her feeble hand and pulled away from her withdrawn face, Merry was begging her to let her escape the hospital. Again.

Julia gently moved Merry's hand, slid the mask back over her mouth. She wasn't falling for it.

For six months now, she wasn't falling for it.

If anybody had told Julia the day before Good Friday that she would be the one traipsing in and out of hospitals, taking care of 59-year-old Merry, she would have slapped them in the face. Merry had a husband, after all.

And by all accounts, him being cheap and a scared straight drunk notwithstanding, Elgin seemed like a responsible enough man. Who knew he was a no good, sniffling weasel who couldn't make a decision or answer a question for shit?

Truth be told, that's the only reason Julia got involved. Well, that, and because of her home training. After she got the call that Good Friday that Merry had suffered a traumatic asthma attack and was bleeding internally, Julia didn't hesitate to put her clothes back on and go down to Harper Grace Emergency.

She wasn't close to Merry by any stretch of the imagination. They hardly talked. On the phone or otherwise. And before that night when Julia went down to the hospital, it had been a month or more since she had actually seen her mother.

Yet, when she got the call, Julia put all that to the side. Merry being a dope-fiend jailbird and abandoning her and Jr. Baby as babies. Not knowing until she was damn near grown that Merry was her mother and then once she did know, it not making a damn difference. Merry not understanding or sticking by her when she was battling cancer and fighting to kick an addiction to Vicodin. Merry's teaming with her ex-husband Boxer and helping to keep her girls away from her. Merry getting drunk and making Jr. Baby's murder all about her. All about her grief. Her guilt. Her pain.

Julia got the call. And she put all of that to the side. Because her momma raised her better than that.

Merry reached for her oxygen mask again. Julia stopped her hand.

"You know you can't breathe without it."

Merry nodded, pointed to the pen and notepad on the nightstand by her hospital bed. Julia sighed, handed her the pen and held up the notepad for her to write on. Merry scribbled.

Take me to the bank. I'll come back. I promise.

Julia read it and Merry grinned up at her with big, pitiful eyes. Julia chuckled.

"Nice try, Merry. Dolores'll be here soon enough. You can play the numbers then."

Julia took the pen and notepad from a protesting Merry, finished tucking her in. Here Merry was lying up in Vincore Rehabilitation Center with a temperamental hole in her aorta too risky to repair and only one functioning lung tattered from years of smoking and chronic "Auto Plant" asthma and all the woman cared about was playing her numbers. So what Merry would hit once or twice a week and was pretty much a genius at it. More than once Dolores hinted at wanting Merry's mini Hallmark calendar books after she was gone. Julia never paid her any mind. She didn't know where the number books were. Didn't care. All she knew was she wasn't about to be drawn into Merry's gambling ring. Elgin had been appeasing her for awhile, but then stopped. Probably after Merry wouldn't tell him where she was keeping her thousands of winnings. Then, one of the nurses and Dolores took over. Every day like clockwork, the nurse would play the numbers for Merry and Dolores - the mule - would carry Merry's winnings back to her from her numbers runner.

What her mother did with the money then, Julia didn't know. More than likely, she was bribing the nurses to sneak her in food. Now that Merry had stopped accusing them of trying to kill her and trying to escape and hide under the bed like a crazy woman, the nursing staff had actually grown to care for her.

With the time they had left, that is.

Julia, because Elgin's spineless ass couldn't or wouldn't - Merry was convinced that the man, if she wasn't there to stop him, would pull the plug - had decided against the doctors operating on Merry's aorta last week. She only had one lung and the doctors said they were afraid that if they opened Merry up to fix the hole and stop the bleeding, her body, ravaged from years of drug and alcohol abuse, would give out.

It wasn't a hard decision to make. For Julia. Merry was dying. She wasn't bleeding internally right now. Thank God. And the morphine drip - an extremely high dosage for anybody else - was managing the pain.

Julia knew that was the best thing she could do. As her daughter. Manage the pain and make sure that her mother was comfortable.

Julia eyed her purse in the chair by the hospital bed, started to leave. Merry grabbed her hand.

"Uh uh, Merry, I ain't falling for it. Now, let me go. I got things to do..."

Merry shook her head, urgent, grasped at her oxygen mask. Julia, already knowing what she wanted, pulled the mask down, away from her mouth.

"What."

Merry, gulping a breath to jump-start her lung, gazed at Julia sincere, grateful.

"Thank you."

Julia paused. She heard Merry. Even felt Merry. A little. But not enough to puncture her rib cage and penetrate her distant heart. Julia slid her hand out from Merry's grasp, more detached than a nurse on the job for too long.

"Alright...See you tomorrow."

Julia said it, already knowing that she wasn't going to be coming the same time tomorrow. Some shifts were lazier, less attentive than others. So to make sure that her mother got the care she needed and deserved, Julia made it a habit to show up at any time.

Julia was assertive that way. She asked the questions that other patients' family members - if they had them -

didn't, couldn't and wouldn't. Plus, she made it her business to buddy up to the two most important women in the rehabilitation center - the head nurse and the administrator. And Julia didn't stop there. Even when she was having a bad day, she remembered names and details and always said hello and goodbye when she came and went. The nurses and orderlies appreciated that. Most folks were so worried about their family members that they hardly looked at the hospital staff until there was a problem. They didn't give a damn about how they were understaffed, overworked and underpaid. Julia didn't either, but at least she acted like she did. Because she knew that made the difference between her mother lying in a pool of stale urine or being cleaned and changed.

"Alright, Gloria. I'm gone."

"Gone?"

Gloria, the 43-year old afternoon head nurse on duty, was the same age and half the size of Julia's 173 pound, 5"2 frame. But she had a voice as gravelly as a man's. Standing up at the nurses counter, she glanced over her shoulder to the clock on the wall. It was twenty after six.

"23 minutes. Julia, if you had visited your mother any longer, I would of assigned you to her room."

Gloria and the young nurse filing behind the counter chuckled. Julia fell right in line with them.

"Girl, you know me. I'm making moves."

"That's right, girl. Doin' big thangs. I hear that. How your smart girls doin'?"

"Good. Good. Neema's hanging on at grad school and just got hired at a newspaper. And Jada made the dean's list again. How your new grandbaby?"

"Talkin', shittin' and walkin'. All in that order. Boy runnin' me ragged. I can't keep up wit' him. You'll know about that soon 'nough."

"Girl, shut up! That ain't even funny."

Gloria and Julia laughed. Friendly chitchat surrounded by sickness. Back to business, Julia put both hands up on the counter.

"She sounded congested. I checked her tubing. It looked alright to me, but when's the last time you checked her lung?"

"Ran a test this mornin'. Didn't see a drop of blood. But she did ask for more morphine."

"Bet she did. She complain about the pain?"

Gloria, wishing there was something more she could do, shook her head.

"As much morphine we're givin' your mother, Julia, she shouldn't be complaining. I can't..."

"I know. I know. Could you just check her?"

"Yeah, yeah, Julia. I'll do it myself."

Julia left, knowing that she would. Gloria was one of the good ones. A nurse that still cared.

Julia walked by Administrator Wagner's office. Everyday, she made it a point to poke her head in and say hello. But Teresa's door was still closed. Julia nodded goodbye to Carl, the security guard.

"See ya later, Carl."

"Alright, Julia."

Stepping outside Vincore's glass doors, Julia felt the warm Indian Summer dusk breeze brush past her face. It was the sixteenth of September. Fall, according to the calendar. But by the feel of it, summer wasn't ready to ride off quietly into the sunset. And that was alright with Julia, because Fall coming meant Winter was right around the corner and she wasn't looking forward to salting and shoveling her driveway and sidewalk in front of her house. Again. By herself.

Julia took out her keys, ripped off the carwash tag still on the ring. She didn't have far to walk to her car - a white Chrysler Plymouth Acclaim. And her spot - on the opposite side of the nondescript two-story beige building away - was safely positioned in a way that she could drive right out the exit without having to back out and turn around.

Julia opened her car door, spotted a runny present a bird left for her on the hood. About to cuss, she heard a familiar horn toot. It was Elgin pulling up behind her. Sixty-one, gray beard stubbled and still spry for his age despite a beer belly, he climbed out of the mini-van, carrying a greasy brown paper bag.

"Hey, Julia."

"Hey."

Elgin eyed the new bird poop on her car hood.

"Got you again, huh?"

Julia, too pissed to answer, motioned to the greasy bag.

"What's for dinner?"

"Merry wanted corn beef. Wanna pickle?"

"No, thanks."

"Alright. She awake?"

"Wide awake. And hungry."

"I better get in there 'fore she starts cussin'. You gone be back tomor..."

Julia nodded before Elgin even finished the question. She and Elgin didn't talk much, but when they did, it was always the same conversation. Bird poop. Merry. Food. And everyday, Elgin would end by asking Julia if she'd be back tomorrow. For six months now, Julia's answer had never changed.

Elgin headed inside.

"Alright, Julia."

"Alright."

Julia turned back towards her car, saw the bird mess on the hood, got pissed all over again.

Flying overhead, she heard a bird taunting. Julia looked up, ready to kill.

"If I had a gun, swear to God..."

The bird whipped past her, flew over the top of the building. Julia followed it with her eyes, stopped, peered closer. The sun was starting to set and it hadn't, from what Julia remembered, rained. Yet, in the sky right above the building, between two fluffy gray clouds was a beautiful, faint pink-yellow-blue rainbow. Plain as day.

Julia paused there, admiring it. Not able to remember the last time she had stopped moving long enough to see a rainbow.

It was already a forgotten memory by the time she drove away.

*

Julia took a last puff of her Salem light snubbed it out in the ashtray. She was sitting in her car, trying to catch up on her English homework assignment. And she was late for class. Again.

Julia turned the page. Good thing she was a fast reader. That was the only thing helping her to halfway keep step with the young competition at the Detroit College of Business.

What the hell Julia was thinking she went back to college, she didn't know. She had always felt like a failure for not finishing back in the day, that was true. She was nineteen, a junior with the world ahead of her and messed around with Boxer and got pregnant. The mistake that it was, she and Boxer were getting married anyway and Neema, their firstborn, was a blessing. But with work and two babies - a new one and a grown ass one who cared more about her washing clothes than rewiring circuits - Julia had to drop her Computer Programming curriculum and walk away from her education.

And here she was again. More than twenty years later, trying to finish what she started. Thanks to Chrysler, Julia didn't have to pay for her books and tuition. She only had to make a few changes to her life. Studying, writing papers and taking tests again when everyone else in the class was twenty years younger? Not easy. Computers had also come a hell of a long way since 1970. Switching to a Business Administration major, despite her deep embedded hatred of accounting, only made the most sense. And getting an associates degree? Julia knew that at the end of the day, the degree wouldn't be worth more than the damn paper it was printed on. But she wanted it anyway. She wanted to finish what she started.

"Nice of you to join us, Julia."

Julia slid into her desk at the front of the class, unembarrassed. She was used to her teacher calling her out by now. One year shy of fifty, wrinkled and his white, pale body battling Parkinson's, Professor Chapman was a good instructor. If his medicine was working. But if Chapman's pills weren't kicking in and he was suffering abnormally from his own personal earthquake, then he would show up to class, ready to tear every student in his quivering sights a new one.

"Langston Hughes' rhythmical, lyrical, pivotal *Freedom Train* written in 1947. Analyze it. That was the assignment. The simple assignment. To think, then transform those thoughts to paper."

Professor Chapman paused, Julia and the entire class knowing what was coming next. Blue eyes flashing, he tossed the stack of papers down on the floor.

"This was offensive to me. To spend my time - what little of it I have left - reading this dribble. These essays show no effort and no respect...and if there were no remote possibility that I could languish on to teach this material again next semester, I would fail you all today. All of you, except one."

Professor Chapman, fighting a battle with his neck, held out Julia's essay. He looked at her.

"Mrs. Gossett. Your essay was excellent. Read it to the class."

Julia, stunned, couldn't move from her seat.

"My...my paper?"

Professor Chapman eyed her.

"Yes. You did write it, didn't you?"

"Oh, yes, sir. I did."

"Then you'll have no problem reading it."

And Julia didn't. In fact, she was proud to. All those twenty-somethings peering at her, jealous, made Julia stand taller. Twenty extra years of living hadn't ruined her ability to reach, to grow.

For herself.

Dropping her keys on top of the glass-topped, wooden corner table in the living room, Julia clicked on the lamp. The light, a dull yellow shining through a beige lampshade, didn't really illuminate much. Not that Julia needed it.

The layout of the room, hell, the layout of everything in her modest gingerbread colonial house, hadn't changed much in the twenty plus years since she, the girls and Boxer first moved in. Her brown and beige couch against the lead eggshell painted wall needed new cushions. Her coffee table that matched both corner tables was starting to crack on the left side. And her 27 inched, mahogany encased floor level television that everybody used to lust after back in the day was an exercise in light and shadows. The picture tube was going.

But that didn't matter to Julia. She had learned to watch it by squinting. Just as she had learned to roll up the first of her living room window shades by hand. The shade, itself, was ripped and the spring on the roll had long since given out. Yet, instead of throwing it away, every morning, Julia stepped up on her footstool to roll it up. And every night, just like tonight, she stepped back up on her footstool to roll it back down.

Her daughters, Neema and Jada had no patience for such things. Whenever one would visit from Chicago or D.C., it was like a checklist:

Momma, it's past time for you to come into the 21st century. Toss out that window shade. Your old chocolate brown drapes, too. And while you're at it, Momma, when are you going to fix the lock on the front door? And don't even get us started on the kitchen...

Julia headed up the stairs, the brown carpet once cushy, now worn down from years of her grown and gone daughters running up and down them.

She had meant to pull it up last year with the rest of the living and dining room carpet when she scrimped some pennies together to redecorate the house a bit to throw Neema a college graduation reception. That evening, she got rave reviews about her beautifully varnished hardwood floors, her new lazy boy chair and elephant figurines. But the biggest hit of the party? The photographs of her girls. A shrine to her daughters, Julia's walls and fireplace mantelpiece rivaled any museum's. Neema and Jada, afro puffs, front teeth missing. Neema and Jada, jheri curls, public school picture day backdrops. Neema and Jada, Toni Braxton bobs, high school graduation caps.

The only picture Julia had of herself - on the second row of a rickety glass and silver metal display shelving in the dining room - was her high school graduation photo. Flanked by both girls' commencement photos - Neema on her left, Jada on her right - Julia, wearing Pershing High School's blue and gold robe and cap, flashed the exact same smile of her daughters. Same cock of the head. Same glint in the eye.

Julia and her girls even sounded the same. It was a running joke that if anybody called that wasn't a part of the family or one of Julia's closest friends, they had better ask who they were talking to before they started running their mouth. Wasn't no telling who they might be talking to.

Julia chuckled. Neema's voice, the deepest between hers and Jada's, sounded scratchy on the answering machine, like she had just woken up from a nap. With her bohemian, night owl self, she probably had.

"Ma! Where you at? I needs to know how we did on the paper. I took time out my very busy schedule, gave you some good stuff, and against my better judgment, I'm allowing you to take all of the credit. But if you don't call me back soon, I'm gone drop a dime on you to your professor. Bye!"

Julia, sitting down on her bed, slipped off her cotton, polyester blend pants, reached for her oversized pajama shirt.

Neema was a fool. A smart fool that she owed a call. Last week with all the drama that went down with Merry, there was no way Julia would have been able to navigate through the poetry that is Langston Hughes without her daughter's late night help- line calls. She eyed the time on her radio alarm clock. Six minutes after nine. Her first-born was an hour behind in Chicago. Julia, smiled, reached for the phone.

Gloria's even voice next on the answering machine stopped her.

"Julia, it's Gloria. I need you to call me right away. After runnin' a test on your mother's lung, we discovered blood from another hole in her aorta. We managed to stabilize her, but... she's lapsed into a coma. Call me."

Julia sighed. Her just-taken-off pants next to her, she yanked them back on with her right hand, snatched up the phone with her left. There was no dial tone.

"Hello?"

"Julia..."

"Elgin, I was just about to call Vincore. Did they call..."

Elgin, his voice cracking, interrupted.

"She gone, Julia. She gone."

LaVergne, TN USA
12 November 2010
204683LV00001B/5/P